"There are so many joys in this para..,
mythologies, religions and magicks are a weight that balances the emotional tenderness."
—*New York Times Book Review*

★"Sparks fly in Tsai's refreshing and enchanting paranormal debut. A sordid family past has driven gifted immortal Elle Mei, a descendant of Shénnóng, the Chinese god of medicine, into leading a quiet, unassuming life. Though Elle's exceptional talent at magical calligraphy could easily earn her a lucrative career, she chooses to cover up the extent of her gift, hiding in plain sight as an "ordinary" glyphmaker in Raleigh, N.C. It's the only way she knows how to protect her family, as using too much power would surely draw attention. But the temptation to use her full abilities becomes too much to resist when it comes to her favorite customer (and crush), the dashing half-elf security expert Luc Villois. When Luc realizes what Elle's truly capable of, he commissions her to create custom glyphs for an upcoming assignment, and, against her better judgment, she agrees. Meanwhile, Luc has a secret of his own, and he knows that Elle would never choose to spend more time with him if she knew who he truly was. Despite their mutual reservations, their friendship deepens into love—but will their trust in each other be enough to save them when their twisted pasts come back to haunt them? With brilliantly developed, multifaceted characters; a clever magic system; and witty prose, the pages of this fantasy fly. This marks Tsai as a writer to watch."
—*Publishers Weekly*, starred review

"The modern Chinese diaspora fantasy that I've yearned for—fresh, exciting, with characters who leap off the page."
—Courtney Milan, author of *The Devil Comes Courting*

"A romp of a supernatural action-romance, *Bitter Medicine* is a sparkling mix of angsty yearning, cool magic, family drama, and intriguing side characters, with a garnish of wonderful use of language!"
—Malka Older, author of *Infomocracy*

"I could not put this book down. *Bitter Medicine* is a slow-burn romance wrapped in an international spy thriller wrapped in supernatural politics, and it's tasty as hell. The deeper I got into Tsai's deeply imagined world, the more I wanted more of her funny, sexy characters with so many feelings—and such intriguing powers."
—Annalee Newitz, author of *The Terraformers* and *Autonomous*

"A lovely, absorbing read with wonderful characters, a perfect romance, and an action-packed plot."
—*Buzzfeed*

"As a contemporary fantasy debut, Mia Tsai's *Bitter Medicine* is an extraordinary and distinct blend of agent thriller, the supernatural, and romance."
—*Asia Pacific Arts*

"Overflowing with effervescent charm and sly humor, *Bitter Medicine* intoxicates with its steamy romance, globe-trotting adventure, family drama mystery, and a fabulously inventive world of magic inspired by cross-cultural lore."
—Angela Mi Young Hur, author of *Folklorn*

"Fans of Sarah J. Maas's epic paranormal fantasies will also find much to savor in Tsai's debut."
—*Library Journal*

"*Bitter Medicine* goes down like a spoonful of sugar with a dash of spice: a dazzling and adventurous romantic fantasy with tons of heart. I can't wait to see what Mia Tsai does next!"
—Hugo Award–winning editor Diana M. Pho

"Creative, tense, and extremely swoonworthy, Mia Tsai's *Bitter Medicine* brings together cultures, mythical creatures, and genres for an unforgettable mash-up debut that will appeal to fans of Fonda Lee and paranormal romance enthusiasts."
—Mike Chen, author of *Star Wars: Brotherhood*

"Magical, sexy, and snarky, *Bitter Medicine* is perfect for grown-up fans of Artemis Fowl looking to scratch that fairy heist itch."
—Lara Elena Donnelly, author of the Amberlough Dossier and *Base Notes*

"I love that this book was inspired by Chinese mythology, in particular 仙侠 (xianxia) . . . The romance between Luc and Elle was steamier than expected . . . Their chemistry was lovely to witness and there were moments that made me audibly gasp because they were just so cute!"
—*Min's Archives*

"An intoxicating blend of mythology, family love and betrayal, and magic, Tsai's debut is an absolute stunner! Mix together one fiercely talented calligrapher, one swoony French half-elf, and a magical world filled with danger and mystery, and you get a breathlessly compelling contemporary fantasy. *Bitter Medicine* is as elegant and potent as one of Elle's spells."
—Sierra Simone, *USA Today* bestselling author of *The Fae Queen's Captive*

"A love letter to code-switching and its many forms: exchanging phrases in multiple languages, finding loopholes, and thriving under restrictive rules, adapting to different worlds."
—*Mochi Magazine*

"*Bitter Medicine* is contemporary fantasy at its best."
—*Shelf Awareness*

"Tsai delights with this fast-paced, romantic-fantasy debut."
—*Booklist*

BITTER MEDICINE
MIA TSAI

MIA TSAI

Bitter Medicine

TACHYON | SAN FRANCISCO

Cover art and design by JiaLing Pan
Interior by Elizabeth Story
Author photo by Wynne Photography

Tachyon Publications LLC
1459 18th Street #139
San Francisco, CA 94107
415.285.5615
www.tachyonpublications.com
tachyon@tachyonpublications.com

Series Editor: Jacob Weisman
Editor: Jaymee Goh

Print ISBN: 978-1-61696-384-2
Digital ISBN: 978-1-61696-385-9

Printed in the United States by Versa Press Inc.

9 8 7 6 5 4 3 2

To me, because I could.

Chapter One

$\mathcal{F}$IRST, THE INK.

Elle pours a bit of water on her grinding stone, sets the end of her ink stick in it. She clasps her hands and breathes out slowly, closing her eyes. When she opens them, her magic rouses, filling the pit of her stomach with familiar, joyful warmth.

She takes hold of the stick and pushes it in small, clockwise circles, her thumb pressing against debossed flowers painted in gold. She's been waiting half her shift to escape to her workshop, needing the meditation of calligraphy to decompress. In the stillness of art there are no outstanding orders or rude customers, no worries over her eldest brother, Tony, no limits on what she can do.

Elle settles into her rhythm, her meridians waking with magic. It unspools with her movements, unwinding in tendrils through her chest and arm, infusing stone and water and stick with whispered potential. *Shh*, the grinding stone says, soothing. The comforting scent of incense rises. *Shh*. Tony is safe under her protection, and though he no longer has his magic, he's happy and healthy. *Shh, shh*.

The ink thickens, growing deep and black and reflective beneath the fluorescent overhead lights. She exhales, lays her stick down, and trails her fingers across the brushes hanging from a rack. Instinct and her century of experience guide her to the correct brush—bamboo handle, wolf hair, sharp tip. Elle murmurs a greeting as she lifts it off its hook and prepares it, then dips it into ink and acclimates it with a few test strokes. There's enough ink for one glyph, a single character on a square of rice paper she'll end up selling. She holds down her paper, saturates each hair of the brush with her magic, and whispers a prayer to Shénnóng, the Chinese god of medicine, her patron god and direct ancestor.

There are nine strokes in the character for "fly," and Elle imbues each one with the determination to leave the earth, to soar into the sky. Three strokes create a beating wing, feathers spread and vibrating, straining against the atmosphere. A second wing takes shape, ensuring speed and swiftness. The final downward stroke becomes the hard line of the horizon tilting vertical as the birds bank sharply to the right.

Elle sits back when she's done, looking at a word crackling with so much energy it almost springs off the page. The original character depicted birds in flight. Whoever buys the glyph will have no issue joining them.

She sighs, disappointed. The glyph is too strong.

Her cell phone goes off. Teresa Teng sings of the moon, her voice tinny and muffled.

That's Tony's ringtone.

Elle scrambles to her feet, her stool screeching displeasure against the concrete floor. Teresa Teng continues, oblivious to her as she hunts for the phone, moving aside rolls of rice paper, stacks of glyphs, jars of dried powders. The phone isn't on the counter by the sink, nor is it by the filing cabinets on the other side of her workshop. It isn't on the other side of her long workbench. Maybe it's on the junk shelf of the bookcase, which doesn't make sense, but it could be in outer space and she'd accept that as long as it was found.

It stops, only to start again, fanning her into a frenzy. "Where is it?" she snaps at herself. Finally, she spots a lone wire snaking its way into a dusty pile by the garbage can. She reels in her phone amid a cloud of particles, her nose itching, then yanks out the charging cable and flips it open to answer.

"Tony?! Tony, are you okay? What's wrong? Are you hurt?"

"Oh my God, calm down. I'm fine." He's either irritated, or patronizing, or both.

"You aren't supposed to call me unless it's an emergency!"

"Maybe I wouldn't call you if you checked your email more than once a decade," Tony retorts. "It's been two weeks and you haven't replied. Maybe I should be worrying about you, huh?"

"No!" Unlike Tony, Elle's magic has never been stronger, and she could take a bullet and survive, thanks to Shénnóng's blessing. "I did check my email!"

"Your work email doesn't count."

"All I get on my personal email is fake stuff."

"There are filters for spam. Aren't you a hundred twenty-five or something? You're too grown to be this ignorant. Even a thirty-year-old knows more than you." He pauses, probably to roll his eyes. "I emailed you two weeks ago to invite you to an event at the North Carolina Museum of Art. You know, the big one outside the loop. It's a Chinese art exhibition. Thought you'd be interested."

"You thought I'd be interested, or you don't want to go alone?" Elle pins the phone between ear and shoulder, stooping to pick up her mess. She dumps papers onto her workbench with enough force to send a sheet on a different stack flying. She snatches it out of the air and hastily unfolds it, smoothing it down.

Tony sniffs. "The first one, of course. You're still painting, right? Not just doing that glyph crap?"

"It's not crap," Elle protests, looking at the paper beneath her hand. It's a charcoal sketch of a handsome man sitting on a couch, engrossed in a book.

All thoughts of the invitation disappear, replaced by thoughts of him.

Luc. Specifically Agent Luc Villois, a tall drink of half-elven water who's been patronizing her shop for the last eight months or so, not that she's counting. These days he's more friend than customer, and a smile curves her lips as she thinks about their late-night chats, his restoratives brewing in the background.

Tony groans. "It's crap because you can do more, but you don't. I don't want to sound ungrateful or anything . . ."

The book in the sketch is the same as the open book on her coffee table. Elle hasn't managed to put it away in the week he's been gone. She can't, she reasons. He'd want his place marked for his next visit.

". . . like the portrait you painted of me. Right? That's your best work, in my opinion."

If she concentrates, she can visualize Luc sitting in his spot on the couch, head of dark hair bent over the pages, long legs crossed ankle to knee, bottom lip tucked into a small frown. It's to keep him from moving his mouth when he reads, he's explained. An old habit.

Elle thinks it's endearing, but she's said nothing. That would cross a line. They're just friends, and they're both not looking for a relationship. Luc is, as he has said, a terrible prospect who is often away on classified missions. And Elle?

"Elle? Hello? I'm talking to you. You're still painting, right?"

She throws a guilt-laden glance at the paintings on her walls. They're all from years ago. "Uh, yeah. Yeah, I'm painting a lot. A ton. I'm super busy."

"You're such a bad liar. Calligraphy doesn't count. Come out with me tomorrow night and get some inspiration. You're welcome."

"You're a dick. Why invite me?"

"I can't spend time with my favorite sister?"

"I'm your only sister."

"Doesn't make what I said not true."

"Tony." Her nostrils flare.

"Okay, fine. I'll be straight with you."

Elle snorts, maybe a little too loud. "You, straight?"

"Got me there. One of my patients gave me her ticket with a plus one to this swanky opening gala—"

"Why are you pronouncing it like that?"

"Don't interrupt. Because I'll be there and I'm gay, lah. Where was I? A *gala* for an art exhibit from New York. I want to go because it's free and I get to dress up and look devastatingly handsome, and if you're with me, you'll benefit from some of my shine."

That can't be all of it, though if it were, she wouldn't be surprised. Suspicious, Elle says, "And?"

". . . and because I think you need to get out more."

Elle folds her lips together, holding back all the reasons why she doesn't go out. Tony knows. "I get out plenty."

"You don't even get off company property to go to the store. You get out once a year to see me. Come out tomorrow night and double your stats."

"I don't want to risk it."

"Risk it? Risk what? It's an art show."

"Your safety."

"Nope, blocked. You're not using me as an excuse. It's been thirteen years since the last time. You've gotta be lonely."

She takes a deep breath, lets it out. Loneliness isn't a factor when it comes to calculating sacrifice. Elle has laid personal goals, ambition, and long-term relationships as offerings on that altar, watched them burn without remorse. "Sixteen years. And two months."

"Sixteen years and two months, which is much too long to not have fun."

"An art show with a lot of people there doesn't sound like fun."

"Going to a gala with free booze and a strict dress code is fun for me. Going to an exhibition of art that you happen to be an expert on is fun for you. Everyone wins." Tony hmphs. "It's decided. I'll see you tomorrow night."

"No! It's too soon! Maybe we can schedule something smaller? Just you and me? In a couple of weeks? I'm supposed to come see you, anyway."

Tony takes a breath like he's about to rattle off a list. "Tomorrow night wouldn't be too soon if you checked your damn email; it's been sixteen years and two months and you have done a stellar job of keeping me alive and you deserve to enjoy yourself; I think you should focus on painting and seeing some classics might inspire you; I miss my sister; this is a black-tie event so wear something nice; I'll pick you up in front of the agency tomorrow at seven. Did I miss anything?"

"The part where I said no?"

A sharp knock sounds at her door. A split second later it swings open to reveal Lira, co-owner of the store and Elle's best friend. Lira is a small, robust Black woman, with hair in a perfect, bouncy twist-out. Her skin is a warm, deep brown, and her face is the definition of round-cheeked. On said face is an expression the definition of annoyed.

"Elle, your break's been over for—wait, are you on the phone?"

"Uh." Elle clears her throat. "Yes?"

"Is that Tony?" Lira pitches her voice louder. "Tony, are you okay?"

"Oh, is that Lira?" Tony perks up. "Tell her I'm fine."

Elle dutifully relays the message.

Lira steps into Elle's workshop. "Why's he calling?"

"I'm calling to invite Elle out tomorrow night," Tony yells through the phone. Elle holds it away from her ear, wincing.

"Good luck," Lira yells back. "She'll never say yes!"

"Should I just give her the phone so you can talk without spilling my business all over the place?" Elle scowls. "I'm gonna give her the phone. Here."

Lira accepts it with a brilliant smile. "Hey Tony! One sec." She cups the receiver of the phone with a hand. "Elle, Ed's out front. It's your turn to handle him. Okay, Tony, I'm here. What's up? How you been?"

Summarily dismissed, Elle leaves her workshop, puts her retail face on over her frown, walks down the hallway, and pulls up short as she sees the oni in her store.

It's burly, with thick, muscled arms. A knobby, oversized club dangles from its hand and drags on the floor. A thicket of stiff hair striped in black and brown grows from its head, as well as two curved horns. A bone-white mask, eyes ringed in dark circles, sits on its face. Behind the creature, a furry tail flicks back and forth. The bite of iron tints the air.

Elle sighs, going to the counter to clock back in. She might be a middling-rank shopkeeper now at Roland & Riddle, the faerie temp agency, but she used to be a high-level agent here. She's familiar with all classifications of oni, and none of them have robber mask patterns.

Tanuki, however, have robber mask patterns. "Ed, you left some raccoon on your face."

"Aw, darn. I didn't even trick you for a second?"

"No, sorry."

The oni's outlines blur like water running over rocks in a stream. A second later, a diminutive Japanese raccoon dog in overalls stands in its place. A company pass clipped to his front pocket reads *Agent Ed Mochi*. It's a silly alias, but everyone in the agency is required to have one, and Ed's is more adorable than ridiculous. Certainly, it's better than a puk named Agent Bucket or a dryad named Agent Chuck.

Elle leans forward over the counter to see Ed better, forcing cheer into her voice. "But you almost got me! Don't forget about your tail next time."

"Oh no, my tail?"

Elle nods, then gives Ed a practiced, warm smile. "You'll get the hang of it eventually. You're a young tanuki, and it takes years to perfect the transformation, doesn't it?"

"Yeah," Ed replies, mournful, "but I want to get it so they can move me up a rank. I'm so bored with my missions."

"What are you now, a C?"

"Yeah. Everyone in my family's already a B or above! It's just me. I can't go out with the humans until I hit rank."

With good reason, but she lets Ed talk. Human interaction is risky, especially if disguises aren't perfect; history skews unkind whenever human and fae clash, and ever since the European schism separated humans from fae some six hundred years ago, the Western fae have kept to themselves. The company policies reinforce the divide and protect the more vulnerable agents.

"You'll get there! Until then . . ." Elle cocks a pointer finger in the air and strikes a pose. "What can I help you with?"

The tanuki heaves a beleaguered sigh. "I need a glamour glyph. I'm on haunt duty again."

"You know, you're the third temp to mention haunt duty this week. What's going on?"

"The ghosts in City Cemetery went on sabbatical." Ed produces his agency-standard faerie identification card from somewhere in his fur and places it on the counter. "I mean, I don't blame them; they work all the time, you know? They're gonna be gone for a few months and need someone to show up and look spooky from afar. Just to keep up appearances and all that. It's not hard to do, I just . . ."

His nose twitches. "I just wish I didn't need someone else's magic to make me turn transparent. Um. No offense."

"None taken. You're house-sitting too?"

"I guess." Ed sounds like a whiny teenager, or a sulky owl.

"O-kay," Elle says, moving things along, "you get to pick two add-ons. Which two would you like?"

"I'd like to be extra see-through, and if you could make me look like I'm dripping blood, that'd be epic." Ed's upper lip lifts in a tanuki version of an evil smile, revealing sharp little teeth. It's more cute than scary.

"Ed, you gotta pick from the menu." Elle gestures to the lists on the wall behind her. "No custom add-ons until the next rank."

"Dang it," Ed replies, his face falling.

Elle gives Ed a sorry-not-sorry look. She's read the agency manual like it's a holy book and knows to the letter what her limitations are. No flashy stuff, no off-list glyphs or potions, and no demonstrations of power above her rank, like the glyph of flight on her workbench. She's being average for Tony's sake, though there are days when she's struck by the compulsion to make something, and her magic boils strongly enough in her to hurt, leaving her sleepless and in torment.

There are also enormous infographic posters plastered on the other side of the counter, explaining what each rank is allowed in their field kit. "It's agency regulation. I can do a standard transparency on a humanoid ghost glamour. You'll need to pick from the menu for your second add-on."

She reaches beneath the counter and hauls out a fat binder, the webbing on the bottom cracked from frequent use, and flips it open. Inside are examples of her glyphs, square and rectangular pieces of paper with Chinese characters of varying scripts crammed onto them. She pushes the binder forward.

"Okay," Ed says, stretching up to see. A second later, a black claw taps delicately on the sheet protector. "This one's good."

Elle glances at the label, then turns to the drawers behind her, pulling one open to reveal rows of glyphs encased in cellophane sleeves. "Ghost," she mutters, her fingers walking through dividers until she gets to the correct one. She plucks it up, then opens another drawer.

By the time she's gotten the second, Ed has elongated his body in order to see over the counter, looking more like a malformed weasel than a raccoon dog. He slides his FID, which doubles as an agency debit card, across to her. Elle takes it and hands the tanuki the glyphs, finishing the transaction.

"Have a nice day." She sends Ed on his way with a smile and keeps it on for the next customer, a Jersey Devil. "How can I help you?"

The devil stomps a hoof lightly on the floor and cracks some gum, which amazes Elle given that bipedal goats with horns and wings usually don't chew gum, much less crack it, but she supposes the New Jersey tendencies are strong.

"I was passing through and saw some reviews that said you do special orders. Is that true?"

"Ah." Elle reminds herself of her no-commissions rule. "It depends on the order. Bulk items might take longer if you order more than we have in stock. What rank are you? What are you looking for?"

"B-rank. I'm not looking for a bulk buy. I need a reusable invisibility glyph that also allows silent movement. Got a misdirection mission in the Pines again. Gotta show my face long enough for the kids to get me on Snap or Insta or something, but then I have to disappear quick."

Elle's shop is rated for ranks B and below, though she gets the occasional A-ranker. There's one glowing review on the intra-agency network and a slew of mediocre ones, which is typical. She'd like to keep it that way. "I can do three or four minor invisibility glyphs with add-ons."

"No, I need it to be reusable. I don't want to open a new glyph every time."

"There're no charms in requisitions that do that already?"

The devil shakes her head. "I put the request in to up my clearance so I could layer the charms but got rejected because some dummy broke the system. Thought I'd try glyphs instead. Can you help me or not?"

"I'm sorry to disappoint you, but I'm afraid I can't." It wouldn't be difficult. It would be a few extra characters on one glyph, and a redirect with some muting and light-footedness on a linked glyph. She hasn't put her ink stick away yet, and her brush is still wet. She could paint the order in a minute.

But she can't show her power. She's no longer the young woman taking A- and S-rank clients exclusively by referral. As easy as the glyph is, she won't abdicate her responsibility to Tony.

"I'm really sorry. You could try one of the shops in New York. They do commissions all the time. If it's a Chinese glyph you're looking for, there are some excellent crafters in the Flushing branch."

The devil sighs in a way that means two stars on the internal rating system, then cracks her gum again. "Thanks."

"I'm sorry I couldn't help you more."

The devil waves her off and walks out, sidestepping a familiar figure coming through the front door.

Elle's breath catches in her throat.

Luc is tall and slender like a soccer player, with chestnut brown hair swept away from his pale face and a jawline begging for her lips and eyes blue enough to be seen from a distance. His features are a symmetrical marvel, with cheekbones that have spent days eluding her pencil, and he moves with a smooth, compelling grace that draws the eye. He is, in short, a beautiful man, one who carries himself in a way that's reminiscent of the royal Chinese princes in her favorite period dramas.

She tells herself firmly not to smile. After all, Luc is a customer first and foremost. She has to treat him like one, and not like a very attractive friend who makes her grin like a fool when he's near. Elle remains as expressionless as possible, determined to avoid said foolishness.

She manages to hold out until the devil exits the shop. Then she grins like a fool, which forces her to cover her mouth with her hand. Luc answers with a sunny smile of his own that turns his elegant, sculpted features into bright boyishness.

Skies, it's suddenly hot. Too hot for her in her T-shirt and jeans and shop apron. Too hot for him in his navy suit, a crisp white collar peeking out from beneath a patterned summer scarf.

"Hello, Agent Mei," Luc says rather seriously once he's at the counter. The smile fades, but not all the way. "Your terrible prospect has returned."

Elle shivers at the way his faint French accent curls around his words. "And your terrible prospect is still here. Hello yourself, Agent Villois." She can't resist tucking her hair behind her ear although it's in a ponytail and hasn't misbehaved. "You're back sooner than I thought. Did everything go okay? Potions and glyphs all worked correctly?"

"Yes, very well. I wanted to thank you for your impeccable work."

Her cheeks tingle. Elle hasn't mentioned it, but she does put extra effort into Luc's orders, customizing them for his body chemistry. Luc hasn't said a word about being half elven, likely for security reasons, but she'd known when she'd performed his first pulse diagnosis that he wasn't fully human.

She's certain he hasn't noticed the difference. "Thank you, but it's nothing special."

"I speak only the truth."

"You flatter me."

"It's warranted."

"You know, you aren't supposed to be here. You're too highly ranked for what I do."

"Your rank is insufficiently high for the work you produce. Are we having this conversation again?" Luc's eyes acquire a bit of sparkle.

Elle warns her knees not to fail her. "What conversation?"

"The one where I compliment you, you tell me it's nothing, and I marvel at why your products are not in high demand."

She bites her lip and smiles. "It really is nothing. Just standard-issue stuff."

"I've seen the standard-issue stuff, as you say."

"And?"

"Yours is better. Your magic is more potent. Your work is more detailed. I cannot see why my colleagues are not able to tell the difference, and I haven't any idea why your ratings are as low as they are."

Elle sidesteps the truth. "Sometimes I'm rude, and sometimes stuff doesn't work."

"Never, in my experience. And I have always found your work to be without fault. Regardless of what others may think, I wanted to . . ." Luc takes a breath. "That is, I saw this, and thought of you. I thought you should have it, given how much of it you spend on me."

He slips a hand into the inside pocket of his coat and withdraws a rectangular wooden case. Elle gasps when she recognizes the size and shape of it, already knows what it is before Luc takes off the lid.

An ink stick. He's brought her an ink stick that's worth at least a month of pay. Elle looks from the box to Luc, then back at the box, then back to Luc. She opens her mouth, but nothing comes out. It might be from the shock, or perhaps the confusion. People who are just friends don't usually give gifts, especially not of this caliber. Elle is of the opinion that she and Luc are more in novelty sock territory.

"I . . ." She's frozen.

"I hope it pleases you," Luc says, his voice dropping into a rare, tender quiet.

Elle reaches out, her fingers tracing first the brand name on the box, then the characters painted in gold on the surface of the stick. There doesn't exist a higher quality ink than what Luc has set on her shop counter. The stick is as hard as stone, the color a deep, pure black, and Elle knows from experience that it can last decades without cracking or losing potency. Grinding it verges on the spiritual. Using it in her work can amplify her magic fivefold, and that's without a blessing.

She makes a fist and puts her hand on the counter, fighting off the urge to sniff the stick. She'd like a moment to puzzle out what herbs have been used in its making. It probably smells divine, which will make it harder for her to turn the gift down.

"Luc, I can't." Oh, but she could paint so many things with that ink. New wards for Tony, for example, or a set of eight talismans to bring peace and prosperity to a home. Ink like that could be painted directly on someone or, if prepared correctly, tattooed. Elle's eyes fall on Luc's arm as she imagines what he might look like with her magic living in his skin, with characters drifting from his shoulder to his wrist.

There's concern on Luc's face. "You can't use it? Is it the incorrect—"

"No, it's the right kind, I just can't—"

"I don't—"

"It's too good for me." Elle means to sound matter-of-fact, but the longing creeps into her voice regardless.

Luc shuts his mouth, his eyes on hers. He pushes the box toward her. "I insist. You deserve it."

She can't refuse again; it would look too strange. "Thank you so much. That's so . . . practical of you. I appreciate that."

It's subtle, but Elle notices it: Luc schools his face back into the more businesslike expression she's come to expect from him. "Yes. I am nothing if not practical. In fact, you might find yourself using the ink rather soon."

If he can be businesslike, so can she. "Oh yeah? You need more glyphs? A bulk order?"

"Not quite. Are you available for commissions?"

Elle slaps away the *yes* which almost leaps out of her throat. Two requests in the same day. The spirits are testing her. "I'm sorry, no."

At that moment Lira strides out from the back, the phone held to her ear. "Elle, pickup is at seven thirty instead."

Wide-eyed, Elle whips herself around, shaking her head frantically at her friend.

Lira stops at the front counter, her eyes narrowing at Luc. Her demeanor cools in an instant. "Oh. It's you."

"Good afternoon, Agent Gaines," Luc greets her.

Lira gives Elle a stern look. "Seven thirty, okay?"

"I didn't say yes!"

"He says you didn't say no."

"I'm saying no now."

Lira snorts. "You wanna talk to him?"

"No!"

"He thought you might pitch a fit. He says if you don't go, he'll go by himself and get in every single news photo. He's got a hashtag picked out and everything."

What's a hashtag? Fear grips her stomach. Tony hasn't ever passed up an opportunity to have his picture taken. "He wouldn't."

"You should get a nice dress. I'll help you with it."

"I can't go." Desperate, Elle seizes the first thing that comes to mind: Luc's order. "Because I have to work!"

Lira flattens her lips into a line and puts the phone in Elle's hand. "You talk to him."

"Have you changed your mind, Agent Mei?" Luc inquires, polite.

Elle holds up a finger, mouthing *one second* at Luc. She puts the phone to her ear. "Hey. Something just came up."

「放屁!」 Tony replies.

「我沒有,」 Elle says before realizing she's speaking Chinese. "I'm not bullshitting you! I just got an urgent commission from a client. Needs to be done tomorrow night. So sorry I can't go, you shouldn't go either, but if you do, please don't get in any pictures, I'll see you when I see you, okay gotta go! Bye!"

Elle closes the phone with a satisfying clack and exhales, relieved.

Lira folds her arms over her chest and lifts an impeccably groomed eyebrow. "Are you making an exception to the policy?"

"Not really?" Elle hedges, thinking of ways to back out of the job. Maybe if she trips and breaks a finger in the next minute, Luc will let her off the hook.

"Looks like it to me."

"Okay, Agent Villois is a busy person and I'm sure he needs to discuss specifics about his not-special, extremely normal work order with me." Elle opens the counter and gestures for Luc to enter.

Lira hmms. "In private?"

"If it makes you more comfortable," Luc breaks in, "we can stay here."

"Nope!" When it comes to confrontation, Elle is in permanent flight mode. "I'm happy to discuss business matters with you in the workshop." She pastes a smile on her face until Luc leaves.

"Elle." Lira speaks softly. "For real, though."

"I know, I know." Elle drops the smile so hard it crashes on the floor. She hesitates before she picks up the ink box.

"You could have gone out instead. I think that would have been better for you."

"I'm such a homebody, you know that."

Lira shakes her head, disapproval in the set of her mouth. "What are you going to do about the commission?"

"Tell him I lied, I guess?" Elle drags a hand down her face. She doesn't want to admit she used Luc to get out of seeing her brother, but she also can't tell Luc about her brother. Either of them.

"Welp." There's sympathy in Lira's eyes. "He's your friend, right? He'll understand."

"I hope so." Elle gives her friend a quick hug and turns toward her workshop.

Chapter Two

THERE'S A LIST in Luc's dossier of the types of missions for which he's suited: guarding or escorting, or any job that requires fighting. When his boss allows him a break from violence, he's sent on reconnaissance because he passes for a thirtysomething-year-old human. At the top of the list of missions for which he isn't suited? Diplomatic missions.

The reason? A weakness in interpersonal communication.

Now, standing in Elle's workshop, he understands exactly how weak his skills are.

He hadn't intended to give her the ink in that manner. He hadn't been sure he was going to give it to her, despite disregarding his doctor's orders and spending half a day of his convalescence hobbling around Shexian County. But it had begun burning a hole in his pocket the second he'd seen her laugh, and a desperate emotion had taken over. Panic, most likely, but his dossier also says one of his strengths is that he doesn't panic.

Madness, he concludes. Temporary madness. That's the only explanation for how he'd reacted to her. He's grown accustomed to the steady flow of her friendship and how he feels in her presence. He expects the pleasant warmth in his chest when she sees him, a spark of recognition lighting her eyes. The brilliance of her smile lifts the weight from his shoulders, causing him to smile in return. This time, in addition, it was as if something in him had broken free, like water bursting a dam, and the movement had carried him along until he and the gift were deposited at her counter.

Elle enters, tucking the box of ink in her apron pocket. Their eyes meet. Luc waits, his response prepared. *It's good to see you*, she might say, or *How've you been?*

She steps past him, turning away.

Luc's stomach sinks. It must have been the gift. He hasn't explained himself. He's miscalculated the value of the ink. He's been too forward in presenting it to her.

"Sorry about the mess." Elle sticks her hands on her hips, her back to him. "Give me a minute."

She bustles around the L-shaped space, collecting scrolls of rice paper from the sofa by the door and stacking them haphazardly on one side of her long workbench. The other side is home to her chemistry apparatuses, with glass tubes and beakers and other things Luc knows nothing about.

"Tea?" Elle grabs an empty flask, filling it with water.

"Yes, please, and thank you." He isn't thirsty, and he prefers coffee, but it wouldn't have mattered if he'd said no. Elle drinks an unrealistic amount of tea.

He watches as she sets the flask over a burner, shuffles away, gathers up a few brushes, exclaims to herself, then puts her things down and shuffles back. She lights the burner with a wave of her hand, twisting the gas valve until the flame turns blue. "I'm so sorry," she says again.

"You don't need to apologize. Is there anything I can help you with?"

"No no no, go sit, I've got it handled." She gestures vaguely at the couch.

Unsure, he doesn't move.

"Luc, really."

He unbuttons his jacket and shrugs it off in preparation for her customary pulse exam, then undoes his cuffs and rolls them up. He perches on the edge of the cushion, arranging his jacket over the arm of the couch to avoid wrinkles.

Out of the corner of his eye, he sees Elle moving clutter from spot to spot. It's about as futile as digging a hole on the beach during high tide. Her workshop is in a perpetually lived-in state, a vortex where things go in and don't come out. Scattered over various surfaces are half-used notepads, each accompanied by an abandoned teacup. Whatever vertical space she has is occupied by stunning ink-and-wash paintings. The only consistently clean area is a wide circle on the floor stained with scorch marks. Otherwise, tidying doesn't come naturally to her, as evidenced by the human architecture book he'd left on the coffee table last week. He's sure it's still open to the same page.

"Everything okay?" Elle asks as she approaches, removing the ink from her pocket, then placing it on the coffee table.

"I feel I should be asking that of you." He does have a lot on his mind in addition to his current stress, but he refrains from mentioning it for now. Luc forces himself to lean back onto the couch cushions.

"There was a lot happening all at once. I'm okay." Elle pulls the ties of her apron and hauls it over her head, mussing her hair. She *tsks* and removes her hair elastic, leaning back to shake out long locks, then re-forms her ponytail.

Luc watches transfixed as she finger-combs her thick black hair, his anxiety fading into the background. Elle is, simply put, one of the most beautiful women he's seen in all his two hundred thirty-plus years on earth. She has flawless, touchable golden-beige skin, and large, expressive brown eyes that crinkle into crescents when she laughs. High cheekbones help frame an oval face with a rounded nose and a full mouth suited entirely to wide, bright smiles.

The ID picture on her agency file reflects none of that. The photo is blurry, showing a Chinese woman of indeterminate age with dark eyes and hair. Actually, her agency file is twenty years out of date, and much of the information is incorrect. For example, the file says her shop is in Vancouver instead of Raleigh, and she's listed as a B-rank despite the skills that should have her at the minimum of an A-rank.

Luc closes the architecture book in order to stop staring.

"Okay." She plops onto the armchair set diagonally from him, makes a face, and retrieves a crinkled cellophane sleeve from underneath her. "About the commission."

"Thank you very much for accepting." Luc ventures a smile.

"That wasn't . . ." Elle sighs, drooping.

Luc holds out his left wrist, expectant. Elle has in the past told him she needs to read his energies before she makes his potions. All he buys from her are agency-standard items, which don't require personal exams, but she's the artisan. He isn't about to question her competence.

Elle takes his wrist in her hands, her touch hesitant. She's always warm, thanks to her pyrokinetics. Luc steadies his breathing, corralling his heart rate as she lines up the long fingers of her hand on his vein. She closes her eyes as she probes, for which Luc is grateful because he likes to watch her as she thinks.

"You've got such incredible control," she murmurs. Usually it takes only a few deep breaths before she's done, but Elle examines him for much longer. A furrow appears between her brows. She probes again, the pressure of her fingertips changing, and frowns.

She opens her eyes. "Can I sit next to you?"

"Of course."

She takes a seat, their legs separated by inches. "Other arm, please."

Luc obliges. Elle turns his arm to show the underside of his wrist, then rests the back of his hand on her thigh as she performs her exam. He tenses. Despite his efforts, his heart rate increases.

She pulls her hand away, gasping, her eyes popping open. "What happened to you?"

That's a question with many answers, some of which he's forbidden to give. "What do you mean?"

"You've been hurt, and bad. Everything's out of balance. Why are you here when you're this injured? You need to rest!"

He needs a moment to gather his words, stunned at her reaction. "I came to give you a gift as thanks for saving my life."

"For *what?*" she yelps.

"Saving my life."

Elle's mouth drops open. When she recovers, she says, "Because of this? What happened? Can you even tell me about it?"

Luc shakes his head. "If I could, I would. You might find it funny."

"Funny how?"

Describing himself as a chew toy for basilisks will violate his NDA. Showing her the bite mark won't. "Would you like to see?"

Her eyes narrow by a hair. "Please."

"Under my collarbone." He unwinds his scarf, hiding his wince, and undoes the top buttons of his shirt, pushing aside the collar to reveal twin scabs surrounded by an area of lurid, angry red.

She leans in to inspect the wound, freezes, then looks up at him, alarmed. She's so close he can see the brown-on-black striations in her irises, so close he can feel the mist of her breath on his skin. "Are those bite marks?"

He nods.

"What bit you?"

"That, I cannot say. My apologies."

She regards him as she straightens. "Can I ask a kind of inappropriate question? You can say no."

On the inside, a hue and cry go up. On the outside, Luc merely lifts an eyebrow. "Yes."

"Did you get bitten because you're tasty?"

He does his best not to smile and fails. "No. It didn't bite me a second time either, so I will take it as confirmation."

Elle purses her lips. "You're high rank and active in the field, which means you have access to the best healers here. You're still hurt. That bite is fresh, and from the looks of it, from a venomous creature. Necrotoxin. Close to your heart too. You survived that?"

Impressive. He'd ask what training she's had, but they've made it a point not to ask about each other's backgrounds. Luc will have to resign himself to Elle being a mystery. It's better that way. If she knew what he did or heard the rumors about him, she'd stop being his friend, like all the colleagues who have gone from cooperating with him to whispering behind his back.

And now, mocking him for botching a routine mission he's completed dozens of times. It's shameful for someone who's seen as the model agent, the perfect Fixer. The original and the best. "Barely. I found life to be more preferable."

"And you thought I'd find that funny because . . . ?"

"My coworkers found it funny." Luc remembers hearing laughter before passing out. "I'm sorry. I shouldn't have said it."

"Almost dying isn't funny. Your coworkers are jerks. Your injury must hurt a lot."

Not as much as the venom had. He's since walled off the pain, acknowledging its presence but not allowing it to take up space. "It's bearable, thanks to you. With more treatment, I should regain full function."

"If it does bother you, try acupuncture. Wounds like that often stagnate, and acupuncture will get your energy flowing again. I can—" Elle takes a breath. "I can recommend a few excellent doctors who could work with your special needs."

Part of the puzzle of how he survived clicks into place. She knows he's half-elven, and has been customizing his order for him for who knows how long. No one save for his boss, his aunt, and his physician know what he is. His full file is inaccessible to all but the founder of Roland & Riddle, and the semi-pointed ears that would have marked his heritage had been docked many years ago.

He speaks quietly. "How did you figure it out?"

She shifts on the couch, looking everywhere but at him. "Your pulse diagnosis. Your energy flow isn't human."

"When?"

"The first time. Right away. I just didn't say anything."

"Thank you for keeping it confidential. And thank you for your concern. Suffice it to say I'm now in good health, in no small part thanks to you. Your glyph of restoration, along with your healing potions, were the difference between mission success and mission failure." He watches as her eyes widen.

"Your skills are extraordinary." After eight months of getting to know her, he's finally caught a glimpse of the breadth and depth of her abilities, and it's staggering. Luc has sat with Elle many times as she's drawn up his order. He doesn't recall her stopping to reformulate his potions; she combines ingredients with a confidence he's assumed was born of routine.

Luc reaches for the ink, presenting the box to her, meeting her eyes before he speaks. This is how he should have approached the situation, and not the shove-it-at-her-and-hope-for-the-best method. "I wanted to give you a gift of gratitude for saving me. You have my deepest thanks."

She takes the box from him, her fingers brushing against his. A jolt crackles between them, racing up his arm and through his body.

Elle's head comes up, her lips parting, her hand stilling against his. Luc looks at the fullness of her lower lip. The longer they stay in contact, the more he wants her touch.

The water begins boiling.

"Excuse me," Elle murmurs, getting up, setting the box on the table.

Luc swallows and lets out a silent breath once her back is turned.

Elle returns with a teapot and two cups on a tray, pours tea for them both, and sits.

"The commission," Luc continues, pretending nothing has happened, "was supposed to be part of it. I didn't know how else to show my thanks."

"Would it, um, hurt your feelings if I backed out?"

According to his colleagues and an anonymous intranet post from earlier in the year, Luc has no feelings. "No. I don't take things personally."

"Really?" Elle looks worried. "Because you just gave me this ink, and if I'm not doing your commission, then I won't need it."

That stings. "It's a gift. It's yours regardless."

She glances at the box, yearning on her face. "Are you sure? It's so expensive."

Luc's mouth reacts faster than his brain. "Measured against my life, it comes up short."

Elle freezes as if someone has hit pause. "You say that to every gal who saves your life? How would your doctor feel?"

He has to recover the situation and run damage control. Perhaps he should open a ticket and request "interpersonal communications" to be bolded and underlined in his file. "My doctor is an old werewolf who's tired of seeing me."

"With a wound like that, he's going to see you lots."

"I'm aware. I have reduced responsibilities until he clears me."

"Reduced responsibilities?" Disbelief is written all over her face. "You aren't on medical leave?"

"Unfortunately, I am not." Dr. Clavret had recommended a minimum of ten days of PTO in his report to Oberon, Luc's boss, but it had gone ignored. Luc could argue, but he knows from previous experience that his position as Oberon's right hand means nothing. No one says no to the founder of Roland & Riddle.

"You should be resting!"

"I agree, but there's the matter of work." Prior to being bitten, Luc had been daydreaming of asking for several months off and renting a small apartment in Strasbourg, then spending much of that time researching curse-breaking. That's out of the question now. Oberon won't reward him for failure. If he wants to escape—no. Calling it escape is a conceit, as he can never leave Oberon's side. If he wants a respite, he needs absolute success on the next mission.

Elle gets to her feet and goes across the room to one of the baskets where she keeps spare glyphs. She returns with a stack of them and smacks them onto the coffee table. "I'm giving you a bunch of restoration glyphs. Use them all. I'm sorry I can't do more for you."

"My commission," Luc reminds her. "It's necessary for my job. I apologize for pressing you. I believe your glyphs would give me the edge I need."

"Luc," she starts.

"Please." He meets her eyes, despair welling up from where he's kept it sealed. He can't leave Oberon, but if he can get that month, he can pretend his boss doesn't exist. For a month, he can devote himself to helping the two children who need him.

Just the thought of it is enough to raise a guilty flush in his neck. Luc throws the intrusive thoughts and emotions back into their boxes and buries them.

Elle wavers, then sighs. "I'll at least hear you out. But it depends on what you're asking for. I have limited ability."

Relief breaks over him. "Please don't undersell yourself. I won't believe it for a second."

"What if I oversell myself?"

"I doubt you could."

She cocks an eyebrow. "An immortality serum would cost you a million cool ones."

"Cool what?"

"Cool ones. You know, money."

He tries not to laugh, closing his eyes briefly, taking a measured breath. He hasn't heard that phrase before. Coming from her, it's adorable. "Do you mean a cool million?"

"No, cool ones. Don't you call money cool ones in French or something?"

"No, and I don't think we call it 'cool ones' in English either."

Elle scowls. "I said what I said. Cool ones. A million of them."

Very seriously, he replies, "I will have to check the cool ones bank to see if I have the funds should I want to live forever. You're still underselling yourself. That's an unreasonably low price."

She dissolves into giggles. "Cool ones bank! What should I charge?"

Luc gives up, laughing with her. Elle's smile is a weapon against which he has no defense, and her laugh is infectious. She, and no one else, has that effect on him. It's been empirically proven. "In which currency? USD or cool ones?"

She laughs harder. "Enough, I get it! What do you need from me?"

He's thought about this a lot, not having much else to focus on during his hospital stay. "I'd like a total of five glyphs or potions."

Elle grabs a pen and a notepad and settles back into her chair, her eyes trained on the paper. "Go for it."

"I would like a restoration potion, a glyph of enhanced strength and agility, a poison ward, a glyph of blurring, and a glyph of edged light."

"It's a tall order." Elle peers at her notepad. "Some of these I don't think I'd be able to do."

"My usual order—" Luc starts.

"Is simple compared to what I'd need for these," Elle finishes. "It would be easier if I knew what situations you were going into, but I know you can't tell me."

More basilisks, Luc almost says. They, along with angry leshiye and the yearly incursion of irritable undead with swords, are a recurring problem, the solution to which requires coordination between no fewer than three agency departments and a lot of misinformation released on the internet in false flag operations. He shakes his head instead.

Her mouth presses into a line. "I've heard you out, and this is a big order. Are you sure you can't get these somewhere else? You've got better access to a wider array of things than I do. You don't need custom work from me."

"I trust you."

"You really shouldn't."

"You haven't given me a reason not to."

She looks away, then back. "You shouldn't go around blindly trusting mediocre glyphmakers."

Luc snorts quietly. "You are anything but mediocre. I would not choose that for myself." As soon as he's said it, he realizes his mistake. His mouth is fired, effective immediately.

"What?"

"I meant," he says, remaining steady because he doesn't panic, "that if you were mediocre, I would not return repeatedly." That isn't much better. "Your work, that is." Still not better, judging by Elle's faint smile.

"Would you like to keep trying, Agent Villois?"

He slumps against the couch cushion. "No, thank you, Agent Mei."

"Let's talk compensation."

"Anything you need, I'll provide. Money is no object." He doesn't have many expenses and he constantly works overtime, which adds up over two hundred years. He also gets a seniority bonus. "You shouldn't need to spend anything but your time."

"Which I will invoice you for. These won't be easy to make. I'm not even sure if some of these are possible. I'll have to leave the shop to Lira. She has her own work to do and can't be covering for me all the time."

"Of course."

"One last stipulation, then." Elle straightens, descending into seriousness. "It's the most important one. If you can't agree to this, I can't do this work for you."

Luc straightens as well. "Name it."

She fixes him with a steely, level stare. "You have to keep me a secret. You can't tell anyone who I am or where to find me. If anyone asks, you send them somewhere else."

Luc meets her gaze, the gears in his head turning. "You want me to keep all of your information confidential."

"Yes. If you can't do that, then this commission won't get off the ground, and you'll no longer be welcome here."

He blinks, taken aback at her words. Not for the first time, he wonders who she is. "At all?"

"At all. I know it's extreme. I'm sorry. I like you, and I've enjoyed our time together, but if you can't agree to do this one thing—and you can refuse, no hard feelings—then you can't come back."

It's an easy choice. Luc already maintains an impenetrable wall between his work life and his private life, not wanting anyone to claim the few parts of him that aren't fully agency property. Elle is one of those few. "I agree."

"I need it to be stronger than that."

"You have my word."

"Stronger."

"I swear it on my laes." There is no stronger oath. A laes is the object that holds a fae's magical essence; it defines them as fae. "Agent Elle Mei, I will keep all your information confidential."

"Then, Agent Luc Villois, you have a deal. You'll get five glyphs or potions." Elle sticks her hand out.

He clasps it, bracing himself for a spark, but there's only her warmth. "Thank you."

"Do you have a timetable for these? How does two weeks sound?"

"Excellent."

"Okay. I'll get started right away, but I need to go chat with Lira first." Elle stands. "Do you mind waiting here?"

"Not at all." As of right now, Luc has only paperwork and a check-in later in the evening.

"I'll be right back, then. Don't go anywhere."

Luc nods and opens the architecture book to find his place.

Elle finds the store blessedly empty. Lira is sitting on a stool, hunched over the counter, her chin in one hand and a pencil in the other.

"That went fast." She places the pencil in the spine of her notebook before closing it. "How long am I covering for you?"

Elle sputters. "How'd you know?"

Lira gives her a flat stare.

"What?"

Silence as Lira leans into the look further.

"Seriously?"

"Elle, please. You've never said no to him."

"What are you—what are you trying to say?" Elle glares. Luc hasn't even tried to get close. She can't say yes when he keeps an ordained distance of at least a foot between them.

"I'm not trying to say anything, I'm just sayin'." Lira holds her hands up, shrugging.

"Just say it then!"

"I did. I said you've never said no to him."

"That's not true!"

"Name one time."

"I—" She shuts her mouth with a click. She's never said no to Luc.

"I mean, I get it. You can spend more time with the white French guy who probably likes you—"

"Lira, no, we're just friends!"

"Just friends, uh-huh, next you'll say some shit about having a business relationship."

"That's exactly what we have!"

"Which is one hundred percent garbage because he never buys any runes from me. If I didn't know any better, I'd be side-eyeing the hell out of that."

"I accidentally saved his life with one of my potions and he's figured out it's me and that's why he wants a commission!"

Lira stops. "Oh, shit. Elle! You were doing work to spec this whole time?"

"No! I mean, yes, but he didn't know, and now he does." Elle puts her face in her hands. "I tried to get out of it, I really did, but he said I saved his life and then I couldn't back out. I told him two weeks for his order and swore him to secrecy or else he couldn't come back."

Elle covers her eyes so she won't see the expression on Lira's face.

"Are you upset that you've been found out, or are you upset that you have to do the commission?"

"Um." The commission is, if she's honest with herself, not as difficult as she's making it out to be. Maybe it'll scratch the itch, and she'll be fine again once she's finished.

"How big of an order are we talking here?"

"Major. I need stuff I can't find here. I have to go to New York." Elle would order if it wouldn't leave a direct trail to her door. "I should have just said I'd go out tomorrow."

"Don't kid yourself. You'd still be here moaning about having to go out. But if you don't think that'd be the case, you can tell Villois no, and we can close early to go dress shopping."

Elle sulks. "What if I do neither."

"You could, but you'll be unhappy at losing the chance to flex, we won't have a pile of money from a commission, and you'll have multiple people pissed at you. I know you hate that."

It's true. Elle has her father's harmonious nature, which has proven useful for a middle child. But valuing harmony, she thinks bitterly, is what's gotten her into her current life: retail drudgery, self-imposed mediocrity, a magic-less elder brother aging prematurely from a broken laes, and a once-beloved younger brother who has vowed to see his older siblings dead.

She has no right to be upset over the consequences of her decisions. She's responsible for Tony's safety, especially after her part in the disaster. His happiness, though—that should matter as well. "What if you went tomorrow?"

Lira considers. "That's not a bad idea, actually. Would that be okay? You've been leery of too much contact in the past."

"He really wants to go. I feel bad about not letting him have his fun. He'll be happy to see you."

"Wow, you're easing up *and* taking a commission all in the same day. Amazing."

"He'll be protected with you." As the daughter of the Black Doctor of the Pines, Lira is a ghost-spirit hybrid who can't be killed and has few weak points. Add in a close relationship with Norse gods and Lenni Lenape spirits, and she's a formidable opponent.

"Yes. I'm sure nothing will happen. It's been years. You've done great. How long am I covering you for?"

"Two weeks at most. Don't worry about it, he said he'll compensate me for everything. I know your family time is coming up, and I won't run into it. Hey, do you think we can work on linking our magic again?"

"Sure, if there's time." Lira taps her notebook. "I was thinking the same thing. Was working out some rune schematics."

Movement catches Elle's eye. It's one of the local lutins employed as cleaning staff for the agency. They're effective, if overenthusiastic, but the agency building is a large, multistory office building shoved into a pocket dimension, and no one else is willing to do the work.

The lutin pushes open the door, dragging the cleaning cart in, and peers around, likely searching for dirt and disorder. He looks directly at Elle. "Hi there! Hello! Do you need any help?"

"You deal with it," Elle mutters to Lira, backing away from the counter. "I've got a client waiting."

"Hey!" Lira frowns and starts fading away.

"Hello?" the lutin calls again. Elle glances over her shoulder as she escapes to her workshop. Lira has gone fully ghost and is invisible. "Excuse me? Hello?"

Chapter Three

ELLE SHUTS HER WORKSHOP door, slumping against it, and exhales.

"Is there a problem?" Luc asks.

She straightens and gives him what she hopes is a reassuring smile. "No, everything's fine. One of the lutins came in and I'm protecting his sanity by not letting him in here. Don't want a code Stiltskin."

He surveys her workshop as if taking a panorama, his head swiveling on his neck. "Yes," he says finally. "You are quite considerate."

Elle laughs, partially in embarrassment. "Thanks. I'm gonna go make my list."

She snags a notepad off the corner of her workbench, shepherding her mind toward what she needs. But Luc's presence looms larger and larger, and after the fourth item, she loses focus. He knows about her. Sort of. He doesn't *know* know about her, which is good, because the last time she checked, her little brother Yiwú was still on the agency's shit list, and Elle wants no harm to come to him.

It's an unreasonable position to take, seeing as Yiwú tried to take Tony's laes and, when that didn't work, tried to kill him, but love is unreasonable. She couldn't choose between her little brother, who'd been her best friend, and her big brother, whom she'd idolized. She can't choose. All she can do is keep Tony hidden. If worse comes to worst, she and Tony can move again. With repetition should come ease, right?

She's overreacting. Elle's paternal grandmother had the temperament of a smooth-running river, unperturbed by small disturbances or mishaps, and it's that temperament she prays for now. For the next hour, or the rest of the afternoon, she'll focus on what she knows she can do: paint glyphs and make potions.

Elle blows out a breath, stabbing the tip of her pencil into her notepad. The edged light glyph is likely for a sword. As for the glyph of blurring, she assumes it's meant to make him harder to see in order for him to gain an advantage in combat, like the S-rank optical illusion charm.

It's a clue as to who Luc is. Elle has tried to look, but her current rank is a B, and she needs to be an A to see more than his name. Based on the extreme lack of information about him, she's sure Luc is S-rank and works for the Bureau, the elite, secretive arm of the agency. He might be part of the Fixers, the special agents who report directly to Oberon, the legendary founder of Roland & Riddle. Everyone else in the Atlantic division reports to Lysander, the COO, who is, if the rumors are true, Oberon's son.

Bureau agents are accessible to executive levels only. Elle used to have those privileges, and two brothers she adored, and a thriving business with plenty of challenge. Now she has a so-so business with a yawn-worthy level of challenge, though Luc being here alleviates that somewhat. If this job goes well, there may be more in the future, which would mean guaranteed time with him.

Slow down. Elle quashes the flutter of excitement at the idea of putting on her jade and letting her full power out. She's getting too far ahead of herself. This is a single job that she'll do once for a regular, and not someone whose company she enjoys, whose humor she tries to tease out. Every time he smiles it's like he's opening a door to a vast, hidden warmth, and she's addicted to it.

Nope, Elle has to swerve around that. She sneaks a glance at Luc, who's absorbed in the architecture book. He has his lip tucked under his teeth again, but there's an expression of wistful longing on his face as he reads.

He looks up, his eyes meeting hers. His voice is uncharacteristically gentle when he asks, "Is something the matter?"

Oh, skies. She could fall into those eyes and never return. "No, nothing. Do you want to borrow the book? You look interested in it."

His answering smile puts a stutter in her heartbeat. He closes the book, placing it on the table. "Thank you, but no, thank you. There are photographs in here that remind me of places I've been. That's all."

"What places?"

"Eastern France, the Alsace-Lorraine region."

"Did you spend lots of time there?"

Luc's smile widens. "I grew up there."

She mirrors him, unable to stop herself. "Do you miss it?"

He glances at the book, then looks back to her. "I do, yes. And what of you?"

Elle had grown up in her mountaintop ancestral home in Shén-nóngjià, Húběi. She and Yìwú had their own joke for it: Shénnóngjià, Shénnóng's House instead of Shénnóng's Ladder-Trellis-Thing. She'll never be allowed back. Her family thinks Tony is dead and she's responsible, which is not the whole truth. More like 90 percent.

"Elle?"

"Oh. I'm sorry. Yes, I do miss it." Elle points at one of the paintings on her wall. "That's from where I grew up."

"That's beautiful." Luc goes over to inspect it. "Who's the artist?"

Me, she almost replies. Alert, alert. She isn't supposed to draw attention to herself, and she doesn't paint anymore. "Nobody important."

He eyeballs her for a full second longer than is comfortable. "A shame she isn't more well known. She does masterful work."

The alert turns into a hamster running frantically in its wheel. "I have some questions about your commission," Elle declares loudly. She's going to change the subject with deftness.

"Yes?"

"Could I modify your order? The restoration stuff you want is mostly covered by the things I already do for you. I could make a potion, but what if I combined it with your strength and agility glyph? Is that okay?"

"You're the artist," Luc replies.

Elle elects to ignore his choice of words.

"You have carte blanche to do what you wish."

"Really?"

"Really. I defer to you, the expert."

She clears her throat, stifling the little flame of delight that has kindled inside her. What she isn't going to do is start clapping. "I can do anything I want?"

Luc chuckles. "Could I truly stop you?"

"Okay. Okay!" Elle snatches up her notepad and pencil and hustles to the filing cabinets on the far side of her workshop. She opens one, her mind racing. "Ginseng," she mutters, hauling out an overstuffed folder. "And elven sage."

She peeks in to check the contents and drops it flat side down with a resounding thump, spilling paper across the floor. Unconcerned, she steps over the mess to wrestle with the handle of another drawer. After some yanking, the drawer opens with an affronted shriek.

"Have you ever had White Rabbit milk candy?" Elle calls over her shoulder. "What if I did something like that? Like a caramel, but with the glyph as the wrapper?"

She pauses, thinking. Her glyphs are touch-activated. Using the wrapper as the glyph wouldn't work. "No, wait. I'll put the glyph on rice paper inside a gummy candy infused with restorative herbs. How does that sound? Activates on chew. I think I have a mold somewhere. Not, like, fungus mold, though I have that too."

"That sounds wonderful." Luc pauses. "The mold for shaping things, not the furry mold."

She claps with glee. "Excellent! I have a schematic for poison resistance in here somewhere. The glyph of blurring and edged light, I'll have to experiment with." Elle searches for her advanced agency manual, which she's not supposed to have anymore but has kept, and dredges it up from the back of the drawer.

"Do I need to be present for that?"

No, but today is a weird day full of possibilities, and she isn't going to throw away her shot, as Lira has said over and over. Given what Elle has overheard from Lira's workshop, there are only five songs and one act in the whole musical. "Yes. I'll need help with the testing."

"Let me know what you need from me, then."

"I gotta get my ingredient list together. I'll have a better idea of how to plan afterwards." She clears out space in the middle of her pile, notebook at the ready, already thinking about what she needs to get in New York. If she can make the trip fast, she should be safe. "I'll start a new invoice for you and bill you for the supplies."

"Better yet," Luc says, checking his watch, "I can go with you and pay for everything."

"Wait a second." She scans him up and down, critical. "You need to go home and rest. You can't be running around with me in New York."

"I'll go after you're finished. Please don't take offense, but I have doubts as to whether you'd invoice me for your full investment into this job."

"I—" She's been outmaneuvered.

Luc's mouth pulls into a lopsided smirk that's gallingly attractive. "Go make your list, Agent Mei."

Luc watches Elle flit around her workshop, chatting absentmindedly to her growing shopping list. She opens a drawer to study a glyph, a dreamy half smile on her face, her fingers tracing the brushstrokes with such loving care that it makes him wish he were the paper.

If only she'd look at him with that same fondness. She has, he's determined, no understanding of what effect she has on him, no awareness that being close to her and her cheerful disposition only makes him want to be closer. No one else in his life treats him with kindness. No one asks about his general well-being, nor do they ask for his opinion. Elle extends to him a basic level of care, without any calculating element behind it, and that's refreshing. All it does is give him the desire to reciprocate and turn himself to her like a flower seeking sunlight.

"Okay, I'm done." Elle slaps her pen on her workbench with finality. The sound of it shakes Luc from his thoughts. "Let's get some food. I wonder what they have at the cafeteria?"

"The cafeteria?" Luc narrows his eyes at her, hoping she isn't considering a meal in a place where liquid albumin counts as fresh eggs. "As in the canteen? This one here? In this branch?"

"Um, yes?" Elle shrugs one shoulder. "I just want a snack. Where else would I go?"

"You have someone else's money to spend and you want to eat at the cafeteria?" Luc leans forward from his seat on the couch and stabs two fingers into the surface of the coffee table. "Here? This one?"

"I heard you the first time. Are you judging my choices?"

Luc has had precisely one pastry from the canteen, a muffin so old and dry that selling it should have gotten their food service license revoked. "Yes. I am. Please reconsider. If it's a snack you'd like, I'm aware of a café in your town whose baked goods are decent and whose coffee is better."

"You're aware of it," Elle says, her eyes gleaming with a hint of mischief, "or do you know from personal experience?"

"Personal experience."

She grins. "Naughty of you. Sneaking out with mundanes on company time? You could be written up if you were found out."

Luc snorts his laughter. "Hardly. My record is pristine, Agent Mei. And I'm allowed exceptions."

"Oh, a model employee stands before me. Do they have your picture on the wall?" Elle sticks a hand on her hip, her other hand describing an arc, like a vista is spread before her. "I can see it now. The corkboard in the back of the office. Employee of the month, Agent Luc Villois. One gold star to you."

He's been the employee of the century, more like. Oberon sends Luc into hairy situations without reservation and expects a finished job, no excuses. Luc delivers every time despite his personal feelings. "I have at least two gold stars. You might undersell yourself, but I am proud of my two stickers."

She laughs, rolling her eyes at him. "All right, fine. I'll make you a deal. I need to go to a bigger branch anyway. How about the cafeteria in New York?"

Luc frowns. "Is this your idea of a compromise?"

"That's a yes, then?" She giggles, but it doesn't alleviate his concern over her taste. "It's a date? I mean, not that kind of date."

He heaves a sigh. "Call it a client meal. I wouldn't lower myself to calling an outing at the company canteen a date."

"A client snack, then."

"That does not sound . . . correct." He's had enough of things trying to eat him.

"A client teatime?" Elle tilts her head, brown eyes thoughtful.

"Tea is at four, and it's barely two. A client meal works well."

"Okay, I'll take it. Makes this sound super professional." Elle waves her list in the air. "Let's go!"

They leave the shop under Lira's appraising eyes, going down several floors in the building to where the port room is located. The transport system is proprietary magic, Roland & Riddle's pride and joy, the secret to its success, run at all hours by carefully trained technicians. The system allows fae to travel instantaneously to any branch in the world, provided it's hooked into the network. In Raleigh, the port room has large double doors, both propped open, giving Luc a view of a half dozen glass tubes, each four meters high and three meters wide, set upon reinforced wooden grates, all on top of glowing rings. Three of the tubes are marked for arrivals, the rest for departures. As they approach, a humanoid agent blinks into one of the tubes, then pushes open the door and exits, bustling toward the outbound turnstile.

Luc is thankful for the upgraded technology, remembering when the system was semi-reliable fairy rings separated by wooden partitions. Occasionally, it resulted in being sent to the middle of nowhere, or worse, some human's garden party.

"Where to?" asks the conductor goblin, perched at his station.

"Manhattan for both of us," Luc replies.

"Rings 2 and 3." The goblin gestures to what looks like a card reader. "Swipe your FIDs, please."

Once they arrive in Manhattan, Elle takes the lead, which should surprise Luc but doesn't. She weaves between crowds of fae, not once looking at the massive domed ceiling, intricately inlaid marble floors, or signposts attached to each corner, heading toward the canteen with the accuracy of a hawk diving for prey. She doesn't glance at the sphinx on her massive stone plinth in the center of the hall, charting a direct path past her. Around the sphinx's plinth are gathered several fae, with more standing at a distance to gawk.

It's another indication that Elle is more than she lets on. Most fae are unused to seeing a sphinx, though they're fixtures in metropolis-sized branches, volunteering their time to answering questions about the agency. There remain a handful of sphinxes in the world, and the only one in North America frequents the Manhattan branch. Her residency used to be in London, but after what Oberon had done to Luc twenty-eight years ago, she prefers to be anywhere Oberon isn't.

Luc smiles faintly when she turns lazy, kohl-lined eyes onto him, her tail quivering the slightest bit, the overhead lights glancing off high, regal cheekbones in a dark-skinned face. He nods to her, respectful, as her mind brushes his.

« *Lucien. Bon retour.* » Her voice is as warm as the desert from which she comes, and always a comfort to hear, especially so when she chooses to speak to him in his preferred tongue.

« *Allo, Tatie.* » He sends her his affection.

« *Comment tu vas?* »

She likely senses a story, but Luc doesn't have the time for an explanation at the moment. He sends her flashes of images and emotions instead, knowing they'll suffice. « *J'suis bien.* »

« *Mm.* » She's unconvinced. It's possible she's detected his suppressed pain. « *C'est qui, ça?* »

He tells her the truth: he and Elle are work friends. There's never any use lying to a creature so telepathically strong. « *Ma collègue.* »

She chuckles as if she knows something he doesn't. « *Ah bon? Et qu'est-ce que tu fais?* »

« *J'vais chercher quelque chose à manger.* » The tips of Luc's ears heat up for some reason. He and Elle aren't doing anything but getting food before work.

« *Avec ta copine?* » The sphinx continues to laugh as he follows Elle down a wide hallway. It's good-natured, of course. Outwardly, all she shows is a Mona Lisa smile.

« *Ma collègue,* » he repeats, firm. Luc bids her a hurried goodbye as he exits her range, promising to catch her up later.

"Everything okay?" Elle touches his arm briefly. "Luc?"

"Apologies. I was thinking."

"Must be some heavy thinking," she says with a smile. "All right, is your card ready to handle my stomach?"

He snorts. "Yes. Didn't you say you wanted a snack?"

"You said client meal, so I'm running with it. I can do some serious damage, just saying."

"You're welcome to try. All meals at the agency are free for me."

"What?! When did that memo go out?"

"You might not have gotten it." He feels a bit sheepish. "It was top-level. Years ago."

"You have an unlimited credit line already. They didn't have to add free meals to that." She grabs a tray and plunks a plate down. It rattles.

"It isn't unlimited." The credit line is simply quite high.

"I've seen your fancy card. You didn't bat an eyelash when you offered to pay for everything. So it might as well be unlimited." Elle bypasses the non-humanoid foods, pauses in front of the Western selection, then slides an enormous quiche onto her tray.

Luc has to laugh when he sees the price tag. "And here you were, trying to eat at your branch canteen."

Freshly squeezed organic orange juice grown in a dryad-tended orchard makes its way onto her tray. "Seems like I've developed expensive taste now that I have a wealthy patron."

"Here, at least, I am the richest man in the world. Outside, it may differ." Luc orders an espresso for himself and a glass of spring water. They find a table for two by the window, where Elle tries valiantly to prevail against the quiche.

"Do you need some help?" Luc sips his coffee, entertained by how she's glaring at her food.

"I might." She makes a face. "I hate wasting food."

"Same." He needs a fork. He rises, but stops when Elle offers hers.

"I'm not sick." She smiles. "Don't worry."

"I wasn't." He sits back down and accepts it, telling himself there's nothing behind the gesture other than practicality. They're friends, and friends sometimes share utensils.

Once the plates are cleared, Elle fishes out her list and navigates the upper levels of the Manhattan branch like an old hand. Luc saunters along in her wake, content to trail behind.

"Can you believe these prices?" Elle mutters after they leave an herb shop. She casts a dark look behind her. "Wouldn't even haggle."

"I wasn't aware one could bargain with dwarves."

"Everything can be negotiated," Elle says, giving him her bag. "Doesn't matter who or what. Price tags are just a suggestion."

"Is that so?" Luc shuffles around the bags he's already carrying to accommodate the new one. "Would you say the same for your prices?"

"Of course." Elle sniffs. "No one's been clever enough to try haggling, though."

"Duly noted. Could I theoretically bargain you down from a million cool ones, then?"

She breaks into laughter. "Stop teasing me!"

"What would make you lower the price? Do you barter?"

Elle spins on her foot, walking backward as she talks. Her smile takes on an impish element. "Only if I like what you have to offer."

He only has himself, which most people would find a poor deal. "I'm afraid I'm stuck with paying a million cool ones."

"Oh, I wouldn't say that." She rakes her eyes over him, speaking before turning around. "I'm sure you have something I want."

He continues to follow her as she forges cheerfully ahead, leaving him in his packhorse role. Luc wonders if he looks like the stereotypically aggrieved boyfriend with shopping bags sprouting from his hands.

He admonishes himself for wishful thinking although the afternoon has lent itself to the practice. For once, he isn't knee-deep in unseelie fae guts or guarding sensitive magical items in transit. He isn't babysitting a naga princess with a crush on him, nor running point on the Wrecking Crew's nutty and often literally explosive schemes. He isn't intercepting rival agents and neutralizing them. He isn't being stabbed, shot, punched, bludgeoned, or bitten (again). He especially isn't doing the stabbing, shooting, punching, bludgeoning, or biting, although Luc can only recall a few instances in the last hundred years when he's had to resort to using teeth.

All he's done is have an unhurried meal with a beautiful woman and hold her shopping bags. There's a small pang of guilt as he realizes how much he's enjoying something this normal and how he'd like to have more of it. His regular life is considered exciting, and a dream for some agents, but here he is, longing for the exact opposite. Stability and routine wouldn't be bad, and he could visit Elle more than a few times a month.

Because he'd like to have more of her time. Luc would like to have more of Elle and the way she's breezing through the supply floor like she belongs there. He'd like to have more of her and the adorable way she passes her shopping bags to him, thrusting her arm out, a toothy, cheesy grin on her face. Luc finds himself unable to mount even the smallest bit of protest. Whatever she wants, she'll get.

If things work out, he might ask her to be his exclusive supplier. The thought of having an excuse to see her weekly, maybe twice a week, causes him so much excitement that he gets embarrassed. *Has no feelings*, he reminds himself, recalling the intranet post as Elle gesticulates at a shopkeeper. *But takes orders and will remember your birthday.*

"That took longer than I thought!" Elle announces after she exits the last store, tearing her list into pieces and dumping them into a bin. "I'm ready to go back. Do you need any help carrying those? I'm sorry I made you hold everything."

Luc shakes his head, facing her. "I will be fine. It's a welcome change from what I usually do."

"You like the boring domestic stuff, then?" Elle flashes him a quick smile.

He's utterly captivated. "Today I do. With you."

Elle's smile disappears in an instant, and the mood crystallizes into one of fear.

Luc's heart sinks. He's spoken too much. "I'm sorry, that was too forward. Forgive me."

She doesn't look at him, going as still and tense as prey when it sees a predator. He isn't sure if she's even breathing.

"Elle, what's wrong?"

"Listen to me." Her voice is low and soft but holds an edge. When she lifts her chin to look at him, her eyes are full of apprehension. "I'm going to step very close to you. Put your arms around me, and I'll explain."

Luc does as he's told, encircling her gingerly, trying not to make too much contact. His heart shifts gait into a wild gallop. He's never allowed himself to be this close to Elle, hasn't entertained the notion of hugging her. He's preserved the space between them as carefully as a curator with a priceless item, wanting to put their friendship in a glass case, afraid to let anything near lest it break. She's his friend, and that's enough. He should be satisfied.

Elle tucks her forehead against his neck, slipping her arms around his waist, curling herself against him like she's hiding. Luc responds instinctively by bending himself to her, tightening his hold until they're pressed together. Her breath unfurls warm against his skin, and all he can think of is how strangely intimate it is. If they were in any other situation, Luc would remark on how well they fit.

"I'm sorry to put you on the spot like this." Elle pitches her voice for his ears only. "Don't turn around. There is someone here I don't want to talk to, but she's seen me. She isn't sure it's me yet. She'll approach. You might hear her shouting a name. Ignore it."

Luc folds his emotions up neatly and stores them in the box where he keeps them while at work. Whatever tightness he's experiencing drains away as his body settles into mission mode, muscles loose but active, ready to act and react. "Understood. Further orders?"

"We might be able to lose her in the lobby, but she's a fox spirit and she'll know me if she smells me." Elle detaches herself from him, turning quickly, and heads for a stairwell at the other end of the hall. Luc feels her loss as a sharp but muted ache.

"She's young. Ninety at most, so she doesn't have all her powers yet. Lucky for me." Elle shoulders open the door, glancing down the hall. "Shit. I've been made."

Their footsteps echo as they descend, accompanied by the rustling and rattling of bags. Elle wastes no time, zeroing in on the ground floor, going down stairs so fast she looks like she's in a controlled fall. Several floors above them, a door opens with an echoing thunk, then a resounding crack as it rebounds off the wall. The fox spirit shouts a name, but the stairwell distorts it, the sound waves bouncing around and running into each other.

Elle shoves the ground floor door open with her foot, escaping into the lobby. Luc follows on her heels, the hubbub of the grand hall washing over him as he takes in their surroundings. In the center is the sphinx's dais, now empty, and to their right is the port room. The building current of the late afternoon rush manifests itself as coalescing clumps of fae that move en masse toward the doors, obscuring the view of the room.

If the woman chasing them tracked by sight alone, they could slip into the crowd unnoticed, but the fox spirit likely has their scents, as Elle has predicted. Luc frowns as he runs through suitable counters, but there are none in this environment.

Elle licks a finger, using the moisture to draw something on the back of her hand. Instantly, a strong gust springs up from beneath them, like they're standing on an active subway grate. Around them, fae exclaim in surprise, feathers and fur and hair ruffling. The wind disappears as suddenly as it had appeared.

"Ugly, but it'll do," Elle mutters, stretching her legs in a faster walk.

"What did you . . . ?" Luc overtakes her, using his larger body to break through the crowd.

"A little wind to make it harder for her to find me." She makes a sound of dismay when the port room comes into view. Through the windows, Luc sees that the room has filled, and with each passing second, more fae add themselves to the massive, zigzagging queue.

Elle grabs his sleeve, distressed. "We aren't going to make it through all of this. She'll catch up and follow me right back home. I can't go there. Skies, where can I go?"

If it's safety Elle needs, Luc can provide it. If it's speed she needs, he can provide that also. His rank gives him executive-level privileges, including the power to jump the port queue when he deems it necessary.

Luc deems it necessary and reaches into his pocket to retrieve his FID. "Don't worry. Stay close to me."

He bypasses the whole room, shoving through the fae in line, ignoring shouts of indignation, undoing worn tape barriers and letting them snap back into their stanchions. He barely notices when Elle latches onto his arm. Her apologies trail behind them like wisps of smoke. Luc angles directly for the nearest conductor, cutting in front of the next fae.

"Hey, what the hell is your problem?" the conductor snaps at him in an oversized Brooklyn accent. "Stand in line like everyone else or I'll call security!"

Luc holds up his FID so the iridescent sticker in the bottom corner gleams and gives his best VIP glare. "Emergency." He indicates Elle with a jerk of his head. "She's with me. Paris. Now."

The conductor sits up straight, eyes wide. "Yes, sir. Right away, sir. Rings 7 and 10 are ready."

Luc leads Elle to the rings; her attention is concentrated behind her. "You take 7, it's closer. I'll see you on the other side."

She nods and steps onto the grate, pulling the glass door shut.

Chapter Four

*I*T DOESN'T HIT LUC until after Elle is in his house that there is someone in his house. He, Luc Villois, notorious loner, has invited another person willingly into his home, and she's standing in the foyer, taking off her shoes, lining them up beside his, and walking goggle-eyed across his chevron parquet floors.

He's made a mistake.

He's been making a lot of those lately. It must be caused by the madness, the same one which had overtaken him earlier in the day. At this point Luc should call it what it is: panic. His dossier will need updating. Oberon will be displeased.

Luc exhales, willing away the tension crowding into his neck and shoulders. His flat is his sanctuary, the one place solely under his control, untouched by anyone but him. Its austerity is due more to a lack of time for decoration than personal preference, but unlike his life, he can call everything within its high-ceilinged confines his own. The modern kitchen is his, the individually selected copper-bottomed pots hanging like ripe fruit from the overhead rack. The enormous four-poster bed lurking in the bedroom is a custom piece outfitted with the finest linens and the fluffiest pillows. In all other aspects of his life, Luc has trained himself away from wanting comfort, physical and emotional, but even he needs somewhere to unwind. He has trouble sleeping when he's away.

"You weren't kidding when you said not to worry. Thank you." Elle sets her bags carefully beside the sleek black leather couch.

"You're welcome." Normally, Luc would relax the second he crosses his threshold, but Elle's presence is like a fine thread inside him, incandescent with stress. She isn't staying, he reassures himself. She needed a safe place, and he has provided it. Why his mind had jumped immediately to his home and not the safehouses scattered around Paris is something he'll need to interrogate later. His house is, firmly put, secure. There is one entryway, and the terraces aren't accessible from outside on account of the building being in a shielded agency space. In the unlikely case that someone is able to breach both the wards on the building and the top floor, he would still be here, and he can navigate the area in total darkness.

The drawback is that Elle is in his personal space and now holds the record as the first person Luc has ever brought home.

He watches Elle turn in a circle to observe the room, her eyes lingering on the classic French crown molding at the top of the pristine white walls. She stops at the French infantry sword displayed over his couch. "Is this a replica?"

"No. It's real. From Napoleon's time." Serving in the army had been one of Luc's first training assignments. He'd spent five and a half miserable months marching forever, sustained minor injuries while thousands of soldiers around him died in battle, learned the expansive limits of his stamina while the survivors starved, discovered his resistance to cold while the remaining soldiers fell to hypothermia, and gained a lifelong enmity toward Russia.

Elle responds with a blank look. "Napoleon?"

"Napoleon Bonaparte." Luc had only seen the man from afar. He'd looked like any other man who thought himself important, his movements brisk, as if everything tried his patience. "A self-styled emperor who seized too much and failed."

"Ah." She nods sagely. "We have some of those too. How long ago was that?"

"Almost two hundred years." It's too personal, too soon. Luc has never in his wildest dreams imagined this scenario happening, having understood decades ago that his responsibilities made association with him distasteful at best. Having drinks with coworkers would have been a stretch. Elle being his friend has already suspended all the disbelief he has. "Do you need more security? We can move to a safehouse."

She shakes her head. "Here is fine. I know you're really private, so I appreciate it. I won't be here long."

He retreats to basic hospitality, having nothing else in his arsenal. "Please sit. Water?"

"I'm good, thanks." She goes from the couch to the leather armchair in the corner, reaching out to touch a handwoven blanket of blues, oranges, and yellows. It's the only spot of color in his otherwise monochromatic living room. As she inspects it, Luc clamps his mouth shut over the words threatening to pour out. Elle doesn't want to know he'd bought that blanket in a souk in Marrakech because it reminded him of the throw rugs he used to pile onto the sphinx's bed. The information is irrelevant.

Beside the chair is a hip-high stone statue of a sphinx in repose, and on the glass-and-steel coffee table, next to two worn cookbooks, sits a palm-sized miniature of the same statue.

"You like sphinxes?" Elle reaches a finger toward the statuette.

"Please don't touch it," Luc blurts out, taking several rushed steps toward her before reining himself in. If she accidentally activates the magic within the statue, he'll have a lot more to explain than a sword on the wall.

She snatches her hand back, alarmed. "Sorry!"

"It's old and very delicate."

"Okay, I won't touch. It must mean a lot to you." She leans down to inspect it, pursing her lips. "Is it me, or does it look just like the sphinx in Manhattan? Right down to the part in her hair. Speaking of, you were pretty distracted when we got to New York today. Everything okay?"

This time, he's unable to stop the words. "Yes. I was speaking to the sphinx, is all."

Surprise lifts her brows. "I wasn't aware they had personal connections with non-sphinxes."

"I'm an exception. She's like my adoptive aunt." There's no good reason to tell her, but he wants her to know, wants to show her things the way a child, inordinately proud of themselves, would show off toys.

"An adoptive aunt!" Elle exclaims, delight sparkling in her eyes. "So this *is* the sphinx! How long have you known her?"

"Since I was young. I came to the agency when I was a youth. The sphinx took pity on me."

"Took pity on you? Why?"

Luc takes a deep breath, unsure of why he's so willing to talk to her, and unsure why she's asking. Very few people know, or care to know, the story of how he came to the agency. "I was young and lost, and my caretaker at the time didn't have the patience to handle someone like me. She took me in."

"So you didn't fill out an application and wait for a phone call like the rest of us?" she asks, her tone teasing.

"Unfortunately," he replies, "that policy has only been active since the last century."

Elle clicks her tongue. "You must have some sweet seniority perks. Do they pay for your cleaning service? The lutins must love you."

Luc blinks. "They aren't allowed here."

"You say you're busy all the time, but there isn't a speck of dust. How do you find time to clean? Did you ban dirt from your apartment? Told the dust bunnies sternly to leave and never come back?"

He flushes, hoping it doesn't show in his cheeks. When he was younger, Oberon had remarked on Luc's propensity for tidying and arranging things just so. He's since curbed the habit except when he's at home. Cleaning occupies his hands and helps him clear his mind, the low demand of menial tasks being enough to push his brain out of work mode and into a state that will allow sleep. "No."

She turns her head sharply in his direction. "You okay?"

When he doesn't answer, she says, "You get angry brows when you're grumpy about something. Just a little. It's hard to tell. They only move about this much." Elle holds up her hand, spacing her thumb and index finger several millimeters apart. "You can tell me to be quiet if I'm bothering you. I talk too much when I'm nervous. Way too much."

"You aren't bothering me."

Elle finally takes a seat on his couch, leaning forward to inspect his cookbooks. "You cook?"

"When I have the time." Luc's enjoyment of cooking is a secret he guards from Oberon, like his visits to Elle. His relationship with the sphinx remains a bone of contention between him and his boss. "I rarely have the time."

"Because you're at work so much?"

He nods.

Elle opens the cover of *La Technique*, then *La Methode*. "Oh. It's all in French."

Despite himself, Luc smiles. Half of Elle's books are in Chinese, but he hasn't said a word. "You're looking at a French cookbook. Did you expect English?"

"I guess not. When did you learn how to cook?"

"I . . ." His first lover, Baptiste, had taught him on the days when they weren't working the back of the restaurant. He'd sneak kisses in, lips tasting of wine, as Luc did the mise en place. "I apprenticed in a kitchen in Paris a long time ago. For an assignment. The books help maintain my skills."

"You didn't learn in the kitchen with your mother?"

Luc's mother had passed of a wasting illness when he was thirty or so, which was the half elf equivalent of fourteen, but he remembers the simple yet hearty food she'd help prepare in the nunnery. For spaetzle with mushrooms they'd spend the morning in the forest, Luc armed with a little knife, filling a woven basket with brown caps. She would often spot them before he did, calling *Lucien, ici!* through the trees. Luc had been too dazzled by the forest nymphs to pay close attention. "She had the nuns to help her. I was not suitable, as a youth."

"Not suitable? Nuns?"

"Yes. I was raised in a church. My mother thought that was the best place for me."

"Because . . . ?"

"Because she thought we would be safest there. She was raising a child without a father, and I wasn't like the other children. I grew more slowly than the others, and the villagers thought I was simple."

He smiles without humor, thin-lipped. His mother hadn't counted on the French government becoming the largest threat to their safety. Those are years he'd rather forget. "At the very least, she thought it would prove that I wasn't possessed or a changeling. She thought the others might leave me alone if I lived in a holy place."

There's sympathy in Elle's eyes, and maybe a little anger, too, living in the furrow between her brows. "Did they?"

He isn't going to tell her the scars on his body were acquired in large part before Oberon found him. He doesn't want her pity. "Somewhat."

She falls silent.

Luc adds, defensive, "I think she made a good decision."

"I'm not judging. I was just thinking it must have been hard for you, growing up. I'm sorry. No child deserves that."

Luc stares at her, rocked back on his proverbial heels. The statement is true—no child should have to endure the hardship and pain he had endured—but no one has ever said it aloud to him. Even his aunt, who knows his history, avoids the topic.

"What's wrong?" Elle stands, coming over to him. She lifts her hand as if she's going to touch his shoulder, but puts it down.

"Nothing." He swallows, discomfited by how close she is, how he'd like to wrap his arms around her again. Or she could have her arms around him. Contrived as the situation was, he'd liked the feel of her against him. "It was a long time ago. It isn't an issue. What about your family?"

She turns away, looking at the floor. "That's a complicated answer. If you mean the kitchen, my ma had recurring nightmares about me using a meat cleaver. I'm this old and I haven't lost a finger yet. If you mean in general . . ."

She pauses, her eyes distant, mournful. "Let's say I don't see them much, and they don't want to see me. I miss them a lot, even the worst of them. My brother, he—"

Her voice hitches. "I used to think about my family every day. It's been so long that I don't do that anymore, and sometimes I wonder if that means I've stopped caring. I also wonder if they think about me." She scoffs, the sound tinged with bitterness and resignation. "Probably not."

Elle sighs, closing her eyes. Luc sees the sparkle of unshed tears caught in her eyelashes. Unreasonably, he thinks of wiping them away. "I'm sorry for getting emotional. You didn't sign on to hear my family drama."

"I'm happy to listen." He truly is. He's curious about her, and every morsel of information she gives him makes him hunger for more.

"Thank you. You're so sweet."

Luc stares again. *Sweet* hasn't been a word used to describe him in half a century. Ruthless, cold-blooded, clinical, and machinelike, but not sweet.

"What?" Elle smiles up at him, earnest and innocent, and something in Luc's chest trips and falls with a thud. "You don't think you're sweet? After doing everything you can to help me? How are you not partnered off again?"

"I work too much." Luc sometimes chains missions together, going from situation to situation without returning to debrief. Unlike other agents, Oberon can rely on him to push himself, and demands Luc do it routinely. The amount of free time he has varies from one sleep cycle to two days, rarely consequent. "And my reputation precedes me."

"You have a reputation? For what?"

Luc's throat tightens. If he could tell the truth, he would. If he could tell everyone the truth without violating his compulsion, he would. "I can't say."

She nods. "Okay. Well, I'd like to think I've gotten to know you, and no matter how gruff you look on the outside, on the inside you really are nice. Which makes what I'm about to say worse. If you were a total asshole, it'd be easier."

Dread. "What is it?"

Elle squares her shoulders. "I should look you in the face. Luc, I'm sorry, I like you a lot, but this is the only commission I'll do for you."

Logically, it shouldn't matter to him. Though he's a client, Elle is the business owner and has every right not to serve him. A hot wave of pins and needles rolls from his head to his toes. He's suddenly sweaty. He reviews all his actions from today through the last month. Either he has upset her, or whatever she's hiding from—whoever spotted her today—has her spooked.

"I'm not going to lie and say I don't have the ability. But if I go to New York to get supplies, I run the risk of this happening again. Unless you plan on going with me every time and hiding me in your fortress, I can't do this on the regular."

"Does this mean—" he starts to say.

"Your usual order will be your usual order, if you want it. But it won't be any more or less effective than what you can get at your local shops. I can't customize it anymore." Elle looks at the floor, twisting her fingers together. "I'm sorry. I really am. I wish we could do this more than once. You've given me an opportunity to challenge myself, which I'm so thankful for. You have no idea. After this, you won't need to go out of your way to see me, but if you want to visit, the door's open. As for the rest, I'll give you referrals for other glyphmakers."

"That won't be necessary." He doesn't want anyone but her, not when she's demonstrated a skill level far surpassing the artists she'd recommend. He doesn't want to build a new relationship with another artisan when the one before him is the best.

"Okay. I understand." Her shoulders sag.

Elle's voice takes on a wounded quality, one that goes directly to his heart, which he had thought was well armored. "I just wanted to say that I'm glad I met you. I'm happy to have been your friend. I'm grateful for whatever stroke of luck brought you to my store last year."

Luc tries in vain to make eye contact with her, but she eludes him.

"My original estimate was two weeks. You'll have your order in one. I'll leave it on the counter in case I'm not around when you pick it up."

Belatedly, it occurs to Luc that she's interpreted what he's said as a rejection, which is the furthest thing from what he's intended. "No, I meant—"

A soft chime sounds, muffled, from his pocket. It's his call rune, a piece of wood carved all over with magical symbols, crafted specially for him to wear. Luc stops mid-sentence, flustered and at a loss. Shit. He's forgotten about his check-in.

Elle looks immediately at his pocket. She's heard the rune enough times in the last year to know what it is.

"Excuse me." He fits the rune around his ear, tapping it to wake it up, and strides into his bedroom to take the call in private. "Villois here."

"You're late." Oberon wastes no time in stating the obvious, his disappointment clear in the clipped consonants of his received pro-nunciation accent. "Where are you?"

"At home. My apologies, sir."

"Don't apologize. Get to London. The fountain room. You have ten minutes." The line goes dead.

Luc measures out a breath, puts the rune back in his pocket, and returns to the living room.

Elle already has her shoes on, her shopping bags gripped in each hand. "You have to go."

"Yes. I'll walk you to the rings since we're going the same way." He'll have to jump the queue again to make it in time. "You said you'd need to experiment. I'll come by to help you in any way I can."

"I might have overstated that need." The bags jostle as she walks, some of them bouncing against her legs. "It's okay, I know what I'm doing. Having you around was a bonus, that's all. I said one week, and I'll deliver."

The conversation hits a dead end. Luc fixes his eyes on the hallway ahead of him, his work persona settling onto his shoulders like a cheap woolen coat, prickly and uncomfortable.

By the time he gets through the ports and up the lift to the conference room, Luc has the mask fully on, his emotions as distant and cold as starlight. Nothing touches him in this state. To others it may seem impressive or frightening, but for Luc it's a means of protection that has served him well in his many years working for Oberon.

He opens the door to the boardroom and strides in. As one, six heads swivel toward him.

"The prince of errands graces us with his presence." A slender, blond elf straightens from where he's leaning against a mid-century modern sideboard, setting down a tumbler with half a finger of scotch and a misshapen ice cube. He's dressed in a tailored black suit, which contrasts starkly with his ivory skin and slicked-back, platinum hair. "We can start now."

"The prince of errands?" At the foot of the long table is Gillen, one of the four members of the Wrecking Crew, sitting in an office chair that's one wrong move away from bursting its screws. Gillen is classified in the agency as fae-touched, a hulking Scotch Irish berserker who's descended from Cú Cuchlainn. Intelligence isn't his forte, but that's why he has the three other members of his unit to help him.

Gillen snickers. The office chair creaks, a plea for help. "We call him Killer over here. Right, Killer?"

Luc fixes his eyes on the middle distance and responds with stony silence. The Crew's nickname for him is well known, as are the other names and titles he holds among his coworkers. Oberon's pet attack dog, masterfully trained. Oberon's sword, a weapon to be used regardless of its condition.

Oberon's right hand, the one that wipes the shit from his ass.

The blond elf—Darcy—sighs. "You're so unimaginative."

Even exasperated, Darcy has a face to launch a thousand European ad campaigns, with cheekbones capable of cutting glass, eyes the color of fresh leaves in spring, and a cruel streak which curls his perfect mouth into an ugly, eternal sneer. Luc has never liked him, nor working with him.

"Fuck off, Darcy." Fern, the Wrecking Crew's svartelf enchanter, narrows warning eyes at him. "Better to be unimaginative than a smarmy shit."

"Enough." Oberon turns from his position at the window overlooking London, his hands clasped behind his back. He isn't as tall as Luc nor Darcy; he's broader in the shoulders and chest, heavier-boned, stocky compared to the average elf. He has a rectangular, ageless face topped with thick hair the color of ripe wheat, and chiseled features that would have been beautiful as a young man but are stately at full maturity. Beneath strong brows are piercing eyes the same shade as Luc's, blue enough to be seen from across the room.

Oberon's aura of power ripples through the air as he walks unhurried toward the fountain on the right side of the room. He's divested himself of his customary jacket and tie, leaving his suspenders visible. His shirt sleeves, wrinkled from a long day at the office, are cuffed messily at the elbow. It distresses Luc to see how carelessly Oberon treats his clothing, knowing that every bespoke stitch sitting on his body has been seen to by the best tailors on Savile Row.

The monetary value of his clothing pales in comparison to the ghostly weapon at his side. The image of it, a scabbarded sword, flickers in and out of existence. A sword as legendary as Durandal should have some kind of decoration, some ornament. But it looks unremarkable, with a workmanlike crossguard and a worn grip. The leather of the scabbard bears fine cracks, evidence of its owner's treatment.

Luc notes how Darcy tenses at the sight of Durandal, how Gillen shifts warily in his chair. Of the people in the room, those two would be the most familiar with the tales. None of them are currently in danger from the sword, which rests within the White Cliffs of Dover. Oberon can recall it with a thought, and God help the poor soul at the end of the blade. But he has no need of it. As old elvish royalty, he's more than enough.

Oberon gestures at the fountain for which the room is named, a wide ribbon of water spilling smooth from the ceiling. It freezes into a solid screen. A picture appears of an East Asian man with a long face and somber black eyes. The corners of his mouth are slightly down-turned.

Pei, at the head of the table, sits forward, their expression flicking from boredom to alertness. They're the greenest member of the Fixers, with a mere ten years under their belt. Like Gillen, they're classified as fae-touched, a descendant of Guan Yu, the Chinese god of war. The youthfulness of their round face with its short, no-nonsense haircut belies the brilliance of their strategic mind, and their slim figure hides how formidable they are with the yan yue dao.

"Here is our latest case," Oberon says. His voice is slightly nasal but mellifluous, gravelly at the bass end, the received pronunciation accent he affects lending the deliberate cadence of his words greater heft. For Oberon, appearing powerful is equally important as being powerful, and the accent of aristocracy gets him automatic respect. He'd tried to instill that same accent in Luc, but it hadn't taken. Maybe there had been too many languages residing in Luc's head, or maybe, as Oberon had mused, Luc was just too French.

"Yiwu Jiang, also known as William Jiang. Wanted for laes destruction and murder. He's been on our radar before, but has slipped the noose. He was spotted in the US a few days ago by one of Lysander's operatives." Oberon waves his hand, and the picture dissolves, replaced by the top sheet of a dossier. "Former A-rank, combat specialty. His sword is his preferred weapon, and from previous encounters, we know he has a sentimental attachment to it. He's fae-touched, descended from Shennong."

"A warrior?" Pei murmurs. "From that house? That's rare. They produce healers normally."

Luc catches their eyes, shakes his head subtly. Oberon hates being interrupted. Pei's nostrils flare, and they look away, mouth set in a hard line.

"Special abilities include flight," Oberon continues, ignoring the exchange. "He is a user of the Iron Shirt technique, meaning he can turn his clothes as hard as stone or infuse them with his energy to use as weapons. He is extremely dangerous, sometimes aggressive. He has few associates that we know of and prefers to work either alone or with a group of two to three people."

Pei's jaw tightens, but they say nothing.

"Twenty-six years ago, for reasons unexplained, Jiang killed the other two members of his cell. The three of them were siblings." Oberon flips to a picture of a crime scene in a dining room. Pieces of green stone are strewn on the floor. "The first victim was Tony Jiang, who died after his laes was shattered."

A shudder goes around the room. There had been a case last year involving a selkie whose lover had shredded her coat. Luc remembers the nonstop coverage, turning what should have been a solemn occasion into a distasteful spectacle. Reporters had crowded the hospital for the standard seventy-two-hour vigil, shoved microphones at the door to record the sound of her constant weeping, and discussed with sadistic glee how selkies never survived these types of attacks. Some of the worst commentators had a countdown clock for when the selkie's magic would fade and she'd collapse into a pile of bones and gelatin.

The last straw for Luc had been the televised moment of her passing. It had been inescapable, broadcasted everywhere. After forty-eight hours, there had been a final wail, followed by a splash. The cameras had zoomed in on the doctors running into the room as seawater leaked from beneath the door. Luc hadn't been sure if he felt ill because of the nature of her death, or because no one had advocated for her dignity.

Oberon keeps going, oblivious. "The second victim was Stella Jiang, also A-rank. As some of you know, Tony Jiang was a Bureau recruit and was in the middle of his probationary period when he was murdered. Therefore, this is a little personal."

A murmur of excitement goes up from the Wrecking Crew. Tony had fallen in with them, where his easygoing personality had been a good fit. Luc had met Tony Jiang twice before his untimely death, first at the all-hands recruitment briefing, second during an observational run. Tony had been proud and assured of himself, more than competent, charismatic. Aside from Luc's evaluation of him, they hadn't interacted much.

Oberon gestures again, and the photograph is replaced by a blueprint of the North Carolina Museum of Art. "Jiang is interested in ancient jade and has already stolen several relics from museums around the globe. This season, the Met and the Chinese government have jointly created a traveling exhibition of fine art and jade. It seems like no coincidence that Jiang would show up now that the tour has left the major northeastern US cities. It will be in Raleigh for three weeks before moving to Atlanta.

"This is our opportunity to apprehend him, but we must take things cautiously. There will be an opening gala for the museum's benefactors tomorrow night. Our analysts don't expect Jiang to make a move yet, but we cannot be sure. We will begin with a surveillance operation. I want zero contact on this mission, regardless of circumstance. Understood?"

"That puts the Crew right out of it." Darcy chuckles.

"Luc, you're lead. You will be working the floor with Pei. Passes have been secured for both of you. The museum will spare no expense for the occasion. Make sure you dress for a black-tie affair. The Crew is on support, Darcy on standby. Ken and Fern, I want every inch of the premises scanned and monitored. Emi will be in the van on comms."

"What about me?" Gillen asks.

Oberon gives him a pointed look. "I need delicacy on this operation. You stay home and guard the shiny new house you bought last week."

Gillen scowls. "I'm not staying home!"

Gillen won't be staying home, and everyone knows it. The Wrecking Crew are a team of four, but move as a single unit. Oberon's conceit is that he can control them. As long as the money flows and there's fun to be had, the Crew goes along with whatever they're told to do. Splitting them up, however, is out of the question. Above all, the Crew stays together, their mutual bonds losing potency with distance.

"I'll take care of it, sir," Ken says.

"Make sure you do, or it'll be on your head again." Oberon glances around. "I want glamours and masking enchantments on everyone on this operation. I will personally see to Luc's and Pei's. Jiang cannot know we're searching for him. Pertinent information will be emailed to your private accounts. Are there any questions?"

Yes, Luc thinks. He'd like to know why he has to attend a ball when he'd rather be at home, asleep, or house-hunting in Strasbourg. Instead he says, "No, sir."

"Good." Oberon breaks the magic keeping the fountain frozen, and water slaps onto the floor. "Dismissed. Except you, Villois."

Luc waits obediently as the other Fixers leave the room and pretends not to notice their disdain as they file past.

Once the door is shut, Oberon addresses him. "How is your wound?"

Luc becomes aware of the tight throbbing in his chest at the mention of it. "Still healing, sir. Dr. Clavret has ordered rest."

"Show me."

Reluctant, Luc rests his hand on the scarf looped around his neck.

"At once, Lucien." The threat from Oberon is, as always, an open one.

Luc tugs off the scarf, pops open buttons, and pushes aside his lapel and collar, bringing the bite mark to light. He doesn't react as Oberon steps close, inspecting.

Without warning, Oberon jabs his thumb into the center of the area. Luc cries out, then gasps, knees going weak as pain slices through him. Blindly, he thrusts out an arm, searching for support while his vision swims, the edges going gray. He finds nothing.

By sheer willpower he keeps his feet, staggering as the pain takes hold of him and shakes him in its jaws. Luc groans once it begins ebbing away, straightening back to standing, anger igniting at being touched without permission.

He slams a lid on the emotion, suffocating it before he can act on impulse.

When he has control of himself again, he glares at Oberon, who's standing with arms crossed, observing him.

"Clavret is too soft on you." Oberon sounds detached. "I've seen worse. Had worse."

"With all due respect," Luc responds through gritted teeth, "I almost died."

"But you didn't. I know you can handle this. You're made of stern enough stuff. See your physician again tomorrow if you must, but don't let him give you a painkiller. I need you alert, not drugged. Am I understood?"

Luc focuses on righting his clothing, but his hands are shaking. "Yes, sir."

"Oh, and tell Pei she needs to wear a dress."

Pei hates dresses. "They would prefer to wear something more comfortable."

"What she wants is immaterial. She has to dress correctly."

The damned top button of his shirt refuses to cooperate. "If you could provide them with one, I'm sure they'd be appreciative."

Oberon waves him off. "That isn't my concern. Either she wears a dress or you put her in one. Whatever it is, handle it. Now go get some rest. You look poorly."

Luc would look less poorly if Oberon hadn't touched him, but he deserves it after failing such an easy mission. "Yes, sir."

"I will see you tomorrow in Raleigh." Oberon regards him, his eyes piercing. "Don't be late. I want no mistakes for the next mission. Or I will question the trust I've placed in you."

Luc gives up on the button and puts on the scarf, swallowing his nausea when it touches his neck. He won't let Oberon down. "Yes, sir."

Chapter Five

$\mathcal{L}$UC STROLLS TOWARD the east building of the North Carolina Museum of Art, pausing to accept a smoked salmon canapé from a liveried server. The hors d'oeuvres were palatable earlier in the evening, but now the cream cheese spread has joined forces with the Carolina summer humidity to turn the cracker soggy. The texture reinforces the extreme saltiness of the fish, and though the meager sprig of dill on top is trying its best, it's a poor match against a stacked field.

The unfortunate combination in his mouth is enough of an excuse for him to approach the bar and get more wine. The cabernet available isn't the best he's had, not by far, but it's big-bodied and as forward as a golden retriever, and that's all he needs to mute the flavors on his tongue.

"Why does he get to drink on the job?" Gillen mutters, his voice faint through Luc's earpiece.

"Special privileges for the prince," replies Darcy, his sneer evident in his tone.

Luc deliberately looks at the wineglass in his hand, his second of the night. The silver spectacles he's wearing as part of his disguise are Oberon's smithwork, the magic layered into them giving both Emi and Oberon a live feed of what he's seeing. He'd like to say that he and Pei are supposed to be playing their roles, that they've both had wine, that he hasn't had much because the servers have been miserly with their pours. But he can't speak. He isn't in some spy movie where he can lift his wrist to his mouth without anyone noticing, and they aren't looking for his excuses.

Instead, Luc swirls the wine in his glass, inhales its bouquet, and lifts it in a toast. *À votre santé.*

Ah, but Oberon would want him to conduct all his affairs in English. "Cheers!" he murmurs, taking a long sip.

"Ass."

He can't tell who said it, but the insult rolls off him like a bead of water on oilcloth. He's been called worse, and he has a job to do, part of which entails meeting Pei at their predetermined rendezvous point. Nowhere in the mission does it state he should care about what others think of him.

"Stop looking at your grape juice," Emi says, her voice crystal clear, a soft Nigerian accent rounding out her vowels.

"Grape juice!" Gillen laughs, snarfling.

"Quiet," Oberon orders.

Gillen hmphs. "I'm just commenting."

"If I wanted your commentary, I'd have given you a mic."

Ken breaks in, the epitome of unruffled calm. "Gill, quiet please."

There's some grumbling from Gillen, but he subsides.

Luc walks on, passing by a large window, catching his reflection out of the corner of his eye. Oberon's glamour is of the highest caliber, strong enough to fool mirrors. Luc has been aged up, with crow's-feet at the corners of his now-brown eyes, and wings of gray at his temples. A short beard covers the bottom half of his face, and silver-rimmed glasses perch on his nose bridge. He's learned not to startle at his glamoured appearances, but it's disconcerting to see him so unlike himself.

But it isn't his reflection he's looking for.

"She's still there," Ken confirms for him. "Been following you all night."

Fern snickers. "Looking like that? Some people have no taste."

"Give me a clear view," Emi says.

Without breaking stride Luc uses his index finger to slide the glasses up, focusing on the small reflection of an East Asian woman in a dress the color of smoke. A chill runs through the earpieces of the glasses, signaling the detection of magic, and a faint halo of light springs up around her.

"I got her." Emi hums. "Either she's fae-touched, or she's excellent at glamours."

"I want an ID on her," Oberon says. "Find out who she is and why she's stalking Luc."

The punchline sets itself up, and Darcy plays the straight man. "Might be she wants to take him home."

There's a second of silence before the Wrecking Crew, plus Darcy, explodes into raucous, jeering laughter.

Luc sips his wine, letting them have fun at his expense. It isn't anything new and hasn't been for over twenty years. He continues toward the east building, scanning the crowd. So far, he's seen a few fae at the party, but they've all been harmless locals.

"Villois." The note in Emi's voice makes Luc take notice. "Look to your left."

He turns his head, slowing his pace. The glasses go cold against his temples, lighting up around a clump of people laughing politely by the valet drop-off.

"The brown woman in the off-shoulder sequined dress. Short and curvy. Give me two seconds."

Luc counts to two and resumes his walk, entering the building. Pei is standing by the gift shop, the stem of their wineglass clutched in their fist. They're strikingly handsome in an intimidating way. The glamour shows pin-straight, waist-length black hair sculpted back from their face, with monolid eyes reminiscent of a cat's. They're in a high-necked champagne jumpsuit over which they've thrown a tuxedo cape. Black-tipped oxfords peek out from beneath wide-legged pants.

The shoes, along with the tuxedo cape, had been Luc's suggestion once he'd witnessed Pei holding a pair of stiletto sandals like they were scorpions about to sting. As for the jumpsuit, Luc couldn't bring himself to force Pei into a dress, not after what he'd experienced.

Lucien Châtenois. A memory. Oberon's voice, forever coupled with the smell of blood. Luc swallows as if it can fend off the chill skittering down his back, and his skin tightens into goosebumps. *I speak your truename, and invoke the Right of Dominion.*

His breath snags in his throat. What an inconvenient time to be thinking about this.

"I thought I recognized her," Oberon says. Her, meaning the mysterious woman in the sequined dress. "A disciple of Hermes. Looks like the collection is a target for multiple thieves. That complicates things. Fern, watch her."

Pei nods at Luc, the motion brusque. All their finery can't disguise their warrior's posture, their coiled-spring readiness. "About time you showed up."

Like Oberon, Pei doesn't traffic in excuses, so Luc gives none. "What did you think of the collection?"

"An unusual one." They put their hands behind their back like they're reciting for school. In a way they are, since the information is meant for everyone on comms. "I can see why the Met needed the Chinese government's permission. There are the standard paintings, which I believe are copies, but the rest of the collection is rare. Did you see the ivory figure of Shénnóng and the jade disks?"

"Yes. I thought the figure was quite remarkable. The disks, less so."

"They look plain, but I don't think those jade disks were ornamental or decorative. They're more important. Laes-level important. A source of power for their users. There's one more complex than the others, and I have a strong feeling that's what Jiang wants."

"How do you know he'll show up?"

"Half the collection consists of items belonging to the Jiang family, and they're stingy with their things. Especially those pages out of their family book, the Běn Cǎo Shū. He might be here to reclaim them, if they're real. In addition to the Běn Cǎo Shū being Shénnóng's own collection of remedies, rumor has it that it contains healing techniques meant for no one but the god's chosen heir."

"If the whole family consists of healers," Luc muses, "it seems inefficient to limit access."

Pei snorts, sardonic. "Then you don't know anything about Chinese culture."

They're right, he doesn't. "Is Jiang the chosen one?"

Pei shakes their head, their loaned silver earrings swinging back and forth with the movement. Originally Emi's, the earrings are intricate, shaped like blooming yarrow albeit upside down, and Emi can work her witchcraft remotely through them. "I can't say for sure, but my guess is no. He's a warrior, not a healer."

"Why would he want it?"

"Maybe it has to do with the siblings he murdered." Pei shrugs. "The family has been quiet about it, but I'm not connected to their circle. The head of the family lives on top of a remote mountain and keeps to himself, which makes it difficult to find out anything."

"Move along," Oberon says. "There's a reporter coming your way."

Luc offers Pei his elbow, but they ignore it. The two of them turn toward the door, sidestepping the reporter and exiting the building into blanketlike air. People are beginning to queue at the valet station, which means the event is winding down.

Luc sighs, rolling his shoulders, giving himself a second to think ahead. It'll be nice to go home and get some rest. If he doesn't, he'll face another upbraiding from Dr. Clavret at their appointment tomorrow. At least his wound is healing well. It'll leave a scar, and he'll never achieve his dream of becoming a swimsuit model, but he's sure he'll cope.

"Let's wrap it up," Oberon says. "Ken and Fern, are all eyes in place?"

"Yes, sir," Ken replies. "In place and open."

"Luc and Pei, do one more sweep."

Luc's glasses light up before he and Pei can start their loop. He looks out over the people gathered by the amphitheater, trying to pick out who among them is fae. With a start of surprise, he realizes he's looking at Agent Gaines, Elle's co-owner, dazzling in a slinky red gown that shows off her round, pear-shaped figure, conversing with a man whose back is turned to him. He hasn't expected to see her here, but perhaps she's gained an interest in Chinese art because of Elle's work.

If Agent Gaines is here, Elle might also be here. Luc glances around, seeking her face, bracing himself. She's already pretty the way she is. Elle in formalwear might kill him.

"See someone?" Pei asks.

"No." Even if Elle is here, he can't compromise the mission by speaking to her. She won't recognize him, anyway. Nevertheless, he continues watching Agent Gaines as he walks toward the amphitheater, hoping for a glimpse.

Shock freezes him in his tracks when Gaines's conversation partner turns around. Her friend, and he's clearly her friend, is a doppel-gänger of Tony Jiang, except much older. They begin moving toward the exit on a path that will bring them near.

"Who is *that*?" Emi breathes into her mic.

"No way," Gill says. "He's an old guy, look. It's not him."

"Who?" asks Fern.

"Tony, if he lived." Emi sounds shaken. "I know it isn't him. But I wish it was."

"China is a country of two billion people," Oberon says, uncon-cerned. "It's only natural they would resemble each other."

Luc bites his tongue, actually does it, at Oberon's racism, but doesn't speak.

"That's not true." Pei breaks the silence with a growl, squaring them-self up in front of Luc and glaring. He knows they're looking at the glasses, but Pei has a stare like a punch to the face, and the fremdschä-men makes him want to avoid them. "Why would you say that when you and Villois look like each other?"

"They really don't, except for their eyes," Darcy chimes in.

"No one asked you," Pei snaps back. They're a firebrand, and a spark is all it takes to start a roaring blaze. It's been detrimental in the field a couple of times, but Pei is supposed to be working on it.

Oberon sighs. "Calm down."

"I'm calm." The glint in Pei's eyes says otherwise.

"Luc, on your seven," Ken breaks in. "Heading directly for you. That woman again. Emi?"

Foreboding makes Luc's muscles tense. All he needs to do is leave the gala for the mission to be a success.

"Got her. She's agency. Lily Wang. Fox spirit."

Luc follows the shift of Pei's eyes before he turns around. The earpieces of his glasses go icy against his skin, and a strong halo of light surrounds the woman as she approaches. She's an otherworldly beauty, her skin as smooth and pale as cream, her eyes deep and dark and alluring, her rosebud mouth lacquered red.

"You!" she says to Luc, warm. "I thought it was you."

"Don't talk to her!" Pei spits, their muscles tensing as they shift into a battle-appropriate stance. "The foxes trick men with their beauty."

"It's so good to see you again. How is Grace doing?" The fox spirit smiles. She has perfect, even teeth with sharp cuspids, and, like Elle, her lower lip is thicker than her upper lip. Luc can't stop staring at her mouth. "I'm sorry we missed each other yesterday. Grace and I, we've been friends for years, but she's never introduced me to you. How do you know her? How did you find her?"

Pei hits him on the shoulder, and it breaks him out of his trance.

"I don't know a Grace," he replies, keeping his voice level.

"Grace Lin. You were with her yesterday in New York." The fox spirit steps closer, but Pei thrusts out a palm, sending her stumbling back.

"I don't know who you're talking about." This must be the fox spirit who sniffed Elle out, but Luc has no idea where the name Grace originates. None of Elle's files list Grace Lin as an alias.

"Stay away, demon," Pei warns her.

"We're just having a chat," the fox spirit replies, her eyes flashing. "Don't be jealous."

"Emi," Oberon says, curt. "Hex her now. Darcy, get in there. You're finishing the mission. Fern, get the car for ex-fil."

The glasses go cold again, and Pei's earrings glow. They trip suddenly, their wine glass tipping. The fox spirit cries out as golden retriever cabernet sauvignon splashes across her chest and bounds in streams down her décolletage. The smell of fruit and alcohol rises into the air. Around them, heads turn, including Agent Gaines's as she leaves the area.

"I'm so sorry," Pei exclaims flatly, but they don't sound sorry in the slightest. "Let me help you." They grab onto the fox spirit's arm and begin dragging her toward the nearest server.

Luc takes his opportunity, making his way to the curb, where moments later, a black sedan pulls up. He opens the door and slides in, expelling a breath, dropping his head back against the seat, wishing for another canapé, the whole tray, and a glass of wine to hide the dusty taste of defeat. He's failed. Again.

Fern casts a look over her shoulder from the driver's seat as she maneuvers the car away. "Boy," she says, smirking. "That sure went well, didn't it?"

Elle pushes away from the computer at the front desk, balancing her stool on its back legs, and rolls her neck. She closes out of the store email, then her personal email, which contains an RSS feed of daily goings-on in western Húběi. When she reads them, she can pretend she's connected to Shénnóngjià, though most of the news is centered on Xiāngyáng, to the east. Recently, however, there have been a few reports of illness cropping up in the rural regions, with speculation it's the same mystery illness responsible for dozens of deaths almost three decades ago—including Yìwú's friend.

Tony should have done something. Elle is good at healing as a result of her upbringing, but good isn't good enough when Tony exists. He'd been the hope of the family, the shining star and perfect heir, groomed his whole life to take over. If he'd gone home, maybe people wouldn't have died. Maybe he'd have found the cure within the pages of the Běn Cǎo Shū. Maybe, if that had happened, Elle could still see her little brother and call him her best friend.

She powers down the computer, whacking the mouse button with her finger. The sound of it cracks like a shot in the silence of the darkened store. She slides off the stool, tears stinging her eyes, and shoves it under the counter. The monitor wobbles on its stand and almost tips from how hard she's jabbed the power button. If there's a computer god, and there probably is, she'll have to apologize tomorrow.

Elle checks the time as she opens the door to her workshop and flicks on the lights. Eleven thirty is much too late to be at work, but she closed on her own because of the gala, thereby delaying the rest of the evening's activities. She flexes her hand, looking at rows and rows of simple glyphs occupying every horizontal surface, then stifles a yawn as she begins collecting them.

Her mind strays to Luc's commission. The faster she gets it done, the faster she can hustle him out of her life and resume living in security. What were the odds of her being caught out for the first time in sixteen years? And by Lily, of all people. She'll have tattled to Yìwú immediately.

As nice as it is to have Luc's friendship, and that itself is in question, it isn't worth putting Tony at risk. She'll be fine without Luc. She's *been* fine without him. She can acknowledge her mistake from yesterday and reorient the map. Luc is a friendly customer, not a friend. She's a friendly business owner and won't read anything other than gratitude into his gift.

"It's gonna be a thrilling Friday night," she declares, cutting a sheet of rice paper and setting weights at the top and bottom. One of her procrastination exercises earlier had been figuring out her crafting timeline, which had been more fun than anticipated. If she spends tonight and tomorrow working through all the rough drafts, she can use the remaining time to make one glyph a day. That shouldn't be too taxing. She should sleep to replenish her energy and her magic, but a little more stress never hurt her, and she's waited all night to start this.

Skies. She's actually going to enjoy herself.

There's a faint series of taps from outside her workshop, like someone rapping their knuckles against the front door.

Elle grunts. Her store hours are posted for a reason, and there is no way she's going to stop what she's doing to cater to some jerk fairy who believes he's entitled to her time.

"Don't rain on my parade," she sings, off-key. She's never heard the song herself, but Lira has belted it enough times in her own workshop that Elle can approximate it.

Back to work. She picks her heftiest, fattest brush, dipping it in water, squeezing drops of it into the well of her grinding stone.

The knocks sound again, louder this time.

Whoever it is, they must think she hasn't heard them. Oh, Elle's heard them all right. She gets off her stool and marches over to her workshop door, grabs it, and flings it shut. *Take that, asshole.*

She's seated once more when the store phone starts ringing. "Oh, for cryin' out loud!" she yells, borrowing an expression she's heard from the staff in the cafeteria. It's so nonsensically adorable. What isn't adorable is the continued ringing of the phone. She's tempted to pick up just to hang up on them.

"Hi, you've reached Raleigh Runes and Glyphs." Lira's prerecorded voice, muffled by the door, greets the caller. "If you're getting this message, we are either with a customer or we're closed. Please leave your name and contact info, and we will get back to you as soon as we can. Have a blessed day."

"Have a *blessed* day," Elle repeats as the answering machine beeps, giving the phrase the knife-in-the-back sarcasm it demands.

"Elle." It sounds like Luc. "It's Luc."

She bolts to her feet and runs for the door, almost slamming into it, and presses her ear against it to hear him better. "I apologize for troubling you so late, but I wanted to talk to you. It's half eleven and I'm standing outside, hoping you're able to hear this. If not, I will look a fool tomorrow morning when you or Lira listen to this message."

No chance of that. Elle hauls her door open, almost tripping in her haste to get out, and hotfoots it to the front counter to see for herself if he's there.

He looks up, startled, smiling as their eyes meet, and tucks his smartphone into the inside pocket of his tuxedo.

Tuxedo. Luc's on her doorstep in a tuxedo. Elle files the information away for later so she can react properly to it. Meanwhile, he's still at her door, and she has to answer it. If she sprints, she'll lose whatever friendly business owner dignity she has. She settles for speed walking to the front, unlocking the door, and yanking it open. Now that she's up close and personal, she sees that Luc is a living magazine spread, wearing an expensive tuxedo fitted to every gorgeous inch of him. Oh, skies. He's too handsome. She doesn't know where to put her eyes. His shoes? His face? His crotch? No, not his crotch. She fixes her gaze on Luc's collar. That seems safe enough.

"Hi." A giant, goofy grin plasters itself to her face. So much for dignity. She clings to the door as if her sanity depends on it. If she lets go, she might have a sartorially induced meltdown. "Okay, hi. Hello. Wow. Um, how's it going? I wasn't expecting you until next week. Did I miss a date or something?"

"Hello," he replies. "No, you haven't missed anything."

Oh. Somewhere in the world, a trombone goes *womp womp*. "I'm so sorry for ignoring you, but sometimes customers think—that saying, you know, the customer is always right? They think because I'm still here it means I'm going to help them, which is totally wrong of course. What're boundaries, you know? And I . . ."

Elle exhales, shaky, her cheeks heating. The air shimmers in front of her, but she snuffs her pyrokinetics out before she can light Luc's tuxedo on fire. That's got to be worth at least two months of take-home pay. "Uh, that didn't go well at all. Can we try that again? The saying hi thing?"

Luc's smile broadens, becoming a grin. "Only the saying hi thing?"

He's going to make fun of her, is he? She deserves it. "I'd like a redo, if that's okay by you." She drops her eyes to the floor.

"That will be fine. I'm here regardless."

"Okay. Good. Thanks. Let's try that again." Elle straight-arms the door shut and locks it, turning away.

Luc bursts into laughter.

Elle ignores him, marshaling her shit so she can get it together. She's in a situation like the thief with the bell, except with vision instead of hearing. If she can't see him, then logically he can't see her through an eight-foot-tall glass door. Elle nods to herself, clenching her fist. She can do it. She can be a normal human who isn't wildly attracted to the guy on her doorstep despite being rejected by him, which, since he's here, was probably not a rejection and she's read too much into it.

She unlocks the door, pulls it open, and steps out into the hall. "Hi."

"Hello again. It's good to see you."

He should be arrested for that smile of his. "I got your message."

"I gathered. I know it's late, but I need to discuss something with you, and I'd rather not do that in the hallway."

Elle clears her throat. "Is it bad?"

"No."

"But not good either."

"Whether it's good will depend entirely on you."

All right, he's going for cryptic today. "Come in. I was just about to start your commission. Do you mind if I finish that first, and then we talk?"

"That should be fine. Thank you." Luc enters behind her and locks the door.

She stops by the front counter to delete his message, then proceeds to her workshop. "So, fancy party tonight?"

"You could say that."

"Did you have fun?" Elle picks up her brush, the smoothness and coolness of the handle an invitation.

"No."

She glances at him. He's in his spot on the couch, already loosening his bowtie and undoing the top button of his shirt. The slight dishevelment adds to his appeal. Luc is so uptight sometimes, and it makes

Elle want to muss his hair, so to speak. See him more relaxed, like at a T-shirt-and-jeans level. "You okay?"

"Better now." His expression softens. "Thank you."

"Don't like parties, huh?"

"Not particularly, but this was an obligation."

"Ah, got it. You couldn't squeeze out of it." She understands. "Okay, I'm about to start. Give me a few minutes."

Elle peers at the amount of ink in the well, now diluted with the water from her brush. It should be enough. Her magic, already roused, sparks with excitement as she tests the viscosity of the ink. It's thin but eager, running out of bounds, blooming across her paper in fast-forward.

Restraints off. She's ready.

Her first stroke splatters wet and messy, drops of gray spraying over her work area. Grinning, Elle yanks the brush down, her magic causing the paper to hiss as if pressed upon by an iron. Ink and water fly, but she doesn't care, caught up in the joy of art, the challenge of making her magic do what she intends it to do. The paper drinks in her ink, the edges of her character growing indeterminate and fuzzy as she describes the last stroke.

Next character. Elle doesn't bother picking up more ink, dragging her brush down so the characters will be joined by a long tail. Her hand flies, brush tip sweeping left to right, up to down, looping around in a messy grass script. She runs out of ink partway through but pushes on, her magic roaring as she grinds the brush against paper.

Her magic seizes control, greedy. Untethered after so many years, it charges into her hand with glee, guides it to the ink stone, brings it back to the paper. Elle paints two more characters in the center of a vortex, no longer looking at what she's doing, her eyes open and sightless in her heightened state. All around her, papers flutter and whisper as her power ripples out. Brushes clack against each other, swinging on their hooks from a sudden wind. The tiny open mouths of her test tubes send up a chorus of hollow moans, echoed by the partially filled Erlenmeyer flask held hostage in its clamp. Elle's ponytail streams out behind her as if being tugged by an invisible hand.

The moment the brush lifts off the paper, her magic winks out, leaving a deafening silence. Elle gasps, slumping, catching herself before her forehead slams into the surface of her workbench. The backs of her eyelids burn a neon green as if she's stared into the sun. With effort, she forces herself up and fumbles for her brush rack. It takes several tries for her to hang up her brush.

"Elle?" Luc touches her on the shoulder.

She starts as if electrocuted, losing her balance. She topples, but Luc grabs her arm, hauling her body against his, counterbalancing until she isn't in any danger of falling. She curls herself into him like an Elle-sized pangolin, unable to do anything but wait until the shock passes.

"Are you okay?" The resonance of his voice buzzes in his chest.

It's strangely comforting, and so is his scent. Yesterday, when she'd given him that abrupt hug, she'd assumed he was wearing cologne because no one on earth could smell that good naturally. She'd been wrong. Today, Luc is actually wearing cologne—is that bergamot?— and he smells even better. "Yeah."

"You're shaking."

"No, that's just an earthquake. Can't you feel it?" She should sit up, but no matter how much she commands herself to do it, she can't.

"Must be a personal earthquake."

"Absolutely. One-person portion size. Like a personal pan pizza." Elle finally gets her muscles to obey her. She regrets the decision when her vision goes double. "Thanks."

He retreats to a respectful distance. "I have concerns."

"I'm good, I swear. I just had a long day, and I wasn't expecting that." She stands, using the workbench for support. The adrenaline is free to kick in whenever it wants. "Tomorrow won't be the same."

He looks alarmed. "You'll need to do this again?"

"Yeah." Elle cruises along the workbench like a baby learning how to walk, aiming for the armchair. Luc hovers close beside her, a space heater radiating worry. "I'll be fine, really. I probably overdid it. A little sleep and I'll be ready to go."

Her left knee gives out on step one of the four steps needed to get to her chair. She drops without a sound, but Luc catches her, stepping in to fill the role her useless muscles have abandoned. "Wow," Elle says. "Your reflexes are real fast."

"Hold onto me." More like he's holding onto her.

"The chair is, like, two feet away."

"In your state, it would be better if you laid down, then told me where to find the store keys."

Elle takes another step, but her other knee betrays her. In one motion Luc scoops her into his arms and transports her to her couch. Skies above. Not only are his reflexes fast, he's strong too. "Store keys? What?"

"Your store keys," he repeats, patient. "Because you are moments from passing out, and I cannot in good conscience leave you here unprotected."

"Ha!" She tries lifting her arm to point at Luc, but it won't work. It must have turned tail and fled, like all the rest of her body parts. "What do you know anyway?"

"Exhaustion, when I see it." Luc adjusts his jacket.

"I'll be up in a few minutes, swear." Elle's eyelids slide halfway closed before she wrenches them back open. "Hey, you said you needed to talk."

He lifts an eyebrow. It's a lovely eyebrow. "I don't think now is the right time."

"You said it was important."

"It'll keep until tomorrow morning."

"You don't know that!"

He gives her a flat stare. "Store keys."

Her eyelids slide down again, and it takes a disproportionate amount of energy to haul them back up. "You extorting me?"

"What's there to extort?" He sounds exasperated. "Do you want me to get locked in with you because you refuse to tell me where your keys are?"

"Would that be so bad? Stuck in a room with one bed? It isn't even a bed, it's a couch."

"Elle, please."

She makes a noise that could be categorized as a whine. "Fine. Under the counter." *By the computer,* she means to say after, but there's a five-second delay on the broadcast. "By the computer."

Elle loses the fight with her eyelids. Her couch is too comfortable. "Can I . . ." Impending sleep presses her words into mush. ". . . ask you something?"

She hears the rustle of clothing, feels the dip of the couch cushion as he puts his weight on it. "What is it?" he asks, his voice oddly gentle.

"Take my shoes off?"

His laugh is the last thing she hears before the world blanks out.

Chapter Six

"YOU WANT the good news or the bad news?"
Elle scoots her stool over to make room at the front counter, wincing at the crick in her neck, and finishes writing an order. "Uh. Bad."

Lira plunks down an extra stool, sits, and anchors her elbows on the table before placing her hands together from palm to fingertip. "Great, good news first. I'm in love."

"Wait." Elle isn't ready. "I said bad, and in love? For real?"

"Yes." Lira draws out the sibilance of the word. A grin spreads over her face. "Her name's Sophia. Met her at the gala. Body like this—" Lira pauses to gesture with her hands. "And a face like . . ." She sighs, moonstruck.

"Go on," Elle encourages her.

"Beautiful brown skin that was extremely well moisturized. She smelled like vanilla all over. She wore this sequined dress that was . . ." Lira shakes her head, waving off the rest of her words.

Elle laughs. "All over?"

"Mm. *All* over."

"A good night, then?"

"I am so tired. Had to ditch Tony, but it was worth it."

"Did you get her number?"

"No, she's only in town a short while. Was checking out the exhibit since she'd heard about it." Lira looks so crestfallen that Elle is tempted to break out the bottle of vodka they keep in the back. "I'm in love with a woman who I'll never see again."

"And that's the good news?"

"Eh, it's about fifty-fifty. But let's talk about you for a sec. I wasn't the only one who got some last night!"

"I didn't—" Elle's eyes widen. "Nothing happened!"

"I'm just playin' with you." Lira snickers into her hand. "Otherwise, I'd have questions about a man who dresses that expensive fucking you in the back room and leaving you with a blanket."

Elle sputters. "We're just friends! Not even! He's a friendly client."

"Yeah, a friendly client who hung out at the front desk all night to make sure you were safe, then gave me the keys this morning before you woke up." Lira snorts.

If Elle's face heats up any more, it'll burst. She used to be afraid of that happening when she was little, when she and Yiwú would compete to see who could hang upside down the longest. "That's perfectly normal behavior."

Lira lets out a guffaw. "Uh-huh. Sure. What happened last night?"

"I was working, he dropped by, I was tired, I fell asleep. That's it."

"What were you doing that you fell asleep here?" Lira waggles her eyebrows. "He even tucked you in."

"Stop doing the thing with your face! I was working and I used too much magic. That's all." Waking up with Luc's blanket had been, to date, one of the most disorienting experiences of her life. She'd had a backache, a foul taste in her mouth, and a blanket that smelled like Luc—but no Luc. Given the time and the right circumstances, Elle might have, before the stuff with her family happened, set in motion a plan to wake up beside him. Naked, preferably.

That was the Old Elle of twenty-six years ago. Now she's New Elle, who is Older Elle, one hundred twenty-four to be precise, and she doesn't do relationships. "It's not a big deal. What's the bad news?"

"Tony says that the exhibit has a piece of jade that belonged to your great-great-grandfather."

Elle's blood drains so quickly she gets lightheaded. "He what?"

"He also said not to worry, because you aren't in danger."

Too late, she's worrying. "Why are *you* telling me, and not him?"

"He was afraid you'd have a bad reaction."

Elle takes a deep breath, gritting her teeth, clenching her hands into fists before releasing them and placing them flat on the counter. Tony is many things, but brave isn't at the top of the list. "Okay. Why did he think we aren't in danger?"

"Because Will doesn't know you're here."

Elle closes her eyes.

Lira's stool creaks as her weight shifts. "Elle."

"When I was in New York with Luc the day before yesterday, I was seen. Do you remember Lily, the fox spirit?"

"Sort of?"

"The one who found me in Vancouver. I don't know what she was doing in New York, but she sniffed me out. Again. I ran. Not here, somewhere else first. But I'll bet my life savings that she's already told my brother."

"What did she look like?"

There's something tightening around Elle's chest, making it hard for her to get a good breath. "Why do you ask?"

"I thought I saw someone familiar . . ." Lira shakes her head.

"She's gorgeous," Elle says, then swallows. "Oval face, perfect cupid's bow lips. A beauty mark under her right eye."

The expression on Lira's face confirms her fears.

"Elle. She didn't know Tony, right? And she doesn't know where you went."

She stretches out her fingers; they're stiff. Being caught out is one thing, but to be caught out and know that Yìwú is coming to town is too much. "We have to move."

"No, you don't."

"Yes. We have—we have to go. I'm sorry."

"Wait just a second." Lira leans forward. "Does Tony know about the fox finding you?"

"Not yet. I thought we made a clean getaway, that I could let it blow over." Elle puts her hand to her forehead as a hot flash goes through her. "I'm so stupid."

"Okay, let's just think this through. Lily doesn't know you're here; she thinks you're in New York. She didn't know Tony. As far as we know, if Will comes, he'll get the jade and leave. You don't have to move."

"I'm not taking that risk." Elle gets up. This time, she goes right to the phone and flips it open. She pushes aside things in her junk basket before she finds the taxi service business card. She dials the number, her heart beginning to race. Tony's going to get what he wants, but not in the way he wants.

"Elle, what are you doing?"

She looks up into Lira's concerned brown eyes. "Calling a cab."

"For what?"

"I'm breaking my rule." Elle hits the call button, holding the phone to her ear. "I'm going to visit my brother."

Tony's house is a modest slate-blue ranch inside the Raleigh loop that sits on a wedge-shaped piece of land overlooking a small pond. It's pretty in the summer when the flowering bushes are in bloom and the tree in the front is bursting with leaves. A small creek bisects the lawn, separating the house from the guest parking area.

Elle's driver pulls into a space next to an expensive-looking car she doesn't recognize. By the time she's handed the cash over and gotten out, Tony is waiting, his arms crossed, one shoulder leaned up against the frame of the front door. He's wearing cream-colored shorts and a cuffed chambray shirt that drapes perfectly over his tall, lanky frame. His face, robust with a summer tan, is distinctly unamused.

She slams the heavy cab door, squaring her shoulders, and goes over the footbridge and up the front walk. Normally, Tony would be delighted to see her, smothering her in hugs, hustling her into his house, and sucking her into his whirlpool of chipperness and self-absorption. Not today.

She stares at him in frigid silence until she's on the front step, looking up at him.

"Tony." It's a statement, not a greeting.

"I'm not moving."

Elle opens her mouth. "How—"

"Save it for after my patient leaves." Tony backs into the foyer, looking over his shoulder. The tone of his voice changes so abruptly it makes Elle do a double take. "Thank you for being so flexible with this, Karen!"

Karen steps into view from around the corner. She's an older white woman, blonde, with wrinkles like clusters of alligators at the corners of her eyes, dressed in a white blouse and khaki pedal pushers. The many charms on her bracelet tinkle when she moves. "Anytime!" she says in a soft twang, putting a hand to her chest. "Family is so important. Oh, is this her?"

"Um." Elle's still outside. "Excuse me."

"Come on in," Karen tells her.

Elle eyeballs the woman as she enters. Bold of Karen to act like she owns the place. "Thank you."

"Tony, you never told me you had a daughter!" Karen's shoes clomp on the hardwood flooring by the door. Elle tries not to wince. "All this time! I never knew! She's beautiful. So exotic."

Elle sucks in a breath, heat gathering at her fingertips. "Say that again—"

"That's because I don't have a daughter." Tony interrupts Elle and her uncharitable comment. "Karen, this is my sister, Elle. Elle, this is my patient, Karen."

"Goodness, I've put my foot in it," Karen says, laughing. "She looks too young to be your sister."

Elle raises both eyebrows, steaming, and waits for Tony's response.

"She got the family genes." Tony lowers his voice conspiratorially. "She's a lot older than she looks."

"Tony!" Elle's voice leaps up at least an octave.

"What do you think? She doesn't look a day over a hundred." Tony gives Elle a megawatt grin, taking her hand, patting her fingers.

Elle glares, tamping down her flames more firmly.

"A hundred!" Karen slaps Tony on the arm.

"Don't worry." Tony drops Elle's hand and points at himself. "I'm a lot older than I look too."

"All this teasin'. Now I know you're brother and sister. Y'all gotta let me in on this skincare secret. Who's your dermatologist?"

"No dermatologist, none needed. It's snail goo." Tony nods solemnly, taking a step toward Elle, getting inside her space so she'll move back. He blocks her body with his as he presents himself to Karen, stretching an arm out to pull the front door open as far as it will go. "Cross my heart and hope to die, it's snail goo. It's all the rage right now. Bet you can find some at Target."

"The Tar-zhay, really?" Karen says, breathy. "I'll definitely have to go. I have errands to run anyway. Well, don't let me keep y'all. See you next week, Tony!"

"Bye!" Tony waves cheerfully. "Don't forget the wine!"

"I won't! Have a blessed day!" Karen burbles a laugh. Tony copies it, and the two laugh obnoxiously at each other until the front door shuts. The second the lock turns, his expression plummets back to normal.

"Snail goo?" Elle asks.

"Don't even know what that is."

Of course. That's Tony, who can charm the pants off anyone while lying through his teeth.

"And the wine?"

"Oh yeah, Karen's totally a wino who likes to share." He shrugs. "Who am I to turn her down?"

"She called me exotic. You let that come in here with shoes?"

Tony winks. "See, that's why the wine is important. I might as well get buzzed while taking her money. She's got lots of it, and it helps me pay for carpet cleaning. That's an important thing, the money. I get it from my patients, who come to see me because I've owned this business for the last fifteen years, and I've built up a nice clientele. Which means I'm not moving."

"How did you know?"

"There's a thing called a phone and you can call people with it, which is what Lira did. And before your paranoid ass asks, I gave her my number." He turns, walking through the high-ceilinged house. Sunlight infuses the air from the many skylights built into the hipped roof. In the sunroom, various potted plants stretch upward, luxuriating in the light. All Elle can think of when she's here is how high the utility bills must be.

Tony goes past two built-in bookcases beside the fireplace where jars upon jars of Chinese medicinal ingredients sit, bypassing the large living area with Craftsman-style furniture. Said furniture is completely at odds with the art on the walls: scrolls of calligraphy, and a large ink-and-wash portrait of him that Elle painted years ago. It's been strategically placed so it can be admired from anywhere in the room.

Elle susses out the strength of her wards as she follows, then switches her focus to her brother. He does look older. If she had to guess, she'd say he was in his early sixties for a regular human, but he wears his age with grace and ease. His face is clean-shaven, his black hair short and styled. The presence of deep crow's feet does little to dim the sparkling light in his dark brown eyes, and the gray at his temples only serves to accentuate his square-jawed handsomeness.

"Get your eyeballs off me, 妹妹." Tony waits for her to catch up, then opens his arms for a hug. This is an American thing, the hugging, but on Tony it feels natural.

Elle squeezes him until he grunts. He doesn't yet have the brittleness found in old age, which is a relief. She releases him, taking his hand. "Have you thought about where to move?"

"What if," Tony says, "and this is totally hypothetical, yes? What if I told you it was okay to ignore that asshole?"

"That asshole is our brother," Elle murmurs.

"Wait a second," Tony blurts in Mandarin, then tries to pry her hand off his wrist. "Aiyah, don't!"

Elle is already taking Tony's pulse, the long fingers of her hand lined up precisely along his vein. She probes each level of it, checking the flow of his blood. "Quit moving."

He subsides with a scowl, which morphs into a pout as she finishes the diagnostic. So far, everything is excellent, except for his usual issues. "Stick out your tongue."

"I don't have to take this from my younger sister."

"Yes, you do. Now stick out your tongue."

He sulks, then does so. "Happy?"

"All the way out. Don't talk." She peers at his tongue, noting its shape, color, and texture. She leans in and takes a quick sniff of his breath. "Just how much wine does Karen bring you, and how much of it do you drink?"

"Don't judge me. I drink in moderation and it's not every day. Your turn."

"I haven't palpated your body."

Tony turns his glare on her, serious. "Jiāng Yiyǎ. It's your turn."

It's Elle who sulks now, thrusting her left arm at him. "Using my full name is cheating."

Tony doesn't reply as he does the pulse diagnosis, his mouth pulling into a frown as he probes. "Other arm."

"Really?"

"Other arm."

Elle sighs and holds it up. Other families—normal ones—would be cutting fruit and making tea for guests instead of examining each other's body condition. But other families aren't full of doctors, like hers. "Done?"

"Tongue."

She grumbles but obliges him, letting him manipulate her jaw and head.

Tony makes a clicking noise. "Working too hard again."

"I had to. I wasn't lying when I said I couldn't go because of work." Only now does Elle realize how near of a miss that had been. If she had been at the gala . . .

"You could be doing so much more than that, you know. What have you made for Lira's family lately? Sit." Tony points at the rectangular dining table.

Elle does so. Lira's nuclear family is made of ghosts and spirits, all less corporeal than she is, except for her father, who passed the ability to choose a form to her. Through a stroke of chance, she and Elle had discovered that the Chinese custom of burning paper offerings to send items to the afterlife worked for the non-Chinese. "Her mom wanted new floral decorations and said my flowers are prettier than what she can buy."

"Isn't that something?" Tony pulls a chef's knife out of a knife block and hones it against a steel, his movements swift and surgical as he works. He speaks, his words punctuated by the metallic slide of his knife. "I can't believe it works for all ghosts. Why aren't you making money hand over fist painting things for the ghost community instead? You could paint an entire landscape. Houses. Cars."

"I like what I do right now." And Elle hasn't been serious about art in decades. What she has in her workshop are practice pieces and doodles. Only the calligraphy remains, and the occasional gift for Lira's family.

"Mm. And it has nothing to do with the circumstances we're in."

"No, of course not." She fidgets. "I'm happy with my life."

Tony puts the knife down with a clack, leveling a look at her. "Bullshit. How can you be this bad at lying to everyone but yourself?"

"I don't understand."

He scoffs.

"Are we fighting? I don't want to fight."

"Funny, because you're the one who came over to tell me we're moving. Which I'm not. Now you're getting lectured. I've been saving this up, so get comfortable." Tony opens the fridge, taking out a huge Asian pear. "These are still your favorite, right?" Without waiting for an answer, Tony rinses the pear off in the sink, picks up his knife, and begins peeling the fruit. "You've isolated yourself from the world. You have no hobbies outside of work. You can't live as if there's a blade to your neck all the time, but you do. Is that happiness? Is that what I should call it when you show up at my door once a year with enough fú to ward off the Mongol horde? I appreciate it, but you should turn some of that energy toward yourself."

"I want to do it," Elle protests. "Especially since . . . you know."

"I'm getting older?" Tony finishes for her, switching back to English. "I am. Looking damn good while doing it too. Wanna see my six-pack? It's Insta-worthy."

Elle doesn't know whether to flinch from the truth or facepalm when Tony lifts his shirt, revealing impeccable abs. There's no way Tony would let advancing age diminish his vanity. She's sure nothing could.

"I have the most delicious trainer who punishes me three times a week." Tony finishes peeling the pear, quartering it with casual ease. When they were young, he had preferred ranged weapons, but he's no slouch at melee combat. Elle, unfortunately, is only proficient enough to keep from cutting herself despite the many years spent training. Too reliant on her magic, her father said.

"You should follow me, by the way."

"What?"

"You know, on social media."

"On what?" Elle bites off the end of the word, leaning forward so quickly that the dining table shifts. "Tony!"

"No, @Tony was already taken. It's @TonyTimesTen, hashtag the same."

"Tony!" Elle can't help the clammy sweat that breaks out all over her body. "What happened to lying low?"

"Got tired of it, and you should be tired of it too. I've been using it for a while, but I just didn't tell you." He leaves the knife on the cutting board, bringing her a bowl heaped high with Asian pear, and shoves a toothpick into a cube of pale fruit. "Now eat. This is the one good thing you've done for yourself, liking a cool fruit. You have too much heat, and I didn't need to touch you to know that."

She's too distraught to give the fruit any attention. "Did you put up pictures of your face?"

He laughs at her as he goes back into the kitchen, takes out a clay teapot, and measures out leaves. "Yìyǎ-ah. I'm self-centered, not stupid. No, there are no pictures of my bare face. No, there are no details of where I live or what I do for a living. Just good, old-fashioned Instagay thirst trapping. You should try it."

Elle doesn't understand precisely what Tony's saying, but she gets the gist. "Aren't you too old to be doing this?"

He rolls his eyes. "Not at all. I guess you didn't hear about it, but there's this fifty-year-old Malaysian man, I think? With abs that are as good as mine, and a face that's less cute. He's got hundreds of thousands of followers. There are plenty of older men to pick from, which means I can hide pretty well." A beat. "Don't you want to put pictures of your beautiful face on the internet for everyone to see?"

She stews in her anger. Maybe there's a bit of jealousy in there too. She'd love to have his lack of reservation. "No."

"It helps me out when it comes to dating apps too. So many more people swipe right when they see a good picture. To tell the truth though, most men are disappointing."

Elle really has no idea what he's talking about except for the disappointing part. She's met her few partners the normal way. "Are you looking for a boyfriend?"

"Lord have mercy, not at all. Me, tied down? Don't you know I'm impossible to live with?"

"Still mad about that, are you?"

"Nope."

"Uh-huh." Tony's last and only serious boyfriend, Arun, had said that to him when they broke up, and instead of being hurt by it, Tony had transformed it into his motto. It's true Tony hasn't ever wanted to be tied down to anything, and after the end of that relationship, his commitment-phobia had gotten worse. He's eschewed diets, long-term partners, and his family-ordained responsibilities. His aversion to responsibility was what started the trouble in the first place, leaving Elle and Yiwú to pick up the slack.

"Life's about fun. It's not worth living if there's no fun, right? And one of us has to have fun. This whole family is full of sticks in the mud, I'm tellin' you."

"You've *been* telling me."

"I'm gonna tell you some more, because I just now got to the topic. I'm not moving, and you shouldn't freak out."

"After what you told me?" Now is the season of Elle's panic. "We're moving. We have to!"

"You can move. Feel free. I'm staying here." He arches an eyebrow at her in a challenge.

"No! Lily found me out. Our great-great-grandfather's jade is at the museum." Elle shivers. The power in that one piece of jade wouldn't just amplify her magic. Holding it would be a mandate for her family's spirits, making them more likely to lend her their strength. Tony's had been one of those. "He's coming. Aren't you worried at all?"

"Nope." Tony finishes cleaning his knife and slips it back into the block. His facility with bladed weapons was only outmatched by Yiwú, and it had taken Yiwú years and years to beat Tony. Elle remembers that day, how brightly Yiwú had smiled, how loudly he'd laughed because no one but Elle had believed in him. How he'd come running to her before anyone else, the words *Look! Look! I'm number one!* tumbling from his mouth. How Tony had put his hands on his hips, shaking his head, wearing his ever-present smile.

And Elle remembers the day she gave Yiwú a sword that had been forged especially for him, the balance awkward in her hand but perfect in his, the blade of it singing a pure note whenever it was drawn from its scabbard. That had been the blade in his hand when he'd pointed it at Tony's heart.

She can't think about all of that, but with Tony in the room, she can't help it. "He's coming and you won't do anything about it."

"No, he's coming and I don't want you to do anything about it. There's a difference. If we continue to fly under the radar, he won't know anything. He'll get the jade, and maybe that'll be enough to fool the book."

"Lily was at the gala with you!"

"Okay, but I'm dead. Everyone knows that. And she didn't know me." He shrugs. Their family has been convinced he was gone, not knowing it was Elle who kept him in the world of the living. No jade means no long life, no connection to their family spirits, no connection to their god.

"Been the best move of my life, being dead. It's true freedom. I have a life of my own, and I don't want to leave it. You should have a life too. A partner. Some joy. You deserve it." Tony flips a chair around, straddling it, and pops a piece of pear into his mouth. It crunches as he chews. "Oh man, this is so juicy. You won't think of it this way, but thanks for doing what you did."

Whatever appetite Elle has disappears. Memory rises, a flood filling her mouth and nose, and she's back there again, in the dining room of the house the three of them had shared, steam rising off the dumplings she'd pulled out of the pot. If they let them sit too long, the skins will stick. The tang of fresh cut ginger permeates the air, as hot and sharp as Yiwú's anger.

It's her birthday.

In her mind she watches Yiwú's mouth move. Tony's shoulders droop farther, duty and a broken heart weighing him down. Yiwú has no choice but to take Tony's jade, force Tony back home to do the job he was born to do, make him cure the illness that has killed so many of the disciples living at the foot of the mountain. One of them had been Yiwú's best friend.

Elle knows, as she always has, that Tony won't. That binding him to a generations-long responsibility before he's ready, if he ever will be, will leech the vitality from his spirit. She knows her brothers believe their choices have dwindled to a single path wide enough for one.

She never remembers how she gets Tony's laes. One second it's dangling from Yiwú's fist, and the next it's in her hand, cool and smooth, a figure of Shénnóng carved into a cabochon of imperial jade. Jade is reluctant to warm up, a stubborn stone that dislikes changing its ways, but once it's hot, it stays hot. The light of the flames in her hand catches in Tony's laes, the transparent depths muting first the reds and oranges, then the whites and blues.

Tony convulses and falls to the floor. Yiwú, stunned, drops his sword, shouting at her. Elle only wants to keep her family alive. She only wants to give Tony the freedom so long denied him, only wants to protect Yìwú the way a big sister should. She raises her right hand. There's something heavy in it, cold and biting, as solid and unyielding as deep winter.

Tony screams when Elle shatters his jade. She thinks Yìwú screams too.

"Yiyǎ." Tony's voice, speaking her name. Tony's voice, speaking to her with the accent of home. "Don't think about that."

She replies, voice low. "If you won't move, then I have no choice but to increase the protections here."

"How on earth can you do that? What more can you add? You're going to put legs on a snake."

"I have new ideas. I've been thinking—"

"What about for you?" Tony interrupts.

"For me?"

"For you." Tony works the words in his mouth like he's tasting them. "Have you been protecting yourself at all?"

The glyphs shielding her door wouldn't be strong enough to stop a cockroach. "Yeah, sort of, but it fades with time, and . . ."

"Jiāng Yìyǎ." There's her full name again. She's in trouble now. Tony rarely gets mad; it isn't in his nature. He's wickedly smart, but carefree and sometimes careless, hard to insult, always upbeat. For him, there's no point in getting mad over things or people when nothing will come of it. But there's a storm brewing in his eyes.

He fixes her with the penetrating stare he inherited from their mother. "I'm going to ask you again, and this time you aren't going to give me any of that runaround shit. Have you been protecting yourself?"

She can't look at him, thinking about the wards she didn't have the energy to reconstruct, saying she'd do it later. "No."

His eyes and mouth tighten. "All this time you've been doing the most to protect me, but you haven't even considered yourself? You're the one who keeps telling me Yìwú is dangerous. Is he not dangerous to you? Did he—"

Tony stands abruptly, his hand tightening into a fist. When he speaks, he switches back into their home dialect. "Didn't we both block him? Huh? You don't think he's looking for you too? You still have power, and I . . ."

"You're still the firstborn. I thought that losing your jade would give him what he needed, but no. You saw him last time. The book was driving him mad. He's convinced he can't do anything without your death."

"He can wait another thirty years. That's nothing to him."

"You know he isn't going to do that." Elle stands too, the frustration showing itself. "I won't let him! I've taken enough from you because of him."

Tony cuts in. "And he hasn't taken anything from you? With your help I've rebuilt my life twice. I have hobbies. I go out, I have friends. What do you do? Who takes care of you? Why do you think that you're so unimportant that you can sit there in your misery and call it noble? Then you have the gall to come here and talk about protection when you won't lift a finger to help yourself?"

Elle covers her mouth with her hand, tears starting in her eyes.

"I'm not mad at you for what you did. You chose my happiness over my duty. I'm mad that you've gotten it in your head that the only way to keep me alive is to not have a life at all. That's shit, Yǐyǎ." Tony begins pacing, impassioned. "No little sister of mine gets to think of herself as unimportant."

"It's you who's at the most risk," she tries to argue. The stinging in her eyes moves into her chest, putting cracks in the wall she thought was sturdy.

"Hey! How about you shut up and let me talk?" Tony points at her. "You are not the least valuable child and you are not naturally mopey and the fact that you're still thinking this way is a damned disgrace. Forget what Ma or Ba ever said about you. Protect yourself because you're important and you value yourself and because you don't want to make me cry. It's a terrible look on me."

The tears spill over. Of course Tony would give her that affirmation and cap it off with his selfishness. "You're such a shit."

"Proud of it. And I'm not going to let you use me as an excuse to be a turtle forever. Unlike me, you've got two centuries left. Live it. Yiwú can go to hell. Let him come. I'll fucking send him there."

"No!" Yìwú had been her best friend, and no matter what he's done to both of them, she can't wish death on him.

"You don't want that? I don't think you know what you want." Tony sticks his hands on his hips and glares.

Elle dashes her tears away, setting her jaw. "Maybe, but don't think you can lecture me when you've got a part in this too." Her voice is quavery and not at all collected.

"I'll do what I want, thank you. He's tried to kill me twice."

"Yeah?" She throws it in his face. "Who drove him there? Who refused to do his job? Who didn't want to quit having fun—" Here Elle pauses, gasping. "Who didn't want to quit having fun and ran away to the Bureau instead, leaving his baby brother to take up a role he was never meant to succeed in? Huh? Wasn't me!" The air starts shimmering around her.

"He still tried to kill me! He won't hesitate to kill you either. He's got to get through two siblings before he becomes first in line."

"And that's why I'm trying to protect you even though you're the whole cause of this mess." Skies, she's angry crying again. Their family's edition of the Běn Cǎo Shū would only respond fully to Tony. Without him, its magic would be unpredictable, uncontrollable. "Have you learned anything about responsibility in these last twenty-six years? Have you learned that running away doesn't solve anything? Reflected on what got us here?"

"Plenty."

Elle claps for him. "Amazing. Fantastic. That's real growth. Did it change anything for you?"

"Yeah! I got an Insta account."

His blitheness makes Elle want to pop him in the face. She clenches both fists.

"Why bother asking me?" He shrugs. "If I could change things, I would."

She narrows her eyes, her teeth grinding together. "Really?"

"Really. But I won't get a second chance. The past is done and you've gotta quit being mad about it. I forgave you ages ago. Just waiting on you."

It's like Tony has shot an arrow directly into her heart. She can't breathe for a full second. "You make it sound so easy."

"It's easy when you've done the right thing, which you did. One day, you'll believe that."

"Don't flip it around on me, Yìxiáng, don't you dare!"

"First, take my name out of your mouth. Second, too bad. We're all fuckups here. All three of us." The bitter truth in that statement burns. "I'm telling you, you still have your jade. You could be doing so much more than what, watching bad Chinese dramas and making baby-level glyphs? That's not even your strongest talent. So, what do you want, Yìyǎ?"

He's flipped it around on her anyway. Elle refuses to give Tony more of her reaction. "I want you to be safe."

"Okay, I'm safe. Now what?"

"What do you mean, now what?"

"I mean exactly that. I'm safe. Goal met."

"How can you be sure?"

He throws his hands up. "I'm arguing with you about it, that's how. Our brother isn't here, that's how. You shouldn't even be worrying about that! It's time you took care of yourself."

"You don't want more protections." Elle shakes her head, a plan formulating. "And you won't move. Okay. Here's my counter."

"You suck at chess," Tony says blandly.

"I move in with you. I'll put in my two weeks today."

"You are *not* moving in with me!"

"I paid for this house! It's as much mine as yours. I'm doing it. You can't stop me."

"I can absolutely stop you, and the only reason why you aren't in a heap on the floor is because I love and cherish my baby sister. You aren't moving in."

It won't be hard at all. There isn't much to upend in her life. Lira will understand, and Luc is just a friendly client. "I'm moving in and I'm increasing the protections here—"

"Hold on—"

"—and it'll allow me to be here if you need me."

"Enough!" Tony snaps. "You wanna haggle, let's haggle. You aren't moving in."

Elle narrows her eyes, fire in her spirit. "I'm moving in, I'm claiming the guest bedroom, and you're teaching me how to drive."

"The guest bedroom stays the guest bedroom because you aren't moving in. Stay away from my car."

"I bought that car, same as I bought this house."

"That gets you less sympathy than you think." Tony sets his jaw. "You can move in temporarily. You don't touch my car. When you're here, you pay for your share of the groceries and bills."

If Tony thinks he's winning this, he's mistaken. "I move in permanently, I take the guest bedroom as mine, and I don't pay a cent for anything. You can afford it."

"You move in *temporarily*," Tony says, steel in his voice, "for as long as the exhibit is in town. You bring with you protections for yourself at the same level as the protections you'd make for me."

A low blow. "And I move in permanently."

"I love you, but no. That's the best deal I can make you. You live here for the next few weeks. I'll cover all expenses. But you can't talk about helping me when you refuse to do it for yourself. Your life is in as much danger as mine. So either you come back with some creative and powerful shit, or I toss you on the street."

Elle matches Tony glare for glare. If they were in a drama, someone would be drumming furiously on the jiàn gǔ in the background.

"Deal." The imaginary drummer finishes with a resounding flourish. Elle grits her teeth. If it guarantees she'll be close to Tony, she'll do it. She'll renegotiate later. "I should be able to finish my project by this weekend."

"No rush," Tony says, completely unenthused.

Chapter Seven

IN RETROSPECT, Elle should have taken the warning from the other night. But she didn't, so here she is, in dire need of her laes, her vision filled with static, holding onto the edge of her workbench as if her life literally depends on it.

She assesses what's wrong. Her heartbeat is erratic, caused by overwork, stress, and low blood sugar from not eating. Her qì is unbalanced from spending too much time sitting or hunching over the sketches carpeting the floor, and there isn't enough of it left after all the tests she's run. On top of that, she's exhausted from staying up late in the workshop fine-tuning the glyph she and Lira have created.

She edges backward inch by inch until her feet hit her stool, dropping onto it like potatoes in a loose sack, bracing herself so she doesn't spill onto the floor. As she waits for her blood pressure to stabilize, she debates the merits of using her laes. She's gotten by without it, but if she wants to move in with Tony next weekend, she'll need the boost to get Luc's commission and her protections done on time.

The drawback is having to face her family and her god, who may or may not answer her call for help.

That's an unpleasant train of thought. Tea is nicer. Yes, tea will help her wake up enough to go home. She stretches a hand toward her flask, still full of water from when she attempted to make tea hours ago, and summons a flame.

It takes its sweet time popping into existence, flickering pale yellow and sullen at the tip of her finger. That's worrisome. Elle concentrates, drawing hard on her magic until the fire burns a livelier orange. Her whole body clenches, and for a few moments she quits breathing. She's left swaying over her workbench, dizzy and gasping, aching for relief.

Her jade would fix this. She's almost willing to get it and face more disappointment from her family.

"Elle, are you okay?"

Her eyes spring open to Luc's worried face. Elle lets out a shrieky gasp as she bolts into a sitting position, her stool rocking beneath her. She must have fallen asleep somehow. She tries to talk, but only a croak comes out. "How'd you get in here?!"

He speaks carefully, bordering on deliberate. "Lira let me in before she left."

"I'm tired, not slow." Elle scowls and rubs her cheek. It's numb, and tingles as blood returns.

"I can see that. Do you need help?"

"No." She clears her throat. "I'm okay."

"Can I walk you home?"

Any other day Elle would shout yes, but she's drained and her defenses are down, and all she wants is to sleep for three days straight. Sadly, she doesn't have three days. "I'm okay, really."

"Were you working on my commission?"

"Yeah." She says it before she can think to lie.

"I appreciate you going through all this for me, but you can't run yourself ragged on my account."

"I'm not—"

Luc gives her a flat look. "I literally found you passed out on your table."

Just because it's the truth doesn't mean she has to be reasonable. "It's Sunday. You need these by Thursday night or first thing Friday morning. I'm almost at the final drafts. A few more and I'll be good. Hey, and then I can use your ink! Thank you again, by the way."

Undiverted, Luc says, "You need to rest if you want to make more."

"I'll be okay, really. I . . ." She takes a breath. She can't say a word about Tony. ". . . I just want to make sure everything will work right before you go. I can't have a faulty glyph messing with your missions."

Luc stays silent, which has the effect of making Elle squirm with discomfort, wondering if she's said something wrong. Eventually, he offers her his hand. "Come on."

She takes it and finds herself pulled into his embrace. Well, calling it an embrace would be an exaggeration. Luc practically drags her to the couch, depositing her onto the nearest cushion with an audible *whumpf.*

Her head lolls back. "Thanks. You're the nicest client ever."

"The nicest?" Luc sits beside her, propping her up, shifting her over until she's supported by the corner.

"Nicest and friendliest." She laughs to herself.

"You think of me as a nice, friendly client?"

All the space inside her is taken up by exhaustion, leaving no room for subtlety or diplomatic talk. "Isn't that how you think of me? A nice, friendly supplier. Very businesslike."

There's a mix of emotions on Luc's face, one of which Elle can't puzzle out until it dawns on her. He's hurt. She's hurt him. She didn't think it was possible for someone that self-assured.

"No." Luc's voice is quiet, unadorned. Raw. He looks into her eyes, expression subdued. "I think of you as a friend. I had meant to talk to you after last Thursday when I said recommendations weren't necessary. I should have talked to you sooner, because the meaning you took wasn't the meaning I intended. I'm sorry. I'd like to rephrase more clearly, if you're willing to give me a second chance."

Elle's willing to give him a second chance, or a third or a fourth, as long as he looks at her like that. "I think of you as a friend too, so yes."

"Thank you." His brief smile lifts her spirits. "When I said no recommendations were necessary, it was because I didn't want anyone but you to make my glyphs. If you won't make them, I don't want them."

He doesn't want anyone but her. The statement shouldn't be sending a thrill through her, but it is. Him sitting close, warm and Luc-ish and saying kind words, is sending a thrill through her. "I get it. That's really sweet of you. Almost makes me wish I could do more custom work." Her hand is the only part of her capable of moving, so she puts it on his knee.

"After witnessing how much of a toll it takes on you, I'm thinking it might be a good thing you've banned commissions." He places his hand atop hers. Somehow, it makes her feel better. "I'm going to help you home and get you something to eat. Please tell me how you clean up your workspace."

Elle half-snorts her laugh. "Clean?"

Luc sighs. "You're right. Clean is too ambitious a word. What essentials do you need me to take care of so you can go?"

Elle rests her head against the couch as she directs Luc through the process of rinsing out her brushes and stone and putting the ink away. The sound of water splashing is soothing, as is his presence. She hasn't met anyone else who's made her feel as comfortable as he has. Her eyes close.

"Elle, wake up."

"I wasn't . . ." She swats halfheartedly at him when he shakes her.

"You were, and it's time to go." He holds out his hand.

Elle is pulled to her feet for half a second before she drapes herself over Luc, who humors her by taking her weight. "Ready?"

She dredges up some words, mumbling them against his neck. "Might have to carry me."

"The probability of that is higher than you think."

On second thought, she'd rather walk. "That's gonna be embarrassing."

"I can't promise I won't drop you."

"That's even more embarrassing. Just leave me here and take your blanket. Make me look like I've been pulling overtime."

She feels rather than hears his soft laugh. "I was going to take my blanket regardless, and you're already pulling overtime. I'm afraid I can't leave you. You haven't eaten, and from the looks of it, you need more than a full night's sleep simply to be functional tomorrow."

He isn't wrong. "I have a deadline."

"Deadlines can be broken or extended. You originally told me two weeks. For now, you need to eat and rest. If you can stay awake, I can get you something to eat."

"This is gonna sound weird, but can you make me a sandwich?"

"A sandwich?" He recoils from her, looking affronted.

"I have some bread and stuff at home. It's easy."

"I know it's easy. A sandwich? You insult me."

"Easy is easy. I'm not asking you to cook."

"I can, if you want."

Whatever energy she's saved gets used up as she straightens, interest piqued. "You'd cook for me?"

Luc smiles, a touch sardonic. "Are you suggesting you'd be able to cook for yourself? You can barely walk. I'm preparing to carry you."

The idea is tempting; she's in worse shape than she thought. Given how she's trembling as she pushes away from him, being carried doesn't sound so bad. Skies, she could take a nap on him. "No. I just need to get home."

"Lean on me, then."

For once, Elle is grateful to live minutes away on company property. The walk back to her apartment is punctuated with frequent stops so she can cling to Luc and catch her breath, her field of vision narrowing to a few feet in front of her. When he unlocks the door, she stumbles in, falling against the couch, and slithers awkwardly onto the cushions. Her coffee table barks as it scrapes along the wooden floor. A few seconds later, pain radiates through her shin.

She spends a minute or two waiting for the world to stop heaving, gathering enough willpower to make it to the tall altar on the far side of the living room where her grandmother's portrait is. On the lowest shelf beneath the empty offering bowl and incense holder is the wooden box that contains her jade.

Wait, no. Standing in Elle's kitchen is one very present and very observant Luc Villois, and though he's busy making her a sandwich, he still has line of sight on her. She can't put her laes on with him around.

Okay, time for a new plan. Elle struggles back upright and takes the few steps needed to get to the altar, thumping to her knees in front of it. For a second she crumples, and it's only the fear of losing consciousness that gets her to push herself back up. She shoves her arm into the shelf and fumbles for the box, taking a few seconds to ensure she has a firm grip on it before forcing herself to stand.

Bedroom now. Her heartbeat pounds in her ears, the thunder of it drowning out all else. Her vision pulses in time to it. Overwhelmed, Elle holds the box against her chest, putting out a hand to brace herself on the wall beside the kitchen pass-through.

From far away Luc says, "Are you okay?"

"Just gonna..." Elle gestures at herself vaguely with the box. There's a silver three-by-five-inch frame on the ledge, the only other photo she has in her home. She looks at it, Tony and Yìwú's smiling faces swimming into focus. It's an old picture in black and white, with both her brothers in traditional robes, hair long, arms slung over each other's shoulders.

An alarm trips in the back of her mind. She should be concerned about this. But if she doesn't get her jade on, she's going to pass out. Elle grunts, supporting herself with the wall, and shuffles to her bedroom. She leans on the door to close it, and it shuts with a slam.

She's too tired to wince. She fumbles with the latch on the box instead, scrabbling at it for an eternity before she digs a fingernail beneath it and pries it up. Elle flings the lid open with enough force to make the small disk of jade inside spill out and skitter away on the floor.

She makes a sound of frustration as she falls to her hands and knees, reaching for her laes. It eludes her first attempts before she yanks on its thin red cord, the stone skipping to her. Elle snatches it up in her fist, pushing her hand against her heart. At her touch, the spirits stir. *Please, 奶奶.*

"Shénnóng," she whispers, his name a prayer. "I'm sorry for leaving you. Please forgive me for what I've done."

A rush of wind lifts her hair. Slowly, her god turns his face to her.

Tears needle her eyes. Her hand goes slack, the pendant falling until the cord catches on her fingers. She bows her head, a current of spirits building in the jade, and puts on the necklace.

Energy bursts around her. Elle gasps as the world sharpens and grows brighter, her senses amplified. Her breath rattles through her body; her vision swims as if she's looking through a fishbowl. The wall on the other side of the room is missing a tiny flake of paint. She can count the threads per inch in the twill weave of her jeans. With the door closed, she smells sliced ham and turkey, commercially made bread.

Heat flowers on her forehead, drawing the nimbus of energy into a single point, directing it into her pathways. Her god's blessing sluices down her meridians, forming brief whirlpools in her major centers before dissipating into the rest of her body.

Her grandmother's presence surrounds her, and Shénnóng's voice echoes in her head. *Welcome back, daughter.*

Elle pours out her gratitude, rubbing the smooth surface of her pendant. When she's able, she'll need to light incense and pile the bowl high with gifts for her god. The flame she conjures comes as easy as blinking, appearing fat and blue before she throttles her magic down to a more normal red-orange.

She gets to her feet, finding herself a manageable level of tired. Stifling a yawn, she changes into her pajamas and tucks the pendant under her shirt.

"You're looking better," Luc remarks when she comes back out.

"Anytime," Elle replies automatically before she realizes it's the wrong response. "I mean, uh, yeah, thanks."

Luc's lips twitch before they curve into a hint of a smile. "Feeling any better?"

Now she has to cover for herself. "Yeah. Just got a little something to help me out. A magic talisman thing. You know, like a battery, but made of magic."

"Yes, I'm aware of how they work."

She's gotta stay cool. Luc can't know the truth about the pendant. Details are the key to a convincing story, so Elle gives them. "I mean, it's not made of magic. It's a real thing, not super powerful." Skies, she's babbling. "I only use it once in a while, not often at all. Don't need the boost most of the time."

Dead silence. Luc's hands pause, then resume cutting her sandwich in half diagonally. "You are," he says, his words interrupted by the tinking of the knife on the plate, "possibly the most unsuitable spy I have ever met."

Embarrassment makes Elle flush. She hopes he's bought into her lie. "Why's that?"

"You've said it yourself. You're terrible at lying, and you talk too much when you're nervous."

"I do not." She does. She really does. This is why she hadn't lasted long as a field agent.

"There's no shame in needing help, especially after all the magic you've used."

Oh, thank the gods he's bought it, whatever it was she was selling. "Okay, phew. Thought you were, like, judging me or something."

"Judgment is the last thing I would, like, do or something to you."

Another bout of silence. Then, incredulous, Elle says, "Are you making fun of me?"

"Yes."

"Wow, you couldn't even lie and tell me no?"

He waits until they've stared at each other for a full three seconds before deadpanning, "I would never lie to you."

"Not better!"

"All right," Luc says once he's done laughing. "I wouldn't lie to you, and I was making fun of you gently. Satisfied?"

Elle scowls. "I didn't want this."

"And yet that's what you got." Luc actually grins at her. "I'm glad you're better, but you still need rest. This sandwich is inadequate, but it'll have to do. I apologize. I couldn't find the mayonnaise."

"It's because I don't have any."

He pauses. "Mustard?"

"Don't like it."

"Elle, your habits are trying my patience."

His judgment is trying her patience. "Then don't look at 'em."

Luc huffs. "Here's what I'll do. You're overworked because of me, so it's only fair for me to ease your way as best I can. I'll cook for you as long as you promise to eat what I make, and rest appropriately. How do you feel about omelets for breakfast?"

Shénnóng's blessings, indeed. He's going to seduce her with caretaking. Of all the paths he could take, like accidentally getting too close and *oops!* kissing her, or doing that stretch that shows stomach between shirt and waistband, he's chosen mother henning. This is how Elle knows she's gotten old. "Why are you so nice?"

"Do you want me to be meaner?" In a flash, his posture changes, his body tensing, projecting violence. His expression, too, goes from soft and caring to cold and dispassionate. He points hard enough at her to cause her to flinch back. When he speaks, his voice is flat, with an edge. "I will provide three meals and two snacks a day. You will eat, no excuses."

Elle stares, aghast. This version of him is unrecognizable compared to the laughing, smiling person from a moment ago. "No. Please don't do that ever again."

Luc exhales and relaxes, looking relieved. "I won't. I apologize."

"Who are you when you aren't here?" Elle twists her fingers to-gether, unable to shake the image of him. Neither can she ignore the bleakness souring her stomach. Luc isn't just Bureau. He might be a Fixer with an attitude like that. Fixers have terrifying reputations and require a certain temperament to succeed, and the recruiter who'd chased Tony had emphasized that fact.

He doesn't respond for a long time. "That's a good question," he says finally, "and one I'm reluctant to answer." He puts the plate on her table and gestures for her to sit, speaking quietly. "Tell me what you like and don't like to eat."

Elle takes the seat across from Luc. Behind him, a shard of light glints off the picture frame.

Chapter Eight

Luc chases the fox spirit through a harpy nest and takes a second to reflect on the life decisions that have led him here to this exact moment. He could be prepping Elle's dinner, but alas. If there were stage directions, they would read, "Exit, pursued by a queen harpy."

"On your ten!"

He skids to a stop, throwing up an arm to shield his eyes, flattening himself against the wall of the narrow alley he's using for cover. A small explosion goes off overhead, washing him in heat and light. The shockwave rattles through him. There's a strangled shriek, muffled by the ringing in his ears, and the faint sound of large wings flapping.

"Target?" he asks once his hearing clears.

"No hit. Might wanna—"

Luc ducks. The queen harpy's talons score the brick just above him before she pulls up from her dive. She ascends, trajectory wobbly. He knows she isn't gone for good. Harpies are tenacious.

"Warn me next time." He straightens, watching as she hovers in midair, shaking her head, eyes glassy. She banks to her left, breaking line of sight.

Gillen's laugh booms through the call rune. "That was your warning, Killer. Emi was being nice."

Luc's jaw clenches. "Be nicer. Fern, do you have a shot?"

"Not yet, but if you put your pretty ass in the open, I might."

Luc isn't sure if Fern means to shoot him or the harpy, and has no plans to stand in the open no matter how pretty she thinks he is. He has to pin the fox down, and fast. He needs a win after the museum disaster. "Target?"

"Went to ground in the building on the corner. Apartments, two stories, green door. Brick and concrete, but old." Ken speaks calmly, a Japanese accent tinting his voice. "I'll work top, you work bottom."

"Hey," Emi says, "we still have the harpy around."

Luc doubles back through the alley to the main street. He spots the green door. "Not my problem."

Three voices burst through the rune at once. "You fucker, we don't do cleanup—"

"—a 'thank you' would be good, you're welcome by the way—"

"—just for that, I won't shoot her when she shows up."

Oberon cuts in. "Quiet on comms."

Gillen rolls on, ignoring Oberon. "Don't we have another target?"

Emi snorts. "Thanks for remembering Jiang. Fern and I are working on it."

Fern picks up the rest of the conversation. "Might have a convergence soon. He didn't like being split from his buddy."

Ken clicks in annoyance. "Oberon said quiet on comms. Convergence acknowledged."

Gillen grunts. "Maybe we should let Killer handle this on his own. Let him fuck it up again."

"That's more work for us in the—" Fern starts to say.

"Hey, how do you say *killer* in French? *Zee keel-ah, hon hon hon?*"

"Are you even listening?"

"Crew, *crew!*" Ken puts steel in his voice.

"Yes, yes!" the other three chorus.

There's a beat of silence. "Shut the fuck up."

"Yes, sir!" they say in perfect sync.

Luc sighs, grateful for the peace. Oberon might think he holds the whip, but only Ken can rein in the Wrecking Crew.

"Okay, assholes," Ken says, calm again. "Set up a perimeter, funnel Jiang in."

"What about the harpy, boss?" Emi replies.

"Don't mind her for now. She'll go away soon."

Luc checks the sky as he takes the direct route to the building, but there's nothing but blue. He's halfway across the street when he sees a shadow streaking across the pavement. He barely has time to roll out of the way as the harpy dive-bombs him again, her face contorted with fury. She hurls curses at him in Greek, gaining altitude before she turns, snapping her wings open, whipping them down, unleashing an attack.

He braces himself, protecting his face with his arms, hoping that Elle's strength candy has given him enough power to withstand the gale-force wind. "Fern, take the shot!"

"Can't, I'm not set up!"

He has no time for this. They've spent the last few days tracking Lily and Jiang, learning their patterns and habits. This is their opportunity to apprehend them both, and if a single harpy ruins the mission, he won't be able to ask for time off until the end of the year. Maybe until next year. That's unacceptable.

Luc opens a pouch on his belt, fingers finding the glyph of flight curled in its cylinder. When Elle had given it to him, she'd told him two things: first, he'd have two minutes before the magic wore off, and second, did he like wuxia movies?

He hadn't a clue what they were, and he still doesn't, but the glyph should allow him to fly like he's in one. Regardless, he'll have to thank her for her foresight. He plunges his thumb through the waxed paper covering the mouth of the cylinder. At his touch the glyph inside falls to ash, sending Elle's magic roaring through him.

He leaves the ground like he's been propelled, rocketing wildly up until he gets over his surprise and composes himself. A simple thought has him rushing forward; another stops his momentum. So far, so good. He sets his sights on the harpy. At this distance he can see her amber eyes, raptor-like and slitted with rage.

"The fuck?" Gillen says, hushed. "He flies now?"

She swoops toward him, harrying. Luc dodges once, twice, but the third time he twists away a hair too slowly, and her claws snag on the sleeve of his shirt, scoring his forearm with a jagged line of red.

He bites back the pain, willing it away, not bothering to look at his arm. Blood is beginning to drip, giving him an idea of how bad it might be, but he doesn't have time to take stock of his injury. The harpy will press her advantage if he stays hovering in the air.

He has to go on the offensive and disable her, find some way of getting inside the reach of her claws. Luc charges her to gauge her reaction; his eyes water from the speed of it. She beats her wings frantically in a climb to get away.

It seems the harpy is slower than he is on the ascent. Luc charges her again, the wind whistling in his ears as he powers through another attack. This time she's ready to meet him with her talons, but at the last second he hurls himself upward past her.

The harpy twists to follow, but it's too late. From above Luc drops like a stone, smashing into the harpy's shoulders. Soft down goes flying as he grabs the first joint of her wing, yanking it back. In half a second Luc has his switchblade out, thumbing the release, opening it with a satisfying *thwick*.

"No!" the harpy screams.

Luc stabs his knife into the thin membrane beneath her shoulder, ignoring her shrill cry of pain, slashing up until he hits bone. With a thrust of his arm he slices into the tendon controlling her wing, her flesh springing apart under the blade. He withdraws, angles the tip of the knife back, and digs it into the joint at the top of her humerus.

Blood wells, spattering Luc's face when the harpy spirals into free fall. He wraps his left arm around her, trying to control their descent as Elle's magic flickers and fades. They crash heavily onto the roof of the building, the harpy taking the brunt of it, her body going limp.

Luc staggers to his feet, stunned and aching, wishing he hadn't used all of Elle's regen glyphs. He loses his footing and falls when another explosion rocks the side of the building. Bricks hit the ground with dull thuds.

"Emi's gettin' excited," Gillen declares.

Fern giggles. "Good news for me tonight."

He pushes himself up, checking for the harpy's pulse. It's weak and thready, but there. If she survives long enough to receive medical aid, she'll recover. Luc uses her intact wing to clean the worst of the blood off his knife before stowing it. Then he stands, wiping his face with the sleeve that isn't torn.

He flexes fingers and toes, shakes out arms and legs, takes several deep breaths. He hurts, but nothing seems broken. "Ken, location?"

"Went in the bottom. Clear. Fox en route."

"Jiang incoming." Gillen's voice darkens into a snarl. "Get ready, Ken."

"Don't let it get personal," Ken replies.

"This is for Tony."

"I said don't let it get personal." Ken's words crackle with command.

"Fine." Gillen subsides. "I won't."

At that moment, the door to the roof bursts open, a slender figure hanging off the handle. She trips but recovers, freezes when she sees him. Her eyes go round with fear. "You."

"Me," Luc replies.

"I'd prefer her alive, if possible," Oberon says.

Luc unholsters his gun, pushing the safety up, cradling the grip in his hands as he brings it to bear. "Help us. It will go better for you."

Lily's chest heaves, color developing in her cheeks. The lines of her body turn fuzzy, as if she's barely able to keep her human form. She hunches into herself, her fear a pulsing, tangible thing, unable to look at him. "You can't take him. He's the only one who can heal my family. Please, I can explain. You don't understand!"

"It's not my job to understand." He pulls the trigger. The report echoes off the walls of the taller buildings surrounding them, the sound mixing with the fox's shrill yelp of pain.

"Lily!" Jiang appears over the side of the building, hair and clothes plastered to him from how fast he's flown up. He lands, bracing his feet, and in one movement, sprints toward Luc, drawing his sword faster than the eye can follow.

Luc shoots again, sure it will hit at this distance. Jiang grunts and staggers, his hand going to his chest, but there's no blood as he resumes running. Light flashes on the blade as he extends. Luc throws himself to the side, avoiding Jiang's sword, pivoting to keep his eyes on his attacker.

Footsteps approach in the cadence of a run; Luc isn't ready to evade. Lily tackles him, sending them both to the floor of the roof. He lands hard on his shoulder and loses his grip on his gun. It skitters away, well out of reach. She puts all her weight on him in an attempt to pin him.

"Run—" she starts to shout, but Luc flips her up and over in a reverse, his enhanced strength and agility making her as light as paper. He registers the sound of a door splintering, but remains focused on Lily, driving her into the roof. He braces his arm across her neck hard enough to choke her, but not hard enough to crush her windpipe. She grabs at him, eyes bulging, fingers scrabbling at his torn sleeve. There's blood on her shoulder from where he shot her, and that's where he punches. She gags on her scream, going limp with pain.

Luc gains his feet, assessing the situation. Ken is fighting Jiang on the far side of the roof, fully in oni form, a corner of the doorframe hanging off his curved horns. Jiang is as graceful as a sapling in comparison, but each sword strike ringing against Ken's thick club carries fatal intent. Luc recognizes the moves from sparring against Pei.

He runs to his gun, scoops it up, squares his shoulders, and waits for the opportunity to present itself. There's a rhythm to Jiang's movements, and though Luc can't predict what Jiang will do next, he's more than familiar with the flow of swordplay.

He exhales into his calm. The trigger eases back beneath his finger.

This time, the shot is good. Jiang's knees buckle but he remains standing, his free hand going to his side, his face a mask of pain. He barely evades a vicious downward swing, stumbling out of the range of Ken's club. The end of it slams into the roof, which gives way and collapses into a shallow crater. Ken roars, his battle ire up, and in three steps has Jiang by the throat.

"No!" Somehow, Lily is on her feet again, charging Ken. Luc knows, as Lily likely does, that the move is futile. "Go!" she cries, her voice hoarse, cracking with desperation.

Ken turns toward her, eyes aglow, the softness in the usual brown replaced by a simmering red. He sweeps his arm in a casual backhand, catching Lily on his club with a bone-crunching *thunk*, and sends her volleying back to Luc. She bounces before coming to a halt at Luc's feet.

He pulls his rune of stasis from his belt pouch, slapping it onto her. He looks up when Ken shouts.

Jiang leaps away, his sword dripping blood, and escapes into the sky.

Luc hopes the rest of the Crew is set up. "Emi, spell the bullet. Fern, take the damned shot!"

In the distance, Jiang's body plummets. The thundercrack of Fern's sniper rifle discharging rolls by.

"Got 'im." Fern's smug with satisfaction.

But just as Jiang is about to collide with the roof of another building, he slows, a nimbus of white light flowering around him, and twists himself around to land on both feet. In the next breath he's back in the sky, streaking away.

Several gasps are audible through the earpiece. "What the fuck was that?" Fern demands.

"Pei. Darcy." Oberon, unruffled as always, gives his orders. "Follow him. Don't let him rest."

"Understood," they say together.

Ken sighs, lifting a blue-skinned hand to thumb the base of his horns. He, like Luc, has a cut on his arm, but he doesn't seem to notice it. He goes to the harpy, kneeling next to her, placing his fingers on her neck. Luc is surprised when Ken produces his own rune of stasis. It seems she's alive. "Gonna need two medports."

"Did you say two?" Oberon asks.

"Yes," Luc answers for Ken. "For the fox and the harpy."

"The harpy?" Oberon scoffs. "I thought you handled her."

"I did."

"All right, I thought you killed her."

"I didn't." Not yet, at least.

"She's badly wounded." Ken shakes his head, rising. "Was that necessary? She has a clutch, you know. One of the eggs is cracked."

His insides go hollow, and his stomach bottoms out somewhere by his knees. He hadn't known. The nest had been piled high with blankets and pillows, and Luc had passed by without looking closely, too intent on flushing Lily out from the house. No wonder she wouldn't leave him alone. He hopes he isn't responsible for the egg. If the harpy dies, or is unable to care for her children, that's on him.

He looks at Ken, thankful for his actions. Luc knows acutely the pain of losing a mother at a young age, but to lose a mother before birth? "We have excellent healers. The mother should be able to return soon. As for the egg, if the crack doesn't extend through the membrane, the hatchling will be fine."

"The nest is damaged as well," Ken adds.

"Like Luc said, we have excellent healers." Oberon pauses. "And we'll throw some money at her. That should help."

Luc exchanges a look with Ken, but says nothing. Throwing money at situations is a classic Oberon strategy. No amount of money will soothe the pain of an egg that won't hatch. Money alone won't keep the rest of the eggs warm during the mother's recovery. And despite the skill of the healers on staff at the agency, there's no guarantee that the harpy's tendon will knit together seamlessly. She might never fly again.

Who are you when you aren't here?

He has no answer, not one she'll like. Not one that will assuage the fear he caused two days ago. And Elle's approval, as opposed to his co-workers, means something. The harpy's fate should be of no concern to him. She's collateral damage, a necessary part of the job. But thinking of her in such clinical terms sends tension into the back of his neck, adding onto the faint nausea he's already experiencing. The harpy is a mother with a nest of eggs. Without her, the whole family is lost.

The responsibility sits solely on Luc's shoulders. The last time he was in a situation involving parentless children, it had been a bloody disaster. This time, he has to do better.

Speaking up goes against all two hundred years of Luc's training and undermines Oberon's command. On the other hand, if he doesn't advocate for the harpy, she might lose all her children. He has the power to change the outcome of a bad situation for the better. He should say something. He has to say something. He opens his mouth.

Reluctance lodges in his throat.

"You're bleeding," Ken observes.

Luc registers the cut—it's somewhat deep and on fire with pain—and the sensation of blood running freely down his arm. He shunts it away a second time. His victims received worse.

Who are you when you aren't here?

He remembers Elle twisting her fingers together, glancing to the side before looking at him, her large, dark eyes wide with fear of him. His horror had broken over him like a rain of glass shards, jagged and glittering.

"Perhaps . . ." He forces each word out. ". . . we can provide a surro-gate to incubate the eggs while the mother is in hospital."

Ken turns toward him, surprise lifting both eyebrows.

"Pardon?" Oberon says. "Was that Agent Villois I heard?"

It shouldn't be harder to say it again, but it is. "Yes, sir. I would like a surrogate to incubate the eggs while the mother is in recovery."

Oberon snorts. "What nonsense."

Ken clears his throat, still staring at Luc. "I . . . second the motion."

"I third it," Fern chimes in.

"Fourthed," Emi adds.

"Yeah, me too." Gillen laughs. "But I won't be sitting on any eggs."

Emi groans. "Nobody asked you to, asshole."

"All of you?" Oberon says. "It's just a harpy."

Ken gets to it before Luc can. "It's the least we can do."

Yes. It's the least Luc can do.

"Also," Ken continues, "there's been structural damage to this building."

"Don't act like you and Agent Boyega didn't cause it. That's coming out of your pay, Agent Matsui."

"The surrogate?" Luc asks.

Oberon's irritation comes through loud and clear. "Yes, fine. I'll get a surrogate."

"In a timely manner."

"I'll get it done." If they were in the same room, Oberon would be flaying him with his eyes. "What's gotten into you, Luc? You handled it. It has no bearing on you personally."

Luc swallows his discomfort. He's had enough of ruined families, his own included. "In a timely manner, sir? The eggs can't get cold."

"Yes, I will get the surrogate out there in a timely manner."

Luc blocks the relief that wants to take over. Oberon doesn't always keep his word. He'll follow up tomorrow, just in case. "Thank you, sir."

"Never let it be said that I am not generous. Now, if you're done being tenderhearted, go wash up and report back in for debrief in an hour. Evac is on the way."

Ken removes his rune from around his ear, deactivating it and folding it into his grapefruit-sized fist. He stares at Luc as he taps a clawed finger against a protruding canine. "What happened to you?" he asks finally.

"Nothing." Luc isn't about to tell anyone about Elle or his history.

"Mm." Ken's nostrils flare like he's scenting something. "If I didn't know you better, I'd believe that."

Luc removes his own rune and deactivates it. "That's all you're getting."

"The others will have fun making up stories about you again."

He shrugs. "What a shock."

"It doesn't bother you?"

The only rumor that bothers Luc is the one he's been forbidden by Oberon to talk about. He'd have the truth come out if he could, in order to restore what little dignity he carries in his name, but Oberon's compulsion remains firm after twenty-eight years. "It doesn't matter."

"So it does bother you, then?" There's a knowing light in Ken's eyes.

"No. It just doesn't matter."

Footsteps pound up the stairs. One after another the rest of the Wrecking Crew pile onto the roof. First is Fern, curvy and brown-skinned like many svartelves, hands clutching the case holding her sniper rifle. After her is Emi, tallish and rangy, dark eyes darting around to check her surroundings, the cool tones of her deep black skin drinking in the sunlight, silver yarrow earrings dangling from her ears. Last is Gillen, who is six-and-a-half feet of black-haired, green-eyed Scotch Irish muscle.

He goes to inspect the harpy, spending a little too long looking for comfort. "You fucked her up. How'd you do that? How'd you know where to cut?"

Luc answers honestly. "It's like breaking down a chicken."

Fern guffaws, then claps a hand over her mouth. "That's awful."

"Sounds about right for him." Emi drapes an arm over Fern's shoulders when the smaller woman nestles close. Gillen joins them, allowing Emi to lean against him, accepting a quick kiss from Fern. For a moment, Luc lets himself envy the Crew's relationships with each other and how openly they display affection. He'll never in his lifetime have someone to come home to, much less three someones.

Emi continues. "Big boss called you tenderhearted, though. What's up?"

Luc would rather tell Ken than tell Emi, and he'd rather face torture than tell Ken. "He referred to all of us in that manner."

"No," Fern says, her head tilting. "Just you. What happened?"

"Maybe he had a come-to-Jesus moment," Gillen suggests.

"Or maybe, when he was almost dead, he thought about all the bad choices he's made." Emi casts a pointed look in Luc's direction.

"Maybe," Ken says quietly, "he has a conscience."

The other three freeze.

"No way!" Gillen hollers, cackling. "Him? That's the dumbest shite I've ever heard!"

Luc takes a measured breath, his heart racing, then takes another. When he looks at Ken, he finds the oni looking right back. They lock eyes for what feels like an eternity.

"You're right," Ken says eventually, pitching his voice so he can be heard over the Crew's laughter. "That's ridiculous."

Uncomfortable, Luc disengages and turns away.

Chapter Nine

THE SPHINX'S OASIS is as it always is: unchanging, a place where time passes through but claims nothing. Luc closes his eyes, the late afternoon light a brand across his shoulders, baking the pure white threads of his loose cotton shirt. He fills his lungs with desert air, smelling clean sand and dryness. He spends a moment basking, enjoying the crisp heat on his skin.

When he can't stay still any longer, he jumps down from the large stone slab that serves as the port zone, sand shifting beneath his boots. Not far off is the sphinx's compound. His shadow stretches eagerly in front of him, leading the way.

The outer wall is knobby stone and mortar, its length gripped by gnarled banyan tree roots. Luc runs his fingers along them, appreciating the dappling of light and shade on the bark, pats the stone post of the front gate as he passes by. Flanking the gate are square buildings that once would have served as guard towers. Beyond that, behind a courtyard overgrown with scrubby grass, is the large main building where he'd slept as a youth. Peeping over the top of the building is the rounded dome of the stone gazebo that sits in the middle of the reflecting pond.

It's eerily, oppressively silent. There are no birds or animals around, not even insects. The first night he'd spent here, he'd been unsettled by the desolation; where he'd grown up, there was always someone awake, often praying. In those early days it was he who spent time praying, pushing the smooth beads of his mother's rosary one after another through his fingers.

Luc no longer prays, instead finding holiness in the stark lines of the desert.

He puts his hands in his pockets as he walks, going under the front arch of the main building, the soles of his boots thumping against the mosaic on the floor. A set of stairs to his left curves up toward his old bedroom. To his right, in front of a sunken area strewn with lambskins, is a small, low table. He pauses before it, then takes a seat on the floor to wait.

He feels the touch of the sphinx's mind before he hears the whisper of her paws on the sand. A few minutes later she arrives, a real smile stretching across her face. "It's been some time, hasn't it?" she says in French.

He stands, inclining his head in respect. "I'm glad to see you."

"He says that now." She harrumphs. "How many times have you passed me in New York without even giving a second to greet me?"

Luc responds in kind. "Tatie, how many times could you have said hello to me as I went by?"

"Were you not in a rush those few days ago? I could think back and count for you. Would you like me to try?"

"Are you ready for me to dispute you?" He's going to lose if he does, but that isn't the point of this game.

"Are you insinuating that I do not know everything?"

"Who can know everything?"

The sphinx leans down to bump her forehead against his. "Ah, Lucien. Thank you. I do get tired of having to answer questions all day instead of posing them."

"You could stop. No one would blame you."

"But who will look after you if I am not there?" This time, the smile she gives him is sharper than a rising crescent moon and shows the tips of her canines. "Oberon?"

She'll scoff at him if he says yes, but Oberon has his own way of looking after Luc. He's responsible for so much in Luc's life. Almost everything Luc has is a result of Oberon's teaching and guidance. Luc's flat. His skills. His obscene amount of money, some of which is now enriching Elle's bank account. Oberon had given Luc a purpose and a place to belong during a time when Luc had none of those things. He had given Luc a chance to make a difference in the world, wielded as a sword or a shield in Oberon's hand.

"You look after more people than just me."

"True, yes."

"I can take care of myself."

"Also true, more or less."

He compresses his lips into a line. "What does that mean?"

She blinks slowly at him, then sits, wrapping her tail around her feet. "I said I was tired of answering questions, didn't I?"

"Tatie—"

She shakes her head. "You nurture the physical, but have you seen to your emotional needs?"

"I don't have—" He shuts his mouth after the sphinx pins him with a scathing glare. He changes tactics, knowing he's at a disadvantage. "And what about you? You look after so many. Who looks after you?"

She gives him the flat stare he's given so many others. Hers is the original and is much better. "You did not come here after so long to talk about me. What has troubled you so much that you would want to return?"

It's the harpy. He's been thinking about her and her clutch of eggs since yesterday, unable to shake the guilt. He's done all he can, has already confirmed that the surrogate is in place, has met with the harpy's doctor and given her Dr. Clavret's number. Luc should be able to put his feelings neatly away.

When he doesn't reply, she says, "Do you want me to look?"

He nods once, then closes his eyes and blanks out his thoughts.

"Ah, Lucien," she murmurs. "You're having a normal reaction. Did you think visiting these two would help you feel better?"

"I don't know."

"Do you want me to tell you you've done the right thing?"

He needs no platitudes. "I did what I did. I accept that. It's a small regret."

"And you being here is what, then?"

It's an acknowledgment of a much bigger regret, one that takes the form of two young children under an enchanted sleep. But Luc doesn't answer. He sets his shoulder against one of the latticed double doors that leads outside, the hinges creaking as he pushes it open to allow the sphinx through, and resumes his walk.

He takes the meandering brick path to the edge of the pond, and when it becomes a series of stepping-stones, he goes from one to the next with ease. He slows as he approaches the gazebo, his heart pumping apprehension through him at the sight of two beds beneath the roof, each occupied by a child.

"Have they been well?" Luc swallows, his mouth dry. He checks the girl first, taking her temperature, observing her respiration. He goes to the boy and does the same. He adjusts their blankets, retucking them until not a hint of a wrinkle remains. He does this even though he knows nothing has changed in twenty-eight years. Their faces are peaceful, their bodies so deeply buried in sleep that their dreams flow past them, carried away by a distant current.

It had been the right thing to do, but it's small consolation. Every time Luc comes back, he has to relive the memories in painful clarity: the children, so traumatized that all they could do was huddle in the corner and tremble; the impossible amount of fresh blood on the floor, on the walls, on the children themselves; the severed head of the redcap, grinning in death; the empty eyes of the parents, arms outstretched in supplication.

And worst of all, Oberon's words stripping the will from him, leaving Luc as a passenger in his own body.

Luc's breath comes shorter, and he squeezes his eyes shut, suddenly dizzy.

"Handle it," Oberon said, tones succinct.

Luc couldn't comprehend the order, his mind going blank. "I don't understand what you mean. The redcap is dead."

"The children have been tainted. There is no known cure for redcap infection. They cannot live. Finish the mission. Do you understand?"

He shook his head, though Oberon couldn't see it. "Sir. The mission is complete."

"As long as they're alive, it isn't. You're the only one I trust to handle this. Do you understand?"

He shook his head again, the movement transferring down through his neck and into the rest of his body, where it wouldn't stop. "I don't. They *deserve a chance. No cure now doesn't preclude a cure in the future. We can summon the best healers to look at them, keep them under observation. They might not turn."*

"I can't risk the agency if they do."

"They've nowhere to go, they've just lost both parents!" His failure burned in his chest. If he'd gotten to the house a few minutes earlier, he could have prevented this. Luc took a deep breath, found it to be too shallow, then took another and another, all short and uneven. Why couldn't he . . . ?

"Everyone, clear the room. Switching to a private channel." In the interim silence, all Luc could hear was the panicked drumming of his heart over the whimpers of the children. He could only say no to Oberon so many times.

"Lucien. You alone deserved the chance I took on you. These two don't. It's for the best that you take care of them permanently. I have faith only in you. Handle it."

"No. I can't. I won't." He shut his eyes, pushing gloved hands against his face. The acrid copper tang of blood filled his nose, making his stomach churn. Oberon had taught him to be cold, but this was cruelty.

"If you won't, I will force you."

Nausea robbed Luc of the ability to speak.

"After all you've done, you balk at this?" Oberon spoke after Luc gave no reply, his voice gone weighty and quiet. "You leave me no choice. Last chance. This is a kindness."

"Not to them." Nor was it kind to him, but that was expected.

"Lucien Châtenois."

Luc went as silent and still as a songbird trapped in a fist, his heart a hundred frantic wingbeats, primed and afraid of the crush. Dread rolled over him, crawled acidic up his throat. Oberon wouldn't finish the sentence. He'd dangle it as a threat, like the last time. As long as he didn't invoke the Right—

"I speak your truename, and invoke the Right of Dominion."

The compulsion took effect, seizing him so strongly it felt like Oberon had plunged a hand into his chest. Luc stood helpless, feet rooted to the floor, no longer in control of his own body, his resistance snatched away.

"Handle the situation. I know you can. Once the children are gone, speak nothing of this mission to anyone. You may not discuss specifics

such as names and locations, nor the actions you've taken here. You cannot tell anyone I invoked the Right of Dominion over you."

The words tightened around Luc, pricking him like thorns. He felt his hand move on its own, watched it reach for his sword.

"Of course they've been well." The soothing calm in the sphinx's voice jars him from his thoughts. Luc relaxes his shoulders, unclenches the blanket, pulls it straight.

"I'm sorry." For insulting her abilities, and for placing this burden on her. The sphinx shouldn't have to stand watch over a mess of Luc's own making. "I'll keep searching. I've been planning to ask for time off. The last lead I had resulted in nothing, but maybe I can . . ."

"Lucien." His aunt is ever patient with him. "There is no cure, and you know it."

"There might be."

"There isn't. You've already done what you could. You refused to do what he commanded and suffered for it. These two live, despite everything." She approaches him, picking a line between him and the beds. Luc shuffles out of her way to avoid being pushed into the pool.

"They have names." *Dominic and Jacqueline.* He'd asked as he washed the blood from their faces and hands. Luc tries to speak, but his neck and chest lock up the way they did when Oberon used the Right. His mouth moves, soundless.

"The compulsion holds, and will for the rest of your life." Anger crosses her face before she sighs, herding him away from the gazebo. "As I said, there is nothing you can do to change this. The past is done. The future—that you can change."

They reach the shore of the pond. Luc twists to look back. When he faces forward, the sphinx stalks in front of him, cutting off his path. "Do you want something like this to happen again? Shouldn't once have been enough?"

It should have been, but almost two hundred years of habit had sent him back to work the next day, and almost two hundred years of discipline kept him thin-lipped and stoic beneath the withering looks of his colleagues. Gillen had confronted him publicly. Luc's silence was the confirmation his colleagues needed.

"What kind of future do you want?"

"Does that matter?" Luc has always assumed he would work at the

Bureau until the job killed him. There's no escape from Oberon, and nothing else in his life.

Elle. If only. And a small apartment in Strasbourg, close to the market.

"Who are you," the sphinx says, each word deliberate, "when you aren't here?"

Luc halts, wide-eyed. He hadn't intended to let the sphinx grasp his thoughts. "What?"

She repeats herself. "Who are you, Lucien, when you aren't here?"

"I'm . . . ," he begins, then falters. "Someone who tries to fulfill his duties as best he can."

The sphinx looks thoroughly unimpressed, flicking a paw at him. "Are you happy with that?"

"It is satisfactory." His reply feels as inauthentic as it sounds. "I have everything I could want."

"You should have what you *need*. What would make you happy?"

Time away from work. More time with Elle. Days—months, years—when his most pressing problems are how to take his coffee and what to have for dinner.

Luc takes a breath, then hesitates. "There is," he says slowly. He takes another breath, trying to prepare himself. "There's someone—"

His call rune chimes.

The sphinx bares her teeth and hisses.

Luc closes his eyes, pained, and slips his hand into his pocket to pick up the rune. The sphinx's mouth fixes itself in a frown as she watches him put the rune on.

"Villois here."

Oberon sounds curt. "I need you to come in again."

"Yes, sir." Luc ignores how the sphinx's tail lashes back and forth. "I'll be there soon."

Elle holds her pendant between her fingers, rubbing the smooth surface in an effort to manage her anxiety. Tony pays her no attention as he sets up their work area, pulling a fresh sheet of paper over the surface of the bed he uses for his acupuncture patients, reaching underneath to ratchet it up to the correct angle.

"You want a pillow?"

She nods, looking at the tattoo stencils on the tray for the ump-teenth time. They've mapped out the schedule, and the first session is going to take hours. "A couple of them, please. Sorry."

"What for? I'll be right back. You want your blanket too? I think you brought half your house."

"I'm good." She takes a deep breath, then another, closing her eyes to better sense the new scrolls of shielding, evasion, and defense that she's painted, all keyed to Tony's energy pattern. As long as he stays in his house, he should be okay. Elle, on the other hand . . .

Guilt slices her open and crawls into her body, making a home in her bones. She doesn't deserve to be protected. She shouldn't need to carry complex glyphs on her body; basic ones are good enough. She's overstepped enough by wearing her jade and showing herself to her family.

She can't back out. Half her clothes are in a pile on the guest bedroom floor, and if she wants to finish moving in by the weekend, she has to go forward with the plan. Otherwise, it'll be a colossal waste of effort and goodwill. That's it, that's the ticket. Instead of feeling guilty over taking Tony's time for something as narcissistic as protecting herself, she should feel guilty over potentially wasting his time and skill.

"If you're having second thoughts, you should stop having them." Tony slaps two pillows onto the bed.

"It's that easy, is it? Just stop?"

"Sure. Whatever you're thinking, that's not how I feel, so you can tell your brain to quit it."

Elle gets on the bed before her mouth can say no and land her in trouble.

Tony helps her adjust the pillows. "Comfy?"

"Yeah."

"Good." Without warning, Tony's hands blur, his fingers stabbing swiftly into several qi points. Elle yelps as half of her body goes limp. She struggles to move, but it's futile.

He considers her, frowning, then brushes his fingers over several more points. "Now you can't go anywhere. Might as well relax."

"That's not fair! You could have killed me!"

"Oh, ye of little faith. If I wanted to kill you, you'd be dead." There's a glint in Tony's eye as he pulls on surgical gloves, snapping them against his wrist in a comically exaggerated fashion. "You should be able to hold the ink container. Wiggle your fingers."

Elle glares, but does as she's told.

"Here. Don't spill." He inclines his head, eyeballing her. "Don't worry. I'll unblock you before it's too late."

There's nothing for Elle to do but stew. Tony's command of pressure points had been second to none in their family, and from his demonstration, it remains that way. He might run a Chinese medicine and acupuncture practice and act like he wouldn't hurt a fly, but in reality, he's incredibly dangerous, especially if he combines his martial art with qì manipulation.

In retrospect, losing his magic probably hadn't affected him as much as she thought it had.

"Let's see. Stencils, check. Green soap, check. A million paper towels, check. Sterile needles, check. Ink, check." Tony takes a seat on a rolling stool and peers at the thimble of ink between her fingers. "That's some sweet ink, have I mentioned?"

"You might have." Elle closes her eyes, focusing inward.

"What's his name again?"

"Luc."

Tony hums. "Wonder if I know him. He really got that for you, eh? The man must be loaded."

She's already told him the story. Tony had reacted as well as she thought he would, whooping like a teenage boy, teasing her mercilessly. "Stop it."

He laughs. "It's a hell of a gift, is all. He's serious about you."

"You don't even know him."

"I could get to know him if you brought him to meet me." Tony waggles his eyebrows at her. "Ink like this? Custom orders? Cooking for you? You pulling out your jade to help him?"

"I did it for you!"

"Nah, you did it for him. Fuck him already. It's a guaranteed score."

Elle's eyes pop open in shock, and she loses her concentration. "No!"

He turns away, exploding into laughter. The sound of it fills the room. "Okay, then find a woman."

"I'm not finding anyone!"

"Good thing the work's done for you. When was the last time you had fun?"

"Before you opened your mouth," Elle shoots at him.

He snickers at her. "I've never met him and I know he's waiting for you to make the first move. Do it. Carpe that diem. Seize the moment."

If Elle could, she'd punch him. "I don't know how!"

"Start by asking him out, dumbass."

She sulks.

"And when you finally get some play, because lord God you need it, tell me without too much detail. We gotta hit the shame trifecta in this family."

"I'm not—"

"Shame trifecta!" Tony chants under his breath, picking up the first stencil. "Shame trifecta! If he's rich, that's different. Money fixes everything."

"Will you shut up?" Elle snaps, closing her eyes as Tony applies the stencil. Tony's glee grates against her. He's never had trouble thumbing his nose at authority. All things considered, he's a poor role model as an eldest sibling.

"Okay, fine. I have to pay attention, anyway."

Elle refocuses, her magic stirring in her gut. She exhales as it billows upward, directing it through her body and into the ink, shunting as much of it as possible into the skin of her left arm. The next breath she takes activates her laes, the power of her god pooling in the jade on her chest.

"Ready." She's as calm as the current running placid through her.

She feels the prick of the needle as a gentle tap. Elle relaxes, emptying her mind of extraneous thoughts, allowing herself to have full confidence in Tony's steady hands and years of knowledge. All she has to do is keep the flow of magic circulating, and Shénnóng's blessings will take care of the rest.

"Looking good so far," Tony murmurs, shifting his weight on the stool to retrieve a paper towel. "How do you feel?"

"Good," Elle replies. The outline of the first character is complete. Ink hovers in strands of black pearls below the surface of her skin. "Keep going."

Silence falls like snow, broken by the occasional crinkle of paper, the spritz of alcohol. Elle slips into a trance, weaving her magic in a rhythmic circuit. At some point Tony unblocks her, but she's so deep in her meditation it doesn't matter.

"Break time," Tony says finally, sitting up with a weary sigh. 「逸雅啊.」

She comes to, opening her eyes to dusk's orange light and the sight of Tony scrubbing an ungloved hand through his hair. In the lengthening shadows he looks smaller, more worn. Elle shuts down the link between her and her laes, quiets her own magic. "Are you okay?"

"Ready to hit the bathroom and eat," he replies. "Look at you, doing your best impression of a cow scapula."

Elle wrinkles her nose as she pushes herself up to a sitting position, holding her arm out to inspect it. Two long rows of oracle bone characters march from her shoulder to her wrist, the pictograms shifting slightly as the magic fills the boundaries of the ink. Her skin is a bit red, but fades to normal as she watches.

"Thank you." Elle gets to her feet.

Though tired, Tony quirks an eyebrow. "Thank you?"

She bows, switching into Mandarin. "Please accept my humble offering of thanks, o great and esteemed elder brother, he who has given freely of his precious time and energy to perform a task for an inconsequential being such as myself."

"You were good up to the inconsequential part." Tony takes off the other glove, gesturing with it. "You aren't. You have the privilege of being my sister. Don't let that Luc guy catch you talking about yourself like this, either. You're not going to get any pity points. He doesn't like you for your ability to put yourself down."

Elle flattens her lips into a line. She'll self-deprecate all she wants. "Just take the thanks."

"Already taken." Tony makes like he's going to stand but collapses heavily onto his stool.

"Tony!" Alarmed, she grabs his arm to steady him, pulling back and bracing herself. Together, they avoid crashing into the rolling tray holding the needles and ink. "You said you were okay!"

"Guess I lied." He leans on his elbows, his back hunching, head low.

Elle goes to her knees in front of him, her concern a wild fluttering behind her sternum. "I worked you too hard! I'm sorry. I'm so sorry!"

"You did nothing of the sort. I did this because I wanted to."

Elle bites down on her lips, holding back the impulse to blame herself. There's no purpose in insisting everything is her fault unless it's to aggravate him. She presses her fingers against his wrist to take his pulse. After so much effort expended, she can finally sense what kind of toll premature aging has had on his body.

She has to make things right, at least a little. Her hand goes to her chest, then to her neck. She hooks her index finger around the red string until her pendant appears, dangling in the air. She isn't sure if her magic can be used to revitalize him, but she can try.

"Here." Elle motions for Tony to take her right hand. She encircles her pendant with the left.

"What are you doing?"

"Just do it." When they were children, Tony used to dare her to climb trees with him, then jump on the ends of the branches to frighten her. Their hands meet, his tremors traveling along her arm. This time, she's as solid as a trunk, unshakeable.

"You don't have to . . ." Tony swallows, looking at her, then at her jade with sudden hunger.

"But I do," Elle says quietly. "For my big brother."

She pretends she doesn't see the shine in Tony's eyes and draws upon the power in her pendant. It's as easy as blinking to reconnect to her ancestors and her god, to let their strength and magic flow into her. But she needs more than that. Elle opens herself up, widening the spiritual channel.

The room grows hazy, fogging with the magic that clings in smoky tendrils to Elle's skin. It creeps down her arm toward Tony's, and when it touches him, he gasps, his breath rasping in his throat. He goes rigid, his hand a vise around hers. A short, stifled sob escapes.

The sound slashes Elle's heart into ribbons. *Shénnóng,* she prays, *I need you. In memory of your lost son.*

She hears a distant shout of recognition right before her god responds with a surge of power. It slams into her, torrenting along her skin, making the unfinished tattoo on her left arm smolder like embers. Elle is unsure whether it's the shimmering of flames or the tears in her eyes that blur her vision. Her family's spirits press up against the barrier of the jade, howling their grief. They always loved him most, and have never forgiven her for taking him away.

For Yixiáng! they call to one another. In seconds, more spirits crowd into her pendant, each clamoring to give a little of themselves to her in the only gesture of mourning they have. There is so, so much. Elle keeps the barest amount for herself, gets out of the way for the rest. Tony gasps like he's been running a marathon, his chest heaving, flinging his head back far enough to bend his spine, his eyes aglow with rapture.

Elle doesn't know how long they sit, eldritch and frozen. When she's no longer a conduit, she shakes herself and looks at Tony, who bears a blank, detached expression. "Gēge?" she says softly, squeezing his hand.

Magic drips from his mouth when he opens it, fumes gray and curling from his nostrils when he breathes out. It wreathes his head, clouding for a split second the brightness of his eyes, the irises no longer rheumy at the edges. His face, too, looks younger, less lined. Elle covers her mouth with her free hand, her shock pushing her exhaustion away.

"What . . ." Tony clears his throat. "What did you say to him? I couldn't . . ."

Elle swallows uselessly, tears cascading down her cheeks at the sound of Tony speaking their home dialect. "I told him I needed him. Could you hear anything from our family? Feel anything?"

Tony touches his forehead to their linked hands, his own tears spattering onto the floor. "Aside from the magic, no."

"Brother," Elle says on a sob. She squeezes his hand again, lowering her head, and bows to him three times. As the younger sister, she must always show respect. "They miss you."

Chapter Ten

「想你呀! 要不然我来干什么呀!」

Elle leans forward, her hand at her mouth, eyes glued to the TV. She's been waiting twenty-four episodes for Qiáoyī to confess her love—oh, it's so obvious, and every time Qiáoyī looks at him, Elle's chest hurts—and the dramatic music has just started. It's gonna happen. This time, they're gonna kiss.

Someone knocks at the door.

She shrieks, jumping a foot off her couch. By the time she finds the remote, the music has swelled, the two leads are kissing, the person is knocking again, and she's missed the Big Moment. She snaps a glare at the door, incensed. There is no reason in the world for someone to come to her house, ever. Especially at 12:13 P.M. on a Friday, in the middle of the most important episode of the series.

Elle screeches internally at the interruption, composes herself before she self-immolates, and calls, "Who is it?"

"It's me," Luc calls back.

Oh, shit. Her chest hurts, but for a different reason. Her house is in disarray, and that's a generous way to describe it. Normally she could panic-clean it in under an hour, but she's used moving as an opportunity to get rid of things, and the junk is piled beside open suitcases and boxes.

She runs the obstacle course to her door and opens it wide enough for her to stick her face out. "Hi."

"Hi." Unlike Elle, Luc is put together, his hair fetchingly tousled, wearing a subtly checked light gray blazer over a white button-down shirt. Sleeves cuffed below his elbow show off muscled forearms, and a leather watch hugs his left wrist. Elle's eyes travel down royal blue slacks to the burnished tips of his reddish-brown brogues. "It's lunchtime, but you weren't at the store. What would you like to eat?"

"Oh. I took the day off." She clears her throat. She'd needed to pack and rest after the double whammy of finishing both her tattoos and the commission. "Your order's at the front counter. Didn't Lira give it to you?"

"She did."

"You got the invoice too?"

"Yes. I already paid." He tilts his head. "I thought you said you'd quote me a fair price."

"I did."

"I feel I've taken advantage of you."

"No, no, we're all clear. Don't worry about me. We're good now, yeah?" Elle doesn't mention how nice it's been to have Luc sending her meals for the past four days. The ones he's cooked personally have been the best. His omelets—*omelets!*—are eyes-rolling-into-her-head, strip-naked-and-proposition-him-level good. Lira herself had tried a bite and immediately cussed.

"I'd still like to get you lunch, if that's okay with you." He runs a hand through his hair, and if Elle didn't know him, she'd call the movement bashful. It's adorable and attractive at the same time, and she has to remind herself that they're friends. It's the drama's fault. She's thinking about romance, and Luc has caught her in a moment of weakness.

"Would you mind if I come in?"

Sweet skies above. Her TV is frozen on the image of two people French kissing. She has her hair down, she hasn't washed her face yet, and she isn't wearing a bra. "I don't think my place is up to your standards."

"It can't be that bad."

"You sure?" she mutters.

"I'm trying to be nice. I won't say a word regarding cleanliness."

"Okay." She steps back, grabbing the remote to turn the TV off before she shames herself further.

He shuts the door, his hand lingering on the knob, eyebrows furrowed as he surveys her apartment. Elle swears he looks a little too long at the photo of her brothers on the kitchen pass-through, but his face remains unchanged. "Are you going somewhere?"

She tucks a lock of hair behind her ear, not meeting his gaze, calculating how much information she can give out. "Yeah. I'm moving."

"When?"

"Tomorrow."

"You . . . didn't tell me."

"I'm still going to be at the store. I'm sorry. I didn't think it would be a big deal."

"Where?"

"Nearish." Elle puts the remote down. "My brother needs help, so I'm going to stay with him for a while."

"I didn't know he lived in town. Will you need help moving?"

"That's really sweet of you to ask. I don't think so. Thank you for offering, and thank you for coming over to ask about lunch. Your commission is finished, so you aren't obligated to do anything." Elle extends a hand, ready to stop being the friendly business owner. It's too much to look at Luc and daydream. Her chest hurts again, probably for a different reason. "I've enjoyed working with you. I'm sorry it couldn't be a recurring thing."

"I, uh." Luc takes her hand, his touch uncertain, and gives it a feeble shake. "Perhaps we can celebrate the end of the job? One last client meal."

Her chest quits hurting. Elle looks at the reality before her. *Start by asking him out, dumbass.* Tony would flip if he were here. In her mind's ear, she hears him shouting, *Say yes, stupid!*

Time to carpe the diem. "Okay, sure. I'm dressed for the cafeteria."

To his credit, Luc doesn't run away. He glances at a half-full suitcase. "I was thinking somewhere more formal, though if you've packed those clothes already, we'll have to try the canteen. I'd prefer not to eat there."

How dare he ask her out and make her get dressed. "Where? I don't get out of my home clothes for just anything, you know."

His face softens. "I was thinking if you're hungry enough for dinner . . ."

"Probably. I haven't eaten breakfast."

"That doesn't surprise me. Might I suggest Strasbourg?"

"You wanna take me to *France?*" Her eyes fall out of her head. She imagines them bouncing on the floor, picking up dust, and rolling under her sofa.

"If that's okay with you," he replies.

Elle's instinct is to say no. She has to remain local in case something happens to Tony. But she's spent two days warding his house, backed by the power of her jade, and the protections have never been stronger. Yiwú, if he could find Tony, wouldn't be able to get through on his own.

She's worked hard and deprived herself for sixteen years. The man she's interested in is asking her out. She can have one date at least.

"A date in France? Of course that's okay." She watches Luc's eyes widen and amends herself. "Or a client dinner. How fancy do I have to dress?"

He points to himself. "About this level, else we'll be laughed out of the establishment. Is an hour enough time to prepare?"

"Yeah, I just need to get dressed and put my hair up."

Luc pauses. "I think you look nicer with it down."

Elle has no reply, having short-circuited. It's possibly the first compliment he's paid her over her appearance. She'd thought he was indifferent. "Um. Thank you. I'd return the compliment, but your hair isn't long enough to put up."

"Would you believe," he says, smiling, "that it was, once upon a time?"

"No way!"

"Long hair isn't practical for what I do. But yes, when I was much younger, I had hair to my shoulders."

Elle giggles. "I bet you were so pretty."

"Perhaps, but you'll always have me beat in that department."

Her mouth drops open.

"One hour." Is that a twinkle in his eye? "Meet me at the Paris rings, and we'll go from there."

"Luc, slow down," Elle complains. "I can't keep up."

He laughs quietly and does as she commands, shortening his stride. "I was already going slowly."

"Slower, then." Elle hooks her fingers around Luc's elbow and hauls herself to his side, glad her long-sleeved navy shirtdress has enough allowance to keep her comfortable. At the moment, she's thankful she had enough foresight to choose a forgiving silhouette.

She lets go of him and pats herself on the belly. "I wasn't joking when I said you'd have to roll me out of there. It was all so delicious I couldn't stop myself."

Luc shrugs with one shoulder, elegant. Most everything he does is effortlessly, maddeningly elegant. Elle has never known anyone so intrinsically beautiful, and that's counting the sirens and nymphs. "I will never judge a person on how much they eat. Food is one of the rare pleasures in life. Eat however much you want. If you still have room, there's dessert."

She blows out a long sigh. "Skies, no. Slow down, please."

"Any slower and we'd be at a standstill." Ambient light illuminates his fond smile.

Elle tries not to turn into a puddle. If she could bottle that smile and sell it, she would. She'd label it *Soft Boyfriend* and make a killing. It'd probably smell like fabric softener, sandalwood, and musk. "Shouldn't have left when we did. Should have stayed to digest longer."

She drapes herself on the railing that runs along the sidewalk, watching the reflection of the city lights in the waters of the canal. Maybe it's the company, or maybe it's because she's far from her troubles, but her shoulders are light, and the absence of weight combined with the magic of Strasbourg makes her want to paint the scene.

"We'd already stayed quite a while." Luc props a foot on the lowest rail, then regards her. "The kitchen was preparing to close."

"I can't believe it's that late." Really what Elle can't believe is how quickly the time has passed. Luc in Strasbourg is relaxed and open, easy to laugh and smile as opposed to the curated stoicism he wears for work. During dinner he'd chatted with the waitstaff as she looked on, charmed, and toward the end the chef had come out for a visit. The hidden warmth she's glimpsed is on full display here, and it's immensely satisfying to see him this animated.

"You are operating six hours behind, so it makes sense."

"No," Elle says, shifting her weight on her forearms, leaning toward him. "I meant that I can't believe it's been a few hours since we got here. It doesn't feel like that at all."

"I agree. I can't think of a better way to have spent my time today."

Elle tells herself her cheeks feel warm from all the wine she's drunk, which was lightly sweet and tasted of lychees. She counts herself a new convert to Alsatian cuisine. "Hey, I've got a question."

"By all means, ask."

"That language you spoke. What was it?"

"Alsatian. It's a dialect of German and was more commonly used in times past than it is now."

"Is it your native tongue?"

"Close enough to be. The language my mother spoke no longer exists. French has been standard for some time and is easiest to use."

"That's sort of like me. Mandarin is standard now, but my local dialect is . . ." Elle frowns. "The closest big city would be Xiāngyáng, though that's not my hometown."

"What is?"

"A tiny place in Húběi. It's not on most maps." She shivers as a breeze snatches up the hem of her dress.

"Are you cold? We can cut the walk short and return."

"A bit," she replies. "If we weren't in public, I could keep myself warm. I can hold out for a while, though. The walk is good for digestion and—what are you doing?"

What he's doing is rolling his sleeves down, pulling off his blazer, and shaking it out before settling it over her shoulders. Elle stares at him wide-eyed, swallowing at the hint of cologne wafting up from the collar, taking in bergamot and sea air mingled with his comforting natural scent. He smells lovely, though what would be lovelier is burying her face in his neck and breathing him in. Which she isn't going to do, no matter how much she wants to right now.

"My apologies," he says, re-cuffing his shirt sleeves. It's such a simple action, but Elle can't help but watch raptly at how Luc rotates his forearm this way and that, streetlights flashing off the face of his watch, his attention bent completely to his task. It's criminally sexy. She wouldn't mind if he looked at her that way. "I should have mentioned the temperature before we left so you could bring a coat. It may be summer, but here the nights are still chilly."

"I—" Elle stammers. Damn the wine, though it's not the wine. It's her reaction to how casually Luc's given her his jacket, how with one gesture he's blurred the line between a client dinner and a date. "Thank you. Aren't you cold now?"

Luc smiles, amused. "No. I feel neither the heat nor the cold if it's necessary. A side benefit of my heritage, I suppose."

"That's cheating."

"Hardly." He finishes folding his right sleeve, then begins walking.

Elle ambles alongside him for a few minutes, immersing herself in Strasbourg at night. "I can see why you like it here. It's charming. Metropolitan, but not too fast."

He nods. "You understand."

"Would you live here if you could?"

"Without hesitation." He keeps his gaze fixed on the sidewalk ahead of him. "I had been planning on asking for some extended time off. I had even chosen an apartment to lease."

"What happened?"

He draws in a long breath. "I failed a mission. Directly after that, I failed another. It erased whatever goodwill my boss carried toward me. I'll have to rebuild my track record before I can ask for time off."

"Two failures?" Elle scowls. "How many successes?"

"More than two."

"How many more? Ballpark it if you can't remember."

Luc considers. "Close to fifty, if not over."

She makes a sound of disbelief. "Two out of fifty-two and that's it, you can't get any time off?"

"Yes. It does sound bad."

"Because it *is* bad. Where is this boss of yours? He's breaking policy!"

To her surprise, Luc laughs. "My contract with him is an exception."

"How so?"

"I came in before policies were put in place. I'm contracted indefinitely and the terms are in his favor."

She scowls harder. "You're saying he can do whatever he wants and you can't quit?"

He turns his hands up and shrugs, grim amusement on his face. "We're close to the apartment I would have leased. Would you like to see it?"

"For what?" Elle grouses. "I mean, yes. Sorry, I'm still stuck on your boss."

Luc points to the second story of an older house with Juliet balconies. "That one. With the wrought iron. There is a market nearby, and a boulangerie and coffee shop. I could live content for at least a month."

"That sounds wonderful." She sighs. "Seems like there's enough to do here to fill that month."

He turns, walking back the way they came. "What about you? Is there anywhere you'd like to go?"

She shakes her head. "I haven't thought about it."

"Why is that?"

"My family needs me."

"I thought you said you don't see them often."

"You're right." He has an excellent memory. She'll need to be careful. "Except my brother, the one I'm moving in with."

Luc looks at her as if he's weighing his options or calculating probabilities. "Permanently?"

"Yes, though he doesn't know that part yet." Her thoughts turn to Tony and Yiwú, which is a bad direction for them to go. She yanks the reins left, figuratively. "You know what this looks like, right?"

"Not at all."

"A date, is what." Elle eyeballs all six feet of Luc, strolling with his hands in his pockets, the wind ruffling his moonlit hair. It's like he's stepped out of a movie.

"I had thought," he replies evenly, "that this was a client dinner."

Elle cackles, then covers her mouth, holding her breath. "Yes. Skies. Yes, a client dinner. What was I thinking? I've had too much wine."

It's a flimsy excuse, but it'll have to do. Tipsy is about as far as Elle will get with her divinely granted constitution. When she was younger, she wondered what it might feel like to be blackout drunk, and once she'd tried getting there with Yiwú and a case of báijiǔ—*oh, don't think about him*—but the next morning, she remembered everything.

"You did drink an entire bottle on your own." Luc had shown more restraint with two glasses.

"I've never had a wine that tasted like lychees! But I'm okay, I promise."

"Truly?"

"Yes, truly. When your patron god is the god of medicine, it's hard to get drunk and stay there. I'm already sober."

"Now that's cheating."

"What was it you said?" She dimples her cheek with her pointer finger, exaggerating her thinking expression. "A side benefit of my heritage."

"Touché. Are there any other side benefits to being a descendant of a medicine god?"

Elle smiles when Luc offers his arm, her fingers finding the inside of his elbow. He doesn't say anything as she pulls herself close to him. It's comfortable and intimate and exactly what she needs. She lives here now.

"I don't get sick, and I heal pretty fast. Faster if I ask for his help. You've already seen the fire thing." Elle purses her lips as she thinks. "Back home I can fly."

"You can fly?" He looks impressed.

"If I try hard enough. Out here I'd need a lot of help to do it." She really needs to shut her mouth before she spills any more information. "I'm also immune to poisons. That one's more my ability, and not a general one."

"Immune how?"

"The fire thing." She motions with her free hand. "I can turn that inward and burn out poisons."

"A useful ability," Luc muses. "Does alcohol count as a poison?"

"We'd have a lot of angry family if it did," Elle laughs. "We go through a lot of Chinese wine at parties."

"I don't believe I've ever tried Chinese wine."

She snorts inelegantly. "It isn't anything like French wine. What's the expression for it? Like jet fuel."

She can tell he's trying to hold back his smile. "That sounds more like a spirit than a wine."

"Bad translation. It's a spirit. And you can also say that it sounds awful, because it is."

"All right," Luc says. "That sounds horrible. I would not mind trying some."

"Are you serious?"

He nods, looking dead serious. "I have been told I should be more adventurous. This might count."

"It absolutely counts." Elle grins, feeling devilish. Luc has no idea what he's unleashing on himself.

They pass into the courtyard of the Strasbourg branch and swipe their cards at the nondescript door, their conversation drifting into silence. It's anything but awkward; rather, it's companionable, which doesn't surprise her. They've spent enough nights in silence in her workshop, she at her workbench, he on the couch, and Elle hasn't ever found his presence intrusive. Luc has a serene and unruffled energy around him, and that's a quality she'd like in a long-term partner.

Which she isn't looking for. Just because she would like one doesn't mean she needs one.

She huddles closer to him. "This has got to be the best client dinner I've ever had, hands down."

The corners of his eyes crinkle as he smiles. "Thank you. Has there been a worst client dinner?"

He can't look at her like that. It's giving her the warm and fuzzies. "This is actually my first and only client dinner."

Luc clears his throat, breaking eye contact. "Well then. I am happy to have provided the experience for you."

"Same. I'm glad we didn't go to the cafeteria. Their pizza isn't bad, but this was better."

He dissolves into laughter. "Elle, you just had dinner at a one-star Michelin restaurant!"

"Is that good or bad? One star doesn't seem like a lot?"

He keeps laughing. "It's an honor to receive even one!"

"Oh." That's embarrassing. She's embarrassed. "Well, there's a fancy pizza place in Raleigh, and I really like pizza. It's one of my favorite things."

"I have only one question, then. New York or Chicago?"

"Both? Why not get both?" It occurs to her belatedly what she's implying. "I mean. Not that we're going to get both. This is hypothetical."

"We can get both." There's a perceptible shift in his demeanor. After a moment he speaks, and his words come out gentle. "How about it?"

"That would be . . ." She pauses. "Fantastic."

The Strasbourg branch office is dark and lonely this late at night, the high ceiling of the lobby shrouded in shadow. In the hallways there are only muted, shallow pools of fluorescent light that leach all color from the floor. They approach the port room, where Elle spies a single conductor sitting, nodding off at their station.

Luc slows, speaking as he does. "I had a wonderful time. Thank you. I know you're moving, but when you're less busy, would you have time for me?" They come to a standstill outside the doorway. He turns to face her, and as she releases him, their hands slip together, effortless.

She grimaces. "I really have to say no to more custom work."

"No, I meant . . . for things like pizza."

"Is this an official date request?" Elle holds onto his hand, vowing to let go only if he lets go first. "Because I don't do client dinners anymore."

It takes him a second to respond. "Yes."

"I'll have to think about it." She can escalate as well as he can. She steps close, lifting herself up onto her tiptoes, and kisses him gently on the cheek. "There are a lot of pizza joints I haven't been to. I wouldn't mind having someone to go with."

Luc goes still. "In France, the custom is to kiss both cheeks."

Elle bites her lip to cover her grin and gives him another kiss. "I'd hate to be culturally insensitive."

He lifts his free hand, brushes her cheek with the backs of his fingers. She closes her eyes, leaning into his touch. This, too, is effortless, and so is the way she moves toward him when he slides his hand over her cheek to curl around the back of her neck.

Elle turns her face up to his and meets his lips with hers.

And skies, she thrums, shudders chasing across her skin like wind sweeping across grassy plains. Everything is a thrilling low electricity with Luc in this moment, her body curving into his, their heads canting to the side. She breaks from him and opens her eyes long enough to see his flick open. Shénnóng help her, the emotion she sees rising in those deep waters undoes her completely.

He breathes in sharp through his nose and wraps his arm around her waist, kissing her again. The blazer falls from her shoulders and hits the floor, forgotten. Elle's mouth opens with his, perfectly in sync, as if they've kissed a hundred, a thousand times before. She tastes need on his tongue, the sharp yearning of it striking directly through her.

Luc holds her like she is precious and adored, cradling her face, touching her as if he could write oaths into her skin with the whorls of his fingertips. Her surroundings fade as she immerses herself in him, her heart soaring, every single fiber in her vibrating with how true and right it is to be here with him.

Elle is speechless when they surface from each other, blinking at him with her lips parted, cheeks heated, blood rushing through her like the infinite wheeling of stars. Luc lowers his head, kisses her again, tender and soft. He strokes his thumb slowly over her cheekbone as they part, a promise of what he might do later.

"I've thought about it," she breathes. "I have to say yes."

He smiles, the corners of his lips curving upward. "Excellent."

He keeps stroking her cheekbone. Skies, she wants him to make good on that promise. She won't forgive herself if she's alone tonight. "Come home with me."

He kisses her once more, bends time with the caress of his hands, the press of his lips, the cream that's his mouth.

"What if," he murmurs, "you came home with me?"

She takes his hand. "I'd love to."

Chapter Eleven

*E*lle Mei is in his house and he, Luc Villois, notorious loner, is okay with it.

Most of it. There's a sense of apprehension, a feeling something will go wrong. He can't shake what his gut is saying to him: Elle is part of the case he's on. He's done this too long to ignore his instincts, and very little is coincidental in his career. He only needs one or two pieces of information to link her with the fox spirit and the old photograph on her kitchen pass-through. He hadn't gotten the best look, but the faces in it had been familiar. If he adds the clues up with the admission that she's descended from a god of medicine . . .

It's circumstantial. He needs confirmation.

"What's wrong?" Elle looks up at him, her brown eyes alight. She hasn't let go of his hand since their kiss, except to get in a port ring.

"Thinking about work."

"Can I convince you to not?"

"Please." He should be thinking about her, and not Oberon and the case.

She beckons at him. "How might I do that?"

He reaches out and traces the shape of that full lower lip with his thumb. "With this."

"Nice save, Villois. C'mere." With gentle fingers, Elle pulls his face down toward hers for a kiss.

Luc closes his eyes, breathing her in, readying himself to focus on her and only her. He needs to concentrate to mute the undercurrent of thoughts and allow physical pleasure, knowing that if he doesn't, he'll lose whatever ground he's gained. It's rare for him, after all, to want this, to want with someone else the rapport he had with Baptiste. But he finds it easy to kiss her, as easy as the last time and the time before that, so easy that he doesn't have to force himself to the task or analyze each second of it.

The mood shifts, growing more concentrated, like a color deepening in saturation. He responds to it, to her. It's surreal to be in this situation, with Elle in his apartment, their mouths joined, her hands pulling the tails of his shirt out from his waistband. From somewhere inside him, a shiny, brassy joy emerges. It's good to be alive, to be here with her.

He makes a noise in this throat when she slides her palms up his back, his skin tightening into goosebumps.

Elle smiles. "For me?"

"For you." He chases her lips with his own, sighing when their mouths connect again. Goosebumps are nothing. For her, the brilliant, funny person who's saved his life and who makes him laugh, goosebumps are nothing.

Oberon can never know about her. He'd see her as a threat to be removed.

He tenses, breaking contact.

"Hey." She cradles his cheek with her hand. "Quit it."

He curls his hand around hers, removing it gently. It's a mystery how she can read him so well. "You're right. Let me put the rune away."

He leads her to the bedroom, keeping the lights off as he enters, bypassing the rosary draped over the plain wooden cross on the wall. A set of French doors leads to a terrace and, with the curtains open, there's a breathtaking view of Paris at night.

"Oooh," Elle says, drawing out the vowel as she gazes outside.

Luc smiles to himself, giving her time to marvel, retrieving the rune from his pocket and deactivating it. He walks it over to his nightstand to hide it, but once the drawer is open, guilt snares him, keeping him bent over the drawer, unable to let go of the rune. Oberon would want to know at the very least what connection Elle has to Jiang.

She comes up behind him, wrapping him in her arms, kissing between his shoulder blades. "Mm," she murmurs. "You smell so good."

Selfish. He's selfish, and wants to keep Elle and her kisses and her smile for as long as he can before she's taken from him. Because she will be, whether by Oberon's decree or through Luc's own actions. He closes his eyes, the rigid wooden rune in his palm at odds with the pressure of Elle against his back. He should put it away.

He drops it into the drawer and shuts it.

Elle turns him. "I'm not doing a good job of convincing you," she whispers, pressing her hand against his chest. "Your heart is racing. Let's have tonight without any worries."

"It isn't you." At her raised eyebrow, he says, "It's me."

She raises the other eyebrow.

"I mean"—how is he doing this again?—"I have many worries."

"Same, honestly," she says. "But I want this. You. And I'm willing to try not giving a crap about those worries as long as you can too."

She's right. He should have left his concerns outside the apartment. He's taken Elle home, not his troubles. "I'll do my best."

"You're always thinking." She begins unbuttoning his shirt, a smile curving her mouth. "Maybe that gets in your way. You're at home, Luc. You're safe."

He blinks at her as the idea settles in, his shoulders lowering. Elle gives him a soft look, then continues undoing buttons. When she gets to his cuffs, she lifts his hands and graces each knuckle with a kiss, making his chest ache ten times in succession. The encounters he's had after Baptiste have been perfunctory and mechanical, a function of his job and dependable anatomical response. It's been a long time since anyone has . . .

She pushes the shirt from his shoulders. It drops to the floor, pooling around his feet. "I want to see you," she says, stepping back. Fire blooms in the palm of her hand, casting flickering shadows over the walls, refracting in her eyes, turning them the color of topaz. "Your undershirt first. I hope you don't mind."

"I don't." He hauls the garment over his head, baring his torso. Elle's responding sigh kindles a warmth in him, the sort of warmth he'd once understood as the delight of being desired. He's forgotten it after so many years.

He'd like to hear that again. He wants, very suddenly, the surety of movement and the singular devotion of being with a lover.

"Take everything off, please." She studies him as if he's fine art, her head tilting one way and another. Otherwise, she remains still.

Luc unbuckles his belt, steps out of his pants. He moves without hurrying, sensing Elle's enjoyment, reveling in her desire. This is how it feels to be devoured on sight, and as long as she's doing it, it's okay.

"You're beautiful," she whispers when he's completely naked. "All of you. Every bit of you." She extinguishes her flame and approaches him, her fingers sliding over bared skin, her lips a velvet caress against the basilisk scar. "Look at you," she murmurs, trailing her fingers up his stomach to his sternum. "How could I not know what you are? As soon as I touched you, I could tell. You have energy channels humans don't have, energy flows that are the opposite direction of ours . . ."

She kisses a line across his chest. "Like that one," she murmurs. She kisses another line over his body, flattening her hand against him as she drags her palm across his skin. Liquid heat pools in the wake of her touch, infusing him. He shudders, his senses enlivening.

"And that one. The way your heart and kidneys—" Elle shuts her mouth, disengaging and breaking contact. The heat drains, and for a split second, a white light flashes in her eyes. "I'm so sorry. I'm not here to examine you, and you didn't ask. I'll hold back—"

"Don't," he interrupts, then kisses her. For a minute there's nothing but the sensation of her, the slow movement of their mouths. He undoes the buttons of her dress between breaths, goes until it's an afterthought on the floor. Her bra and underwear follow closely after. The curve of her neck calls him and, unable to resist, he kisses it.

And then he pauses when he brushes against something unfamiliar. It's the thin cord of a necklace.

He pulls back, looking at a flattened disk of jade much like the ones at the exhibit. The apprehension he thought he'd chased away comes galloping back. "What's this?"

She tenses under him. "It's nothing."

It isn't nothing, and neither are the fresh tattoos adorning the entirety of her left arm.

"I had that done earlier in the week." Elle bites her lip, growing distant.

"I like them."

"Thanks." She glances to the side, her shoulders hunching.

Absolutely not. He will not let this opportunity escape them, not after the effort it's taken them both to get here. Not when he's this close to being in a headspace where he can move without overthinking. His mouth firms while he stuffs his concerns into a box. He has to bring Elle back from wherever she's gone. They're already nude, and he refuses to put his clothes back on.

"You said you could tell what I was as soon as you touched me." He takes her hand, placing it on the center of his chest. "What's here?"

Elle blinks, and a soft huff escapes her. "You," she replies after a moment of silence, using her pointer finger to draw a loose oval down to his navel and back. The heat from before returns. Elle continues drawing, tracing unseen lines across his shoulders and up past the pulse beating in his neck. "That's interesting," she murmurs. "Did you know you have a knot here? Here too." She taps a spot directly over his heart.

"Is that a problem? Can you fix it?"

"I'm not sure. Qi shouldn't flow like that. It's inefficient. Do you want me to?"

He nods.

She leans forward, her palm flush with his chest, and kisses his neck.

Luc gasps, energy lighting up in him. Whatever she has done—whatever magic she's doing with her hands and her mouth and her surprisingly devious tongue—unlocks something. For a single breath, his senses heighten, his awareness of himself expanding outward like paint splattering. The light in the darkened room becomes painfully bright; the air currents against his skin are suddenly unbearable. He hears the accelerating beat of Elle's heart before everything fades, leaving only unrestrained desire.

"I fixed it," Elle says, then glances down. She grins, impish. "Shower?"

She really does understand him, but he's not ready to go, not when there's an inexorable need to touch her, to breathe her in, to know the chemistry of her skin. But Elle has somehow produced an elastic and is already sashaying toward the bathroom, putting her hair into a messy bun as she does.

"Oh, skies above," she says, clicking on the lights. "You have two showerheads and can fit, like, four people in here. And there's a shower seat. What have you been doing?"

"Showering," Luc replies dryly; it's all the response he can muster. He doesn't elaborate on the necessity of multiple scrub brushes, choosing instead to watch Elle as she opens the shower door, cranks the water on, and steps directly under the spray. "Elle, it's—"

Luc stops before he can say the word *cold*. The water spits and hisses, rising as billowing steam around her, wreathing her in gauzy white as if she is a demigoddess manifesting. The steam swirls itself into tendrils, following the air currents created by the sudden, hazy shimmer of heat surrounding her, at turns hiding and showing parts of her body: the lower curve of her breast, an expanse of leg, the movement of her tongue licking her lips.

She turns her eyes on him, amused. "You were saying?"

"Nothing." He joins her in the shower, shuddering when she touches him and heat sluices over his skin, turning the water a perfect temperature. In a second, she gets the soap and works up a lather. He can only laugh at her expedience. "Impatient."

"I am not." Elle gives the bar to him, rising to kiss him on the cheek. Her hand slicks down his shaft.

His breath stutters.

"*That's* impatience." Her other hand joins in, applying pressure in long, firm strokes. Luc goes still, focusing only on the evenness of his breath, closing his eyes, blocking out everything else.

Her breasts touch his chest just before her teeth close on his earlobe. "Luc," Elle says, the pitch of her voice sending electricity downward, making him twitch. He fumbles for the soap dish to put the bar away. She releases him, changing course to kiss his neck, her tongue curling up drops of water.

The inexorable need returns. There's no question he wants answered more than how she likes her pleasure, no directive more pressing than how good he can make her feel. He turns her to face the other showerhead, surrounding her with his arms, breathing in the scent of soap and steam and her. He places a hand right under her breasts, brushing against her nipple in passing. "Your lines, Elle. Show me."

She puts her hand over his, aligning her fingers. "Here." She slides her hand down; beneath his fingers, Elle's skin is faintly slippery with soap. Luc kisses Elle's shoulder, following the perfection of it up to her neck, lingering beneath her ear. She gives him what he can only assume is a quiet, happy hum as he trails his hand between her breasts, then down again to her stomach. She's warmer there than the water running in rivulets over their bodies, and when he closes his eyes to kiss the other side of her neck, he gets the sensation of energy moving.

The line deviates, no longer straight, meandering from hip to hip and over the enticing curve of her figure. He breaks from the path when Elle starts moving back up, lets the coursing water carry his hand until it settles between her legs. She turns the slightest bit to glance at him. Luc catches the edge of her smile, feels for himself the keenness of her desire.

"Tell me how to touch you," he whispers into her ear. She rewards him with a shudder, widening her stance. With her guidance, he learns her body, memorizes what she shows him, circles and rubs and traces until she's flushed and dripping between his fingers.

"Am I . . . ," she breathes.

Mouthwateringly so. "Yes."

Elle moans and arches, her body sinuous. Luc tightens his arm around her to keep her in place. She whines, her hand leaving his, and reaches behind her to curl her fingers around the length of him. "Luc, please—"

He surrounds her clit with his long fingers and slides them down, and that's what gets her to gasp and buck within the circle of his arms, a cry escaping her. Her weight shifts, the tempo of her breathing increasing. He closes his eyes, a sound of his own pressing up at how fantastically erotic it all is. Elle's silky and wet while her hand is tight around his cock, and the flicker of her magic is around them, and there is nowhere else he'd rather be than here, right before she shivers apart for him.

"Luc, I'm gonna—please, don't stop, don't stop." She leans forward to brace her arm against the wall. He does exactly as he's told, matches her as her moans grow in speed and pitch and intensity, smiles when she lets go of him to dig her fingers into her thigh, her muscles beginning to shake. He's going to love this.

Elle comes soft and beautiful cradled in his arms, the sound of water subsuming the frantic pace of her breaths. Her fingers flex against the wall, her knuckles going white as she trembles. There isn't a word to describe his satisfaction. He was right. This is his new favorite thing.

"Not done, keep—" Elle gasps. Luc redoubles his efforts, and she climaxes again in seconds, her body drawing taut, her cries going ragged, the air around her charging with points of heat. This orgasm snaps through her rather than unrolls, and even as he takes joy in the moans falling from her mouth and bouncing off the tiles, he groans at how much he wants to slide into her and end it. He can't. He doesn't have handrails installed.

He twists off the other showerhead when Elle straightens. She steps gingerly out and snags his towel for her use, grinning at him when he emerges. He dries off once she's done, then goes into his bedroom where she's got a hand partially wrapped around one of the smooth, dark posts of his bed.

Luc's mind immediately falls in the gutter. Rather, it settles in, seeing as it hasn't wanted to get out.

She slides her hand up and down. "It's huge."

"So I've been told."

Elle inhales sharply. "By who?"

"You, and everyone else who's seen it."

"Who else has been seeing it?" Elle demands, putting her hands on her hips. "Tell them to square up. I just wanna talk."

He laughs. "Only you."

"You said everyone else!"

"You and me and the people who sold the bed to me."

"Oh, are we talking about that? For a second I thought you were being . . . cocky." She giggles, covering her mouth.

He indicates his erection with a nod. "Pardon, but I was being cocksure."

She hoots at him, laughing until she has to lean against the bed. She dabs at her eyes. "Luc, what the hell! I've never seen you like this. When did this start?"

It might be too much to say she's the cause of it. He's had a wonderful night at an excellent restaurant in a favorite city with someone he cares for, and each step he takes toward her reveals a possible future where there are mornings after and sunshine and breakfasts taken together. "Just recently."

"Well, I like it and I'd like to see more of it."

"My apologies for disappointing you, but this is all of it."

She cackles. "What makes you think I'm disappointed?"

Elle picks up the box of condoms they'd bought on the way back, opening it, then rips into the box containing the lube. Off comes the safety seal. She pours herself a generous amount.

He doesn't stop her as she comes back and wraps her fingers around his cock, squeezing. Luc tries not to let his eyes roll back in his head. "Elle."

"Someone told me I should seize the moment, or something."

He speaks, strained. "The moment appreciates being seized, though the moment thinks it's longer than that."

"Luc!" Her fingers tighten as she laughs.

He has to bite his lip and monitor his breathing.

Elle releases him briefly to clamber up on the bed, taking the bottle of lube and a condom with her. "Sweet skies above, what kind of magic is this?"

"It's custom—" Luc starts.

"Don't answer that. Just get over here."

He obeys, climbing onto the bed. She welcomes him with a kiss, and in the back of his mind, Luc finds himself incredibly amused at how she's commandeered his space and how he's allowed it. Eventually she nudges his shoulder, indicating he should lie down.

"Are you okay with this?" She rises to her knees and places the condom in his hand. He hears the click of the bottle cap opening.

He is more than okay with this, with her. She's a vision, one side gilded from rib to thigh with Parisian light. "You don't have to ask."

"Yes, I do."

She looks at him, and he can't do anything but stare back at her, shocked. He's already said yes. It hasn't occurred to him that he could say it again.

"Are you okay with this? Is this what you want?"

"Yes." The next words appear before he can help himself, his mouth opening before his brain has a chance to review. "You. More than anything."

She kisses him before she straddles him and guides his tip against her. "Ready?"

Luc nods, incapable of speaking.

The first inch is delicious torture. Elle bites her lip and tosses her head, moaning as she sheaths herself on him, sinking onto him like it's the only answer to an inevitable question.

"Oh, you are . . . ," Elle mutters, her hands gripping his shoulders. White light leaks from beneath her closed eyelids, and Luc thinks if he looks hard enough, he'll be able to see the undulating shift of her energy, its motion in her calling to him.

"Don't hold back," he reminds her.

Elle's hips move. The action makes his throat close so that all he can do is growl at her, at the perfection of their fit. His hands settle around her hips as she finds the angle and depth of penetration that she needs. Luc grits his teeth, thankful for the condom that's keeping him from ruining everything.

Wisps of Elle's hair, escaped from her bun, hang silvered with light. Luc watches her, in love with the tilt of her head, the rapturous look on her face, the little smile she wears as she gives herself a particularly swift downstroke followed by a voiced exhale. He gives himself over to her as she builds a current of pleasure for them both, touches her stomach to discover how she shivers, draws his palms over the bell of her hips and holds them, anchoring himself in her. Elle cries out, her rhythm faltering, and the amount of satisfaction it yields him to see her respond that way to him—to *him*—only increases his need. He takes the weight of her breasts in his hands, reaches up to follow the line of her jaw with the backs of his fingers. She smiles at him, turning her head to kiss the inside of his wrist.

"Come up."

The change in position gets him deeper in her, and at this, Elle moans, clutching at his shoulders, arching back. Luc holds onto her, bowing his head to her like a supplicant, dipping his lips into the hollow of her neck, tasting her skin. There's a hint of salt, the vibration of her voice. He trails kisses down her sternum and over to a breast, circling her tight nipple with the tip of his tongue before closing his mouth and sucking.

Elle voices her approval with a low moan, pushing herself at him, grinding on him. Eventually she stops, tips his chin up with a finger, leans down to kiss him.

Luc melts, made completely vulnerable by the intimacy of the moment. He's so deep inside her he can't tell himself apart from her and she's kissing him so tenderly and their bodies are so close and no one, *no one* has ever been with him the way she is now, has ever found in him a magic of his own, has ever checked in on him like this and asked what he's wanted.

"Mm," she murmurs. "I have to . . . I hope you don't mind . . ."

"Please," he rasps.

Elle leans back and gets a hand between them, working her fingers against herself. She drapes herself over his shoulder right before she climaxes, and Luc embraces her, awash in the moans spilling down the planes of his back.

"Yes, Elle," he says, growling encouragement into her ear. She cries out, full-bodied shudders running through her and into him, and Luc has to suck in a long breath to keep from losing himself in her. "Yes, just like that."

She's pliant against him, sacred and helpless. "Oh—skies, Lu—"

The end of his name disappears into a hiss, and for a second Luc can imagine that it's his real name that's come out of her mouth, that Elle is murmuring *Lucien, Lucien* over and over instead. The thought of it is so unreasonable, so far-fetched, and yet it makes him tighten up, surging against her, on the verge of finishing. He wants that, and her. He wants her to know his name.

"You," Elle whispers once she's liquid in his arms. She lifts her head; there's a faint outline of a red flower on her forehead, fading rapidly. "You can't look at me like that and not expect me to . . ."

"Not expect you to what?"

She kisses him briefly. "It's your turn. I'm sorry I've been selfish."

"You haven't been. I don't keep score."

"Oh, good," she says. Shakily, she lifts herself off him, collapsing onto her back. She tugs the elastic band out from her hair, flinging it to the side. "What would you like?"

"You, still."

She kisses her fingertips, touches them to his lips, to the pulse in his throat, to his heart. "Then have me. I want what you want."

No one but Baptiste has ever said that to him. It's so simple a thing, consideration, but Luc hasn't had much of that in his life.

She kisses him when he lowers himself to her, his chest touching hers. "Skies," she whispers, and Luc can only agree at the long, thick slide of him in her. "You keep doing that and I'm going to come again."

"A terrible fate. I cannot imagine it."

Elle laughs. Luc withdraws almost all the way and thrusts back in. Her eyes roll back in her head. "Guess I'm doomed, then," she says, cupping the side of his face.

Luc kisses her. There isn't anything else to say. Elle's in his bed, it's nighttime in Paris, and there's nothing but their bodies in glorious motion, and the light in her eyes when she smiles at him, and the fullness of his heart when he smiles back.

He shuts his eyes, driving into her, unable to stop himself from vocalizing when she lifts her knees, allowing him to hit a deeper, toe-curling angle. She gasps each time their hips meet, her fingernails digging into his shoulder, then his rear, helping him go faster, harder. It's the sudden sharpening in her breathing pattern that sends him up and over, his long-delayed release smashing into him. Luc holds her as tight as she's holding him, grinding his head into the pillow as he empties himself into her, sparks on the backs of his eyelids, bereft of thoughts and words.

Elle sighs when he comes to a rest, laughing weakly. Her lips drift over his temple. Luc can't react; he's done. All he wants to do is lie here with Elle, with the lines of their bodies blurred together and her giving him languorous, affectionate kisses.

He withdraws, blissfully heavy-limbed. Elle rolls onto her side, blowing him a kiss as he gets off the bed. He stares at her, struck, as she yawns and stretches. She could do this a thousand times and he'd never tire of it.

She catches him watching and blows him another kiss.

Not a thousand. A lifetime. A lifetime of stretches, or waking up to her, or mutual bad jokes. Of tolerating canteen food and tea brewed in beakers so long as it's with her.

Everything slows to a standstill. He'd do anything for Elle. He'd fetch the stars themselves and lay them at her feet if she asked. As long as she looks at him with those shining eyes and that adoring smile, he's hers completely.

But he cannot give her something he doesn't own, not as long as

Oberon knows his name. And the cure for Dominic and Jacqueline remains his goal. His freedom from the agency, whatever life he could have with Elle, they both fade in comparison to what he needs to do. He knows how things will end. He knows how things must end.

No. Tonight is a suspended moment, the high point of a pendulum swing where there is zero acceleration. There are no worries in his weightless state before he falls. Only he and Elle and whatever they create together. Tonight, and tomorrow, and maybe even the day after. That should be enough.

They trade kisses as they clean up. Luc folds her clothing, arranging it in a neat stack on the bathroom counter as she goes back into the bedroom. After he puts on fresh undergarments, he comes out to see her wearing his undershirt, gazing at the dark wooden cross and rosary on the wall by the bedroom door.

He tenses, alarm skittering up and down his spine. Elle leans forward to study it, and Luc has to take a calming breath to make his muscles relax. She won't know what it is as long as his behavior doesn't give it away.

She glances at him, then back to the rosary, no longer playful. "I didn't know you were religious."

"I'm not."

The corner of her mouth quirks up. "Do you believe?"

"That depends." He goes over to her. "If you mean this one, then no."

"And the others?"

"I think that the difference in power between them and us make it so that it's easiest to think of them as gods."

"It's a difference of consensus." Absently, she touches her jade pendant, the one that looks like the Jiang family artifacts. "Where I'm from. That's harder to say than 'god,' though, so calling someone a god is easier."

"Consensus?"

"Godhood by committee, basically. By the people's mandate. If enough of us think someone new should be worshipped, then a new god appears. That's very different from the idea of an all-powerful, infallible single god here. I hear he's a zombie god."

"He isn't—" Luc starts, then bites his tongue. "A little. Don't say that to anyone else. It can be sensitive."

She turns back to the rosary, her hand dropping to her side. "If you don't believe anymore, then why is this here?"

Luc considers his answer. He could say no, or divert her. He could say something about his mother or his childhood. Or he could take a risk and tell her it's his laes. If his suspicions are correct, she's wearing hers, and has been since the night he escorted her home.

He finds the words eventually. "Because I have no safer place for it."

"No safer place?" she murmurs. Her head snaps toward him, eyes widening. "Do you mean . . ."

Luc softens as he holds her gaze, touching his fingertips to her cheek. Then he rests his index finger upon the red string of her pendant.

She stares at him, her lips parted, and the atmosphere in the room solidifies to one of palpable tension. "You know."

He nods. "I had guessed, and you've confirmed. Now you know about mine. That's my mother's rosary."

She looks from him to the cross, her breath quickening. Her hand goes up to encircle her pendant as her face crumples into a stricken expression, her head bowing, her shoulders slumping as she folds into herself.

Luc's heart sinks. It was too much to hope the pendulum would hang in the air and surpass natural laws. Like all good things, they end too soon, and so his time with her will be a measure of hours and not days. He stands motionless, preparing for the inevitable, feeling every dragging second like the prick of a needle.

Elle doesn't respond. The closing move falls to him, then. Luc braces himself, and his heart.

"Elle."

She won't look at him. "Yeah."

What should he say? What can he say? "I'm sorry. I shouldn't have . . ."

She still won't look at him.

"I've kept my word regarding you."

"Yeah."

He crumbles, preparations be damned. *Breathe,* he commands himself. As long as he does that, he'll get through this, same as always. "I swore on my laes, and I'll do it again. I will keep you a secret. You're free to go."

Luc can tell to the millisecond when Elle stops breathing, can hear the scrape of air in her throat when she restarts.

She swallows, her eyes glistening. "I'm not leaving."

Luc stays silent, balanced on a knife's edge.

"I'm sorry. I reacted badly. It's not about you at all. It's . . . Well, first I should say thank you for sharing that with me." Elle finally looks at him, her eyes unreadable. "I'm not leaving, Luc."

He speaks haltingly. He's sure he was clear, but maybe he hasn't communicated well. "You don't need to stay. I don't want to force you. That would be the last thing I want. If ever I . . ."

Elle shakes her head. "You never have and I don't believe you ever would. Listen to me. I'm so sorry. This is all on my end, not yours. I've got . . ."

She blows out a breath. "There's a lot that I should probably tell you. I've been avoiding it because I've been scared. Of a lot of things. But." She takes his hand. "I'm not leaving. Okay? You've just placed even more trust in me. How could I walk out after that? What kind of person would I be?"

He has no response. She's a better person than he is.

"I care about you." Elle steps close to hug him. "A lot. More than I can say. You've been better to me than I deserve, and it's the least I can do to give it back."

I care about you. Luc lets that resonate, closing his eyes. "You already do," he says into her hair, returning her embrace. "I think quite highly of you for it."

"Don't be so quick to say that. Not before you know the whole story."

It's as if she's stolen the thoughts right out of his head regarding himself. "Okay. But you should let me be the judge of that."

"That's what I'm afraid of."

"Again, I'll be the judge of that. You don't have to do this alone." Why is he offering her an exchange of information? He has no reason other than he wants her to know, wants to be known by her. "I'll tell you what I can about me, provided it isn't under an NDA. Understand that loopholes exist, as they do in any contract."

"So." Her eyes narrow in thought. "If I asked you specific questions?"

He nods. "I may not be able to *say* yes or no."

"I understand. But I'd like to go first, if that's okay with you. If you don't mind deferring for a little bit." She touches her shoulder, rubbing her fingers up and down her tattoos.

He kisses her on the forehead. "Let's go to bed."

"What, so I can confess to you there?"

"Yes. There is very little you can do to make me think less of you, and if you fall asleep, I will still be here when you wake up."

"Okay." She eases herself out of his arms and into his bed.

He joins her. "What is the first thing you want to tell me?"

Her hand seeks his, her fingers tightening. "I want you to meet my brother Tony."

Chapter Twelve

Here is the confirmation. Luc's training establishes itself as a shock of cold water, washing away soft sentimentality. Certainty grows like a tumor in his gut. It's still possible this is all one big coincidence, but probability of that is in the single digits, trending toward zero.

He prepares a mental checklist. Elle will need to say how many siblings she has, what the birth order is, what had happened to Tony, and mention Jiang by name.

Elle sighs. "I should back up and start from the beginning. It's complicated. There's a lot of family drama. When you meet Tony, I just want you to know that he's not like me. I mean, he is like me, but he isn't anymore. Am I making sense?"

According to the file, Tony hadn't survived. There had been no mention of a body, but not having physical evidence was common, if frustrating, in fae forensics. "As in something happened to him?"

"Yes." She shifts onto her side to face him, grasping her pendant. "He doesn't have one of these. Not anymore. It was destroyed."

He breaks into a cold sweat as the first item gets checked off. Elle's brother is Tony Jiang, and they really saw him at the gala. "And he lived through it?"

"It was . . . touch and go for a while. I wasn't sure if he would. I did everything I could, put everything I had into . . ." She trails off again, clearly agitated. "He lived. He's a regular human now. Getting older. A lot older. Don't mention it to him."

"I understand." No one likes being reminded of their weakness.

"No, you don't. He's vain. He's the most puffed-up, self-important asshole on the planet. He has a portrait of himself in his house and he makes everyone look at it."

Surprised, Luc lets out a snort. "Really?"

"Really. But he's always been charming and funny, and apparently his patients are all buddies with him because of it. One of them brings him free wine. I don't like her. She's racist."

"To him? You? Both?"

"Does it matter? She's racist."

Luc presses his lips together and nods. "Where I work, we keep a list of targets. I will add her. What's her name and address?"

"Is this a hit list?"

He declines to answer. "A partial name is fine. I have an intelligence team."

"Luc, are you serious?"

Completely serious, he says, "Yes. Is this actionable?"

"Um. I'm not sure what that means. Can we go back to talking about my brother?"

"Of course." He'll ask her about it again later. "His patients?"

Elle snuggles closer, which sends a thrill of delight through him that's quickly submerged by anxiety. This is his chance, and he won't let it go. "Tony runs an acupuncture clinic out of his house. He's actually a doctor and can do a lot more than acupuncture."

"Much like you can do more than these glyphs?"

"Yeah. When it comes down to it, I don't even need paper."

He runs his fingers over her left arm. "Like these?"

"Mm-hmm." She presents it to him, and before he can stop himself, he kisses her wrist.

"So you saved your brother's life after his laes was destroyed, which is something even the most highly skilled doctors cannot do. You've saved my life. You don't need paper to perform your magic. What else are you hiding? Why have you been holding back all this time?"

She reclaims her arm. "You gonna chew me out too? I've had enough from Tony. You don't need to pile on."

Luc tries to imagine someone scolding her, and fails. Sweet as Elle is, he can't see any situation where she's passively being upbraided. "I'm sorry. What did he chew you out over?"

She gestures vaguely to herself. "Being me."

"I like you rather very much, so that can't be true."

"Well played." Elle chuckles. "No, I deserved it. He wants me to be more me than I'm being. He told me I should be seizing the day. So I seized something."

He laughs despite himself. "I didn't mind. What about your tattoos?"

"Like what I do on paper, just on myself."

"What sort of magic?"

"A mix. A defensive glyph or two, a summon, some protection . . ."

Concerned, Luc asks, "Protection against what?"

She pauses. "My little brother. It wasn't enough that . . . well, he's looking for Tony. For Tony and me. There's some unfinished business I can't let him finish."

Luc pushes her just a hair. "What's your little brother's name?"

"He went by William sometimes. By his real name most other times."

Another check. Of course. "His real name?"

"It doesn't work for us the way it works for you. He flaunted it. He didn't want to change his name."

"Huh." Luc takes a sidebar to sit back on his proverbial haunches and digest. It's simple enough after all his experience ignoring his feelings. "It doesn't work on you?"

"Not the way it does on you. It varies by culture, doesn't it?"

He hasn't given it much thought before. Conceptually, Luc is aware that not all fae have truenames. The same can't be said about a laes. "Theoretically."

"Not theoretically. It's more common than you think. Our names are private because they're only for close family."

He can't imagine what it's like not to worry about keeping a truename secret. If only that applied to him. It would have changed the trajectory of his life. "And what about you?"

"Tony and I felt . . . what's the word. Didn't like it. Will thought we should at least keep our surname. He was proud. He won the argument. Jiāng is rare."

The checkmark gets bolded, italicized, and underlined. "You mentioned unfinished business. What sort?"

"The kind that keeps me where I am, doing what I do." She cups his cheek, stretching toward him to give him a kiss so soft and tender that it slips a knife between his ribs and straight into his heart. "The kind that keeps me from doing what I really want to do."

Hope leaps in him before he quashes it viciously. With him? It can't be. Luc has told her enough times that he's unreliable, unable to commit to anything.

He covers her hand with his, wishing for enough light to look into her eyes and see for himself what's there. Luc swallows, his throat thickening with suppressed emotion. "What is it that you really want to do?"

She takes such a long time to answer that, if not for her hand rigid against his face, he would think she was asleep.

"I'm afraid to say it out loud," Elle murmurs. "Because it might come true if I do, and I wouldn't know how to handle that. Tony would cheer me on. He and Lira have been trying to get me out of all this." She pulls her hand back.

She's definitely not thinking about him and being a hopeless romantic.

"Luc." Elle tugs at him, embracing him tightly when he closes the distance, returning the gesture. Her breath suffuses the fabric of his shirt, warmth spreading over his neck and collarbone. "Maybe the spirits won't hear me if I'm quiet," she whispers against him. "I haven't thought about what I've wanted for so long, other than keeping Tony safe. What I want . . ."

She gathers herself, her ribs expanding beneath his palms. ". . . is to be me without anything or anyone holding me back. I don't want any more regrets."

Neither does he. Luc aches at the realization that it's also something he wants. "I'd like to see that someday," he says, sincere. "You without anything holding you back. I think you'd be magnificent."

He feels the uneven hitches in her back, the flare of her jaw muscles as she fights with herself. "Elle?"

"I'm sorry!" she says, her voice breaking. "I'm so sorry, I didn't mean to—"

She's crying. Whatever remaining defenses Luc has—if he's ever had any against that face and that smile—burn away like fog under the sun.

"Oh," he says, his heart going out to her. She only needs to claim it. An endearment almost inserts itself, but Luc intercepts and blocks it before it can escape. "It's okay. Don't hold back."

She shakes her head rapidly, unwinding herself from him to lie on her back. "Shénnóng, help me," she says, choked up. "Is this what's going to happen every time I try to tell you something important?"

"What does it matter if it does? You have strong emotions." He pushes himself up on an elbow, brushing his thumb over her cheek, carrying a tear away. "But if you would rather return to our previous discussion, we can."

He remembers the file from the briefing in the fountain room. *Classified as fae-touched, descended from Shennong.* Luc's tongue refuses to make the proper sounds. It's shameful. "Did you say Shennong?"

There's a long, ugly sniffle. When she speaks, her voice holds the barest edge of control. "He's my patron god. A lesser-known god here. God of medicine, and acupuncture, and lots of other things."

What was that about him bringing Elle home and not his troubles? He would laugh if he could.

"The three of us," Elle continues, "are his descendants. We're not the only ones, but Tony is the firstborn of our generation. Which means that when he consults our copy of Shénnóng's journal, he gets special privileges."

A short lapse. "Let's just say that he can ask for things we can't. Shénnóng's journal has in it hundreds of remedies and antidotes. Anyone can look at that. For Tony, tonics will appear in the pages only he can see. Acupuncture techniques. Cures for things we don't know about yet. He only needs to pray."

"If you're thinking it's a powerful item, you'd be right." Elle pauses. "My family uses the book to help others in need. Tony would have taken it and gone traveling. Should have."

"But he can't now."

"Right. He can't, because of his . . . condition. Even before that, he had no intention of doing it. So my little brother picked up the slack, though he's never wanted to be a doctor. He thought he could take

Tony's place, but he can't use the book because Tony's still alive. Still firstborn. I thought that if I—" Elle clicks her mouth shut.

"If you . . . ?" Luc prompts her.

"The book isn't meant for anyone but Tony. We found that out the hard way. My little brother suffered the consequences. Probably still does. All to do a job he . . . I don't want to make it sound like he's innocent. He's never liked failing. He's convinced it's not his fault, that we're the problem, and . . ."

He detects a faint trembling through his mattress. "Elle? You don't have to tell me if it's too difficult."

"No. Whatever happens . . ." She clears her throat. "Whatever happens, I have to protect Tony. Because he's in danger."

There's more to it than she's saying, and her involvement goes deeper than being a guardian. Elle is, as she has said, the middle child, the next in line. "What about you?"

"I want to say no."

"But?"

"But yes. I am, a bit."

Luc frowns. "A bit? It seems you're in as much danger."

"I can protect myself. Tony can't. I don't expect you to understand."

He understands she thinks less of herself than she should, which is ludicrous. Someone with her power and ability shouldn't be hiding, nor placing herself second. "Is there a way for me to help?"

"No. This is family business. I'm sorry."

He's asked the wrong question. They have the same goal of removing Jiang from the field. If Elle were willing to show herself, lure Jiang to where he could be captured, that would kill two birds with one stone. She would be safe, and a criminal would be in custody. "Let me rephrase. What if I could help you?"

She tenses. "You don't understand. This has nothing to do with the agency. Stay out of it."

"I'm sorry." Luc means it. But he can't remain uninvolved. Somehow, he's going to have to alert Oberon to the situation without mentioning Elle. "About Tony. Can I ask how you kept him alive?"

"A lot of prayer and seventy-two hours of being awake." She laughs without humor. "The first forty-eight were the hardest. Being human makes it easier. Whatever that means." She burrows against him.

Finally, she relaxes, yawning. "I'm sorry for crying on you."

"You can cry on me as much as you want."

"Mm." She sounds like she's fading. "I hope this is the only time. When I get back . . . Tony wants to meeting you. To meet you. I call him tomorrow. I can't . . . your bed is too soft."

Luc squeezes her hand. "Sleep, Elle."

"Okay. One more thing."

"What is it?"

"Thanks for listening. To all this. I didn't think it'd be this easy to tell you. It's nice."

"I'm grateful, and I will listen any time you want to talk."

"Night."

"Good night." He settles into his mattress.

Elle shuffles near, wedging her shoulder under his arm, leaning her cheekbone against his shoulder, resting her hand on his thigh. It's so casually intimate, so sweet and familiar an action that he can't do anything but be overwhelmed by it.

His thoughts whirl, clashing against each other. Luc stares into the shadows of his ceiling, trying not to let himself sink into despair. If he stays here, he can have his morning after. The forecast calls for clear skies and cool temperatures, a perfect excuse to stay in bed, arms and legs woven together beneath the covers. If he stays here, if he allows his heart to lead and not his head, Oberon will be none the wiser. He doesn't have to make a call. He doesn't have to be bound by duty.

Lucien Châtenois. I speak your truename and invoke the Right of Dominion.

He shuts his eyes and dozes, waking every few minutes to check on Elle. Eventually she rolls away from him, her hair a mess of scattered, inky tendrils on the pillow. He observes the rise and fall of her breath against the backdrop of Paris, the many lights of the Eiffel Tower peering over her shoulder.

Luc waits a minute longer to ensure she's well and truly asleep. He gets out of bed, moving carefully so as not to disturb her, retrieving his call rune with hardly a rattle from the drawer. He pauses before he exits his bedroom, his hand hovering above the door handle, turning to look at Elle. The diffuse light makes everything hazy and ethereal, otherworldly and dreamlike. Watching her, Luc feels like he did the first time he glimpsed fairies in the wood outside the convent, before he'd known he was fae: awestruck, afraid that by simply breathing he'd break the spell and they would fade away, never to be seen again.

He counts to ten, then opens the door.

It's pitch dark in the apartment, but Luc navigates it as if it's filled with sunlight. The call rune awakens at his touch, the symbols glowing with sleepy reluctance. He fits it around his ear and runs his fingers through his hair, as if doing so will push away his apprehension. It refuses to be ignored, surging back each time he clears the tension from his shoulders and neck.

He ought to sit as he delivers the news. His blanket, too, might provide a measure of comfort.

Oberon shows no sign of tiredness when he picks up the call. "Where have you been?"

"Sir. Following a lead." Luc arranges his blanket over himself as he leans back, the leather of his couch creaking. "I apologize for being uncommunicative, but it's been necessary."

"Your lead had better bear fruit."

"It will." He closes his eyes, swallowing against the ache rising in his chest. In any other situation, he wouldn't betray her. Technically, he hasn't said Elle's name, nor given any indication she exists. His vow holds, but only just. "I guarantee it. There's something I must investigate on my own, but if my calculations are correct, there will be a convergence soon. I know what Jiang wants."

Oberon grunts his surprise. "It isn't jade?"

"No. That's secondary. Maybe he'll try an attack on the museum. I wouldn't rule it out. I can't say more on the topic. Please trust me on this, sir."

"How soon is this convergence?"

"Within a few days at most. Possibly sooner. I'm preparing to push the situation regardless. Are there eyes on Jiang?"

"He lost us, but Pei is on it. Darcy is interrogating the fox."

Luc would have preferred the opposite arrangement, but it isn't his place to speak up. "Once I have confirmation, open communications between us and Jiang. He won't pass up the opportunity to get what he wants, and we can take him with a minimum of effort."

"Efficient and practical. That's the Lucien I trained. Close this mission out cleanly and make me proud."

"Yes, sir." He's too empty to accept the praise. If he succeeds, he might get that apartment in Strasbourg, but Elle won't forgive him for involving himself. He can rationalize the hurt away later, but right now every move he makes feels fundamentally wrong.

"Will you need support?"

"No. I'll continue to run dark. Contact only if it's urgent."

"Understood. I look forward to our success." Oberon hangs up.

Luc removes the rune from his ear and covers his face with his hand, rubbing at the crease between his brows as he reorganizes the information. Jiang's victims are very much alive, and one of them is sleeping in his bed. In place of murder, William Jiang should be wanted for attempted murder and laes destruction. It doesn't lessen the severity of the crime, nor absolve him. According to Elle, William is intent on rectifying his mistake. If he's successful, then the two murder charges on his sheet become real.

Then there's the matter of Tony. He might remember Luc. The redcap incident had been recent enough to drive rumors around the workplace. He thought he'd weathered the worst of it, but he's wrong. If Tony remembers and tells Elle, she will for certain never want to see Luc again.

He grits his teeth and sets the blanket aside, getting to his feet, returning to his bedroom. All Luc needs is Tony's location to bait Jiang out. His feelings for Elle have nothing to do with his job or his duty. He can sleep soundly beside her and act as if everything is normal.

He can't bring himself to touch her. He closes his eyes, unable even to look at her.

Between his work life and personal life, Luc is in a unique and unenviable position of being, to put it colloquially, well and truly fucked.

There is a phrase in French that, when translated into English, becomes "so far, so good." Luc finds that insufficient to describe his current situation, the phrase lacking both the charm and the fatalism of the original. *Jusqu'ici tout va bien*, he thinks. Until now, everything goes well. And then, in the next second, it will be a catastrophe.

Luc exits the port room in Raleigh and stops by the transportation office, then makes his way down to the garage, where he's supposed to pick up Elle. He covers a yawn with the hand he's using to hold the car keys. Unlike her, Luc had spent the rest of the time trying in vain to enter deep sleep, finding it mere moments before Elle had woken with a jolt, almost falling out of bed in her haste to get to work or pack. He hadn't been sure which.

He affects a nonchalant lean against a wall, taking a position that allows him to view the doors at each end of the hallway, regulating his breathing in order to dispel the jitters rattling around his body. He'd offered to help her move, and in her desperation, she'd accepted. So far, she suspects nothing. All he needs, he reminds himself, is a confirmation of where Tony is. Whether or not Tony remembers him is immaterial. But Luc would feel better if Elle were fully briefed. Like it or not, whether she wants it or not, he's involved. He closes his eyes, running each possible scenario to its logical conclusion. All of them end with him alone.

This is what it must feel like to be tied to the tracks with a distant train approaching.

He slips his hands into his pockets. His right hand touches the switchblade clipped to the inside of his pocket, the shape of it cold, clinical comfort. His left hand touches his call rune, the wood of it warm from his body. Discipline is what he needs now. There is no threat to him yet.

Movement catches his eye. Luc sees Elle approaching through the half window of the far door, each hand grasping the handle of a suitcase, her shoulders loaded with bags. She smiles at him and he waves back, going to the door to open it for her. He should enjoy his last few moments with her.

"Ready?" Her smile holds an undercurrent of tension.

Jusqu'ici tout va bien. He'll act like it too. He takes the bags she hands over. "As much as I can be."

"Me too." Elle's face settles into a resolute expression. "You got the directions I sent?"

Luc nods. He should joke around with her. "I can't express enough how shocked I was to get a text from you."

"Hey!"

"I thought perhaps you'd draw me a map."

"Luc!"

"Welcome to the twenty-first century, Agent Mei."

She puts her hands on her hips, but laughs. "I'm not that backwards! I use my phone!"

"Once per year, or is that too frequent?" He smiles in response to her scowl.

"I use my phone more often than that!" She starts to take a tally, but stops.

Luc chuckles. "Ah, no? You don't?"

"Shut up! Where's the car?" Elle bulls her way through the door to the parking garage and stalks toward one of the many nondescript black compact cars in the Roland & Riddle fleet. "The sass of it all. I never knew it was part of the package. You were just the hot French guy friend who would read all my books."

"I enjoyed your company and your books, and you enjoyed the package. I thought it was a good bargain."

"And the dick jokes! Who knew? I didn't! Did you?" She jabs her finger toward a car. "This one? Where's the driver?"

Luc presses the unlock button on the key fob so that the car lights flash. He gets to it before Elle does, popping the boot open and dropping her luggage in. He's certain she's snuck cement blocks in. The better to tie him to and drown him with when she finds out. "Should I stop the jokes?"

"No!" She throws herself into the seat. "You're the driver? I didn't know you knew how to drive."

"I don't do it as much these days, but yes, I do."

"So you're rusty?"

He walks around and gets in the driver's side, starting the ignition. "No."

"But you said you don't do it as much these days."

"That doesn't mean I'm rusty. I don't see why you'd jump to that conclusion."

"But you said—"

Luc flicks a glance at her, tamping down a spike of annoyance. "You can trust me. Roland & Riddle requires that I have advanced driving skills with multiple vehicle types, and I renew my international license in France. We also train in the UK. Not being in a car chase in a while doesn't mean I lack the means to drive."

She subsides. "Okay."

He finishes his adjustments, puts the car in reverse, and backs out of the space. "Do you drive?"

Elle shakes her head, then drums her fingers against the armrest. "Never learned. Never needed to. Turn left to get out."

"Elle." He gives her a meaningful look. "You've already given me directions."

"I know."

"And I have memorized them."

"Really? Are you sure? I can pull them up right now just in case—"

"Yes. Please—"

"Don't tell me to relax! I'm relaxed! I'm as relaxed as you!"

Luc barks a laugh. He isn't relaxed at all.

"Skies, no. I'm not relaxed. Could you tell?"

He snorts, then says dryly, "No. You have an excellent poker face."

"Was I talking too much?" Elle heaves a sigh. "Okay, I'll be quiet. I just . . . I'm nervous about this move. I know he doesn't want me to live with him, but there's something wrong with the spirits. Like they know something I don't. And I've never brought anyone to meet Tony. He's never asked to meet anyone either."

She drops her head back against the headrest. "This is all new. You and me, and seizing the day, and Tony. I don't want anything to go wrong."

He's more pessimistic than she is, but he says, "I understand."

She touches him on his arm. "I can trust you, right?"

He almost breaks down and tells her right then and there. "I've said it already, but I'll reiterate: I won't lie to you."

Elle slouches into her seat, closing her eyes. "That's not an answer, but okay."

They arrive at Tony's house with an embankment of clouds looming thick and broody behind them, promising a tantrum. Elle exits the car ahead of him in order to wrestle with her luggage, shuttling her suitcases to the footbridge, using it as a staging area. She's visibly anxious, tapping her index finger against the railing of the bridge, shifting her purse forward and back.

Luc can't fault her when he's feeling the same way, but he can't let his own anxiety get the better of him. He holds out his hand.

She takes it, but only to give him a short squeeze. "Deep breath, you've got this," she mutters, then marches up to the door, suitcases in tow, and rings the bell.

A moment later the door opens wide. Luc goes on immediate alert, fighting the urge to put his hands in his pockets. It's definitely Tony.

Luc approaches slowly. Tony might not remember him. *Jusqu'ici tout va bien.* Nothing has happened.

"Elle!" Tony exclaims, throwing his arms wide for a hug, which Elle gives. He stands aside to allow her passage. "Come in, come in!"

"Hello," Luc says, extending a hand.

"Not you!" Tony says, not losing a step, retaining the chipperness in his voice.

So much for that. Tony definitely remembers him.

"I thought it might be you, and I have to say I'm a little disappointed. Okay, I'm a lot disappointed. I'm gonna need to have a talk with my sister. You're not allowed in."

"Tony!" Elle sounds scandalized.

Tony braces his arm across the width of the door, effectively barring both Elle from leaving and Luc from entering. Luc scowls before replacing the expression with the neutral one he uses on missions. This was an expected outcome. He can stay rational.

"Stop trying to push me," Tony orders Elle, looking over his shoulder. Beyond him, visible even from the door, Luc can see a large framed picture on the wall. It is, as Elle has said, a portrait of Tony, but younger, in the same style as the paintings in her workshop.

"What is wrong with you?" Elle's voice climbs in volume. "Why are you acting like this? You said you wanted to meet him, and here he is!"

"Yeah, about that." Tony cocks his head, a dangerous gleam in his dark eyes. "How about you back off a bit, Agent Villois? Maybe to the end of the walk. That seems safe enough."

Luc retreats partway to the sound of Elle's loud gasp.

"I didn't tell you anything but his first name. How'd you know?"

"Stay in the house."

"No."

"Elle—"

"You don't get to boss me around, Tony! How'd you know?"

"I figured it out, obviously!"

"Who'd you talk to?"

"No one. I have a brain. Thank God one of us does."

"How much do you know?"

"Enough. Stay in the house and quit fighting me."

"If you think I won't lay hands on an old man—"

Tony whips his head and shoulders around. "I'm not old!"

Luc gains a perverse sense of satisfaction at watching someone else wrangle with Elle, as well as a bit of pride at how much fire she's showing.

"I won't quit until you tell me what's going on. Or I'll ask him myself. Luc, what's going on? Why's Tony acting like he knows you?"

Tony stares defiance at him as if to say, *Go ahead, lie to her.*

He won't. "Because he knows me."

"What, from the Bureau?"

"Yeah," Tony confirms.

"We met a couple of times before his untimely death," Luc continues.

"Ah, yeah. That's what happened, isn't it? I hope I got a nice memorial. What happened after?"

"A case file was started on your brother."

"Oh, there's a file now?" Tony grins, sharklike, his teeth showing. "Am I in it?"

"Yes, but your file is classified, as is your sister's. She's done an admirable job faking your death."

Elle folds her arms across her body, the expression on her face not one of appreciation.

"She has, hasn't she?" Tony glances at Elle. "Oh, come on. We're complimenting you."

She spits out something in Chinese that sounds rude.

Tony sighs. "I guess the secret's out, then. Has she told you everything?"

Elle pokes Tony in the ribs, and from the way Tony flinches, she hasn't done it gently. "I'm not stupid. I haven't told him all of it. We need to have a discussion inside, instead of outside for the whole world to see. We, as in the three of us, and not the two of you doing whatever weird thing you're doing."

Tony hip checks Elle so that she stumbles away. "Take your shoes off, and no. Over my dead body."

Elle lets fly another something in Chinese, which Luc assumes is an invective.

Tony laughs. "And waste all your effort these last twenty-odd years? Don't do his work for him. On the other hand, Villois is trying to catch him, right? So he can come."

Fingers wrap around Tony's wrist. "Tony, move yourself or so help me, I will move you instead."

"Sorry, little sister. No can do. You've been in bed with a dangerous man. You *did* fuck him, right? Don't wanna assume."

"*I'm* a dangerous man!" Elle explodes. "What the hell is this? He's been in bed with *me*."

"Well, you're a woman," Tony starts, "unless you've discovered something about yourself, and let me just say I am supportive of that. Pride was last month, but it's never too late."

"Will you be serious for once in your life!"

Tony yelps, his body popping through the door like a bubble bursting. Luc figures he's been kicked. Judging from the way he rubs his behind and the amount of anger on Elle's face, he has.

"Will someone please tell me what's going on? How long have you two known about this? How long were you planning to not tell me? Luc?" She levels an accusatory finger at him.

"Since this morning."

Elle glares hard enough for him to feel it as a slap to the face.

He amends himself hastily, recalling that Elle is pyrokinetic. "I've been working your brother's case since last week. I've known about you since last night, and I was looking for the right time to tell you—"

"I told you to stay out of my family business!"

"I'm sorry, but I was assigned to the case. I'm bound by confidentiality clauses."

Tony watches them like a spectator at a tennis match, his head turning from Luc to Elle and back to Luc.

"I should have spoken to you about it before we arrived. I'm sorry. I know you didn't want my involvement."

"And you?" Elle rounds on Tony. "Luc's said he won't lie to me, and I believe him. You, on the other hand."

Tony's reply is mild. "Yeah, you can't trust me. I was hoping I was wrong."

Elle's voice takes on a warning tone. "Don't."

"But because I'm never wrong—almost never—I've known since you left. Started suspecting when you told me he was hot and French and all." Tony breaks eye contact with Elle to look at Luc, then whistles appreciatively. "He's still hot and French, so you assessed that correctly, but you left some information out. Bet he didn't tell you."

It's Luc's turn to stiffen, his gut tightening into a knot. It will be the worst-case scenario, then. "Don't."

"Whatever it is that he didn't tell me, it's because he hasn't had a chance yet."

Tony sighs. "Told you I'm never wrong. Do you know who he works for, and what his reputation is?"

"No."

"I thought you two had a good relationship built on mutual trust and honesty. I guess not!"

There's no time to prepare. No extraction plan, no saving grace.

Elle speaks with the cool calm that is often the sign of true fury. "Don't do this, Tony, I won't forgive you if you do. This is outside our family. Whatever he hasn't told me, it happens on Luc's terms, not yours."

"I was going to tell her." Luc speaks softly. He can try one last appeal. "In time."

"No time like the present, then." Tony steps back, vicious triumph lighting his eyes. "No hard feelings, right, Villois? You understand. You'd do it for your sister if you had one."

Luc closes his eyes, unable to watch his life going up in flames.

"Elle, my darling baby sister, you've been dating the top Fixer at the Bureau. He reports straight to the founder of Roland & Riddle. Oberon's right-hand man, they call him. Killer. His pet attack dog. Does what he's told and never questions it. Hey, have you ever met his friends?"

He flinches, the knot in his stomach souring. He hates that nickname so much.

"Tony, *please*. Stop."

Tony ignores her. "It's because he doesn't have any. Want to know why?"

Luc feels like he's falling even though he's standing on solid ground. He looks at Elle, seeing nothing but her as time grinds to a halt around him. It's the same slow motion he experiences in a fight, the same precognition he gets when a hit is coming and he knows how hard it'll land, how much damage it'll do.

"Because no one wants to be friends with someone who murders children."

Her head snaps up, eyes meeting his. Luc holds Elle's gaze, his body hot with shame. The world narrows down to the dawning horror on her face. *I'm sorry*, he wants to say. *Elle, I'm sorry*. But he can't speak. He's going to be sick.

"That's what he does. Whatever Oberon needs done, Villois does it. Ask him about it. Did you kill those two kids, Villois? In the red-cap case?"

Luc's throat closes up, the compulsion taking over. His eyes widen, the only part of him that can move while the rest of him is gripped with Oberon's command. *Once the children are gone, speak nothing of this mission to anyone. You may not discuss specifics such as names and locations, nor the actions you've taken here.*

"Look, Elle. He's not denying it. If he didn't do it, he'd be yelling about his innocence."

His neck cords out with how strongly he tries to shout no, but nothing happens. Speak nothing, Oberon said. In this moment, Luc wishes desperately that he had the sphinx's telepathy, signal flags, Morse code, anything, to tell her the truth.

Elle leaves Tony's doorway, walking toward Luc like she's moving through water. "Luc," she says. "What happened?"

He shakes his head, and even that costs an immense amount of effort. Each word he speaks, he forces from his mouth. "Can't. Talk."

"Because it's classified?" Tony laughs, mocking. "From what I heard? Villois was sent to take care of a redcap that had attacked a family. Oberon wanted the redcap gone and the family obliterated, kids included. Your hot man here? He did it. Probably thought it was noble. For the greater good and all that shit."

Elle reaches him, looking up at him with her big brown eyes. The look of hurt on her face is as good as condemnation. "Is it true? Did you do it?"

"Why bother asking? He can't even deny it."

Luc wants to. Father God, he wants to, but he can't even summon a growl of frustration, much less a prayer to a god he abandoned long ago. His chest constricts as his body wars with the compulsion, denying him breath. Luc wants to say no with every fiber of himself, but he can't. He can only stand here, helpless and suffocating, wanting to tell a truth he's held close for the last twenty-eight years. In the back of his mind, he's known that the situation would someday come back to haunt him. He'd envisioned it differently, though. Elle was never part of it.

Now she is, and the prospect of not only losing her, but her regard, is more than he can bear.

Who are you when you aren't here?

In a second, the answer to that won't matter.

He would beg if he could.

But Elle touches him, her hand curving over his shoulder, sliding up his neck to cradle his jaw. Luc can't relax, his body locking up even further. It hurts, every shallow sip of air he takes in sending a chorus of pain through him.

"I don't know what you have to do for him," she says, tremulous. "But I have a hard time believing you'd do something like that."

A flicker of hope kindles inside him.

Tony sneers. "You've never seen him at work, that's why."

"Go away, Tony."

"Have you considered that maybe he's been faking it for you all this time? Pretending to be a nice guy?"

"What for?"

"To get in bed with you, what else?"

Elle stares at Tony, rage rolling off her shoulders. "You're an asshole. You deserve a punch in the face for that."

She turns her attention back to Luc. Her fingers probe his skin, pressing gently into the muscles of his neck. "You can't even look at me. Why aren't you breathing?" she mutters. "That knot—"

Suddenly, concern breaks over her features. She grabs his left wrist, places three fingers along his pulse. "Tony, there's something wrong with him. Something's wrong with him!"

The flicker roars up, becoming a beacon. Stunned and confounded, Luc tries to understand what's going on.

"Ya think?" Tony sounds sarcastic but looks less sure. "He kills kids and sleeps well at night. There's a lot wrong with that."

"Who told you that? Why did you believe it?"

"Because he's refused to answer the question, just like he's doing now. If that isn't an admission of guilt of some kind . . ."

"Luc, breathe," Elle says. Luc claws down a breath. "You've said I have to ask you the right questions. Is now one of those times?"

He strains forward, nodding slightly.

"Are you allowed to talk about this?"

There's no energy to spare. He gives her silence.

"Can you write it down?"

Luc swallows, then shrugs and shakes his head.

Elle turns to glare at Tony. "I told you there was something wrong with him. Is there evidence that you didn't do it?"

Luc's breath rattles to a stop.

"Okay, wrong question. What can you show me?"

The oasis, the one place untouched by anyone else but the sphinx. The ruins, where he learned to come to terms with himself. The banyan tree, its every branch known to him. The reflecting pool with its gazebo, where he sometimes spent the night.

Luc's breathing restarts, the compulsion loosening, leaving him gasping like he's sprinted several kilometers. He almost collapses onto Elle, but catches himself at the last minute. She steps into him and hugs him anyway, lending him strength.

He lets her have some of his weight, overcome with gratitude. He doesn't deserve her faith, or her trust, or her brilliance after what he's done.

"Luc?" she whispers.

He finds a reserve of energy and straightens. "You'll have to come with me."

Tony says something in Chinese.

Elle's expression firms with resolution. "I'll be the judge of that."

"Thank you," Luc says, having no other words.

"Go inside, Tony." Elle cuts her eyes at her brother. "I'll call you later."

Chapter Thirteen

*E*lle stumbles as she and Luc appear in the desert, her feet scuffing against the stone of the landing area. The sphinx's teleportation feels like an abrasive wind compared to the sleek elongation that she associates with the port system at Roland & Riddle. She breathes in the desiccated air, the skin of her face tightening in the arid climate. Luc holds his arm out for her to steady herself, and as he does, she offers him the thinnest smile of thanks.

If only it were so easy to steady the many emotions whirling in her head. *It's complicated* only scratches the surface. "We're alone, right?"

"Yes. Aside from porting with the sphinx, the statuette is the only way to get in here."

"I need to ask you a question."

Luc glances sidelong at her. "I will do all I can to answer."

"What did you tell your boss?"

As if on cue, his call rune chimes. He silences it and speaks without hesitation. "I told him I was following a lead, that I knew what Jiang wanted more than the jade at the museum. I did not mention you or Tony by name or give him any indication of your involvement. As far as he knows, I am investigating something on my own."

It gives her no comfort. "Did you think that counted as keeping your word to me?"

He looks pained. "I had hoped it would."

Avoiding betrayal on a technicality has never worked, neither on reality television nor in her personal experience. "Were you planning to tell me?"

"I had not yet decided on the right time."

"That's a no, then."

Luc says nothing.

She scrutinizes him the way she would a test tube in her workshop. "What were you planning?"

"I told my boss I would see him soon, as I expected your brother and my team to meet. We'd already fought once, before I knew you were his sister. He's a formidable opponent."

Elle inclines her head, no longer surprised, grimly proud. "I've never won against him. There came a time when Tony couldn't beat him either."

"I also told my boss I was prepared to push the situation into a confrontation. We were at the gala Friday and spotted Tony, though we didn't realize it was him. I needed Tony's address and was prepared to lay a trap for your brother in order to take him into custody."

She shivers when the wind blows, but not from the cold. Goosebumps spring up over her arms. "You were going to sacrifice my brother for my other brother. Now do you understand why I didn't want anyone involved? I never wanted my brother to be hurt." Neither of them. Because neither of them deserve to be hurt when it's her fault.

"Even though apprehending him would solve all of our problems?"

Elle isn't prepared to admit to her part in it. "People give him a disproportionate amount of blame. Does your team know where Tony is?"

Luc shakes his head.

She takes a deep breath, lapsing into silence. Wherever they are, it's nighttime, and overhead a graceful crescent moon shares the sky with an ocean of stars. She looks up, following the current of the Milky Way, held captive for a moment at the beauty of it all.

A flood of sudden homesickness washes over her. Elle clenches her jaw against it, her eyes stinging. She hasn't been back to her ancestral home in half a century. The constellations loomed closer on her family's mountaintop, and when the moon was at rest she imagined she could reach up and touch them. On summer nights, when no one was looking, she'd set magic beneath her feet and fly as high as she dared, dreaming of a crown of stars. After her little brother was born, she made mirrors out of basins of water and gifted him the heavens.

She'd have done anything for Yiwú. She saved him the best peaches, the most beautiful plum blossoms. She tutored him at the expense of her own studies when he couldn't make heads or tails of various healing techniques. She defended him to their family when no one else would. They explored the mountain together when Tony had extra lessons, chased swallows on the wing as they returned home to roost, cut down lengths of young bamboo and took turns whacking each other with them.

"Are you okay?"

She blinks her tears back and returns herself to the ground, reminding herself of why she's here. "Shouldn't I be asking you that question?"

"I'm more than fine." Luc pockets the figurine.

"Really?" She can't forget the stricken look on his face, nor the way he fought so hard against his compulsion that he couldn't even breathe. The buildup of energies in his pathways had been unnatural and immense.

"You're here, and that by itself has given me hope. Are you cold?"

"Yes, but you said no one's around, right? So no one will mind me doing this." Elle concentrates, bringing her magic up to the surface of her skin, letting it build without allowing it out. The air around her shimmers before she finds the right temperature and dials her energy back. "Much better."

His eyes linger on her before he turns and leaps off the slab of rock, his feet landing firmly in sand. "This way."

Elle follows. Aside from answering her questions, Luc hasn't spoken much since leaving Tony's house except to express, in his own words, his most heartfelt gratitude. The rest of the time has been spent in silence, though whether it was by choice she doesn't know. It's hard to describe, but Luc feels on edge, like a piece of paper about to rip or the thinning of a soap bubble right before it pops. Beneath his outward stoicism she can detect the subtle cycling of his emotions: the chitter of anxiety; the press of determination; the rush of relief. The fact that she can tell is disturbing. He's always been calm and assured, unflappable.

It only speaks to how deeply Tony's affected him. Elle scowls. A point of flame ignites in her palm before she snuffs it out, seething. When she gets back to Tony, she's going to kill him. He had no call to behave that way, to put in the open information that was clearly private. She has no idea whether Luc would have told her about it on account of his binding, but that doesn't erase the fact that Tony has violated Luc's privacy.

Oh, Tony's gonna get it. The second Elle finishes things up here, she's going to make him holler so loud the ancestors will hear him. She's gonna make Tony *cry*.

"Hey." She hurries forward, reaching for Luc's elbow. He touches his fingers to hers for a second. "I'm really sorry for my brother."

"You don't have to apologize. It wasn't your fault."

"Okay, next time I see him, I'm going to make him apologize to you because he's a dick."

"No need. I understand where he's coming from."

"He was really mean for no reason."

"Again, I understand where he's coming from. His reaction to me wasn't unexpected. It's within parameters. A risk of my job." Luc speaks with a practiced flatness that makes Elle's heart ache. Gone is the gentility she's used to hearing, replaced with a detachment that razors off the peaks and valleys of his speech. This must have happened to him so many times that he's resigned to it.

Frustrated, she says, "But you aren't your job."

Luc raises an eyebrow at her. "Neither are you."

"Where are we?" she asks, changing the subject, not wanting to argue, trying to channel her emotions into something constructive. Being mad does no good right now. She needs to focus on the immediate thing: figuring out what's affecting Luc. She isn't familiar with the many forms of compulsion in the West, but she does know that the strongest ones have a physical effect.

Anger spikes up as she thinks about it. It's unbelievable that no one has noticed him having trouble before. Then again, with Luc's reputation, Elle suspects no one cares enough about him to see the signs.

She reels her energy in before she lights up. This not being mad thing isn't working out.

"We're somewhere in Ethiopia, most likely." Luc doesn't turn to look at her, gesturing instead to the craggy, striated cliffs in the distance. "I've never asked. This is a small space that the sphinx has maintained for hundreds of years, if not thousands."

They approach an ancient, gnarled tree, which Luc greets as if it's an old friend. He lays his hand over one of the exposed roots.

"You know this place well?"

He nods. "I spent a lot of time here when I first came to the agency. Things weren't so developed back then. We didn't have on-site housing, and the main buildings were no place for a youth to live. So the sphinx brought me here."

"She thought this place was better?"

"Yes, and I agree." Luc resumes walking, following the low wall. His head cants to the side. "She's awake. She'd like to see you."

They pass the front gates and enter what Elle assumes is the main building. There are no lights inside, only what starlight and moonlight can come through the doorways on either end. Luc is a shadow beside her, slipping through the dark with ease, the lack of light bothering him about as much as the cold does. She wonders if it's because he's so familiar with the building, or if it's because he can see better than she can.

"You can keep a light on if you'd like." His footsteps slow beside her. Elle hears the scrape of his shoes on the floor as he turns. "Tatie, we're here."

Elle holds up her hand, a small tongue of flame rising from her palm. In the dimness she can see the outline of the sphinx sitting up, pinpoint reflections in her eyes.

"Welcome to my home," the sphinx says.

Elle kneels, then touches her head to the floor in the deepest gesture of respect that she knows. "Thank you for allowing me the privilege of being here."

The sphinx rises to her feet, padding silently toward them. "I understand you have some questions. This will go faster if we can speak directly. Do I have your permission?"

"Via telepathy," Luc supplies helpfully.

"Oh," Elle says. "Yes, of course." She closes her eyes.

No need for that, child.

Elle's eyes pop open. *Yes, ma'am.*

She detects amusement from the sphinx. *You can call me Maryam. Luc has already shown me what happened. He is under a geas and cannot speak on the matter, so he has asked me to intercede on his behalf.*

Under a geas? Elle thinks, confused. She looks at Luc. *The compulsion?*

The same. Are you ready? I will warn you that Luc's memories are both graphic and intense.

She braces herself. "Okay. Show me."

But she isn't prepared for the deluge of emotion that slams into her. The smell of blood. The guilt of not arriving in time. Two pairs of eyes, glassy with shock. The grief over the parents and the lost innocence of the children. The memories engulf her, dragging her down. Elle gasps, shaking, her eyes unfocusing. The argument with Oberon. The unfathomable command followed by the threat. And then—

She comes back to herself with a painful snap as the sphinx lets her go.

Luc cannot speak because Oberon spoke his truename. Maryam's tail lashes from side to side. *Under his command, he cannot discuss the redcap case nor the children, nor tell anyone he is under a geas. Until now.*

Elle clenches her hands into fists. "How dare he," she says, her voice low. "How dare he do something like that." She looks at Luc again, but his face is unreadable. "That's your boss? The head of the agency?"

Luc nods. "And the one who found me when I was lost. I am able to do all that I do through him."

Thanks, she hates it. In her opinion, Luc owes him nothing. "And you've been living with this inside you for how long?"

He shakes his head.

"Twenty-eight years," Maryam replies for him. "A blink of an eye, and yet far too long."

"What happened next? What did you do?"

"That is what I wanted to show you," Luc says, strained. "Walk with me."

Elle takes hold of his hand, snuffing out her flame, keeping her magic tightly leashed before it roars up and out of her. The injustice Luc has had to face makes her insides prickle with enough heat to keep her warm. The violation of his trust is likely to make her explode. To use a truename that way, committing one of the worst crimes of the

Western fae world—it's horrific. And there's no telling if Oberon will do it again. If she were Luc, she'd be terrified to leave.

Luc holds the door open for her. "The stepping-stones there." He indicates them with his head. "They go out to the gazebo."

Elle squints as she navigates the stones with ease. "Are those beds?"

"Yes."

"Are they . . . ?"

He steps onto the floor of the gazebo as if it's sacred ground, walking toward the beds like he carries a thousand tons on his shoulders. He comes to a stop between them, then turns to face her, the sadness on his face sending a pang through her chest.

Luc nods once.

Wide-eyed, Elle approaches the first bed, which is occupied by a young girl that looks to be no more than seven or eight in human years. Her heart-shaped face still carries the last traces of baby chubbiness; sprinkled over her light brown skin is a scattering of freckles. Her dark hair is bound in two perfect braids. She's steeped in so much magic that Elle can smell it, catch the dry heat of it on the back of her tongue when she inhales.

"I put them under an enchanted sleep," Maryam says from behind her. "They are tied to the same magic of the oasis. Time passes, but the effects are not felt."

"Oberon never told you explicitly to kill them, did he? He told you to handle the situation." Elle looks at Luc, who stands as straight and unbending as a sword.

A muscle in his jaw jumps as he grits his teeth. "He often does."

"But you brought them here instead." She notices that he's closed his eyes. "Are you okay?"

"This is difficult for him," Maryam says softly. "He is reminded of his failure when he sees them."

"You didn't fail, Luc." Elle takes his hand.

He starts, his eyes flying open.

Elle speaks in a soothing voice. "It wasn't a failure. You've saved these children. Breathe."

Maryam shakes her head. "He says he hasn't saved them."

"Why?"

"They are children out of time, with no place in either world.

Oberon spoke true. There is no cure for redcap taint. Luc has searched for one and hasn't found it. To keep the children from turning, I watch over them here."

"But what if there were a cure?"

"Child," Maryam says. Elle pushes away her annoyance at being called a child. To someone as old as Maryam, 124 is nothing. "I have to my knowledge never seen a cure for redcap taint, and Luc has found nothing in almost three decades of searching."

"Well then." Elle puts her hands on her hips. "I don't know if you went searching in my part of the world, but I happen to be descended from the medicine god himself, and we see things differently." Undeterred, she gestures to the girl. "May I examine her?"

"You may try. I caution you against too much optimism."

"Luc?" Elle turns to him.

He sighs like a spell has been broken. "Go ahead."

Elle folds back the blanket until it's at the girl's waist, then quiets her pyrokinetics. She hovers her palms about an inch away from the girl's body, getting a preliminary read on her energies. They're cool, moving slow but steady along her pathways, spiraling back around as a result of the sphinx's stasis magic. But there are a number of hot spots in random places, and over her chest, her stomach, and her forehead.

She picks one of those places to explore, taking in a tiny bit of the hot energy through the open channel in her left palm. Immediately she tastes bitter metal, sharp like pepper on her tongue. "Ugh!" she exclaims, venting the energy out through her right palm, turning away to spit the foul taste out.

"Elle?"

"I'm good." She can cleanse herself with Shénnóng's qì if she needs to. Elle continues, lifting the girl's left wrist, and places three fingers to her pulse.

She frowns. The pulse is slow and elusive, fighting back only when she presses harder into the blood vessel. That's strange even for a girl who is essentially Sleeping Beauty, so Elle decides to go further. She prepares her qì for the next roll of blood, slipping it into the girl's pathway in a split second before the pulse writhes away again.

She's met with an alien energy, wrapped thorny and vine-like around the girl's vital organs. Her heart and liver are the most affected, and as she probes, Elle can sense how deeply the redcap's energy has integrated itself into the girl's organs. Without the finest touch, the most sensitive manipulation, there's no way to extricate it.

Troubled, Elle goes to the girl's other side and picks up her right wrist. Here she can feel how the redcap's energy affects the rest of the girl's body, fine filaments of it threading like a malevolent fog through the lungs and stomach. She's never experienced anything quite like this, but when Elle concentrates, honing her thread of energy into an edge, she can find a place to separate them.

She attempts slicing the redcap's energy away. It recoils but counters, slapping back at her. Elle hisses at the sting, retreating. Her level of expertise isn't enough for this. She can't heal the girl.

But, she realizes, excitement striking through her, Tony can. Or rather, Tony could.

She deflates. Shit.

"What is it?" Luc has hope and fear written on his face.

She braces herself. "I don't want you to get too worked up."

Even the sphinx is interested, her black eyes drinking it all in. "Daughter of Shénnóng, what did you find? Can you cure them?"

"I can't cure them, no. I don't have the skill." Elle doesn't wait for the crestfallen look to settle fully on Luc. "But Tony could. If he had the book to help. Back when he . . ."

"But he doesn't have the book," Luc says, forlorn. He exhales, an old, weary sound, putting his hands on his face before scraping them through his hair. "And he can't do it."

"No. But Shénnóng isn't the only god of medicine, just the most worshipped. There are other gods, other families who can do similar things. So that's hope, right?"

Maryam chuckles at herself, rueful. "I suddenly feel foolish. To be humbled at this stage of my life by a child! All this time, if we had only searched farther east . . ."

"Don't feel too bad. You would have needed someone like me to show you the path." Elle glances at Luc. "And with Luc's restrictions, the search would have been difficult anyway. I don't know how you managed to get far at all."

"Museums," Luc says. "Historical records in libraries and churches. Strasbourg has an old repository, hidden to non-fae. It has treatment records from werewolf and vampire attacks dating back a thousand years. The afflictions have similar symptoms."

"That's why you wanted to live there? Why you needed time off? For research?"

"Yes."

"But you couldn't get time off because . . ." Elle can't finish. Because Luc had failed twice and Oberon wouldn't allow him a break. He needed to rebuild his track record, he'd said.

"Luc. Does rebuilding your track record mean capturing my brother?"

She doesn't need his affirmation to know the answer is yes.

"This is the only thing I have wanted for a long time," he says, resigned. Luc looks and sounds exhausted, his shoulders bent, head lowered. There's something else unspoken, but Elle has no idea what it might be. "To make amends for mistakes I made. But it seems all I can do is make more mistakes. I'm sorry."

Her chest twinges, and her eyes burn. She understands that sentiment more than he knows. She's here twenty-six years later, having gone from mistake to mistake. "Maybe I can help."

He turns to the sphinx. "Tatie, could Elle and I have a minute?"

They look at each other, and something passes between them.

"Let's go to the tower," Luc suggests.

They leave the gazebo and pass through the main building, then climb up to the roof of the tower. Elle puts her hands on the low wall and leans forward, stretching her body out, turning her head to the sky, feeling like she's falling up. Already she's going through a mental Rolodex of old contacts, figuring out who the best consultant would be. There are a few renowned Ayurvedic practitioners, and hidden away in the Taiwanese countryside is an estranged branch of her family.

Behind her, she hears the scrape of sand beneath Luc's shoes. For a few minutes nothing happens except for a faint bloom of heat coming from her pendant. Elle puts her hand to her chest, pressing the jade against her skin, but it remains vaguely cool and smooth, a comfort. Perhaps she's imagining things.

"Elle."

"Mm?" She turns, ready to say something else, but words fade when she sees Luc in front of her, the expression on his face hesitant, his brows slightly furrowed. Starlight from above descends onto his hair, limning the brown strands, and moonlight washes out the blue of his eyes, turning them a luminous silver, giving them an eerie, otherworldly beauty. Around his shoulders he wears the night sky like a royal mantle, and like this Elle can believe that Luc truly is elven, coming from an ancient eldritch land.

"I want to apologize." He steps forward, taking her hands in his, lowering his eyes. "I'm sorry for betraying your trust. I know better than to ask forgiveness. I don't know what else to say."

"This is a good start."

"I also want to thank you, but I don't know if it's something you'd want to hear."

She squeezes his hands. His contrition feels genuine. If she were in his position, she might have done the same. She waits until he raises his head. "How will you know if you don't say it?"

"Let me say what I can first."

"Okay."

"You have my unending gratitude. For everything you've done for me, for all of your time and effort, for being you. For being someone who's treated me well despite my poor treatment of you. For being someone who has believed in me when I was convinced no one would on a matter this sensitive."

The warmth of affection blossoms in her. "You're welcome, but—"

"Elle, hush. Let me finish." He smiles faintly. "I owe you tremendously. I don't think I can begin to comprehend how much. You have saved my life. You've given me trust when I have done little to earn it. You have given me hope even though the task before me is enormous. But it isn't impossible. I have something to look forward to now. A new goal."

"I can help with that. I think I have the right network for it."

"Please, can I—"

"Finish? I'll shut up, I'm sorry."

He lifts her hands to his mouth, kisses them like she's given him a blessing. Elle shivers, and once again, it isn't from the cold. Luc is looking at her with such an intensity that she aches from it. "I understand you may not want to see me again. I accept that consequence. I want you to know, whatever happens . . ."

There's another surge of heat from her jade. Elle blames it on the sudden apprehension squeezing her stomach. Is this it, is he leaving her? Are they breaking up after a single day?

Her jade begins pulsing with warning.

"... that you've made me happy, and that's something I never thought could be possible. Elle, I—" He cuts off, then swallows.

"You what?"

"I'm sorry." Luc cups her face with his hand and leans down, halting an inch from her, closing his eyes. When he breathes, she feels it as a coolness against her lips. Elle holds herself still, her own eyes closing, the space between them as crystalline and fragile as spun glass.

Luc kisses her.

He kisses her with enough tenderness to break her heart, as if he's trying to tell her through his actions what he can't with his words. Her head spins as she brings her hands up, cradling his face. He makes a sound in his throat like he's giving up, right before he deepens the kiss.

Elle sighs, opening herself to him, all things forgotten but for the taste and feel and warmth of him, the rightness of his touch, the safety of his arms around her. If not for Tony and Yiwú and the burden of her mistakes, if not for the compulsion which tethers Luc's life to the agency, she would want this—him—for a very long time.

She's never thought that about anyone else. Her eyes spring open.

"Elle?" Luc murmurs, his eyes opening, the depths of them now mirroring the color of the sea at night.

She kisses him, pressing herself to him. "I appreciate your apology. But don't—"

Heat lances from her jade, stabbing straight through her. Elle breaks off with a gasp, her hand going to her chest, finding her pendant. Energy roils, pressing against the barrier of the jade. Something's wrong.

Tony.

"No," she whispers.

"No?" Luc repeats, hurt flashing across his face.

Elle shakes her head, taking a step back. It's hard to focus through the alarms she's set, hard even to get her bearings when she's being overloaded with spirit energy. Her jade flares so hot it burns her hand. "No, I mean—"

At that exact moment the wards surrounding Tony's house shatter, the recoil snapping across time and space, smashing into Elle like a fist, dropping her to her knees with a scream.

Elle doubles over, gagging, shuddering with the force of the impact, wrapping her arms around herself, trying futilely to contain the magic that spills from her veins. There's a second barrage of energy, and she screams again, smoke billowing from her mouth. Through a whoosh of fire she hears Luc exclaim something, but it's all she can manage to vent her magic upward so it can't hurt him, the night disappearing under a flash of incandescent flame. With her eyes closed, she holds her laes flush to her sternum, gasping and rocking back and forth on her knees, trying not to let the overflow burn through her. She can't sense anything else about her glyphs, only that the outer layer is gone. Impossible.

Tony is in trouble. She has to get to him now.

"Elle?" Luc tries to help her up but she refuses him, getting on all fours before she stands. "Elle, what's wrong?"

"It's Tony!" She sprints unevenly for the stairs, shouting as she descends. "Maryam! Maryam!"

The sphinx bounds up to her, sand bunching around her feet as she skids to a stop. Elle reaches out with her mind, her panic searing through the connection. She's breathing too fast. Shénnóng help her, Yìwú has found him.

Hold onto me, Maryam says. *I'll bring you as close as I can.*

Elle slings her arm over the sphinx's shoulders as Luc hurries out from the door of the tower. "Elle, I didn't—" he starts, his eyes round with alarm. "It wasn't me, I never gave his location—"

"Take this!" Elle gropes around in her purse until she finds her phone. "Call Lira, get her to Tony's. I'll meet her there. I gotta—I'm so sorry, I have to—"

A swirl of sand, a wrenching of time, and the desert disappears.

Elle will fly.

It's the fastest way to get to Tony, a straight line between two points, compressing a drive of fifteen minutes into a journey of a few.

It also breaks one of the cardinal rules in the agency manual regarding human-fae interaction: no displays of magic around humans. That includes unnatural flight, fire starting, and summoning, all three of which she's going to do.

Elle bursts through the door leading to the topmost level of the parking garage in Raleigh, drawing power up and through her jade. In this, she doesn't ask anything of her god or her ancestors. She demands, and then she receives. Raw power floods her veins, and without thinking Elle concentrates it in her forehead, her heart, the space between her hips. It's raining, drops sluicing down from a sky made prematurely night from thick cloud cover. Each drop that hits her hisses into a changed existence, dying on her shoulders and head and skin, rising anew as steam.

With a sweep of her hand the character for flight appears, written in flame. She needs no brush, has never needed one for herself. Elle leaps, landing lightly with one foot on the concrete wall, leaps again, passing through the character, wreathing herself in it as it takes effect. She shoots upward into the sky, unbound from gravity, her hair streaming behind her like a phoenix's feathers, a meteorite streaking unerringly toward Tony's house.

She ignores the cries of her ancestors, creating a mandate with her will, grabbing each spirit and emptying it of power before casting it away. Elle had thought she was angry before, but she is furious now because skies, Shénnóng, she's at fault for this. Again. She never should have reconnected Tony with their family; what did she think would happen? She's furious at herself, and at her ancestors for being themselves. News always travels fast where gossiping aunties and uncles gather, and the spirits are no different. Beneath the rage is the fear, and this is what Elle uses to fuel her flight, dragging the power of her god and the spirits to her until she's in a state of divinity. Yiwú will know she is coming. Her whole family will.

The tears burn down her cheeks, leaving behind a tight salt patina. In the distance is Tony's house, an unfamiliar car in the driveway. The door is wide open, yellowed light spilling across the threshold, a sodden glyph lying in a heap just inside. She bears toward it, the fear thumping through her, and softens her landing with the roof of the car.

"Yìwú!" Elle screams her brother's name as a challenge, stalking toward the door, the tattoos on her arm coming to life, glowing and shifting over her skin. She screams again. 「你給我滾過來！」

His response comes as a surge of energy, directed not at her but at the eastern point of the inner defensive perimeter. There's a source of power in the house, as bright and blinding as a supernova, and she realizes a split second too late that it's her great-great-grandfather's jade.

More energy hammers at her wards. The aftershocks hurl Elle to the ground, her fingers clutching at the wood of the bridge. Within moments, Yìwú collapses the southern point, the west, the north. The combination of destruction and backlash crushes her repeatedly against the bridge. She sees stars.

Elle gets to her feet, teeth gritted, struggling upright though her body feels like a rung bell. It's frightening how quickly Yìwú is going through her wards, how much power he wields. Something trickles onto her lip. She wipes it away, tastes the metal of blood.

She hopes that he's got it worse. If there's anything she knows about her brother, it's how unsubtle he is. Brute force will be met with brute force, and Elle has designed her wards to break outward and injure the attacker.

She pushes herself through the ruin of Tony's door, the frame splintered and warped, sees two figures in the house. One of them is lying on the floor. "Yìwú!" Elle shouts.

Her brother turns toward her. Elle gasps, her heart tearing in two, tears starting in earnest. Yìwú hasn't aged a single day. He's built like a willow branch, slim and unassuming, with a narrow, angular face that holds a perpetually serious expression. His eyes, black and hooded, meet hers. Blood drips from one nostril, connects with the blood at the corner of his mouth. Strewn across the floor are the broken remains of Tony's medicinal jars, and the dining table where she's drunk tea for so many years lies toppled on its side, cracks running lengthwise through it. Elle's scrolls hang tattered from the walls, fluttering in the soft breeze caused by the power rippling up from her brother's shoulders. Ghostly flame dances along the length of the sword leveled at Tony's head. Dangling from the hilt is a jade disk inscribed with bull horns.

"Big sister," he greets her, his voice rising and falling in the dialect of home.

Elle covers her mouth, choking on a sob. Memories from a lifetime ago pile into her mind one after another, threatening to drown her with sheer volume. Her family had always said that Yixiáng—Tony—had been born with an abundance of luck and cheer, while she, Yìyǎ, had just enough. When the youngest had been born, there was nothing left for him but despair. Yìwú the somber, whose smile was rare and whose laughter was far rarer. As a child Elle hadn't cared, and had included her little brother in everything she did until he gave up that bit of smile.

She makes a guttural noise from somewhere in her chest.

"He's still alive. For now. Your magic has gotten a lot stronger. But I've gotten a lot stronger too."

"Little brother," Elle says, her throat thickening in response to the fight she doesn't want. "Don't do this."

"If I don't," Yìwú replies, his eyes endless black wells, "I will never be able to atone for my mistakes."

Atonement. It's something she and Luc and Yìwú are all chasing. Elle doesn't think she understands what it means. She had thought it was bitter medicine to be cooked and choked down, with the understanding that it would make her better eventually. "You can do that without hurting us."

"It's two lives against many." Yìwú's head tilts. "I did the math a long time ago. As long as he lives, people die. People have already died. It's his selfishness that forced me to take action, to do something he could have done easily."

Elle closes her eyes, pained. There had been a boy of similar age to Yìwú at the foot of the mountain, who lived with the disciples there. The two had been close. When the boy had fallen ill, Yìwú had begged Tony for help. When Tony selfishly refused to come back, Yìwú had done what he thought was right.

Against all caution, he used the book. He never could have guessed his actions would lead to his friend's death.

"Tony didn't want his destiny." The words are flimsy, hollow. She knows who is at fault. "You know how happy he was to be away from our family. To finally have control over his own life."

"I wanted *my* destiny." Yiwú's voice is so loaded with resentment that Elle's mouth puckers. Yiwú would have been a glorious warrior. "But all of that is in the past. What matters now is that I seize my future. It starts with both of you."

There's no use talking. There hadn't been any use twenty-six years ago, and there's no use now.

Whatever she does, she can't let his sword touch her.

Elle summons fire, blasting it at her brother to gain space and force him away from Tony. It roars through the foyer, leaving scorch marks on the wooden floor.

There's a metallic flash. Yiwú slices the flames apart, charging through the breach. The air leaves her as his palm strike connects with a meaty thunk on her chest, barely missing her jade. She opens her mouth, a glyph forming, and spits needles at Yiwú's face even as her back connects with the doorframe.

He turns away, the needles embedding themselves in his forearm. Without missing a beat he plucks them out of his skin and flings them at her. Elle propels herself sideways toward the portrait, dodging, her right hand touching her left arm and unspooling a string of characters. They hang like smoke in the air before she inhales, then exhales a stream of wind that carries them toward her brother.

Yiwú yells wordlessly as the characters find him, his hands coming up to cover his eyes. When he pulls them away, his eyes are unfocused, and as he goes still to listen for her, Elle levitates off the ground, readying her next attack. Another string of characters comes off her arm, melting into each other, forming one long transparent ribbon.

She sees Yiwú sketching a counter-glyph as she grasps the handle of the ribbon, whirling it overhead before snapping it toward his sword. The end of it wraps around the hilt. Elle tries to yank it out of Yiwú's hand, but he keeps it in his grip as the counter goes into effect, dissipating the blindness. Instead he flows with her attack, extending himself at her sword-first.

Elle winds the ribbon around her elbow so that it goes tight, grabs it with both hands, and heaves, sending her brother flying past. She leaps up, gathering her energy around her, and hurls herself feet-first onto her brother's back, smashing him into the ground. His sword cuts into the wood of Tony's floor and through to the concrete foundation below; Elle hears the crack of Yiwú's teeth snapping together.

She has to end things fast. The longer the fight goes on, the more of a disadvantage she has, and the less she'll be able to overcome his Iron Shirt techniques. The next glyph flashes under her touch. Elle snatches it up, leaving half her skin bare, rolls away from her brother, and throws it toward the ceiling, hoping desperately that the link to Lira's Nordic magic works. In a blink the glyph morphs, turning into a series of indecipherable runes.

A translucent spear flashes down, stabbing through Yiwú and pinning him to the ground. Elle cries out with her brother as it happens, wanting to shield her eyes but unable to look away from the vibrating black haft that crawls with runes. The sound of hoofbeats from a six-legged horse rolls through the house like thunder, rattling the potsherds on the floor. Elle hides her face in her elbow to keep from making eye contact with an ancient god. Yiwú grunts as the spear disappears, reclaimed by its owner, leaving behind a wound that wells with blood.

Elle yanks on her ribbon again, this time dislodging the sword from Yiwú's grip. It clatters away, skidding across the floor into the sunroom. She should grab the jade, but her eyes are full of only Tony.

"Tony!" Elle yells, racing toward her older brother, turning him so he faces up. They only have a minute before Yiwú starts healing. "Tony, talk to me. Are you okay?"

He groans. "No."

"We gotta leave. Come on. Let me—" She lays her hands on him, praying. *Shénnóng, your son needs—*

"Stop! No more running. We finish this now." Tony groans again, then shoves her away so he can stand. "Fuck. Why'd I get rid of my meat cleaver?"

"I'm not killing him. I can't. Come on, we have to leave." Elle grabs hold of Tony's arm, hauling on him.

Tony's eyes widen. It's the only warning Elle gets before something punches into her body, making her grunt and stagger forward.

"Yiyǎ!" Tony shouts, trying to catch her.

Yiwú's kick slams her face-first into Tony's cabinets. A knife—it has to be a knife in her back, nothing else would hurt that way. She screams as Yìwú grabs it and thrusts it deeper.

Short of breath, with legs suddenly weak, Elle slides down, trying to grab for drawer handles as she collapses. *Shénnóng!* she begs. Beside her are muffled thumps as Tony and Yìwú exchange a flurry of blows. She can't pay any attention to that; pain rocks through her body. Her god responds with healing energy that erupts from her jade, cascading over her skin until it finds the knife. Elle reaches behind her, moaning, and pulls it out, the magic filling the wound, beginning regeneration.

There's a glyph on her forearm for healing. Elle holds the knife and brushes her fingers over the tattoo to activate it, inhaling with the rush it brings. Renewed, she rejoins the fight, where Yìwú has the upper hand.

Primal fear grips her. "Get away from him!" she shrieks at her younger brother before she sets her feet and launches herself at him.

She tackles Yìwú into Tony's armchair, which spins and topples, sending them both onto the coffee table. By some miracle Elle manages to hold onto the knife; she slashes toward Yìwú's head. It's a terrible angle. He takes the cut on his cheek, his skin springing apart, then seizes Elle's wrist in both hands and twists the knife out of her grip.

In the next breath he stabs her three times in the side, rolls out from under her, then grabs her hair and bashes her head against the table. Pain explodes through her, and for a second she blacks out. When she opens her eyes again, the pain like a million screams, she finds all she can do is lie on the coffee table, bleeding, and watch as Yìwú takes Tony down.

"Inelegant," Yìwú says, breathing hard as he stands over Tony. "But it'll do."

Tony opens his eyes. "Fuck being old," he groans.

"That won't be a concern for you for much longer," Yìwú says conversationally.

"Fuck you," Tony responds just as conversationally, and gives Yìwú the biggest shit-eating grin Elle's ever seen in her life.

No. Elle reaches toward her brothers. *No, no, no!* Her right arm moves a fraction. She whimpers but tries harder, digging into herself to find more magic, more fire, a prayer to her god to heal instantaneously, anything. The inevitable is coming.

Yiwú leans over, and with an almost tender gesture, shoves the knife up under Tony's ribs.

"No!" Elle howls the word over the sound of Tony's loud grunt, the air in his lungs leaving him. "No!"

"I am sorry it's come to this," Yiwú says, retrieving his sword, returning to where Elle lies. Tears blur her vision; she can't get a good breath anymore. Her pain diminishes before the magnitude of her many failures. She couldn't stop them from fighting last time. She almost killed Tony. She's led Yiwú here and hasn't stopped him. She's tried and failed over and over and yet nothing has come of it. Tony is still dying on the floor of his house.

Soon, unless she does something, she's going to join him.

"I will send you with the mercy you deserve," Yiwú says as he approaches. "This isn't my preference. You were my big sister. But as long as you're here, you'll always stand in my way."

Elle can't reply, her tears running freely down the sides of her face, gathering in her ears, splattering onto the floor. Her body won't heal fast enough for her to move.

Yiwú stands over her, and there are tears in his eyes as well. He gets on his knees, setting his sword aside, and bows to her, his forehead brushing against the floor three times.

Elle sends up one last prayer, and a request. *Grandmother,* she says, sending her farewell through her jade. *Please.*

As one, the ancestors wail.

"Revered elder sister." Yiwú stands, brushing her mussed hair back with gentle fingers, the bloodied knife held to her throat.

囚。 A character that means prisoner, to imprison. Four walls with a man trapped inside. The word looms large in her mind.

"Beloved younger brother," Elle mouths, fresh tears cascading over her cheeks. The character rides her breath into being, flashing like a spark.

"What—" he begins, but the magic takes hold. Thick walls spring up around him, slamming into place. One last glyph sloughs off her arm, a glyph of stasis. She touches it to the prison. It spreads over the walls in an instant, like oil across water.

Inside, all motion stops.

Elle sobs with long, low moans, moving little by little, begging her body to do what it must and bring her to Tony's side. She flips herself onto her stomach, whimpering through the pain of multiple partially healed stab wounds and probably a concussion, throws all dignity aside to crawl to her brother. The pool of red beneath him looks altogether too placid.

"Brother," she cries, her chest too tight for words.

He stirs. "Not the angel I wanted."

Elle half laughs, half weeps. Skies, that hurts. "You aren't . . . dying today."

"Funny," he says, breathing out. It's a moment before he breathes in again. "Sure feels like it."

"You'll live. You have to." Darkness creeps into the edges of her vision when she pushes herself up onto her elbows, a shaking hand going to her laes. There isn't enough time or energy for her to heal herself, not if she wants to save Tony's life. Her family has always loved him best.

The ancestors cry out again as they ascertain her intent.

Elle works the string over her head, then reaches out, pressing the plain jade circle into Tony's hand. "I'm sorry," she whispers. "This is all I have left."

Tears leak out from beneath Tony's closed eyelids. "Making me waste my last words . . . why?"

"Because." Her hand tightens on his, their fingers interlacing. Elle calls out to her family, living and dead. They must take Tony back. This is, after everything that has happened, the right thing to do. If only she had done it all those years ago. "I've failed you. So many times. I've taken too many losses. If I can . . ."

She pauses, unable to stop crying. "If I can turn one thing into a win, I'll do it. I took this away from you. Now I'm returning it."

The power transfer starts slowly. Elle keeps her hold on Tony's hand and curls herself into the fetal position beside him as her connection to the spirits dwindles and wanes, draining from her and into him. One by one they disappear until her only her grandmother is left. Then she, too, is gone.

Tony coughs. His clothes rustle as he rolls himself onto his side, his hand gripping hers tightly. "Yǐyǎ. Jiāng Yìyǎ, are you still with me?"

It takes her a minute to answer, like she needs to surface from deep waters. It's so much effort to open her eyes, but she does for a moment. "Nn. Not for long."

"Bullshit." Tony swears again as he hauls himself onto his knees, his hands moving over her, pushing her onto her back.

The pounding of feet interrupts him, followed by a hoarse shriek. Tony looks over his shoulder, his mouth moving. "Lira! Help me!"

His voice comes to her after a long delay. Weirdly, he's speaking English.

"Elle!" someone else shouts, panicked. It's Luc, but it can't be. He wouldn't panic.

"Yiyǎ!" Tony slaps her on the cheek. Her head rolls to the side. He sounds urgent, which is out of character for him. Everyone is acting strange. "Stay with me, baby sister. Stay awake."

"No," she replies, dreamy. Her heart beats, a hummingbird. "I'm going."

"Yiyǎ, I beg you." Is he crying? She can't turn her head to see. "You can't go. Stay just a bit longer, I only need a minute. C'mon."

"Sorry." Lassitude claims her, blanking out the pain. Elle drifts on currents of gray, her vision closing in around her. It's cold, and she's so tired. She's looking forward to rest.

She can't say anything more. Her wounds have reopened without her ancestors and her god to help her. It's too silent without their voices, and too empty without their presence. Elle floats toward nothing, her heartbeat a weakening rush in her ears. She hears Tony praying, his words washed away by a calming sea.

Chapter Fourteen

Luc answers Oberon's summons late in the afternoon, pushing open the heavy wooden door of his boss's top-floor office. It's a beautiful day in London, clear of rain, and the floor-to-ceiling windows welcome the light in with wide-open arms. Outside, the temperature is warm but not cloying, unlike the eastern United States. If he decides to pick up a coffee at the fancy shop down the street, it'll be a pleasant walk.

As he enters, he wishes for the hair-plastering heat of North Carolina. His body might be here, but his mind is an ocean away. He ought to be happy on account of closing out the Jiang case. It's a big notch on his belt, exactly what he needs to get back in Oberon's good graces. But it's been almost seventy-two hours since he saw Elle dying, soaked in her own blood, and though Tony swears she's going to make it, she hasn't yet woken up.

Oberon glances at him before flicking away the glamours serving as computer monitors. "You're dressed casually."

"My apologies. I was not expecting to come in today."

"Have a seat."

Luc settles himself in the single chair in front of Oberon's broad oak desk. It's practical and plain, incongruous with the plexiglass and steel modernity of the office, and would be a better fit in Oberon's smithy, located many floors below.

"I've finished reading your report. As always, you've been thorough. I am especially intrigued by the details of your relationship with Elle."

Agent Mei, Luc corrects him silently.

Oberon wiggles a finger, and a display shimmers into existence. "On one hand, I'm disappointed you didn't notify me of this. On the other hand, I'm impressed at the level of work that went into cultivating her, and I see the necessity of keeping it quiet. To plan something for eight months and have it come to fruition the way it did . . ."

Oberon chuckles. "I might get to retire earlier than I thought. Don't worry, it won't be soon. You still have a long way to go before this office is yours, but what you've done here shows promise. I previously thought you'd be unable to develop relationships in this fashion, but your seduction of Elle proves me wrong."

This time, Luc says nothing out of shock. Alarm klaxons go off inside him, but his emergency measures kick in, keeping his face neutral and sending him into the cold, empty space where he can operate without emotion. He understands why Oberon thinks this way. Objectively, it does look like Luc seduced Elle in order to pry her secrets out.

"I'll change it on your dossier. You've maximized efficiency and yielded excellent results. I would say this earns you a reprieve, but unfortunately, there have been complicating factors. The Jiang family will arrive soon. I'll be tied up in negotiations for William."

Oberon levels a look at Luc. "Take my place. Run the operations I have marked as crucial."

Taken aback, Luc says, "Sir?"

"Yes, I share your concern over how long it'll take, but this isn't a standard release. Jiang has a long list of offenses and several governments who would rather have him than yield him to his family."

Luc shifts his weight forward. "What about Agent Mei?"

Oberon half shrugs. "They haven't mentioned her."

"And Tony?"

"He's overseeing his sister's care and has made it clear he won't be available until she's recovered enough to be discharged." Oberon drums his fingers against the surface of the desk once, then sniffs. "He's insisted on her staying in Raleigh despite her violating agency regulations as a mundane. But he's agreed to pay Elle's hospital bills and has signed our liability waiver. It covers her death, if that happens."

If that happens. Luc hears the subtext. "The Jiang family won't take over her care?"

"No. Our agreement extends to William only. Let's circle back to that. I'll need you to step in for me for several days at least."

"I . . ." Being interim Bureau chief is quite possibly the least appealing idea on earth when Elle is clinging so precariously to life. He'd rather be with her, even if all he does is sit in her room. "Agent Pei has an excellent strategic mind and would be a better fit."

"You are too modest." In Oberon's mouth, the word is an insult, not a compliment. He narrows his blue eyes into a glare. "You have been here the longest. I trained you myself. You have helped build this enterprise. You closed a twenty-six-year-old case with minimum damage to our agents."

But not minimum damage to Elle.

Oberon continues. "Pei hasn't done that. The Wrecking Crew would never do that. Darcy would have left a trail of blood behind. The other Fixers are on long-term assignments and are unavailable. Who better than you to oversee missions?"

"Surely," Luc starts.

"I'm offering you a rare opportunity, something I should have offered earlier. You should have a real stake in this company." Oberon's face softens. "I know you and I have had disagreements before in how operations were carried out. Walk a mile in my shoes. Perhaps you'll see things differently, do things differently."

Perhaps isn't the right word. Luc *will* see and do things differently. "I am not sure whether I'm ready."

"Let me put it this way. Would you rather sit in a conference room with the vampires and haggle over numbers?"

Luc goes still. Oberon has a point. "Yes, sir. You said only a few days, correct?"

"For now. I'll send the memo out. You're dismissed. Keep the rune on you. Starting tomorrow, I'll have calls forwarded."

He nods, getting to his feet. In the back of his mind, the memory of the sphinx whispers to him: *You should have what you need.*

He can have until tomorrow to check in on Elle.

"Oh, and Lucien?"

"Yes, sir?"

Oberon smiles warmly, his teeth bright and white and even, but it doesn't reach Luc. His skin tightens, and chills lift the fine hairs on the back of his neck.

"Good work."

Elle has the longest and strangest dream on her way to heaven. At least, she hopes it's heaven. She isn't sure whether her sacrifice has been enough to redeem her. Maybe it hasn't, and she's going to one of the eighteen hells instead, but the visions she's having don't look anything like a maze full of torture implements. First of all, there are no demons. Second, what should be a maze full of screaming and violence is instead a cozy room poured full of sunlight, where the only implements aside from her bed are an IV pole and a gallon jug of hand sanitizer.

The scene shifts every time she opens her eyes. Tony is young again, always smiling at her, chatting with her despite the way she fades in and out of his words. Lira's changed her hair into sleek braids, which Elle loves but doesn't have the energy to express. It's okay, though. Lira isn't really here.

So when Elle sees Luc, she doesn't react. He's in a chambray suit that accentuates the blue of his eyes, with a cream linen pocket square completing the look. Elle sighs and smiles, glad that whoever's in charge is being nice to her before she arrives at her final destination. She could use a visit from her grandmother. Hopefully in her next vision.

The gods send her parents instead. Consciousness arrives as relentless and steady as the tides. Elle registers two figures, the lines of their forms sharpening as her pupils adjust to the light. She must be dreaming. Her parents haven't said a word to her in decades, believing she'd killed Tony, not knowing he was alive. To protect him, she'd kept silent.

Instinct makes her jaw move, her dry lips peeling apart. "Ma?"

No sound comes out, but her mother turns to her, her pale, ageless face as beautiful as ever, her large brown eyes growing larger. "Yìyǎ!" she exclaims. She motions to Elle's father. "Hémù, she's awake!"

Elle looks at her unfamiliar surroundings. "Am I in hell?"

"What kind of question is that?" Ēnlián's eyebrows draw down in annoyance. "Is this how you greet your mother?"

"Am I dead?"

"What nonsense." Ēnlián scoffs. "Of course not."

Elle's father appears in her field of vision. She should feel comforted, but all she has is pain, building slow and heavy in her body. "What are you doing here?"

Ēnlián recoils. "Why wouldn't we be here?"

Elle's so fuzzy-brained that she can't sort out all the emotions piling up inside her. Unable to articulate anything, she starts crying. "Where have you been?"

"Here, of course. Don't cry." Her mother plucks up a tissue and dabs at Elle's tears.

"I'll cry if I want to!" Elle sobs. Images shouldn't have weight, but the sight of her parents is enough to shatter the fortress where she's jailed her resentment, making it pour out. "Where have you been? Why didn't you come earlier? Why didn't you intervene? Why didn't you . . ."

She gulps down breaths like knives, cries harder. Something pulls against the skin of her stomach. It feels like tape.

"We are very sorry," her father says. Elle can't look at him, can't stand how gentle he sounds, or how even-keeled he is, or how he exudes peace and safety. "We didn't realize the truth until it was too late. Yiyǎ, you've done something extraordinary."

Her parents should have been there for her and her brothers twenty-six years ago. "Why are you here now?"

"Watch your tone." Elle's mother speaks quietly, but there's a steeliness to her voice. There's a steeliness to all of her, from the intensity of her stares to the way she holds herself. "You need us. We came to see what we could do for you now that you're . . ."

Elle tries to conjure flame, but nothing happens. It hits her then, lands on her so hard she can't breathe. She's alive after what she did for Tony. She wasn't supposed to live. Not like this, with no magic, no grandmother, no *god*.

"Ah, Yiyǎ. Please don't cry." Her father rests a hand on the bed rail, sympathy on his face. A long time ago, Elle would have given an arm and a leg to hear her father speak to her again, but that desire has been rotting in its grave for decades. "Of course we had to come. We didn't understand the extent of your ability. The family couldn't lose that."

That. Not her. If possible, she cries harder. It's already lost.

"When you're well again," her father continues, "we can take you to the temple at the base of the mountain, and you can teach us how you restored Yìxiáng."

"You can't come home without your jade," her mother interjects, "but you can be as near as possible."

"I can't—" Her brain betrays her, sending images of the great court-yard filled with snow, ice riming the branches of the peach trees. She used to study them, painting as fast as she could, using her magic to keep her ink from freezing.

Ēnlián dabs at Elle's face again. "You can still be of use to the family. You can still help."

"There are many possibilities before us," Hémù says. "You can show us new paths."

She doesn't want to hear it. "I don't want to help."

"You must." There's her mother's steel again, a contrast to her father's running water. "Who else do you have but family? You have a duty to us."

Elle finally understands how Tony must have felt back then. No wonder he'd rather wallow in his heartbreak and pursue a career as a Fixer instead of returning home. But he's the rebellious one, not she. She has always been a good and dutiful daughter.

Despair claims her, oozing up in tendrils, wrapping around her heart. "Did I not do enough?" She must have something left, some scrap she hasn't yet given. "Mama, was it not enough?"

The door opens loudly, drawing attention. Tony—a younger version of him—stands in the doorway, a scowl on his face. Elle gasps in shock, her chest heaving.

"Ma, Ba," Tony says, acknowledging them with curt nods of his head. "You're disturbing my sister."

"Your sister is also our daughter," Hémù says serenely.

"A fact you've conveniently remembered only after she's brought your sons back." Tony moves into the room and stands to the side of the door, his meaning clear. "She's just woken up and has to stay calm. Visitation is over. As her doctor, I have to insist you leave."

"Yìxiáng, your brotherly devotion to Yìyǎ is admirable." Ēnlián smiles, appeasing. "But your father is a physician also, and I think he'd know how to manage your sister's stress."

Whatever she's tried to do, it doesn't work on Tony. His expression doesn't change a hair. "I'm listed as one of her primary physicians on her chart, which I know you've already consulted. I'm ordering you to leave the room, as Yìyǎ is in the early stages of recovery."

"Of course." Ēnlián inclines her head, as graceful as a tulip swaying in the breeze. "We'll wait outside. What an excellent take-charge attitude from you."

Tony bangs the door shut behind them. "The nerve," he mutters as he approaches, hooking the leg of a rolling stool with his foot, propelling it to Elle's bedside. He sits.

She gapes at him. "Tony?"

"The one and only. You couldn't delay waking up an extra five minutes? I wanted to be the first person you saw." He presses his fingers to Elle's wrist, holding her hand in a way that keeps him from jostling the IV taped to the back of it. "Let's see how you're doing before we start talking."

"What happened to your face?"

"That's why I wanted to be first. I got it back, thanks to you." Tony scoots around the bed to the other side. "We'll get to that later, since you'll probably forget what we're talking about now. No worries, it just means you can see me for the first time all over again." He shakes his head. "What a shock waking up to Ma and Ba, huh? Absolute hell, if you ask me."

He returns and lifts the blanket covering her, prodding at her left side gently. He leans down to sniff. "Getting better. You should be able to drink later today. I'll get some medicines started for you."

"You're so serious."

"Yeah, well, the other option is rage."

"Are you mad?"

"At you? Never. At our parents? Eternally." Tony switches into English. "You'd think distance would make the heart grow fonder, but nope. Nothing has changed. They're still assholes. Did they tell you they were here to see you?"

Elle nods.

"It's all bullshit. They're here to negotiate the terms of Yìwú's release."

Tears flood her eyes. Here's her answer. What she's done hasn't been enough. *She* isn't enough. Yìwú, though, will get the attention he's always wanted. "He's okay?"

"Thanks to you, again. Our family is mighty glad no one died."

She can't help what comes out of her mouth. "Can I see him?"

Tony scowls. "You're fucking kidding. After all this, the first thought you have is to see him? Look to yourself. Christ. No, you can't see him. It'd make me happy if you never saw him again and forgot him forever. I'm not answering any more questions about him."

Silence.

"What happened to me, Tony?" Tony says in a squeaky voice. "Glad you asked, 妹妹. In classic Chinese tradition you tried very hard to die, and you almost succeeded but for the enormous efforts of both me and Lira. I cried prettily for the camera, and maybe I yelled at Shénnóng a little, and Lira said every cuss word known to man in English, Danish, Lenape, and Faroese, and the two of us told the god of death, 'Not today.' You're welcome."

When Elle doesn't reply, Tony flaps his fingers at her and says, "C'mon c'mon c'mon. I'm waiting."

She's having trouble following. "I died?"

"A bit. Makes a good story for speed dating."

"Speed . . . what?"

"Dating. A thing you should do. I still don't hear a thank you, by the way. You're fortunate to be alive. You've got four stab wounds, definitely a concussion. Needed a blood transfusion and surgery. You're also pretty hopped up on pain meds." Tony looks disgusted. "I'll make you something to fight the morphine. Technically it's hydromorphone, but whatever. I hate that shit. Go easy on it, you're gonna be sensitive."

"How long have I been out?"

"Almost three days. Our parents arrived earlier today after I knew you'd make it, so no thanks go to them. They're going to ask lots of questions about what you did."

"I know. I don't want to see them. They shouldn't have come here."

"That's the most sensible thing I've heard you say all day. Say something else."

"They said they underestimated my ability. I think they're pretending to care about me." And she might fall for it.

Tony lets out a low whistle. "You're two for two. Amazing. Consider more near-death experiences in the future. The clarity you have!" He cranes his neck up, eyeballing the clear bag hanging from the IV pole. "That'll serve you well in the next stage of your life."

The brain fuzziness makes it hard to follow him. Tony moves fast, but right now he's quicksilver, rolling right out of her grasp. "What?"

He sighs. "I won't joke around. You have a chance to do whatever you want once you recover, and I'm going to give you as much support as I can so you can take that chance. You took care of me for so long. Now it's my turn. You didn't think I'd abandon you, right?" Tony scoffs. "I'm gonna sell the house—"

"Sell the house?"

"—sell the house," Tony repeats himself, "and then—"

"It's my house. I paid for it." She'd lived off cup noodles for years for that house. Like hell Tony is going to sell it.

"Sell the house," Tony says a third time, "and send the funds to you, and get you a sweet setup where you can do whatever you want."

"Whatever I want." That's a new concept, one she greets with dread. "I don't know what I want."

"Now that this business is over with, you'll have plenty of time to figure that out. I've got a friend of a friend in San Fran who wants to go back to China for a few months. Could use some help from you."

"Why does everyone want me to help them?" She means to ask in a regular tone, but the question comes out as a wail instead. "I don't want to help! I shouldn't have to help!"

Tony snickers. "Three for three! Astonishing. You could work on your delivery some, though."

Elle does her best to glare at her brother. "Your bedside manner sucks."

"I know."

"I don't want to help your friend."

"Then don't. Stay here until the house sells. Your stuff is already in the guest bedroom, but Ma and Ba are taking that over. I'll put an air mattress for you in the living room." He shrugs.

"I haven't even finished moving in and I'm getting kicked out already?"

Tony shrugs again. "Family first, right? Whoa, no crying. I'll be here for you, okay? Don't give yourself extra stress. Your job is to get better. Thankfully, you've got me, and the doctor that Lukey called in is pretty decent. Lira was about to get on the phone and ask her dad to come down, but I told her not to. So she's got every inch of this room carved with restorative runes instead."

Bewildered and somewhat lost, Elle asks, "Lukey?"

"Yeah, we're on a first-name basis now."

"But Lukey?"

"He hates it," Tony says, blasé.

"I hate it too."

"Of course you'd take his side on this." Tony sniffs, then grins. "He's the one who knocked Yìwú out after you died and your magic stopped working. You should have seen him. Threw the heaviest punch I've ever seen in my life. That man is poetry in motion. It was beautiful." Tony pats his chest, looking wistful.

"My magic?" Elle's lip trembles, more tears forming. She should feel different without her magic, but so far all she has is numbness.

"No, don't cry! I'm a sympathetic crier."

"You are not!" Elle retorts, her voice cracking. She sobs, and pain lances through her side. "You just hate feelings!"

"Damn, got me there. You've got a real hot streak going. You're going to pull your stitches if you don't calm down."

The increasing pain she's feeling is a testament to that statement, but Elle can't seem to stem the tide.

Tony heaves a sigh. "I told our parents not to stress you out, but look at me doing the same thing. Just concentrate on getting better. Depending on your progress, I'd say you've got another week of being here."

There's a knock at the door.

"No visitors!" Tony hollers.

"It's me!" Lira yells back.

At the sound of her friend's voice, Elle's tear ducts find a second wind.

"Fine, come in." Tony hauls himself off the stool.

Elle shuts her eyes. Over the sound of her own crying, she hears her mother say something, and Tony's reply. Footsteps approach.

"Hey, girl. I'm glad you're up."

Elle looks at Lira. Her friend is wearing a shop apron over her work clothes, along with an expression Elle assumes is supposed to be comforting. "Are those your parents out there?"

She manages a nod, sniffles, and winces.

Lira finds the morphine pump, then pushes the button. Tony grunts in disapproval. "Don't skimp on this stuff. You don't need to deal with the pain at this moment."

"I have to be careful with it now." Without the blessing of health, she'll have to be careful with a lot of things.

"Be careful with it later."

A round of wooziness hits her, making her head swim. "Was it that bad?"

"You died, friend. How are you asking me if it was bad? Is there something worse?"

Elle holds her laugh in, ending with something that sounds like a geriatric wheeze. "Could lose money."

Lira throws her hands up, laughing. "I can't with you!"

"How's the store?"

"Fine for now. I can't stay long, I'm on break. I'm holding on to your stuff until you get back."

"I'm not—" Before she gets back. There's no going back for her. "I'm pretty sure I'm not allowed."

Lira clicks her tongue. "Okay. You rest." Whatever else she might say is left dangling when there's a knock on the door.

"I got it," Lira tells Tony. She opens the door, revealing Luc, as well as a blistering, laser-focused stare from Elle's mother. Elle's heart leaps at the sight of him while the rest of her withers beneath said stare.

"Hi." Lira lets him in and closes the door on Ēnlián, then looks Luc up and down. Elle does the same. Luc is wearing a white linen buttondown with the sleeves pushed up, paired with fitted jeans which are cuffed at the ankle to show off his polished tan monk straps. "Is it Casual Friday?"

Elle knows Lira's intent is to show her surprise at Luc dressing less formally. Luc, however, replies, "It's Tuesday morning."

His dry humor cuts through enough of the brain fog for her to register it as a joke. Elle laughs, then hisses at the stab of pain. "Lira's just shocked to see you wearing jeans."

Lira nods vigorously. "Yeah, I didn't know you owned any. Thought it was all suits and blazers and stuff."

There's a hint of a smile on Luc's face. "I am full of surprises. Wait until you see my sneaker collection."

"It's huuuuge," Elle drawls, holding up her hand, forming it into a C-shape.

"Elle!" Lira yells, covering her eyes and laughing.

"Elle!" Luc exclaims, red flooding his cheeks.

"Dang with a capital D," Tony says, looking impressed.

Elle hits the button for more morphine so she can laugh without it hurting so much, then hits it again just in case.

"Okay, I gotta work," Lira announces, not looking at Luc, clamping her lips shut. "You two, uh." A snort escapes. "Behave yourselves."

"He doesn't actually have a sneaker collection!" Elle calls out.

"Yeah, I got that part!" Lira calls back, grabbing Tony by the elbow, hauling him out of the room.

Luc waits until the door closes before he approaches.

"Hi," Elle greets him, trying to smile through her puffiness. Everything seems a bit brighter now that he's here. It could also be the morphine. She resists the desire to press the button a third time.

"Hi." Luc takes a seat, then takes her hand. "It's good to see you awake."

"As opposed to seeing me not-awake?"

"Yes, as opposed to seeing you not-awake."

Elle chews on that for a second. "Been spending time here?"

"A lot, yes."

"The doctor didn't stop you?"

Amused, Luc says, "He's a werewolf with a sharp nose. He already knows."

"Knows what?" Then it comes to her. "Oh."

"So, yes. I have been spending time here." Luc gestures to the corner of the room. "I've brought my blanket, so you know it's serious."

Elle doesn't look where he's looking, spending a moment admiring the softness in his expression, her eyes following the lines of his face. His structure has eluded her so many times before, but if she can get her hands on some charcoal, this time she'll be able to capture him. The next time she's alone, she'll try it out. It'll be a good way to test her memory for when they're apart.

Because they'll have to be. Happiness drains away like the movement of the sea before a big wave and returns, inexorable, as crushing heartbreak. Before, when she still had her jade, they might have had a chance to build something lasting. Now, her path and Luc's will diverge. They had one night in Paris, and that's all they'll ever have.

Oh, that's a hurt no amount of painkiller can soothe. She frees her hand from Luc's and clicks the button several more times anyway. The machine fires off three warning beeps.

"Elle, are you okay?"

She shakes her head, unable to speak for the tightness in her throat, not wanting to see the concern on Luc's face. He shouldn't be here. He shouldn't see her like this, not when she can't think right, not when her emotions are like one of those game show wheels, and every human interaction results in a spin.

"What's wrong?"

"Hurts," she lies, sniffling. That causes more hurt, so technically she isn't lying.

He gets up, bringing several tissues over, pressing them against her cheeks to soak up her tears. "It will improve," he says. "I promise. Tony and Lira and Dr. Clavret are doing all they can to ease your recovery. Another couple of days and the pain should diminish significantly."

In between sobs, she asks, "Personal experience?"

He smiles. "The first day after you saved my life. I feel, after what we've been through, that I can break my NDA on this small detail. I'd been bitten by a basilisk, and your curatives were all that stood between me and a horrific death. I laid in bed and cried from the pain. The venom had to clear my system before the healers could restore me. I thought of you often."

Elle stares at him, then clicks the morphine button furiously. She needs more brain fog, stat. The machine beeps at her again, angry. "What's wrong with this thing?"

Luc glances at her hand. "It won't release a dose more than once every five minutes."

"That's *stupid*. I want one *now*."

Luc reaches out, brushes the backs of his fingers over her cheek, and leans over to kiss her on the forehead. "What's really wrong, Elle?"

What the hell. She's been found out. "I don't know what to do."

He gives her a sympathetic look. "Recover first. Worry about the rest later."

People keep telling her that. "Maybe I want to worry about it all at once, like a BOGO sale. Good in bulk. Cheaper."

Luc laughs at her. "You're three days from death's door and somehow you're still making jokes. Unbelievable. What's wrong, truly?"

It takes a while for her to answer. "I don't know what to do."

"Because?" he prompts her softly.

"I don't have magic anymore." Elle clenches her jaw. She's said it out loud. It's real.

"And?"

"My family is here." Skies, her brain feels like a hundred marbles dropped onto a hardwood floor, bouncing everywhere. The rattling makes it hard to think. "And I don't want to be a burden because I'm mundane."

"You aren't a burden, but go on."

"And." She blinks, exhaling as a comfortable, calming numbness begins spreading outward from her chest. Her next words come out soft as porridge, with the consonants all gooey. "I don't . . . know why you're here. The case is closed. Your commission is done."

This time, it's Luc who takes a while to speak. "Anything else?"

She fixes her eyes on the ceiling, then unfixes them because they've decided focus is for suckers. "I'm tired."

It's a relief when she starts floating.

"Are you finished?"

Elle allows the slightest of nods.

"Can you look at me, please? Let me try to address everything you've said. I'll be brief."

"Okay."

"You're right about your magic. Everything in your life is going to change. I'll do what I can to help you there. Regarding your family, my opinion is that you should stay as far away from them as possible, with the exception of Tony. As for why I'm here, it's because I care about you and I'm invested in your survival. But you're in no condition to discuss this. I don't know if you're able to listen."

Elle doesn't say anything, distracted by the shape of Luc's nose and the color of his eyes. He really is quite good-looking.

Luc stands, shaking his head, a deep frown distorting the handsomeness of his face. He wraps his hand around hers, dislodges the morphine button, and sets it somewhere too quickly for her to follow. He then disappears from view long enough for Elle to start thinking that she's been speaking to an apparition.

He returns, flanked by her parents.

"Ba," Elle murmurs. The world is turning hazy and soft, blurring like she's used her thumb to smudge all the lines. Somewhere inside her is a kernel of distrust, a hard pit she feels through the many stacked mattresses of the morphine. She presses on it, using it to hold on to the fleeing bits of her lucidity. She has to escape. If she talks to her parents, she doesn't know what'll happen.

"Luc?" she slurs. "Can you get Tony? Tell him I'll help?"

"Yes. I'll be right back." Luc's eyes tighten before he pivots to leave.

Elle turns to her parents. The sunlight frames their faces with gold. Her father smiles at her, and she's reminded of the times he'd praised her for helping Yìwú with his acupuncture techniques. She'd felt good, then. She feels good now.

Passing clouds cast fleeting shadows, dimming the room before it fills back up with sparkling, beauteous light. Her father keeps smiling at her.

Chapter Fifteen

*E*lle stands inside a doorway, out of breath, sharp aches ricocheting around her body from climbing up several sets of stairs. Like ripples in a pond that clash and join together, the pain escalates until everything hurts, from her toenails to the hair she hadn't the strength to tie back before signing herself out of the hospital this morning.

"You're very lucky. I was going to list this tomorrow." The tenant she's subletting from sweeps her arm in an arc, showing off the apartment. It's small and dingy, with scuffed wood floors and yellowing walls. To the right, there's a tiny card table shoved against frosted windows that open to the fire escape. In the oddly shaped far corner is a boxy fridge and a kitchenette, which has a sink, three inches of counter space, and a meager four-top gas range covered liberally with foil. Above that is a greasy hood, also covered in foil. The living room has a decent-sized TV on a rickety stand and a plastic-covered love seat of indeterminate color. There's a single plain bathroom and a bedroom down the hall. All told, it can't be more than 500 square feet. So much for Tony's sweet setup.

"Lucky?" Luc mutters. Elle feels the barest touch of his hand on her back, a signal to her that she can lean against him. She flinches away, the contact overwhelming, her nerves responding with a wave of pins and needles that cascades outward and turns her limbs into crackling static. She breathes out, on the verge of breaking down and crying.

"Yes, lucky for Chinatown. Come in." The tenant begins speaking in rapid-fire Cantonese.

Elle won't cry. She straightens, putting every complaint her body sends her into the trash can, and walks in. She reminds herself that coming to San Francisco to work in a Chinese medicine shop was her choice. It's preferable to recuperating in Tony's living room, or having her parents take her to the threshold of the home she's barred from entering so she can spend the rest of her truncated life being dutifully useful.

"Elle." Tony ahems.

"Yeah," Elle says. "I'm sorry, my Cantonese isn't good at all."

Tony grins and speaks to the tenant in excellent Cantonese, and the two share a laugh.

"No washer," the tenant tells her. She's exactly the kind of person Elle pictures when she thinks of a Chinese auntie, with round glasses and permed black hair, wearing khakis and a T-shirt underneath a fleece vest. She moves with purpose, wasting no motion. "Laundromat is down the street. No cable. Rent is three thousand a month."

"Three *what*?!" Elle splutters, turning to the auntie before she goes tight with pain. The woman is also the owner of the Chinese medicine shop downstairs and has been living in San Francisco for almost two decades. She might own the apartment at this point. "Three *thousand*? This space isn't worth half that!"

"Elle." Luc taps her on the shoulder, leaning in to murmur into her ear. "I can—"

She cuts him off with an angry shake of her head. Luc has no idea what he's doing, and she won't let the auntie prey on him. It's not his fault he doesn't understand the haggling process, but he's a liability just being present.

She draws herself up, ignoring the way her wounds scream, and turns back to the auntie. The pain adds an extra dimension of horror to her scowl, she's sure. Elle shakes a finger. "I heard housing prices were high, but this is ridiculous!"

"Ai," the auntie sighs. She's known as Dr. Ma to her patients, but Elle isn't a patient. "Aiyah. The youth are so entitled these days. But because you're doing me a favor, I can lower it for you. Twenty-eight hundred."

The *youth*? The auntie is the youth, not Elle. She counters. "Because I'm doing you a favor, twelve hundred."

"No can do. I have costs. You want me to go bankrupt?"

"You'll be in China, what do you care?" Elle fires back. She's already out of patience for this shit. "You want me to die of starvation because I can't afford to buy my own groceries? Look at me. I can barely walk. I left the hospital today. I've been stabbed four times and you want me to give up all my money and watch your store for you. You don't even have to train me. I could run your practice this second. I should have this apartment for free! If I die here, it's bad luck for you!"

"Eighteen hundred," Auntie Ma says tersely, "and you can reduce the store hours to four days a week while I'm gone."

"Deal." Elle takes a bank envelope out of her purse, pulls a wad of hundreds from it, and fans them out. She counts them out loud, then hands the stack over.

Auntie Ma's face creases with her smile. "Pleasure doing business with you."

"Same," Elle replies, grimacing in return.

Luc's call rune goes off, but he silences it within a ring. It's been doing that nonstop since he picked them up at the airport.

"Must be very important." Auntie Ma nods approvingly. "You're a big businessman, huh?"

"Somewhat," Luc replies.

"Ah, he's modest. Good, good." Auntie Ma addresses Elle again. "Feel free to have a look around. I'll be downstairs when you're ready to learn how things work."

Auntie Ma waits until Luc moves out of the doorway, then clomps her way down the stairs. The door to the outside shuts with a slam.

"Came in under market," Tony says with a grin, shaking his head. "Nice job."

"No thanks to you. You didn't negotiate with her?"

"I did, but she forgot. You got the best of her anyway."

Elle snorts. "Forgot, my ass." She slips off her sandals and winces as she goes to the sofa to sit. The plastic sheeting creaks. "She wasn't even trying that hard."

"You invoked the death and bad luck clause, that's why." Tony sits beside her.

Luc walks the perimeter of the apartment to inspect it, his face carefully neutral, which means he's annoyed.

"Hey," Tony calls out. "Your shoes."

Luc's rune goes off again. He frowns, leaving the room to take the call.

Elle clenches her teeth, willing the pain to subside. "Tony, I'm going to assume that your sweet setup is forthcoming. Because this isn't my idea of a sweet setup. It's a really not-sweet setup."

"The house hasn't sold yet, okay? Give me some time. You woke up yesterday. This is the best I could do under short notice."

"You told me a few months. A few is three."

"Did I say a few? I meant six. Or less."

Six months (or less) of being on her own in an unfamiliar city, running a shop, trying to figure out what to do with her life now that she's got no magic. Only one of those things is something she's familiar with. The rest? Fabulous. Wonderful.

"I'll visit you, I promise. Every day until I have to go back."

She sighs, weary. "Should we go downstairs?"

"How are you feeling?" Tony asks.

Elle sits on both her hands so he can't take her pulse. She holds her breath, wincing. "I'm fine."

"You should be resting."

"I'm *fine*. Can we go downstairs?" She sets her jaw, preparing herself to get up. It hurts the worst whenever she has to use the muscles in her torso.

"Just a moment." Luc comes back into the room and picks up a dining chair, bringing it over. He sets his folio in his lap, opening it. "We have some things for you."

"Oh yeah," Tony says, getting up to retrieve his messenger bag. "Okay, Lukey, you go first."

Luc shoots Tony a dirty look before he speaks. "I know this has never been high on the priority list for you, but it is for us." He withdraws a slender, pricey-looking phone. "All of our contact numbers are already on it, including my private number. Call that any time you want. I'll pick up."

"Even if you're at work?" Elle holds the phone gingerly, eyeing it with distrust. She's not sure what to do with it. It's probably too high-tech for her.

"Even if I'm at work."

Tony sulks. "You didn't give *me* your private number."

Without missing a beat, Luc says, "And I never will."

"How are we supposed to have heart-to-heart chats, then?"

"My suggestion is that we don't."

Normally Elle would find the exchange funny, but today it's irritating. "Tony?"

"You didn't say thank you."

She glares. "Shut up."

"Fine." Just like that, he turns his cavalier attitude off. "First, Lira says she's going to send you a package once she has your address. Don't ask, it's a surprise. Okay, my turn. I know this isn't your place, but a little bit of decoration will go a long way to making it feel more personal. So!" He hauls out a framed photograph of himself and shows it to her. "Ta-da!"

Elle glares again. Luc, on the other hand, snorts with laughter.

"I couldn't save the portrait you painted." Tony is dead serious, mournful even. "I'm really sorry about that. So I got you the next best thing until you can paint another."

"Tony, no."

"What do you mean, no? You're an artist and have always been. Even your boyfriend knows that. You've probably got a drawing of him hidden somewhere."

"*No.*" It's likely she won't get her art supplies back. Knowing that her brushes and ink and inkstones are gone is a blow Elle hasn't yet processed. As for Luc, things have been strained between them. A boyfriend he is not.

"Oh, quit. It ain't cute." Tony goes back to addressing Luc. "All the artwork you've seen in her workshop or her house, Elle's painted those."

She looks down at the phone in her hands, uncomfortable heat prickling over every inch of her skin. She wonders if she can give it back without looking too ungrateful. "That was a long time ago. I don't do that anymore."

"You should."

"I agree," Luc says.

"I don't want to talk about it." Elle sets the phone on the love seat, her mood galloping toward a cliff and plunging straight down. It's been doing that often, the negative feelings coming on her suddenly, forcing all other emotions away.

"Okay." Luc stands. "Let's go downstairs."

Elle pushes herself to standing using the arm of the love seat, glad that the fall of her unbound hair is hiding how her face contorts. She squares her shoulders, not wanting Tony and Luc to see her being sad. "Can you guys get my stuff while I'm down there? Please."

"Move you in? Yeah, sure." Tony stands. "It's just a couple of suit-cases."

"Yeah, but they're heavy."

Luc gives her a searching look, but follows Tony to the door. "We'll return soon."

"Okay. See you in a bit."

She sits back down once they leave, a few tears sliding down her cheeks. She wipes them away, gritting her teeth, not wanting a crying session to start. There are things to do on her list, and nowhere on it is hiding in the apartment, feeling sorry for herself. She needs to go downstairs and start learning the ins and outs of the store.

She feels sorry for herself anyway. Everything that's happened from the moment she woke up has been real, no matter how desper-ately she's wished for it to be a dream. Elle holds up a hand, the gray remnants of medical tape on the back of her palm grounding her in reality. She tries to make fire appear, concentrating so hard she gives herself a headache. *Maybe this time.*

Nope. She closes her eyes, praying to a god who can't hear her, begging to go to heaven, for a reversal, anything, as long as it's not what she currently has, which is nothing. Well, that's not exactly right. Elle has one thing: a hole inside her, a roaring emptiness that can't be filled. Physically, she isn't any different from when she did have magic, which is a betrayal. Her body hasn't changed; her qì still flows from the same place. She just can't harness it to make what she imagines into reality.

"Go downstairs," she mutters. Her eyelids pulse in time to the throb of her headache. It's the kind that saps all energy and puts itself in front like a tall person blocking the view at a movie theater. "One thing at a time. Downstairs. Work."

Elle swears she'll rest for only a minute, but when she next opens her eyes, she's met with thick beams of afternoon light and the feeling of her bandages sticking to her stitches.

A chair scrapes across the floor. Tony sets his phone on the table and says, "You're up. Sleep well?"

Elle smears her hand across her face, blinking slow and unsure. "How long?"

"A few hours. We just finished putting your stuff away."

"Luc?" She thinks she hears him, but it could be her imagination.

"On the phone in the bedroom." Tony supports her as she sits up. "You need to change your dressings. Can you do that on your own?"

Elle has no idea. "Yeah."

「胡說。」 He slings an arm around her uninjured side, shuffling with her to the bathroom where he makes her sit, chattering at her as he peels off bandages. "The secret is rubbing alcohol. Keep the area clean and dry, okay? Your back is the most healed, but you'll still need at least a week."

"I know what to do." She swallows, light-headed, as Tony dabs at her stitches. "You don't have to—"

"Shut up," he interrupts her pleasantly. "Let me be your big brother for five minutes. Then I'll get out of your hair so you can rest."

Elle hobbles out of the bathroom when Tony is done, finding Luc seated on the couch, legs crossed ankle to knee. Resting on his thigh is a tablet computer, and nestled around his ear is his call rune. He's so focused on what he's doing that he doesn't notice her. She watches him for a minute, observing how he's reclined against the couch cushion, how he's alert and keyed into his task. He's speaking German, probably, and sounds unmistakably like someone in command.

It would be easier for him to be in the office, with all his resources available, instead of working remotely from her crappy apartment. He can't be limiting his ability to work if he wants to win time off from Oberon. It's her fault he's here.

Luc glances at her and ends his call.

Guilt gnaws at her. "You didn't have to."

He shakes his head. "It isn't a critical situation yet. They don't need me."

But she does, apparently.

"I've stocked your kitchen. Your dinner is in the refrigerator." Luc gets to his feet, stowing his tablet in his folio, pocketing his rune. "I've also taken the liberty of setting up a meal service for the next couple of weeks. I hope the selection is to your taste. You have fresh linens in the bedroom and closet, and your bed is made."

She fidgets, dropping her eyes to the floor. "Thank you. You've done a lot."

He frowns at her, his dissatisfaction evident. "It's a start. You've already paid your rent, but I can look into better accommodations for you next month. Or a helper, perhaps, until you regain your strength."

"No." Elle doesn't know what a helper would do for her, and she doesn't want anyone around. "You've done more than enough. I really appreciate it."

She looks at everything in the room but him, unsure what to do next.

"Oh-kay, I think that's it for today." Tony breaks in, saving Elle. He gives her a careful look before putting on his shoes. "Your meds are on the counter. Take them with food. I'll be back tomorrow, okay? Go rest. Lukey, you coming?"

"In a minute. Go without me."

An awkward silence stretches between them as Luc waits for Tony to exit the building. Elle stretches it out further, not shutting the apartment door, her eyes lowered to avoid Luc's gaze. The overhead lights cast her shadow, faint and watery, across her threshold, and that's how she imagines she looks: magic-less and broken, a ghostly husk of herself.

Finally, he says, "Do you want me to stay with you tonight?"

Last week, in the oasis, Elle's impulse would have been yes. Yes to long nights and mornings after; yes to fresh omelets and jokes and his secret, warm smile. Now it's no because she isn't herself any longer, and on top of that, she's injured and needy. He's had a long day and is probably as tired as she is, but he's too polite to ditch her. Therefore, he's doing his due diligence before he extricates himself.

Elle turns so hot with shame she begins sweating. Outside, the sounds of cars and passersby grow unbearably loud.

She must take too long to answer, because Luc gathers her close to him, kissing the top of her head. That gesture alone is enough to start her trembling. Any more and she's going to fall apart.

He lays his cheek against hers. Instantly, pain of a different kind strikes through her. Skies, she can't take it. It's too intimate an action for the relationship they have. He has to leave before she starts crying.

Luc's voice drops into the private, gentle tone that renders her defenseless. "I know it's been difficult for you, even if you try to tell us you're okay."

"I am, I swear." She doesn't return his embrace, refusing to bend herself to him, trying to preserve the distance she's worked hard to cultivate.

"You almost died over the weekend."

"See, and I'm alive. I got better."

"Elle," he chides her.

"Luc," she chides him right back. "You don't have to worry about me. I bet you're exhausted. You've already done a lot, and I can take it from here myself." Alone, without the nagging feeling that he's here because of a misplaced sense of duty.

"You can hardly move without wincing. I'll stay."

Elle refuses again. "Really, you don't have to. You've been very thorough, but you aren't responsible for me. The case is closed."

That lands. Luc looks at her in dismay, hurt in his eyes. "This has nothing to do with the case."

"Doesn't it, though? I was part of it, wasn't I?" She's being unreasonable, but there's nothing the reasonable side of her can do. Reasonable Elle is locked in another room, pounding on the door and shrieking at her to stop. "You don't have to pretend, or use me for information, or do what you think you need to do to make it up to me. I forgive you. It's done. I've got nothing left."

"What?" Luc pauses, a telltale sign that he is feeling more emotions than he's willing to express. "I *want* to stay. I'm not asking you for anything but your permission. I'm here because I care for you."

She tries to push away, but she's too feeble to break out of his arms. The movement causes a whiff of his scent to rise, and Elle stops, her throat constricting. That's not fair. *Nothing* is fair.

"Elle, look at me please. I'll go if you demand it, but I want to stay."

She tries to say no, but her traitor mouth refuses to obey her. It seems Reasonable Elle has picked the lock and assumed direct control. "Okay," she says instead. Her brain chimes in with a backing argument. She's given him plenty of opportunities to leave and he hasn't taken them. Maybe he really does want to be here.

Elle sighs at the flutter of hope and allows herself to rest her head on his shoulder. He responds with his own sigh, his muscles relaxing against hers.

Luc's call rune chimes.

His body tenses in an instant. Neither of them moves.

The rune chimes again.

"I'm sorry," Luc whispers. "Elle, I'm really—I'm so sorry." He steps away from her, the call rune appearing as if by magic in his hand. He fits it to his ear as he strides toward the bedroom.

Elle's heart plummets through her rib cage, past her stomach, and lands on the floor with a wet plop. She stands there, her body hollowing out, the walls of her apartment closing in on her, Luc's voice distant and unintelligible. Of course this would happen. It was foolish of her to think otherwise.

Luc apologizes again when he comes back. "I have to go in. The situation turned critical more quickly than I anticipated."

"It's okay," Elle says, subdued. She shouldn't have gotten her hopes up. She shouldn't be surprised, or hurt, or mad, or feeling any kind of emotion. Luc isn't her boyfriend, or anything long-term. He's a friendly ex-client who has been upfront with her about why he's a terrible prospect. At the time, Elle hadn't understood what it meant because it hadn't impacted her life.

If she could flake off and crumble into ash, she would. She'll always be secondary to his job. Secondary to his boss, who has the knowledge of Luc's truename, who can use that power at any time. Secondary to service to the agency, which forms the sum of Luc's life. Second. Never first.

There is absolutely nothing Elle can do to change that. Her heart, already cracked, gives up trying to hold itself together, and falls apart. "It's work. I get it. You're pretty important."

"You are also important," Luc says, narrowing his eyes at her.

"No, it's fine." Disappointment scours her insides bright and clean, reflecting clarity back at her. She knows what to do: end it, send him away, allow him to excel at his job so he can gain the grace to find a cure. That is, above all, the most important task for him. There's no room for her to be selfish. She'll get by on her own.

"Go," she says, stepping aside. "It's okay. I'm pretty tired and all I want to do is go to bed."

He kneels to put on his shoes. "I'll come back as soon as I'm done."

She shakes her head, trying to ignore the twinges in her chest. It's really unfair how there's no upper limit to pain, no end to the number of tears she can shed. "No. I'll be asleep soon, and you don't have a key. Even if you did, there's no place for you to sleep. Just, um."

She's already devastated, so this won't hurt as much. "Don't bother."

Luc's hands still. Elle watches him process her words before he breathes out, his shoulders slumping.

Eventually he says, "I understand. I'll see you at another time. Sooner rather than later, I hope."

Elle stands wordless and stiff, her insides feeling like grinding glass.

Luc touches his fingertips to her cheek. "Be well, my heart."

Whatever expression he has on his face, she misses. She can't look at him. It's game over if she does. "Bye," Elle chokes out, then shoves the door closed and escapes to the bathroom, where it's okay to get everything wet.

Luc squeezes his eyes shut and stands on the landing, his fingers curling into claws as he tries to retain control of his calm. He hears Elle's receding footsteps followed by the slam of a door, and right then he almost barges in to stay with her. She's far from okay and shouldn't be left alone.

Anger stretches him tight like a steel string, with each breath bringing him closer to snapping. For a second, he wonders why he doesn't quit his job. All he'd need to do is walk into Oberon's office to tender his resignation. Ah yes, then Oberon would use the Right of Dominion to ban Luc from leaving.

He exhales noisily in lieu of a scream and rattles down the stairs, trying to figure out when he might return, but it's of little comfort. The damage is done, and he's facilitated it. What he needs to do is mitigate that damage and prove himself.

As he exits the building, he's greeted by a low whistle. It's Tony. He's leaning against the wall separating the storefront and the building door, a hand in the pocket of his leather bomber jacket, the other holding a cigarette. He takes a drag and blows a cloud of smoke into Luc's face.

"Not even ten minutes. She kicked you out with a quickness."

"I got a work call. I aim to come back." He narrows his eyes at the cigarette, then at Tony. He doesn't care for the smell of smoke, although he's conditioned to it. "Keep that out of the apartment."

"I plan to. It's just an experiment." Tony grinds out the cigarette and flicks it away. "We need to talk."

"About what." Luc retrieves the car keys and unlocks the doors.

"My sister, what else?" Tony slides himself into the passenger seat. "I'll get right to the point. How serious are you about her?"

"I don't understand the question." He jams the key into the ignition and starts the car, then takes half a second to calm down, thinking about how he'll have to research housing in San Francisco at some point in the day. Luc hits the turn signal and merges smoothly into traffic.

Tony arranges himself casually in his seat. "I think you understand it fine. How serious are you? I've seen how you look at each other. I'm going to assume the rumors about you aren't true, because what you allegedly did is a total dealbreaker and Elle wouldn't associate with someone like that."

Luc keeps his expression still, the car jumping as he taps the accelerator to make it through a yellow light. "I'm serious."

Tony snorts. "Does she know that?"

"I hope so."

"I wouldn't be surprised if she didn't, because you sure aren't acting like it."

Luc's hands tighten on the wheel, his anger returning. Tony's accuracy is deadly.

"You need to figure out what your priorities are. Is it work, or is it Elle? She's too nice to say anything about you taking calls and leaving her when she needs you. Unfortunately for you, I'm a dick."

"You're her brother, and she needs your support as well."

"Don't deflect. She has it and she knows she has it because it's been the two of us against the world for almost thirty years and I'm loyal as hell. You, on the other hand, she doesn't know about. If you're serious about her, you need to show it. No half-assing. She deserves the best, and if you aren't willing to do that, you can kindly fuck off. She'll get over you eventually." Tony reaches into the inside pocket of his jacket. "Oh yeah, forgot to mention."

Luc throws a warning glare and growls, "Don't smoke in the car. This is company property."

"That's hot. Yes, *zaddy.*" Tony bites the tip of his index finger, coy.

Luc's eye twitches. "Call me that again and I will toss you out of this vehicle into a busy intersection. I know you won't die, so it's worth the peace I'll get."

Tony sighs. "Fine. Where was I? Right. I forgot to mention." His expression shifts, and suddenly he's exuding murderous intent, his dark eyes as keen as the edge of a blade. "If you hurt my sister, I'll kill you myself. Then I'll find your spirit in the afterlife and kill you again. Understand?"

This is the most dangerous Luc has ever seen Tony. If the stars had aligned, he would have made an excellent Fixer. "I understand."

"I want her to survive this," Tony continues. "I want her to thrive. I don't want to get a call that she's gone splat on the sidewalk because she thinks the only way out is to jump. If I didn't have my family breathing down my neck, I'd move in with her and babysit her the way she did for me. But I can't be there as much as I want to, and neither can Lira. This is a team effort. If you're serious, you need to do more than give her a phone she's terrified of using, then run out on her."

They make the rest of the short drive without speaking. Luc pulls into a parking space in the garage and cuts the engine, hunting for all the places in his schedule when he can be with Elle. There aren't enough. There can be, if he makes a new deal with Oberon.

Luc gets out of the car, addressing Tony over the roof of it. "There are things you don't understand about my relationship with the agency that Elle does. I'm not making an excuse for myself. Ask her about it the next time you see her. I will do my part on my end."

"That's not good enough." That dangerous look is back. "I need something concrete."

"You'll have it soon."

"You should have just said you don't know what to do yet, but you're figuring it out. Give me your phone number so we can coordinate."

A staring contest ensues.

"Come on, we've already had the heart-to-heart."

Luc doesn't blink.

"Give me your phone number, or you're headed to beatdown town in three seconds. I remember your file, I know what you can do. You don't know what my new powers are. You willing to take that chance?"

He grits his teeth, a muscle jumping in his jaw. "Hand over your phone." Naturally, Tony's phone background is a photo of himself. Luc inputs his number and returns the phone. "Abuse this privilege and you'll regret it."

"Sure. Good talk, Lukey. Looking forward to our texts." Tony grins at him, blows him a kiss, and saunters off.

Chapter Sixteen

*E*lle eyes the open parcel on her table as if it contains a five-pace snake, maintaining a healthy distance of at least ten feet in case it bites her. She cranes her neck to peer inside it again to check if the contents have changed, but they remain the same: a set of four new brushes and a rack, a heavy grinding stone, a stick of ink, and a roll of rice paper.

"Well?" Lira asks over the phone. "I know these aren't your old ones, but I thought you could start fresh. Surprise!"

Oh yeah, Elle's surprised. "Thank you."

"You probably aren't ready for them yet, but you can't go without your art stuff. It's been almost two weeks. How're you feeling today?"

She couldn't get the stove to light on the first try and she's cried into her tea so much that it's salty, but at least her stitches are out. "Great. A lot better."

"Elle, you know how you're really shitty at lying?"

She answers with trepidation. "Yeah?"

"Turn on your camera."

"What?" She pulls the phone away from her ear. "No! I don't even know how to do that!" She yelps, startled, as Lira's face pops up on the screen.

"There's an icon of a video camera. Tap that."

There are dozens of icons, many of them at the top of the screen. Somehow, Elle finds the video camera button, then almost drops the phone at the sight of her own face. She screams a little. "How do I turn it off?!"

"I swear to every god, even my parents know more about technology than you do. You are not doing better. When is Tony getting there?"

"In the afternoon."

"Good. I'm sorry I haven't been around too much. I'm gonna visit you soon, I swear. Before I go, show me around. Tony told me it was, and I quote, 'shitty.'"

He isn't wrong. Elle holds the phone with both hands and gives Lira a tour. "It's a good price. This is a super in-demand area. Here's the bedroom. I have a closet."

"Whoa, a whole-ass closet. You're living the high life now. Heard you bargained down the landlord."

Elle scowls. "I should have made her go lower. Hold on, I need to get dressed." She wiggles into a pair of jeans and a shirt. "Lira, you still there?"

"Yep."

"Lemme show you the store." Elle locks up, then goes out the main door and into the shop door to her immediate left, sidestepping the large orange cat that's been hanging around for a week. She likes to think they're buddies. "Okay. What do you think?"

"Welp," Lira says, sucking on her teeth. "It's a store, all right. It's very . . ."

"Disorganized?" Elle suggests. The store looks narrow on account of all the jars crammed onto shelves and the square bins clumped in the middle of the floor, creating a fire hazard. Add to that the low tables for tea and a glass display counter for the expensive medicines, and the store is the definition of high-density chaos. "I've got a lot of work to keep me busy."

"Good. That's good. You need that right now. Take some time to paint too." Lira looks away, past the screen. "Shit, I've got a customer. Been busy here without you, and I'm thinking of retiring. I'll talk to you about it later."

"Retiring?"

"Yeah. It's not the same without you. But I gotta go. I'll call you later, bye!"

"Bye." Elle pokes around for the hang-up button, then goes back upstairs, powers the phone off, and chucks the thing under her bed before returning to the store.

Auntie Ma arrives and puts Elle to work, perching on a stool behind the glass counter as she barks orders. She's leaving for China in a few days, and Elle will have to run the store on her own. Despite a headache and her difficulty concentrating, Elle does everything she's tasked with and doesn't complain. She spends the morning filling online orders and running errands, which helps her learn the layout and topography of Chinatown. The cat meows at her each time she leaves and comes back, purring loudly when she pets him. He follows her into the store.

"Auntie Ma!"

"What?" Auntie Ma yells from the back.

"Is this your cat?"

"What cat?"

"This cat! He came in." Maybe he's a shapeshifter customer. Elle hasn't seen any fae yet, and as a mundane she might not be able to see them, but there is a robust community in San Francisco.

Auntie Ma comes out, jaw working around a mouth full of noodles. "Not my cat. Get it out. It's dirty."

The cat looks rather clean and well fed, but has no collar. It twines around Elle's legs, chirping at her like it's begging to stay.

"Ugh." Auntie Ma opens the door and grabs a broom, shooing the cat out.

The rest of the day passes as a contradiction, time sprinting by when customers arrive, moving through arctic waters when no one's around. That's when she's reminded of everything she's lost, and that emptiness yawns itself open and beckons her in. Elle wipes away tears as she tidies, not hearing the jingling of the bell on the door.

"Now *that's* not going to attract any customers."

Elle spins around. "Tony?"

"You should smile more." He grins before smothering her in a hug.

She glares and sniffles extra loudly. "What are you doing here?"

"Is that any way to greet your family? Hey, Auntie Ma!" Tony switches into Cantonese and hollers something. She responds, also hollering.

"Sweet. Let's go, you're off for the day." He takes Elle's arm.

Elle jerks away, then groans as her wounds protest. "What are you doing?"

"Taking you to early dinner. You didn't pick up when I called. Are you gonna adopt that cat? He followed you home and has been here for days. He's probably decided he owns you."

"Auntie Ma said no cats, so that means no cats." Elle rubs at her face, then sighs heavily. "Why are you here again?"

"Checking on you, like I do every day. Where's your phone?"

"Told you I was fine."

"And I told you that you can't lie to me. You've *never* been able to lie to me. Where's your phone?"

"Somewhere in the apartment." It's half a lie, so Tony will halfway believe her.

"You don't even know? Good lord, Elle. Okay, let's go get your phone, and we'll go eat."

"I'm not hungry."

"That's cute. You think I care." Tony herds her out the door, grabbing her keys on the way, and practically drags her up the stairs. "Where's the phone?"

In keeping with the theme, Elle gives him half a shrug. He rolls his eyes at her and starts opening drawers and cabinets, checking behind and under things. Elle folds her arms and waits in the middle of the living room, not saying a word.

After a good five minutes of searching, Tony emerges triumphant from the bedroom. "Got it! You could have just told me where it was. Okay, I'm gonna need you to turn this on and leave it on."

His sunny attitude is grating and makes Elle wish for the morning fog to return. "Why?" she asks, pointed.

"Because if you pick up, it means you're alive," Tony answers, just as pointed.

Elle's lips flatten into a line. No crying in front of others, she tells herself. It's her new motto. *No crying, no crying, no crying.*

Tony places the phone in her hand. "Turn it on."

She glares at him, sullen. "I see you every day. I don't need the phone."

"It's a nice phone, real expensive. Turn it the fuck on."

When she doesn't move, Tony moves her fingers for her, squeezing them over the correct button. The phone powers on and dings several times, then begins flashing blue.

"Okay. You're leaving that on and charged. If I call, or Lira calls, or Luc calls, and we find that the phone is off, we're showing up to raise hell."

Luc. He's unlikely to call, and with her phone mostly off, there's little chance of them reconnecting. She thinks of him more often than she should, enough times that she should be conditioned to the pain. She isn't. "Why Luc."

"Why not Luc? Haven't you talked to him?"

"No."

Tony groans. "Really? How can you be this smart and this stupid at the same time?"

Elle glares again.

"Check your messages while we walk to dinner. Should be a good Thai place a few blocks away."

She has no idea how to check her messages as she's never had any except for on the store's answering machine, so she puts the phone in her back pocket and follows Tony, resigned to his company.

"You have no idea how to check your messages, do you?" he says once they're seated at a table, his own phone in his hands.

Elle would rather say nothing than open her mouth and tell Tony how useless she is, so she keeps quiet as Tony orders for them both.

"Hand over your phone, I'll get it set up for you. God, you did yourself no favors while you were hiding from the world." Tony swipes and taps the screen with both thumbs. "There. I put everything on the home page so you can get to it easy. How did you not know you missed calls? It says right here. Texts too."

He peers at the phone, grins, then gives it back to Elle. "Who's *Looshin?*"

She tilts her head, not understanding, and looks at the screen. There are two missed calls and a text message from someone named Lucien.

Elle throws the phone on the table like it's on fire, her eyes wide, the blood draining from her face. "I don't think you were meant to see that," she manages.

Tony snickers, taking a sip of his water. "If you'd kept your phone on like you were supposed to, this wouldn't have happened. Anyway, that aside—I won't tell him I know—I've been meaning to have a talk with you about life after your jade. Because there is life after it." Tony rubs his hands together in anticipation as their food arrives, sending the waiter off with a wink and his thanks.

She's got no appetite. Elle stares at the plate. "I don't want it."

"Yeah, I figured. But you know there's life after it. I'm sitting in front of you as proof. Oh man, the food's pretty good. You should try some."

Elle shakes her head, still staring at her plate.

"Listen. Get yourself past this phase, which is when you're super depressed and everything you do reminds you of what you used to have, and you wish things didn't happen the way they did."

He's got her attention now. "I don't remember that happening to you."

"Because it didn't."

"What the fuck, Tony."

"I did grieve over not being able to talk to our ancestors." Tony's voice gentles. "That did happen. I did wish things hadn't happened the way they did. Who doesn't? I wished I'd never gone through that. It sucked, and what you're going through sucks. But I was glad to be free."

"Because our family thought you were dead."

"Exactly. I was sad, but that's not the same as being depressed. I'm too selfish for it. I realized I could go and do all kinds of things I couldn't do before. Because I think of myself as the most awesome, I was ready to be awesome in my new life. You could use some of that."

Elle's brows furrow. "Thinking you're awesome?"

"That too, but thinking of yourself as awesome and deserving."

"Of what?"

"Life. Being happy. Chasing your dreams." A grin. "Sounds cheesy, but it's true. Life is a gift, 妹妹. The good and the bad. You showed me that. Can't appreciate the good without the bad. You've had a lot of bad. You've gotta be ready for the good."

She shakes her head. "I don't think I'm ever going to be ready."

Tony chews and swallows. "You need time. One day in the future you'll wake up and feel like the grief is a little further away than it was the day before. That's recovery. It helps to set some goals. What do you want to do with your life?"

Elle's eyes sting, and before she can think about not crying, two tears fall directly onto her pad see ew. "I don't know what I want."

"I know what *someone* wants," Tony says under his breath.

"What was that?"

"Nothing. You can choose anything, be anything."

More tears. "I don't know who I am anymore."

"You're you and you've been you." Tony says it with a confidence that's alien to her. "You're my kick-ass, brilliant sister who thought she had to pretend to be someone she wasn't. You not only survived something that'd kill most people, but you were gutsy enough to do it voluntarily. Now you're my kick-ass, brilliant sister with nothing holding her back. Absolutely nothing, right? The world is your oyster and you should steam it and serve it with black bean sauce."

"Has anyone ever told you," Elle says, dabbing at her eyes with her napkin, "that you're terrible at this?"

"Yes, you. The house is under contract, so you'll have money soon. You've got a life ahead of you and you're healing up and if you wanted to, you could find someone and settle down."

Elle thinks about the Luc-shaped elephant in the room. "There aren't any mundanes who'd believe . . ." She gestures at Tony, then herself. "This."

"You could just lie. People build whole lives on lies all the time."

It's meant to be reassuring, but it doesn't work. Elle cries harder. "I'm so bad at lying!"

"Then don't. As it so happens, there's someone who already knows all about you."

Elle drops her gaze to the table. It blurs before her eyes. "It didn't . . . work out."

Tony sucks air through his teeth. "Yikes. It's worse than I thought."

"Is everything okay over here?" Their waiter cuts in, wearing his customer service smile poorly. "Everything taste okay?"

Tony, on the other hand, wears his smile well although Elle knows he hates being interrupted. "It's great, thanks! Could we get a box and the check?"

They walk back to her apartment afterward. Tony is absorbed with his phone, sending and receiving messages nonstop, leaving Elle in blissful silence. Once they're at her door he puts the phone away, then accompanies her upstairs, stowing the leftovers in the fridge.

"Look, Elle." He sighs. "You probably won't believe me, but this is not the worst thing that could happen to you. Have patience with yourself. You didn't give up on me, so you shouldn't give up on you. Accept help. And really do stuff because you want to, not because you think you have to. I'm gonna give you a homework assignment from the Book of Tony and I'm checking your work when I get back."

"Get back from . . . ?" The Book of Tony. What shit.

"Family stuff. Big meeting has been called. All-hands-on-deck sort of thing."

As if on cue, the tears start up again. "Do I have to be there?"

Tony looks at her, studying her as if he's weighing her soul, all traces of playfulness gone. That's the real Tony, quiet and perceptive, and if he has showed up, the situation is dire. "Do you want to be there? We'll be discussing you."

She doesn't answer, doesn't know how. Her parents are likely furious with her, but they're still her parents. Her mother is correct. Family is all they have.

Tony hums. "That's what I thought."

"How mad are they?"

He chuckles, shaking his head. "Pretty mad. You dangled the biggest carrot in front of their faces and pulled a disappearing act. They are of course blaming you and not themselves. They're annoyed at me because I keep saying I don't know where you are. They really, really want that carrot."

"You'll just make them more annoyed if you keep pretending."

"That is entirely the point. I'll run interference until I can't anymore. I'll give you a heads-up when that happens. I predict there will be strategizing at the meeting, and I wouldn't be surprised if they came back with a counteroffer. It's some real 琅琊榜 shit, but I'm 梅长苏."

It's shocking Tony knows what it is, but not shocking he fancies himself as handsome and smart as Hú Gē's character. "You watched that?"

"Literally everyone watched that."

"You don't like period dramas."

"It was all anyone could talk about when it was airing, so I had to watch it. Like that thrones show. Anyway, don't think about that. Book of Tony, got it? Here's your homework: Be selfish."

"Be selfish?"

"Yes. Be selfish. Quit telling yourself no and start telling yourself yes. If that inner voice of yours says no, you can't have this, you tell it to shut the fuck up and say yes instead. Understand?"

No. "Yes."

"I've gotta go and start prepping. Lira's gonna take over daily check-ins."

Elle frowns. "You make it sound like I can't be left alone."

He points at her. "Ding! Because you can't. By the way, Luc's gonna be here every Friday at six p.m. starting this week."

Elle blinks, horror sheeting over her. "Today's Friday."

"Yep. And it's six o'clock!" Before Elle can react, Tony gives her a quick hug and a cheerful *baibai~* and is out the door, thumping down the stairs.

"Tony, wait!" Elle shouts, grabbing the doorframe, pivoting onto the landing. "No!"

Too late. All Elle sees is Tony's retreating back and a flash of daylight, followed by Luc's tall, familiar figure outlined in the doorway.

She stares at him, frozen with dread.

He returns her gaze, his expression hopeful, soft. "I said to you I'd come back as soon as I was done. Here I am."

Every stair Luc climbs ratchets up Elle's anxiety until, by the time he reaches her, she's a shaking ball of panic, ready to do something drastic like crash through the windows by the fire escape and fall to her death. She can't be here. Or he can't be here. Whatever it is, they can't be in the same space together.

"May I come in?"

Her voice sounds so small, so pitiful. "What if I say no?"

"Then," Luc replies seriously, "I will have no choice but to camp on your doorstep tonight and try again tomorrow morning."

"You wouldn't."

The determination on his face tells her that yes, he would.

"Okay. You can come in. Just for a minute, though. I'm . . ." Any excuse will do at this point. ". . . getting ready to wash my hair and go to bed."

"I'll take that minute."

She steps back, keeping her eyes on the floor. Luc shuts the door behind him and kneels to unlace his shoes. She puts more distance between them when he stands, retreating to the love seat. She has to get rid of him, and fast.

"Are you okay?"

Elle's mouth tightens, doing its best to hold in the swell of her emotions. "I'm fine. You can check off all the boxes. I have food and I sleep eight hours a night and I'm doing better. Thank you, you've had your minute. You can go now."

"According to Tony, you aren't fine."

The two of them teaming up had been, until this moment, an impossibility. "You talked to him?"

"He messaged me. We've been keeping in touch."

"On your private number?"

He lets out a long-suffering sigh. "Yes."

Elle smiles, though there's no humor in it. "Looks like he got what he wanted."

"We share a mutual goal, so it was the logical thing to do."

"Ah," Elle says, and a bit of emotion leaks out. Seems like bitterness is first in line today. "To make sure I'm getting better?"

He looks like he's choosing his words carefully. "That's a part of it."

"Well, job done. I'm fine, see? Obligation fulfilled. Go chase your dreams."

"I'm here, and you aren't an obligation."

"Yes, I am," she snaps. Oops. Anger shoulders its way forward. "You are repaying a debt you think you owe me. It's been repaid. I'm fine. Here's your change, have a nice day. Leave me alone. Go back to work or something."

Elle is so sick of crying, but it seems her eyes aren't. Curse her traitorous eyes.

Luc looks away for a moment. "You have my deepest apologies for that. It won't happen again. I've left explicit instructions not to contact me between Friday evening and Saturday morning, Pacific time."

"That sounds specific," Elle replies. Nastiness steps up, taking its turn. "Enough time for a booty call?"

Luc narrows his eyes. "Elle, stop."

"Aren't I a bit far for you? I'm sure you can find someone willing much closer to home."

"I said stop."

"Then again, maybe I'm the perfect candidate because unlike other humans, I can keep your secrets—"

"That's enough."

"—and I'll be out of the picture soon, and you can move on to someone better!"

Luc steps forward, his eyes a burning blue. "I said *enough*!"

Elle shuts her mouth. She hears her tears hitting the floor.

"If you were only an obligation, I'd be out the door already. But I'm still here even though you are being a complete shit right now."

She folds her arms tight across her body and hunches her shoulders. "Runs in the family."

"So it seems."

The nastiness bleeds away, leaving room for resignation. "What do you want, then?"

"I want to be sure you can recover and have a fulfilling life, whatever that means for you."

Elle lifts her head, challenging him. "Even if you aren't in it?"

His jaw flares. Quietly, Luc says, "Regardless of whether I am in it."

There it is.

"I'm glad," Elle says eventually, "that we're on the same page on that topic."

The silence bears down on them, heavy. Elle looks resolutely away.

Footsteps approach. "I didn't say I didn't want to be in your life, Elle. I very much do."

"What for?" Elle says, her voice small. She uses her arm to swipe away tears. "What for? I'm nothing. I can't do anything for you. Before, I could at least make things for you. Now I'm just a weird, hot mess who can't fit in anywhere and will die way before you. You thought you were the terrible prospect?"

She sniffles, then starts laughing wildly, which is difficult because she can't get a good breath. "It's me. It's me! I'm the real terrible prospect. It was me the whole time. Elle, that's not even my *name*, the terrible prospect. Hi, nice to meet you, I'm Jiāng Yíyǎ, but you can call me Terrible Prospect!"

She breaks down, shoulders sagging, completely defeated. Elle covers her face with her hands and sobs into them.

Instead of replying, Luc steps near and wraps his arms around her in a tight hug, closing himself around her as if to shield her. He's steady and secure as he offers himself to her, undemanding. The simple act of his touch brings with it comfort, and a promise of safe harbor.

She sags against him as she weeps, her mouth open and slack against his shirt. This time, unlike all the other times, she doesn't tell herself not to cry. This time, as the grief rises high enough to drown her, Elle gives herself wholly to it. Within the protective circle of Luc's arms, Elle surrenders and mourns, her body shaking with the strength of her sobs.

When her knees buckle, Luc doesn't waver, supporting her as he maneuvers her onto the love seat. Elle calms down for as long as it takes him to sit beside her with a box of tissues. She promptly tucks her face into his neck and ugly cries for a good, long time.

She finally subsides, dazed and exhausted, listless with catharsis. Luc holds her in the waning light, and after a while, murmurs, "Nice to meet you. I'm Lucien, also a terrible prospect."

Elle manages a pathetic laugh.

"You can call me Luc. After hundreds of years, I have found the only other terrible prospect who understands me. She's brave and funny, but she thinks she's only valued for what she can do instead of who she is. After a traumatic life event, she's convinced I don't want her. I have no useful skills to benefit her and a job that constantly disrupts my life. I am also going to outlive her by at least a hundred years."

"Yeah," Elle mumbles. "That's pretty terrible."

"Maybe even two hundred."

She makes a face. Skies, her eyes are raw. Better to keep them shut. "Don't rub it in. You can join the club. The San Francisco chapter of Terrible Prospects International."

Luc laughs softly. "What's the first order of business?"

She doesn't even think, she's so tired. "Get pizza?"

He laughs again. "And after that?"

"Sleep."

"The junior member would like to amend the motion on the floor."

"The, uh. Chair. Recognizes the junior member."

"I would like to finish the discussion of our relationship before we get pizza."

Elle cracks one eye open. "Are you extorting me?"

"No," he replies. "If I were extorting you, I would say no pizza unless we talk about us. Are you ready to be reasonable?"

"Was I being—" Elle clicks her mouth shut at seeing Luc's sudden, ferocious glare. "Yes, sir."

He lifts an eyebrow, but continues. "I hope I've made it clear that I do want you in my life. Do you want me in yours? Yes or no answers only."

"Yes, but—"

"Yes or no only."

There's no fight left in her, so the truth comes out. Besides, if she says no, she'll have to get up and leave the warmth of his body, the soothing familiarity of his scent. She hasn't the energy for that. "Yes."

"Okay. I'm glad. Now for the rest." Luc shifts, pushing Elle upright bit by bit. "Please sit up, my arm is asleep."

Elle groans; the plastic creaks as she readjusts. "Sorry."

"Might I ask you a question?"

"Sure."

His eyes search hers. "Why do you like me?"

Elle blinks, taken aback. "Because you're you. You're sweet and funny."

"Are you aware that I am a security expert and am the best-rated, most in-demand Fixer at the agency?"

"Uh, I probably could have guessed since you're the boss's favorite and all."

"Did you know I am fluent in seven languages?"

"Sort of?"

"Do you like me for those skills?"

She sees where this is going and doesn't like it. "No."

"So why would you think I like you for the things you did or the skills you have, and not for who you are?"

With effort, Elle scowls. "You're really going to make me say this?"

"Yes, I am."

"Is this payback for last week?"

A fond smirk plays over his lips. "Perhaps. Go on."

"What was the question again?"

The smirk widens. "Why do you think I like you for the products and services you provide, as opposed to your personality?"

There's no answering a trick question, though it's more of a rhetorical one. "Because I'm a shit."

It takes Luc by surprise. He throws his head back, laughing, eyes crinkling at the corners.

She feels thoroughly ashamed of herself and how she's treated him. "I'm sorry for being a shit."

"Apology accepted. As long as you work on seeing yourself as a person and not a vending machine."

Elle blows out a breath. "I can't make any promises."

"Any time you need a reminder, I will be happy to provide you with one." Luc holds out his hand, and she takes it.

As the light fades, Elle thinks about how he's turned her around, how he's de-escalated with his humor and steadfastness a situation that could have spun out of control. She thinks about how natural it is to be with him, how easy and uncomplicated. He isn't uncomfortable with witnessing the worst crying jag of her life. He isn't judging her for being emotional or telling her how to cope or pitying her for being weak. He's just sitting with her on the couch in a companionable silence, asking for nothing, ready to give her whatever she needs.

"Luc?"

"Mm?"

"Thank you for being here for me. Even if I'm a shit."

He squeezes her hand. "You're welcome, despite you being a shit."

"I'm sorry I've been so stupid. Thank you so much for putting up with me."

He laughs at her. "It hasn't been the easiest—"

"Hey!"

"—but you're welcome. And you aren't stupid. Thank you for putting up with me as well. You didn't have to let me in. I'm very sorry for hurting you."

"So we're just going to try working things out? With your job and all that?"

He closes his eyes briefly. "My job is something I need to work out, not us. If I may, I'd like to request some time to put plans in motion. So that when I'm here, you can have my undivided attention."

"What if . . ." Elle glances away, unsure of how to broach the topic. Anything more than hugging and being close is a concept that's far beyond her. "What if all I want is for you to do this? Sit here. Hang out. I'm not ready for . . . client dinners."

"No," Luc agrees. "You aren't."

"Is that okay with you?"

"Elle, anything we do together is okay with me."

She actually wibbles. Her eyes get watery and her lip trembles and her insides do their best gyroscope impression. "Why are you like this?"

Luc takes a breath. If it's possible to be both fierce and tender at the same time, that's how he looks. "Do you want the full answer or the one that will help you stop crying?"

"The full one, please," she whispers.

He speaks without hesitation. "I'm like this because you deserve the same compassion and support you've given to others. Not only because you've held everyone up, myself included, but because you, as a person, are worth it. You've given so much that you have left nothing for you. It isn't right or fair to let you deal with this alone, even if you think you should. I will be here to help you, and once you're back on your feet, you can make the decision on whether you still want me around."

Maybe she should have chosen the answer that would have helped her stop crying, because the tears start for the umpteenth time. Elle burrows against Luc once she's done, ignoring the discomfort of his damp shirt until she can't anymore.

"You're going to need to change your shirt."

A heavy sigh. "I know, but I don't have a spare."

She touches her fingertips to his cheek. "Bring one next time. Bring a few."

Luc takes her hand in his and presses his cheek to the inside of her wrist. "I will."

The room darkens, the city lights muted through the frosted glass of her windows.

Elle stirs, her body aching. She should move so that Luc can get his circulation back. "Did you know that I really hate this couch?"

"Same."

"I'd be asleep now if this thing weren't so awful."

"I've slept on worse, but this ranks fairly low. Points docked for the cover."

"Sorry about that. We put plastic on everything. Supposed to preserve it."

"Do you ever take it off?"

She purses her lips, thinking. "As far as I know, no."

"Then what is the point? Martyrdom?"

She laughs, and somehow that makes her feel immensely better.

"If I'm to spend the night here occasionally, I'm buying a new couch."

Elle pushes herself up to look Luc in the eyes. "No. I'll do it. You can come with me to shop, but I'm getting this one."

He nods, acquiescing. "That's fair. I'll purchase the blanket."

Luc is probably going to buy the most expensive made-with-unicorn-hair blanket he can find. The idea of it is adorably fussy. If they visit fewer than five stores, Elle's gonna be disappointed. "Deal. What should we do now?"

"Hmm." Luc straightens, then stretches. "How about that pizza?"

"That sounds great." Elle's stomach rumbles.

Chapter Seventeen

"Hold it like this." Elle leans across the table she's placed in front of the store's picture window and selects a brush from her rack. She models an upright grip for her customer, a young Asian woman who's stopped over the last few weeks to watch her paint. It isn't anything special, just some calligraphy commissions and basic birds and flowers to restore her skills, but Elle consistently gets spectators. "You want to hold it firm but not too tight, or you won't be able to tilt the brush freely from side to side."

Elle dips the brush in ink and demonstrates by using the tip, then the side, pressing it into her scrap paper. "You can make a leaf like that. Why don't you try?"

The store bell rings, and Elle shivers as another customer lets in the fall chill. She's been in San Francisco for four months and she's still not used to the weather. Her customer is an older Asian man, his hair thinning on his head, wrinkles in a halo around monolid eyes, his face wide and kind. He's stopped to watch her as well.

She puts on her best retail smile. "I'm sorry, we close at six."

"I'm just observing. I've seen you painting here lately. You're very good."

"Thank you." She looks at her paper, where the other customer has drawn several blotchy, uneven lines. "That's not bad! Take up less ink, and don't hesitate mid-stroke."

"Okay," the young woman replies. After a few tries, she puts the brush down and goes to the door. "Thanks!"

"Are those yours?" The man indicates the art Elle has mounted on the walls of the shop. They're her paintings from her workshop, which Lira had framed and shipped as another surprise. Elle might have cried when she opened the packages.

"Yes." She flips the sign on the door to closed. "Do you have a favorite?"

"The mountain landscape," he replies immediately. "It draws the eye."

It's Elle's favorite too, but if she thinks about home, she'll get sad again. She hasn't had a horrible day this week, and she doesn't want to break the record.

"I've been enjoying your afternoon painting demos." The man smiles. "I'm Alan."

"Elle." She shakes his hand.

"I work with the San Francisco Asian Arts Society. We show in galleries twice a year, and if you're interested, there's room for one more artist in the winter lineup. You'd fit right in. Here's my card. Come visit us sometime." He turns, pushing the door open. "Nice to meet you, Elle."

"You too!" She locks up, still processing what just happened, her fingers tightening on the card. She lifts it up to read it, and the information leaps out at her: Alan Matsuyuki, president.

She blinks at it, blinks again to be sure. Holy crap. She's been informally invited to join an art show by the president of the San Francisco Asian Arts Society.

The sound of purring heralds the arrival of the big orange cat, who Elle has secretly adopted and named Grant Avenue. "Look at this!" Elle waves the card in the air, tentatively excited. It's likely not a big deal, but it's something. "I gotta tell Luc when he gets here."

She begins the closing process, opening the register, lifting out the till, unsure whether she can concentrate enough to cash out. She still gets headaches if she thinks too hard, and there have been days when closing takes hours because she's pushed herself too much. Dr. Clavret had told her she'd need a minimum of four months to be completely well in mind and body, but to Elle, it feels like an overly optimistic estimate.

She could use Luc's help right about now. He sweeps and organizes, does inventory, cleans windows when she's at the counter swearing at the e-commerce system. He takes over for her when she's exasperated by numbers, citing his lack of a concussion as a reason why he's better suited to the job. As reasons go, it's pretty decent.

"Get out of here, you big lug," she scolds Grant when he jumps on the counter and plops himself onto her receipts. He meows at her and rolls over. She pets him, compelled. Grant has that effect on everyone, even Luc, who doesn't care for animals. "You're a baby. He'll be here soon."

But the minutes tick on without any sign of him. At seven o'clock, Elle finishes hauling out the garbage, washes her hands, and gets her phone. She's about to dial when she spots him coming down the sidewalk. Her heart leaps, doing its best to leave her body and join the rest of the stars in the sky.

"Hey!" she greets him, opening the door. Grant hurtles off the counter and bounds toward Luc, chirping. "I was worried about you. Everything okay?"

He lowers himself onto one of the stools beside the tea table, wincing, and accepts Grant's enthusiastic hello.

Elle frowns, observing the shadows beneath his eyes, the slumped body language. He looks freshly changed, in a camel cashmere sweater and untucked collared shirt paired with medium gray slacks. Over the outfit is a dark brown leather racer jacket. None of it hides the air of exhaustion around him. "I was going to ask to see the sea lions again, but I think it's best if we stay in tonight. I can cook. Sound good?"

"Yeah." Uh-oh. Something's really wrong if he's saying yeah. "Sea lions next time, perhaps. I wouldn't want to deprive you of their company."

It's true Elle has fallen in love with the lumpy, rude pinnipeds at the pier. Luc, on the other hand, barely tolerates their shouting. "I can watch the livestream." She offers her hand to help him up, narrowing her eyes when he shakes his head. "What's wrong?"

"It's nothing."

She levels a look at him. "You're usually tired when you get here, but you're more than tired today."

"Heavy workload." He tries to smile.

Elle isn't having it. Luc hasn't said anything, but based on his history, she can guess how he's managed to carve out consistent time with her. "I know. What kind of deal did you strike with Oberon to be here?"

"One that works."

"He's running you ragged."

"That is part of it, yes."

"Luc!" Elle glares.

"You don't want to know."

"You're right, but I'm gonna ask anyway." She folds her arms across her chest.

He presses his mouth into a line. It's a moment before he replies. "I work six days of seven, usually in the field. When I'm not in the field, I have managerial duties and training to complete. I'm on call if I'm not at the office."

"What about sleep?"

He laughs. "What about it?"

"Okay." Elle's irritation skyrockets. "Tell me where this shit boss of yours is. I wanna fight him."

This time when Luc laughs, it's real.

"I'm serious. Tell him to meet me in the pit. I will punch him, light him on fire, stab him, whatever, to get you some rest. I will haggle. Elves love that, right?"

"That's not how it works, but I appreciate the sentiment."

"I've got nothing to lose. I'll fight him." Elle sets her mouth in a scowl. "You gonna show me what's hurting you, or what?"

"You noticed." Luc sighs and straightens, pulling up on his sweater and shirt to reveal a three-inch square bandage dotted in crimson, covering the perfection of his left obliques.

"You're still bleeding!" She closes the distance, dropping to her knees, pushing his sweater higher, fingers brushing against bared skin. Luc stiffens, and the dots bloom larger. "We have to take care of this now. What hurt you?"

"A dead man with a sword." Luc sounds strangely tight.

She lets go. "You were fighting the undead?"

"He wasn't dead at the time."

Skies, Luc's job sucks and she hates it. "Please tell me he was a bad guy."

Luc swallows, reaching out to grip the edge of the tea table. "It was his life or someone on my team. I chose my team."

Elle can't think about the broader picture when he's bleeding this much. Triage first. "I have Yúnnán Báiyào in the case. It stops bleeding and stagnation." She becomes more and more distraught as she talks. "I'm going to patch you up, and you're going to head right back to the agency to get some real healing. You shouldn't have come. I wouldn't have been mad if you canceled on me."

She turns away and goes to the counter, fumbling for the key to unlock the back panel. Sudden tears prick her eyes. If she had her magic, she'd write a glyph of restoration and fix him. If she had her magic, she'd have made Luc a glyph of shielding to protect him. If she had her magic—

"Elle." She tenses at the weight of Luc's hand on her shoulder, but doesn't pull away. "I'll be okay. Please don't worry."

She slides the panel open and grabs a bottle and a small white box, then closes it so hard it rattles in its track. "It's all I can do. Let's go upstairs. I can work better there."

He's right in front of her when she straightens. She hears the creak of his jacket as he touches her upper arm. "You've been trained in medical techniques your entire life," he says gently. "You saw I was injured and knew immediately what you needed to get. That is healing as real as any magic."

"Can we please go upstairs?" Panic rises, fluttering, in her chest. She isn't sure whether it's because Luc is bleeding, or if it's a reaction to his affirmation. "Grant, c'mon."

She washes her hands thoroughly once they're in her apartment and directs Luc to lie on her new couch. Elle turns on her electric kettle, then brings out her trusty bottle of rubbing alcohol. "Here's a trick Tony taught me," she says, filling the silence with something, anything. She opens her first aid kit and retrieves some gauze. "Ouchless Band-Aid removal."

Luc doesn't speak, only looks at her. Elle's cheeks heat up under his scrutiny, but the second she removes the bandage she forgets to be embarrassed. He has a two-inch-long gash that's already been butterflied shut, but it's inadequate. "Who treated you?"

"Me." He exhales, measured, as Elle presses gauze against the cut. "It should be clean."

"Try the agency clinic instead," she says, terse.

"I will, tomorrow morning. I needed to see you tonight."

Shocked, she presses harder. Luc doesn't use words carelessly. Needed, he'd said. Not wanted.

He hisses in pain. "Elle!"

"Sorry!" She puts the gauze down and rips into a package of Yúnnán Báiyào paste, squeezing it onto a bandage and applying it to Luc's wound. She turns his words over as she tapes his dressings with an expert hand. He'd needed to see her more than he'd needed to take care of his health. He'd prioritized being with her.

"You have to take a pill as well." She gathers the trash and dumps it, then washes her hands again. In the minute it takes for her to finish that task and get a glass of warm water, he's already dozing off.

"Luc," she calls softly. "One last thing, okay?"

He nods in slow motion. Elle slides her hand underneath his shoulders to help him up and slips the báiyào pill into his mouth. She tilts the glass of water carefully against his lips, listening for the sound of him swallowing, then eases him down. He's so tired that he's asleep before his head hits the cushion.

Elle watches him, resting the bottom of the glass in the palm of one hand. It really would have been better if he'd gone to the clinic for healing, but with the báiyào on the wound and in his body, he'll be okay until the morning. She exhales, her worry abating.

Warmth and affection rise from where they've lain dormant, filling the space. She puts the glass on the coffee table and kneels beside the couch, reaching out, cupping his face. She rests her thumb on his cheekbone, her heart lifting on a rising tide of gratitude. Luc has been tireless and amazing in his support of her. He's been a shoulder to cry on as well as a friend to goof around with. When something happens, he's the first person she wants to tell. A snarky comment from him can leave her in stitches from laughing. Anyone can make a snarky comment, but Luc's sense of timing when it comes to redirecting her negative emotions is unparalleled.

He's been patient with her and respectful of her continuously shifting boundaries. Luc hasn't touched her except for the occasional long hug, which she initiates. He has only touched her cheek that one time to say goodbye. She wouldn't mind if he did that again. She'd like to see him more often.

It seems like the right thing to bend herself to him and press her lips gently to his forehead.

Luc stirs, his hand coming up, fingers curling around her wrist. Elle straightens partway, stops when he murmurs her name.

"Let me get you a pillow." She kisses his cheek, freeing herself reluctantly. On her return, she sees the glittering of his eyes through the veil of sleep. She puts the pillow beneath his head. "Better?"

"Yes. Thank you." His mouth curves into a smile.

"You're welcome," Elle replies, struck by the wistful longing on Luc's face. He's told her he has trouble sleeping away from home, but here he is, on the cusp of dreams, open and vulnerable and looking at her like she's the only person in the world. In another situation Elle might try to find excuses, but even she in her general obliviousness can't deny that he wants her. Not only in a sexual way, but as a friend and companion, someone to spend time with.

And Elle can't deny that she'd like nothing more than to spend unlimited time with him, to laugh at his jokes and be in his presence and figure out how to face the future together. She'd like to invite him to her bed and curl up next to him, holding his hand. She'd like to wrap herself around him as he drifts off to sleep, and wake up full of happiness knowing that he's beside her, and tell him multiple times a day how much she loves him.

Because she does.

Elle reaches for the blanket and tucks Luc in how he likes it. "Good night," she says as sleep leads him away. "I love you," she whispers when it's safe, testing the words. They fit like they've always been there. Like they've been waiting.

Grant hops onto the couch, turning circles until he finds a comfy spot between Luc's feet. "You like him too, huh?" Elle murmurs. She strokes Grant's head, scratches his ears. "You'll have to get in line. I had him first. Though if I don't say anything I might forfeit my place."

Grant's purr rumbles to life.

"I think it's time too." She'll need to figure out how to say the words for real, out loud. She'll have to be careful with them the way Luc's been careful with her. She gives Grant one more pat, one more nose rub. "Watch over him, okay? He's hurt."

Elle turns off the lights, eats dinner quietly, and goes to bed.

The next morning, a soft knock rouses her. Luc pushes the door open. "Elle?"

She makes a noise that's supposed to be a word, then opens her eyes. "How do you feel?"

He stops next to the bed. "Better. I'm going to the clinic. Thank you for taking care of me and letting me stay."

Elle sticks a hand out from under the covers, groping for his. "You can stay over any time you want. Not just Fridays."

A genuine smile grows on his face. "Really?"

Her own smile mirrors his. "Really. I'll even get a key for you."

"I'd like that."

She ought to make it more explicit. Elle struggles up to sitting, then flips the covers aside and stands, sucking in a breath at how cold the floor is. Luc begins to step back, but she keeps her hold on him. With her other hand, she brushes his cheek, drawing him close until their lips touch, light and sweet.

She opens her eyes to a brightness in his. "Come back tonight?" she suggests. "I'll have better breath by then, I promise."

"I really don't care about that," Luc replies, and kisses her back.

The dishes in the sink have been sitting for at least an hour, but Luc is unable to move. It's Friday evening and Elle is lying with him on the wide sectional, tucked against his side, the two of them pleasantly lumped together like a pair of sea lions on the pier, and not even the thought of grease solidifying in the pan can make him disturb her.

"Tony texted me today." Elle sighs. "The family meeting is over, at least for now. He's coming back soon."

"How do you feel about that?" Luc reaches for her hand.

She takes it, lacing her fingers between his, then lifts his hand to her mouth. He can't help but smile at the small gesture. Something has changed. She's been surprisingly affectionate with him in the last week, giving him fleeting touches and quick kisses. She steals hugs, folding herself around him, slowing the world down until it reaches a single still moment of equilibrium.

He thinks about that often when he's at work, putting a hand to his chest, where sometimes the ache of missing her rouses a physical pain. He wonders when, and not whether, the line attaching him to Oberon will snap.

Elle's voice brings him back. "Worried, I think."

"Because of your family?"

She nods. "The last time they saw me, I ran away. There's unfinished business."

"You retreated to regroup," he corrects her gently. "You needed to. You were in no condition to do anything but recover."

"That's what I keep telling myself. I can't help but feel bad about how I did it. Now Tony's going to be back, which means my parents will also be back. I can't let him take the heat for me much longer." She shifts her weight, retucking the blanket around them. "I'm feeling better these days. I think I'm ready to face them. I just don't know how. They don't know my number or anything."

"Call Tony. He'll be your intermediary. Your best strategy is to go on the offensive and catch them off guard. Engage them on terrain favorable to you, in a situation you can control, for maximum advantage."

"Whoa, you sounded ready. Have you been thinking about this?" Elle kisses his hand again.

"No." Yes, a lot. "It's a sound strategy when you have something the other party wants."

"It's not like I'm going to war." She looks amused.

He scoffs. "I've met your mother. It's war. You should prepare for the worst while stacking the odds in your favor."

"Sounds like cheating."

"It isn't cheating," Luc starts to say. "It's—"

"I'll take it."

"What will you say?" They've discussed her options before, and apprehension worms its way into him at the thought of Elle going back to her family. If she does, it's likely he won't see her again unless he asks for Tony and Elle's help in the oasis. There doesn't exist a scenario in which the Jiangs will welcome him, and even if they do, he's being optimistic if he thinks he has something permanent with her. Her concerns over mortality are valid, and their relationship remains undefined. They're more than friends, but less than lovers.

"I'm not sure. Probably something they won't like."

"And if they offer you a deal?"

She snorts. "I'm *tired*, Luc. Short of giving me everything back and leaving me alone, there isn't anything they can offer me. Do you think I'm going to leave you?"

He stares at the ceiling, reminding himself he has no claim to her, and gives voice to his fear. "You might. I would understand."

Elle props herself up on an elbow, wedging herself against the couch cushions. She looks down at him, her dark eyes unreadable, a lock of hair falling partway across her face. He can't help reaching out and tucking it behind her ear. She closes her eyes, leaning into his hand.

When she opens them she holds his gaze, a tremulous smile on her face. "I'm not leaving you. I guess I should tell you something important."

His heart leaps with hope. "What is it?"

"Last week, when you showed up injured . . ." She exhales as if she's bracing herself. "It made me realize something I wish I'd realized sooner. I was so worried about you and all your work, and I got to thinking about this situation and how grateful I am that you're here. I wanted to let you know—"

She lifts her head from her hand, her eyebrows furrowing. To his complete disappointment, Elle gets to her feet. "You hear that?"

Luc grabs at the blanket as the heat flees, watching Elle disappear into the bedroom. She returns with his glowing call rune displayed on her open palm. As she approaches, it emits its usual chime.

Before he knows it, he's standing, the hem of the blanket crumpled in his hand, light-headed with anger. The heat of it hits him like a shock wave, and he tenses to withstand it, his breaths suddenly fast and sharp, his heartbeat whipped into a frothing gallop. He launches himself at her and snatches the rune up, squeezing it to the point of breakage.

Elle cradles his face in her hands, her eyes wide. "Luc, no."

He's shaking and has to unclench his jaw to speak. "I asked for one day. *One* day. Not even one."

"I know." She strokes his cheeks with her thumbs. "He's not supposed to call. I'm sorry he keeps doing this to you."

"I turned this off when I got in, I swear it."

"I believe you." She sounds entirely too calm for the situation, freeing the blanket from his grip, tossing it back onto the couch. The chime continues.

"I'm so sorry."

She shakes her head. "Don't be. This isn't your fault. I'm not mad."

"I wish you would be." The words come out before he can process them enough to stop them. Elle knows how intrusive Oberon is now that Luc is with her more. She's taken the interruptions in stride.

"Would it make you feel better if I were?" Elle gives him a tiny smile. "I'm not mad at *you*. What's the point of showing you that? It'd just get you more worked up. You have one of the shittiest bosses in history. If I could get at him, I would." Her smile turns predatory. "Tell you what. Let me answer your call. I'll shove my opinion down Oberon's throat until he chokes on it and dies."

The glint in her eye makes Luc back up several paces. As tempting as it is, he won't risk revealing her to Oberon. He'd given his word.

"See? That right there. Anything I do will come back to hurt you. I'm not mad at you, I promise. You answer your call. I'll get your socks." She goes back to the bedroom.

Luc inhales, exhales, fits the rune over his ear, taps it to activate it. "What."

He can picture how affronted Oberon is. "Watch your tone, Lucien."

There's too much emotion in him for the threat to work. "I'm not taking calls."

"You're taking this one. It's an emergency."

"I'm on PTO."

Oberon's voice is cold. "I know exactly how much your personal time is worth. A situation has developed and Darcy's been cut off from his second option. You'll need to extract him."

"Need?" What Darcy needs is a bullet between the eyes, not a rescue.

"I know there's no love lost between the two of you, but Darcy has his uses. As do you. Be in Bratislava at the top of the hour. I'll have a car and file ready for you, as well as Castor and Pollux."

Luc sucks in a breath. It really is an emergency. "I thought you shelved that experiment."

Oberon grunts. "You'll be in rusalka territory. I'll risk it."

Elle pads up to him, holding out his socks. Luc sits on the arm of the couch to put them on. "I do this, and you find someone else on Fridays. As promised."

"I don't make promises. One last thing, Lucien."

"What is it?"

"The Oldcastle case."

"I declined it yesterday. We don't help people like him." Luc had recognized the photo in the file immediately as the elf who was wanted for the destruction of the selkie's coat. Oldcastle was asking for an escort to a faerie portal, and the chance of attack was highly likely. The pay was ludicrous, but no amount of money would get Luc to touch the case.

"Please," Oberon says, derisive. "We *are* people like him."

Luc jerks his head up, pain spearing him through. It's a second before he can speak. "Perhaps *you* are."

Elle touches his shoulder, concern on her face. She mouths his name. He shakes his head.

"Don't delude yourself. I taught you. I know who you are." Before Luc can react, Oberon continues. "We're out of time. The Twins will be in a box keyed to my voice. Call when you get in the car." Oberon hangs up.

Elle stands in front of him, looking at him steadily. Luc meets her eyes for one long moment, saying nothing, wrestling with the enormous knot of emotions in his chest. There's frustration and hurt, anger and shame.

He swallows. "What was it you wanted to tell me?"

"Don't worry about it. It can wait for a better time." She leans down, pressing her lips to his in a kiss that's placid and mild. It isn't enough. Luc stops her with a hand on the back of her neck as she pulls away. He stands, drawing her to him, returning her kiss fiercely, as if his love for her—because that's what it is, love, and he's been in love with her for some time—can disprove Oberon's words.

He knows it can't.

"Come back in one piece," Elle murmurs against his lips, slipping her arms around him. "I lo—"

She freezes.

"You what?" Luc prompts her.

"Nothing. Don't worry about the dishes."

Despite everything, he smiles. "How did you know?"

"You always worry about the dishes. It's fine. They don't breed."

"I'm convinced they do."

"We're missing out on the show, then. If they are, I expect to hear more banging. That thick rolling pin of yours . . ."

He laughs, touching her cheek with the tips of his fingers. The anger within him clears like a temporary break in the clouds, allowing a single beam of sunlight. "Be well."

Luc puts on his shoes, steps out of Elle's apartment, and descends the stairs, trying to calm himself enough to put his work face on.

Who are you when you aren't here?

Chapter Eighteen

The vegetables Elle ordered have arrived, set on the table by a server. Arranged on the plate are bright red slices of bell peppers, the one pop of color among a vast field of greens. A plate of tofu and mushrooms follows. Elle picks up a wad of chopped napa cabbage and drops it into the boiling broth in the hot pot.

Steam rises, obscuring for a second her mother's form on the other side of the table. Ēnlián sits as straight as a sword, her expression betraying nothing, reflecting collected coolness at her daughter. To her right is Tony, whose demeanor has been unusually subdued. He's barely spoken a word.

"Do you want these?" Elle indicates the thick clusters of maitake mushrooms on the plate.

Ēnlián nods, holding up a hand when Elle has loaded enough into the pot. Lotus root, oyster mushrooms, and silky tofu all disappear beneath the roiling surface of the broth.

"Your brother says this restaurant is well reviewed."

"Yes. I hope you like it." She's done her research. Last week, after Luc left, Elle had spent the rest of the night formulating her plan. She had called Tony to set up a meeting, knowing her family would come, and quickly.

Her mother will have no advantage here and no choice but to be on the defensive until Elle finishes her combination of opening moves.

Ēnlián peels a strip of beef off the meat plate and slides it into the pot, repeats the action with several more strips. "Your father would have enjoyed this."

"I wish he could be here." Instead, Elle's father is sequestered with Yìwú. House arrest is too light of a punishment, but she'd had no say in the matter, and all Tony could tell her was that the spirits had not yet finished debating and might not for some time.

"I wish you would come home." Ēnlián's gaze pierces her. "It would be good for you to see familiar scenery again."

That's Ēnlián's way of insinuating Elle doesn't belong in San Francisco. Neither does she belong in Shénnóngjià. She's been through too much. "I see it when I look at my paintings. Maybe one day I'll go back, but I'm busy with things here."

Like running the shop, although Auntie Ma is returning soon from China. Or figuring out how to gain more time with Luc. He's been a ghost, entering and leaving at odd hours, and sometimes the only evidence of his presence is her clean, empty sink and the chime of the rune haunting her dreams.

"Can I tempt you to come home sooner?" Ēnlián adds rolled pieces of pork to the broth. Tony, still silent, begins fishing out vegetables and dividing them evenly.

"With what?" Elle prepares herself for the counteroffer, the carrot Tony predicted months ago. Whatever it is, it's going to be a big, honking carrot. "I'm getting used to my life."

Ēnlián glances around, leans in. When she speaks, she uses the language of home, her voice softening, reminding Elle of summers in the garden, of stories told while gazing at clouds. Elle's heart constricts, robbing her of breath. Skies, that's such a dirty move. "You being without your birthright is like being a dolphin in a fish tank. You survive, but you would be happier in the ocean with others like you. Come home. Tell us how you saved your brother, and we can work collectively to help you."

"Help me how?" She takes a bowl from Tony, then pulls beef from the pot.

"What you did can be reversed, most likely."

"And if it can't?"

"We won't know if we don't try." Ēnlián eats her meal without a single drop of soup flicking away, a show of true skill.

"And after you try, what happens if you can't reverse it? Do I live at the bottom of the mountain and teach disciples?" Some people would jump at the chance to live in isolation with a bunch of students. Not Elle. "Do you think I'd be happy to sit in front of the gates and know I can never go in?"

"Better to sit closer to a fire for warmth than to think about it from afar." Ēnlián gestures dismissively with her chopsticks. "These people here have no idea who you are, what you were capable of. Your knowledge is wasted. You have a place at home."

Elle glances at Tony, whose mouth is pressed together in a sharp crease. She could play this game with her mother, but she'd lose. She should speak clearly and directly. "I have a place at home only because you've determined I have something you want. I didn't have a place before."

"You did. You just did not appreciate it."

"What was I supposed to appreciate? Living down to your expectations? Being blamed for things that weren't my fault?" Elle takes a breath.

"That is all history now." Ēnlián's dark eyes remain trained on her. "We did not understand what happened, and you didn't tell us."

Anger flares inside her. Elle slaps her chopsticks on the table, incensed. "I didn't tell you because I was afraid for Tony's life. I didn't tell you because you never cared enough to ask. All you want is to keep your legacy going, and look at how that's ruined us. *You* did this. It was your duty as a mother to help resolve the situation. You and Ba chose not to. Your inaction did this to my brothers and you refuse to take responsibility for it!"

"Yìyǎ," Tony says quietly. "You don't need to fight for us."

Seething, Elle sits back in her chair.

"You are like your father in so many ways." Ēnlián's voice cracks. Finally, the dam holding her emotions fails, and sorrow floods across her features, seeps into her voice. "Making hard choices, doing your best to preserve harmony. Stubbornly doing what you think is best. He thinks it's best you come home. He didn't get to say goodbye before you left the last time, and it broke his heart. Would you break his heart again, Yìyǎ? You are his only daughter."

She refuses to cry or be manipulated. "If Ba is so sad, why are you here, and not him?"

"He's with Yìwú," Ēnlián replies.

"You could be with him. I doubt he's going anywhere. You and Ba are matched in strength. I'm going to assume he doesn't know what you're offering me, and that's why he didn't come." Elle folds her arms, holding her fury in, and tilts her head slightly. "You're right that I'm like him. I don't like discord or stress in my life. I could go home, but someone told me lately I should be more selfish."

A hint of a smile makes the corner of Tony's mouth quirk up. He puts a piece of bok choy in his mouth.

"I realize that he was wrong. I shouldn't be more selfish. I should be more self-assured. That begins with setting boundaries. No, Ma. I won't go home."

"Even if it means you lose your chance to regain what you lost?" Ēnlián draws herself up, and Elle has to remind herself not to buckle underneath that steely, pointed stare. "What could possibly make you want to stay here? Are you seeing someone? Is there a man?"

Without hesitation, Elle says, "No. I'm not interested."

Tony chokes and coughs into his bowl.

"Yìxiáng!" Ēnlián grabs a napkin, wiping up spots of soup. "Are you okay?"

"Yeah," Tony ekes out, his cheeks a dark red beneath his tan skin. "Went down the wrong pipe. Go on. Yìyǎ isn't seeing anyone."

She takes a page from Luc's book, putting herself in a space where she can act and react as objectively as possible. It's the feeling she used to have at home on the mountain, where the sky was an endless blue bowl and the ground was nothing more than a memory. Elle breathes in slowly, detaching herself as she looks at her mother. It's easy. "It may be hard to believe, but I'll find my way out here."

"I was afraid you would say that." Ēnlián picks up her purse and withdraws a box tied with a ribbon. "I thought I would offer you a gift in good faith, as proof that we will do what we promise to do. Come home, Yìyǎ. Your family needs you."

Elle doesn't touch the box. "What is this?"

"Open it and see for yourself." Ēnlián scoops a piece of tofu out of the pot and eats it, unflinching at the scalding temperature.

"Tony?" She looks to him, questioning.

"It's your carrot." He's distinctly unhappy, but that's it.

Elle undoes the ribbon and lifts the lid off the box. There, nestled in styrofoam netting, cradled in a clear plastic half shell, is a peach of immortality, perfectly red and yellow, a single vivid green leaf stuck to the stem. The smell of it rises, cutting through the savory aroma of the hot pot. Instantly, Elle's mouth waters. She can taste it, the firm flesh yielding beneath her teeth, the burst of juicy sweetness muted by the fuzzy skin. Her family has a tree in the courtyard, one of the lesser varietals that confers hundreds of years of life as opposed to three thousand. It's fruited three times since she was born, and she remembers each one of those times. She used to gorge herself until she was sick.

"Our tree bore fruit this year." Her mother smiles briefly at Tony. "As if to celebrate the return of our Yìxiáng. This will not give you back what you lost, but it will give you time to help us learn how to reverse it."

To be long-lived again, to bring back her magic—hope leaps forth, a torch in hand, showing the way. If Elle eats the peach, she buys time to spend with Luc. She'll have a chance, however small, of feeling the spark of fire in herself again, to paint a glyph and let her magic shape it into reality.

But. Doubt is like a tiny stone in a shoe, tumbling around with each step, impossible to ignore. Even if she gains hundreds of years, she and Luc remain on borrowed time. Maybe, if Luc does well enough, Oberon would allow a month without work here and there, but a month in a lifetime spanning centuries means nothing. And whether Elle would be able to see him remains in question. Taking the peach means taking on a new debt to her family, and she's debt-free.

The next realization comes to her with the clarity of a struck temple bell, the tones augmenting one another, expanding. Elle inhales through her nose, holding the scent of peach in her lungs. When she exhales, she lets go of her expectations, bids farewell to the things she's believed for so long. It hurts, but temporarily, like the sting of bandages being ripped off. Her family needs her, but she doesn't need them. She isn't who they think she is.

She is no longer Agent Elle Mei, or Stella Jiang, or Grace Lin. She isn't a glyphmaker, a steward, or a martyr. She isn't a vending machine. She's Jiāng Yíyǎ, also known as Elle Jiang. She's an artist, a terrible prospect, and the architect of her own life, which she would like to live gracefully, with Luc at her side.

She really ought to tell him.

Elle lifts her chin, matches the strength of her mother's gaze. She speaks with the calm that accompanies internal harmony. "What I did cannot be reversed. I did it willingly, out of love. Who among you will sacrifice for me the way I have sacrificed for Tony?"

Her mother doesn't answer.

Tony lifts his napkin to his mouth, muffling his snort of laughter.

Elle places her hands on the table and rises to her feet. She feels so light she could float. "Big brother, please take care of our mother and ensure she has a safe trip back home. Feel free to eat as much as you want. I have already paid." She bows, turning to leave.

"Yíyǎ." Ēnlián stands as well. Elle pauses, looking over her shoulder. Disbelief is painted across her mother's face in an elegant hand. For a second, she thinks she sees regret. "Your gift."

Elle smiles, beatific. "Keep it."

"I hereby call this meeting of Terrible Prospects International to order," Elle says, patting the spot next to her on the sofa. "First on the agenda is roll call."

Luc snorts as he dries the last bowl and stores it in the small and entirely useless dishwasher. "I was not informed there was to be a meeting."

"It was a last-minute decision made by the president. Didn't you get the memo?" Without her family to burden her, she's been able to think about how to tell him she loves him. Elle has taken all day to figure out how to have this conversation and she isn't going to screw it up. She's prepared, dammit. She's clean and doesn't smell like ginseng and has washed all the linens and is nervous as hell.

"No, and I'm afraid I'm booked, so I can't attend."

He's joking, though there's a chance Oberon will ruin everything. It's Friday, after all. "Cancel it. This is more important."

"Somehow, I doubt it." There is an actual twinkle in his eye. "I was supposed to celebrate an emancipation tonight."

"Just sit!"

"As you wish." He folds the dish towel and comes over. "I'm ready."

"Jiāng Yìyǎ, otherwise known as Elle Jiang, present. Lucien Villois?" Elle pronounces it as terribly as she can.

Luc's face creases with pain. "No!"

"Okay," Elle says, trying not to laugh. Luc has several aliases, so she picks one. "Lukas Kestenholz?"

He folds his lips in. "Not here."

"Who's at this meeting, then?"

"You could have just asked me how to pronounce my name."

"Less fun that way." She grins. "Looshin."

"Elle, *please*." He speaks slowly, enunciating each syllable. "Lu-ci-en. Lu-cien."

Elle claps. "Rhymes with goosey on!" She cackles, pleased with her own brilliance.

Luc journeys through half a dozen expressions before saying, "Why?"

"Okay, okay." She makes several attempts and judges her success by the contortions of Luc's face.

"You have to forget the *N* is there."

Irritated, Elle says, "What the hell is wrong with your language?" She tries again, because part of her plan hinges on being able to say his name correctly. Eventually, she puts her hands on either side of his mouth to copy how it moves. "Lucien."

He lights up with excitement, which gets her excited on account of how cute he's being. "Yes! Okay, one more time. Listen carefully. Are you ready?"

She nods, watching his mouth, fighting the temptation to kiss it. "Châtenois."

Elle goes still with shock, her eyes widening, her heart pounding.

"Châtenois," Luc says again, voice low. "Go on."

"Is that . . . ," she whispers, ". . . your truename?"

He nods.

Learning how to say his given name had been part of the plan. Learning his truename? *Not* part of the plan. "Luc, I can't—if something happens, if I do something . . ."

"It's different when you say it." He takes her hands in his and looks into her eyes. "And you'd need to invoke the Right."

"I'd *never.*" The idea of it is abhorrent.

"There are two people alive who know my name. My aunt, who never asked but found out through my memories, and the other . . ." He shifts his grip, interlacing their fingers. "I was a youth when I told him. I had no understanding of it. And so I had no choice in the matter. I understand now. I have a *choice* now. I want you, the terrible prospect who gets me, to have that knowledge. To save me with it. I trust you."

Elle hardly breathes. With three words, Luc has laid himself bare.

"Lucien Châtenois." Elle waits for something to happen, some flash of light, some tremor in the earth. But the only tremors she feels are from her, and the only light she sees is in his eyes.

Elle takes her plan, wads it up into a ball, and chucks it out the window. There's only one thing left for her to do, and that's to tell him. "You've ruined my plan."

"I—what?"

"I had," she says, bowing her head so she can kiss his hands, "a whole entire plan for tonight. I spent all day thinking it up. And you just . . ." She shifts closer. "You've just ruined it."

Luc clears his throat, bewildered. "What were you supposed to do?"

She thought it'd be hard to say the words, but it's so easy. "Butter you up, speechify a little, then tell you I love you."

It's his turn to go still with shock, his eyes widening. After a long, hanging moment, which Elle spends grinning cheesily at him, he swallows and says, "And now what?"

"Now I just do the last bit. Lucien Châtenois, I love you."

The smile that spreads over Luc's face is sunshine itself, bright and joyous and full of everything good that exists on the planet. "Could you please say that one more time?"

"I." Elle frees her hands, placing them back on Luc's face. "Love." She brings herself so close that she feels the warmth coming off him. "You."

And then she kisses him, putting into it all the strength of emotion she has, because a four-letter word like *love* is too meager to express how she feels.

Luc makes a noise in his throat and returns the kiss, cradling the back of her head, pressing her to him. Elle wonders, as her mouth opens beneath his, if he understands how she's feeling, how if she doesn't kiss him she might burst and die. She closes her eyes, focusing on him and only him, immersing herself in the taste and scent and feel of him.

"I love you too," he says when they part.

"Somehow," Elle replies, her smile undimmed, "I already knew that."

He laughs. "You got all the clues, finally."

She has. His laes. The kiss in the oasis. His truename. Skies, even the ink that started it all. "I'm sorry I didn't realize sooner."

"You don't have to apologize for anything."

"What if I never realized?" Elle swallows against the sudden pain. "Would you ever tell me?"

"Perhaps. Or I would love you unrequitedly from afar. It's very French, no?"

She narrows her eyes. He hasn't watched enough historical C-dramas, evidently. She can fix that. "No, it's very Chinese too, and also very stupid. I've waited too long for things in my life. You shouldn't wait either."

"Advice noted." He leans forward to kiss her, applying the slightest bit of pressure to her chin with the pad of his thumb, parting her lips. She sighs into him, melting. His fingers graze the sensitive skin beneath her jaw.

Elle shudders at the spark of heat, stretching her head away so he can place his lips on her neck. She wraps her arms around him as best she can, needing to feel his skin against hers. She's already moaning before she realizes she's doing it.

"Elle." Luc pulls back, putting distance between them. The desire in his eyes matches hers. "I don't want to do this if you aren't ready for it."

"I'm ready. I've been waiting all week." She stands and holds out her hand. "Yes. Whatever you're asking, it's yes."

He smiles and lets her lead him to her bedroom.

Elle doesn't know how she's managed to live without this: the passion of his kisses, the reverence with which he touches her, the electricity that jumps between them when his lips are hovering over skin. She hasn't had any fire in so long that she thinks it's gone, but Luc coaxes it out of her with his fingers, breathes it to life with his mouth.

It runs along the paths he lays with his hands, burning so hot that for a second, she's afraid she'll hurt him. But he's fireproof as he tips back her head, kissing her neck, working moan after moan from her.

"I love you," she says once she's on her bed. Oh, what a thrill to speak it freely.

"I love you too," he replies, lying beside her, kissing her. He slides his hand under her shirt, the fabric riding up as he follows her curves. Luc stops when her bra is revealed, detours in order to push the cup down, his palm molding to her breast. The sheets rustle as Luc shifts to place his mouth on her, his hand spreading open. He flicks the tip of his tongue against her nipple, then sucks. His moan vibrates through her flesh, sending her arching.

She needs to be naked immediately. Elle strips off her shirt and throws it across the room, repeats the action with her other clothes, all of them impediments. Luc does the same, his movements ink on shadow in the streetlight-slashed darkness of her bedroom, and Elle has to laugh at it, at how he must be feeling to be so recklessly untidy. She clasps him to her when he's fabulously, splendidly naked, pulling him back to the bed, giddy with delight at how warm his skin is against hers. She's always been the one who runs hot, and it's lovely and new to experience and appreciate Luc's body like this, with nothing but the scent lingering by his neck, nothing but the flash of his smile and the curious puzzle of fitting their bodies together.

With nothing but him.

"Elle?"

She blinks against the sudden stinging in her eyes. Without warning, a tear escapes and rolls across the bridge of her nose.

"We don't have to do this." Luc starts disengaging from her.

"No!" Elle grabs his arm, hauling him back, sticking herself onto him, twining her arms and legs with his. If there's an inch of her skin that isn't touching his, she'll count herself a failure. She burrows against him in desperation, embracing him so tightly that she thinks their bodies should give up their earthly constraints and meld, like two soap bubbles meeting, or two lumps of clay mashed together. Anything. Anything to anchor herself, to keep from tipping into the ferocious chasm of grief opening beneath her, echoing with the absence of her magic.

Luc shifts, adjusting himself and pressing close enough for them to share breath. It's humid and a little gross, but it's fully theirs and exactly what she needs.

"Elle," Luc murmurs. "It's enough, this."

"No, it's not." She sniffles, the sound of it hollow in the egg of space between them. Maybe she can't have her magic back, and maybe she'll never know the particular misty hum of another person's qi, but she can still feel, dammit. She can still see and smell and hear and taste, and she can still dedicate herself to learning Luc in every sense of the word. And she will.

Elle peels herself from him briefly. "I want you," she says. "And when I say I want you, I *want* you. In a way that I want back from you."

Luc considers her. The headlights of a passing car gleam silver in the depths of his eyes, fading quickly. His hands slip down, smoothing over her skin, coming to a rest on the cluster of scars between her rib cage and her hips. "Do these still hurt?"

"Sometimes," Elle admits, not wanting him to hesitate but understanding why he has. "I don't know what sets them off."

"And this is what you want?"

Elle takes his hand, threading her fingers between his, squeezing until her knuckles pop. "Yes. I want to *live*."

He pauses, and when he speaks, his voice attains a rough burr that has her instantly ready. "Then let's do that."

They come together in a clash. Luc meets her halfway; more than halfway. Elle throws herself at him, wringing moans from him as he does from her. The only end she can see for herself tonight is the dreamless sleep of the exhausted, the sourness of muscles pushed past their limits, the ache in her of a thirst well slaked. If Luc has an issue with her setting her teeth in his shoulder, he says nothing, simply returns the favor. That'll leave a mark.

Luc kisses her, carding his fingers through her hair before gripping the roots of it, his hand tightening into a fist. Pleasure cascades over her. She moans into his mouth, the sound downright shameful in its wantonness.

He does it again, with the same result. He looks at her, hunger written across his face.

All Elle can think about is having him inside her. "I don't want to wait. Condoms are in the drawer."

"Was this part of your plan?" Luc tugs her head back, exposing her neck. He kisses beneath her jaw, spends an extra-long moment on her pulse.

"Not the crying part," Elle says, strung tight, breaths shallow. "But yes."

"Cocky, are we?" He lets her go.

She laughs, reaching for the handle of the nightstand. "No, cocksure."

"Not so fast." Luc plucks up her hand, redirecting it so he can nibble at her fingertips. "Not yet. Not until I get to do this."

"Do what, bite me more? Please. Yes."

Luc laughs and flips the covers off the bed, then climbs over her, pushing her knees apart, settling between them. "I mean this. You have no idea how much I've thought about it."

Elle might scream with excitement. Well, she should, but not too loud. She compromises with a teensy scream. "Really? A lot?"

"Really." He drags his lips over her stomach. "A lot."

She makes a happy noise when his fingers dip into her, testing her wetness, sighs when he spreads her slick over her, his touch amplified. He must remember what he did in Paris, because every movement is just right and exactly what she needs. She moves her hips in what she hopes is an encouraging way. "Please," she says, the pleasure already spiking high. She's a live wire. "I want your mouth."

Luc kisses his way over her inner thighs. He gives her a throaty chuckle, eyes glinting with wickedness. "You go too fast, my heart."

"No, I don't! Luc, please—"

His touch as he draws circles over her clit serves only to hone her pleasure, sharpening it until it gleams. He kisses everywhere but between her legs, and works her open stroke by deliberate stroke, touching her arousal back to her until she's sure she's dripping.

Elle whimpers, lifting her head. "Let me live!"

He smiles. "No."

She whines. Of all the times to stop listening to her. "Luc, I swear by—by all my ancestors, I'm gonna—"

"Going to what, my heart? Leave?"

He laughs at her. He actually laughs at her, then swipes his thumb over her clit.

Elle twitches at the heightened pleasure, moaning as he does it again.

The words tumble out. "I'm gonna come and then you'll be sorry!"

He laughs again and kisses her inner thigh. Elle jumps out of her skin at the touch of his teeth. "That isn't the threat you think it is."

"Please." Desperation lends her voice shades of neon, searing yellows and pinks and oranges that broadcast her desire so brightly that she wouldn't be surprised if people outside suddenly began falling upon each other. "Luc, please, your mouth on me *now*. Please, Lucien, I love you."

She hears his gasp. Then Luc surges forward, licking into her with a groan. "Yes," Elle whispers. Her hands go to his head, and she pushes herself against him, her fingers tightening in his hair the way her body tightens under each stroke of his tongue. Luc looks up the length of her body with blue eyes gone dark and half-lidded with pleasure; his hum of approval goes straight through her. She tries to speak, but he licks the words from her, makes her breathe them back down her throat when he slips his fingers inside her.

He seals his mouth to her and finds the particular spot that makes everything synergize and amplify. She's so close, so close, but Luc is a natural expert at keeping her wound up, a savant at calculating the exponential curve of her pleasure. Elle claws toward her release, determined to wrest it from him, but Luc shifts her into a higher gear, a more glorious plane. Elle screws her eyes shut as Luc's fingers move in her faster and faster, her chest heaving as the ground shears beneath her and all stability is lost.

"I'm gonna—" Elle manages. She's a millimeter away from coming. A fraction of that. Her thoughts are unraveling, shredding with every breath, distilling down to single words until she loses them completely and reaches that split-second stillness before—

The orgasm breaks over her like the crack of a whip. Her little apartment has no hope of containing the sounds of her moans, especially not when Luc adds his voice, groaning and riding her release out with her. "Luc," she gasps, not yet wanting the floating, the bliss.

He doesn't stop, and Elle summits again, sweat breaking out as her pleasure coalesces into a bright, shining point. The second wave picks her up roughly and flings her pieces across the bed. She clutches the covers, her body responding to him, her head lashing side to side, her feet sliding up and down the sheets, heels digging in.

"Fuck," she whispers when Luc lies beside her, so smug she can feel it even through the residual shakes.

"Yes," he replies, kissing her. His mouth is velvet warmth and tastes of the two of them together, which only makes her deepen the kiss. Elle slides her hand down his stomach before she changes her mind and hauls her unsteady self up, scooting to the side of the bed, yanking the nightstand drawer open, fishing out a packet and a bottle of lube. When the condom is on, she straddles him, pressing the tip of him to her. Luc's hands curve over her hips.

Elle takes him in, reveling in the depth and width of him, her head hanging down, mouth going slack. She moans, undone, when their hips connect and she feels how luscious he is inside her. Luc has his eyes tightly shut, his soft growl unrolling behind his teeth, and all she wants, both right now and forever, is this closeness with him, the vulnerable, light-streaked length of his throat, the beat of his heart beneath her palm, and the promise of infinite tomorrows.

"I love you," she declares.

The sound he makes in response defies words. It's a combination of a gasp and a moan, and beneath her, his body moves like an oath. Elle presses her chest to his, still stretched around him, nips a pinprick of pain into his neck, then kisses him so fiercely their teeth click together, which makes her laugh. Elle gets back up and begins riding him, closing her eyes to better feel the movement of him within her. Luc helps, pulsing his hips up against hers, taking her hand and telling her, "Touch yourself."

She braces one hand on Luc's chest, the other going to her clit. She's still wet from before, and now she can feel the seamless meld of his cock in her. It's so arousing that Elle's already halfway to an orgasm when she fingers herself.

"Lovely," Luc murmurs between her gasps, holding her hips, grinding her down until the base of him stretches her to the brink.

Elle doesn't want to be *lovely*. She wants to be fucking *destroyed*. She wants to be destroyed with him and by him, to crash headlong into him like they're celestial bodies and turn into powdery, glittering dust in the sky, to be immolated and burn with feeling in a way that magic could not and cannot ever touch. "Luc, I—"

"Anything you want, my heart. Yes."

It's not romantic to say that the best thing she can think of for them is to be completely wrecked by each other. And it isn't as if she has the ability to speak it aloud, anyway. "You'd better go with me, then."

"Don't hold back."

She should've known he'd anticipate her. "I won't."

Luc is relentless, setting a rhythm that Elle feels from her hips to her neck. She braces herself over him to match him, sweat filming the back of her neck and behind her knees. The pleasure crests, gathering itself before shattering her. Elle tosses her head, her moan starting in her chest and pouring from her as Luc drives into her beautifully, his muscles bunching, burying himself in her.

Elle eases down, breaths normalizing, lost in him. She drapes herself on Luc, skin to skin, half-blinded with stars. This is home.

"I love you," she whispers.

"I love you," he whispers back.

Elle shimmies up until she can kiss him unhurried and languorous, delirious with happiness. Yes. This is what she wants, what she claims as hers.

From somewhere on the floor, Luc's call rune chimes.

"No!" he shouts, every muscle in him contracting as he sits up partway. Surprised, Elle grabs him to hold on, feeling the white-hot blaze of his fury as her own.

She winces, climbing off him as quickly as she can.

"Elle, no. I'll ignore it. Fuck Oberon. I'll ignore him."

Her heart aches. Luc rarely swears on account of keeping himself so tightly leashed. She shakes her head as the rune sounds again, reminding her of her hubris. She can't claim Luc when he belongs to someone else.

But it won't be like this forever. She's done rolling over and waving white flags. "It's okay. I'm not mad."

"I am." He gets to his feet, making a beeline for the bathroom, leaving the rune still chiming. For seconds and seconds it goes on, and though Elle knows it's not possible, it feels like the sound is getting louder, more strident. It's clear Oberon expects to be heard and answered.

Luc isn't any less calm when he returns, his face a thunderhead. He talks over the chime as he gets dressed. "I'm not going to do it, but right now I want to break this piece of shit and throw it as hard as I can."

Elle gives him a hug, trying her best to soothe him. He's brittle with frustration and it's all she can do to hold him together. "Go take care of it. I'll be here."

Luc's eyes are flinty with anger when he looks at her, stooping to retrieve the rune, fitting it around his ear. "One day, you might not be."

They stare at each other. The rune keeps chiming as Luc turns away and exits her apartment.

Chapter Nineteen

"Villois here," Luc growls the second he steps foot on the sidewalk. Long strides eat up the distance to the car parked a block away.

"Took you long enough. I expect promptness from you."

He speaks through gritted teeth. If Oberon doesn't like his tone, so be it. "I expect you not to call me on Friday nights."

"Tone, Lucien. This is a special case. I need you to do the Oldcastle escort."

He stops cold, causing the pedestrian behind him to exclaim and shuffle around him. "I told you, I declined it. You gave me that responsibility. He didn't pass the checks."

"Overridden," Oberon replies casually. "You're taking the case. Off the books. Get yourself back to New York. He'll be waiting for you in your office. He'll be wearing a glamour—"

"No. If he wants a personal favor from you, you'll need to do it yourself."

"Did you think I wouldn't?" Oberon snorts. "I am already in the Heiligensee reserve outside Rostock, preparing the ring. I cannot leave. Your job is to get him here."

"Why him?"

"It's important to me."

Luc opens his mouth to argue the subjectivity of importance. His time with Elle is more important than Oberon's errand.

Oberon continues. "Stop wasting my time and energy. Do this freely, or do it under the Right. Do you understand, Lucien Châtenois?"

Fear coils around his throat, constricting.

"I believe I have your attention now. It's your choice."

He has no idea what will happen if Oberon uses the Right to command him except that it won't end well. He shudders, chills sheeting up and down his body, ashamed of his weakness, how he's capitulating. "I'm on my way."

"I knew you'd choose wisely. Call me when you're in Rostock."

Luc arrives at the top floor of the Manhattan building twenty-three minutes later and shoves open the door to his office. There's someone lounging in one of the two chairs in the darkened room. Oldcastle's glamour casts him as an average-looking white man of indeterminate age, with brown eyes, limp brown hair, and the threat level of a used tweed jacket. But the instant he stands, all traces of being unremarkable slough away. There's a chilly emptiness to Oldcastle's expression which, in combination with his looks, immediately pings Luc's instincts. Here is a man who would be better off six feet under the ground than walking on it.

He wonders if others feel the same way about him.

"Took you long enough," Oldcastle says as Luc sizes him up. "At least he sent someone reliable. Trust Oberon to keep family business in the family. You should fix your glamour. You missed your eyes."

"I'm not wearing a glamour," Luc replies, going to the safe beneath his desk and withdrawing a gun and holster. He shrugs out of his blazer and straps the holster on, then checks his firearm before loading the magazine and redonning his blazer. His switchblade is in its ever-present place in his pocket. "No talking. Let's go." The faster he does this, the faster he can get back to Elle.

"You're a fun one," Oldcastle says. "I can see why Oberon keeps you around."

Luc doesn't dignify him with an answer. If he had his way, he'd lead Oldcastle straight into the ocean and hold him under the waves until the selkies came. He opens the door, fluorescent light from the hallway cutting across the carpet, and allows Oldcastle out before he locks up.

He sets a brisk pace, wanting to keep his contact with Oldcastle to a minimum.

Oldcastle hustles a little. "So you're the Big Guy's second, eh? I can see the resemblance."

"We aren't related."

Oldcastle grunts. "You look like his kid, but rougher."

Luc has never heard Oberon mention a family or children, though he knows logically that they should exist. According to rumor, Lysander is Oberon's son, but Luc also does not speculate based on rumors. He ignores the insult. "I said no talking."

"And with the same excellent manners."

They turn in to the hallway leading to the lifts. At the opposite end, a lift door opens, revealing the Wrecking Crew. They step out in a cloud of laughter.

Luc grinds his teeth. A Scotch Irish berserker who grew up among merrows and selkies is exactly what he needs right now. If Gillen finds out who Oldcastle is, there will be bloodshed *and* property damage to deal with.

"Hey, Killer!" Gill's voice rings out across the space. "What are you doing here?"

"Don't you have Fridays off?" Emi asks, her head tilting. Her earrings catch the light as they swing. "You made a big fuss about not coming in."

"He's supposed to," Fern answers. "If you're here, there's no point in us covering for you."

"You mean we could have been at home?" Gillen glares.

"One-time job." Luc keeps his walk purposeful as he and Oldcastle pass the Crew on the way to the lift. He pushes the down button. "We're leaving."

Fern takes a deep breath, her golden eyes flaring. "A job that needs a glamour?" She exchanges a look with Emi. "What's going on that you need something that strong?"

He stays neutral, balanced. He can get Oldcastle through this unexpected gauntlet. "Nothing."

"I thought you wanted more transparency," Ken says. "At least, that's the impression I got from your memo. That's your policy, isn't it? To be open about what we're doing."

Luc fixes his eyes on the numbered display, urging the lift to get to his floor faster. Naturally, it's at sub-level 2.

Ken hmms. "I understand. This is outside policy."

Luc turns just in time to catch the flash of Emi's earrings.

Oldcastle's glamour blurs and fades, revealing a wiry elf with dark blond hair, a long face, and eyes the same rare, striking blue as Oberon's. With a haughty gesture, Oldcastle reasserts his magic, but it's too late.

"You!" Gillen snarls.

Luc shoves Oldcastle behind him, but otherwise takes no action. "Don't," he warns.

"Of course you'd protect a *murderer*. You know what he did!" Gillen's face contorts with hatred. He spits at Oldcastle.

Luc flinches, thinking of seawater flowing beneath a door, and responds through clenched teeth. "I do."

"Then get out of my way so this cunt can get what he deserves."

"I can't." His breath catches at the thought of the Right. He can't go through that again. Death would be preferable.

An idea sparks and flares to life. Elle and Tony have both—

"You'd go down for him?" Gillen's breathing heavily, his eyes beginning to show white all around.

"I don't want to fight." But he will if he has to. Luc looks at the rest of the Crew, his eyes lingering on Ken. Ending things as quickly as possible will be his objective. Ken is the heart of the Crew, the center of their mutual bonds. Luc will have time for one shot before Emi's magic can land. He'll make it count.

"What does he have on you?" Ken asks quietly. "Why do this?"

It's clear to Luc that Ken is speaking of Oberon. He selects his words, hoping Ken will understand the hidden meaning. "Because I must. Tell Gillen to stand down before it's too late."

"You don't fucking tell me what to do!" Gillen lunges forward with a roar, his fist cocked.

He doesn't have time for this. Luc slips to the left, redirecting Gillen's arm. Concrete crunches and buckles as Gillen's fist smashes into the wall between the lifts, the aluminium control panel popping halfway out in a flurry of paint flakes. Luc steps into the bigger man's space, bracing his leg for a throw. With a twist of his torso he catches and grabs Gill's jaw, shoving him backward. Gillen topples heavily, and as he hits the floor, Luc follows, controlling Gillen's arm, whipping his knife out and pressing the blade to Gillen's throat.

The Crew tenses, but they don't move.

"You've drawn a weapon on your colleague." Ken speaks mildly, but there's no mistaking the red glow in his eyes. "I thought you were better than this. Let him go. Have a heart."

Without missing a beat Luc responds, "I left it in San Francisco."

There's a tangible pause from all four members of the Crew. Fern clears her throat. "Was . . . was that a joke?"

"No," Luc says flatly.

"It kind of sounded like a joke," Gill mutters from the floor. His Adam's apple bobs against Luc's hand.

Ken looks thoughtful. "I don't think it was."

"Will you all focus?" Emi snaps, lifting her hands. Her magic shimmers in the air like a mirage. "Get off him, or else. You can't fight all of us at once."

Luc switches the knife to his left hand without changing the pressure on Gill's neck. In one smooth motion he unholsters his gun, flips the safety, and aims it directly at Ken. "I don't have to."

Behind him, the lift doors open.

"Get in," Luc commands Oldcastle. "Hit the lobby button." He stands slowly, keeping the gun trained on Ken. As foolish as Gillen is, even he won't make a move when his team leader is at risk.

"You're going to regret this," Gill says in an undertone. The doors close on his look of murder.

Luc already does.

The lift begins its descent. He closes his eyes and replaces his weapons, suddenly exhausted.

"Nice work," Oldcastle says. "Put them in their place."

Luc opens his eyes, staring straight ahead, his voice devoid of inflection. "I'll put you in yours if you keep talking. I was not given instructions on how I should deliver you, only that I should."

Oldcastle shifts on his feet. "You'd do that to one of your own?"

"I'm not one of you." He'd rather die before becoming like Oberon. In fact, he might have to.

Luc sips at his Calvados as he waits for the oven timer, trying to relax in Elle's dining chair. Calling it a dining chair is a conceit, as it's actually a folding chair with aspirations. He crosses his ankle over his knee, drumming his fingers once on the table as he thinks about San Francisco's exorbitant housing prices in combination with the paperwork involved in the Wrecking Crew's latest disaster.

"Luc, can you help me?" Elle calls.

There's only room for one person in the kitchen, but he joins her regardless, glad for a distraction. He accepts a kiss on the cheek as he shuffles awkwardly around her to put plates away. Now that Dr. Ma has resumed her occupancy in the shop downstairs, he can discuss living arrangements with Elle. High on the priority list is a kitchen that functions as a kitchen and not as a torture chamber where there is no counter or storage space.

She stacks pans in his arms, but there's nowhere to put them while the oven is occupied. He uses the dining table as a makeshift holding area instead. Elle has maintained order in her kitchen by keeping her pots and other miscellany in the oven and warming tray, but Luc has introduced chaos by using the oven the way God intended.

He's also introduced half his wardrobe to Elle's inadequate closet, as well as an essential collection of shoes and accessories. After Oberon's disastrous call last month, he's shifted the bulk of his funds away from agency-approved banks in preparation for the worst. If it comes down to it, he knows what he needs from his flat. Everything else can be replaced.

"Thank you for cooking." Elle brings over more crockery, then pats her belly. "It was delicious."

Luc had opted for simple, comforting fare, making chicken in vinegar sauce, serving it alongside fresh bread and salad. There's clafoutis in the oven, although Luc has used apples, therefore it's properly a flaugnarde. It's as much for his comfort as hers. It won't be easy to ask for her help in executing his plan, and if she decides to leave him because she thinks he's gone mad, he'll at least have a solid meal in him.

Both of their phones buzz, abandoned and forlorn by the TV. Luc ignores them.

"You're welcome." He returns to his brandy for another sip, swirling it in the glass to redistribute the water. In addition to not believing in ovens, Elle doesn't believe in ice.

"Care to tell me what's bothering you?"

He shouldn't be surprised at how perceptive she is to his moods, but he's surprised.

She smiles. "You've been brooding all night."

"It's work-related." That isn't a lie. In a word, work is hell. The Wrecking Crew is completely out of control. He still has training and managerial duties, and having Oberon micromanaging his job doesn't help. On top of that, he's cut valuable sleeping time to visit the oasis for long talks with his aunt, and has drunk so much coffee he's ready to swear it off. A true tragedy.

Oh, and there's the small matter of quitting the agency and asking Elle to destroy his laes. The heat of the brandy in him dissipates at the thought.

"It usually is. No more dead men with swords, at least?"

The oven beeps. Luc arms himself with mitts and pulls the flaugnarde out, inspecting it. "No more for a while."

"Want to go for a walk while that cools?"

Both their phones buzz again. Elle clicks in annoyance before turning hers off. "We can go down to the pier and find an empty spot."

Empty and quiet, which is perfect. She really does understand him. "That sounds excellent."

They pull on jackets and leave the apartment, crossing Grant Avenue, charting a course to the piers, passing the Transamerica Pyramid. Luc observes the twinkling holiday light displays as they stroll, and with Elle at his side, the two of them part of the crowd, he can almost pretend there's nothing to worry about.

She smiles up at him once they're on the other side of the Embarcadero, her brown eyes soft with affection. Small waves slap against the pylons in concert with the muffled thunking of shoes against wood. She slips her fingers around his elbow as they walk toward the sea, pressing a kiss to his shoulder that makes him melt.

He cannot lose this.

"Let's try this again," she says. "What's bothering you? What's stressing you out?"

The possibility of ending his life in order to escape his boss is the main thing, but he should start small. He'd planned to follow Elle's strategy: butter her up, speechify a little, then have an important conversation. Time for the speechifying.

"You remember what I told you about the Wrecking Crew?"

"Um, four people I'd never want to meet in the pit?"

"Something like that. The legal department is ready to murder them. They caused several hundred thousand dollars of damage during their last mission, which they've expensed to us. The meetings with legal, PR, and cleanup have fallen to me while my boss continues daily operations."

"Let me guess. You love meetings."

"I would rather be presented at a grand fête than be trapped in conference rooms with vampires who have number fetishes."

Elle laughs. "Anything else?"

Luc's phone buzzes yet again. He checks it out of reflex, only to see two lines of eggplant emojis from Tony, then a line of water drops.

She peeks over. "I'm so sorry. He's being an asshole."

"That is his perpetual state of being. Giving him my number was a mistake. Not leaving the group chat was a mistake."

"Tony was a mistake."

Luc stares at her.

"What?" Elle shrugs.

Luc puts his phone on do not disturb.

"He's testing you, is all. But we aren't talking about him." She snuggles up against his arm, causing him to melt again. "You've barely been home, you're asleep on your feet when you are. The last couple of Fridays, you've knocked out the minute you get in the door. Your rune is about to catch fire with how many calls you get. I know work is busy for you, but this is on another level. So, for the third time, what's bothering you?" Elle stops in a pool of light, lifting herself up on tiptoes, kissing him. "Lucien."

A frisson of delight runs down his spine. That's been a dream come true, having a lover use his real name. He kisses her back, then wraps his arms around her as she rests her head against him. Luc shifts his weight subtly from one foot to another, syncing bit by bit to the beat of the faint music coming from a restaurant the next pier over. She sways with him.

"Are we dancing?" Her voice gets lost in his scarf.

"You call this dancing?" Luc makes a note to get himself and Elle out more often. A small jazz club would be a good start. Or maybe the Christkindelsmärik, despite the number of people.

"You're stalling."

"I am."

"Must be big. Is it bad?"

"Not . . . necessarily." But it could be. He's discussed the probabilities with the sphinx, looking at what might happen to him from as many angles as possible. She's done her own research, but there aren't many half elves, and none on record who have given up being elven.

"Can you just tell me, or do you need to work up to it?"

"The latter." He presses a kiss to the top of her head. "I'm following a blueprint you've laid out. I'm speechifying."

"Ah," Elle says sagely. "You're much better at that than I am, so go ahead. I'm listening."

"I wanted to keep this a surprise until I had more of a concrete plan, but I dislike surprises, and you deserve to know before I burden you with me."

Elle cocks a skeptical eyebrow at him. "If you're asking to move in, you practically have already. My time at the shop is done. I've been considering where I might go. Maybe somewhere we both haven't been to."

He'd love to go traveling with her. "It's a little more than moving in. I've begun transferring funds away from my agency accounts."

Elle's other eyebrow lifts.

"I was wondering . . ." *Jusqu'ici tout va bien.* "I've been considering a new vocation. Personal chef. Do you have any openings?"

"Let me check." She pretends to consult an agenda. "You're in luck. When can you start?"

"Not soon enough." Deep breaths. Deep breaths to stave off the emotions he's bricked up behind a wall, the ones that are about to burst through. "I can't do this anymore, Elle."

"This, meaning your job at the agency?"

"Yes. I have to—I have to quit. There is so much outside the job that—I don't know—what am I doing, what's the point, how is this helping, why—"

"Hey." She cups his cheek. "It's okay. Let it out."

He runs both hands through his hair, then tightens them into fists and looks up at the sky as if the stars can help him. His shoulders lift when he breathes in, fall as he breathes out.

The words start slow, then gather steam. "I have no interest in work. Nothing matters, nothing is important. I don't care one way or another what happens to our clients. Someone could die by my negligence and I'd shrug and say 'c'est la vie.'" He begins pacing, aware of how Elle is watching him, sympathy on her face. "I feel I've been wasting my time. I have a path to a solution in front of me and I'm not taking it because all my missions are now critical and I can't say no. Oberon is insufferable. Every time I see him, all I can think about is—"

The air snags in his throat.

"The children," Elle finishes for him, stroking her fingers over his cheek. She keeps doing that until he can breathe again.

"And how I cannot be here with you. You said I shouldn't wait. Then why am I making you do that? You are the most important. You won't always be here. I don't expect you to wait a lifetime for me. I don't expect you to wait another week or day for me to make a decision that should have been clear a long time ago. I have to quit." Luc has to move forward for his own sake. He has to walk away from the last two hundred years of his life so that he can live the next however many with her.

"I understand, I really do. Please don't take this the wrong way. But do you think Oberon will let you go? If he doesn't, then what? I move to Paris to make it easier on you? London?"

"I don't want to be anywhere near work," he replies, vehement. "I never want to think about it again. I've had it, it's nonnegotiable. I can't in good conscience continue working for someone like him when I love you and want to be with you. I can't compromise myself like that."

Elle tilts her head, her expression troubled.

"Let me elaborate." He looks into her eyes, holding her gaze. A flash of heat raises a sheen of sweat over his skin. "Months ago, after you'd finished my commission, you asked me a question. Do you remember what it was?"

Elle shakes her head.

"You asked me who I was when I wasn't with you."

"I remember now. Did you find an answer?"

"Yes. And it wasn't one I liked. I have to hurt people as part of my job, and there are consequences. I visited my aunt after one such mission and she asked me a question as well. She wanted to know what made me happy."

He continues before she can say anything. "You. You make me happy, and the way I am when I'm with you makes me happy. I'm not pleasant at work. I've done things I regret. That's still me, but when I'm with you? I much prefer that. Before you, all I thought I could do was work."

"Like me."

"Yes." He and Elle are not that different. "I thought the only value I had was in how well I did my job, how much I pleased my boss. And then I met you, who never asked anything of me except to be myself. We laugh together. Elle, no one at the Bureau thinks I even know how to smile. We enjoy each other's company. I want that more than anything else. Time with you makes the two hundred years at the agency look empty by comparison."

"You're going to make me cry," Elle whispers. "That wasn't in my blueprint."

There's another swell of emotion in him, which he tries to hold back by shutting his mouth tight. If she cries, he's going to cry too. "Sometimes, during operations, the plan has to be modified."

"So, you're gonna quit, huh?" Elle clears her throat, breathes out, fans her face with her hands. "You had to have thought this through."

"Yes. I need your help."

"You've got it."

Luc places his hands on her shoulders, wishing he could borrow some of Elle's inner strength to say what he needs. "No. Don't rush into this. I'm asking you to help me destroy my laes."

Elle goes stock-still, and in the wan light, Luc sees that she's ashen beneath the tan color of her skin.

"Elle?"

"You're right." She keeps her voice low, but it trembles. She ducks out from beneath his hands, and they fall to his sides. "I shouldn't have rushed into it. My answer is no."

Her refusal reverberates in the air, then hovers between them.

"It's the only way." He hasn't arrived at this decision lightly, but if he goes through with quitting, he can't allow Oberon to override him.

She won't look at him. "No."

"I have to."

"Absolutely not. You'll die. I won't—I won't be a part of that."

"There's a chance I won't. That chance increases if I have help. I've discussed it with my aunt. I could survive, like you."

Her head snaps up, sending tears streaking down her cheeks. "No! I will not be a part of this! I don't want you to die, I won't—"

Wounded, Luc says, "Elle, please, I need your help—"

"—be able to handle it if you do—"

"If we can get Tony and Lira to join—"

"—and I don't want to do it again!" She's shouting at him, fully shouting, her fists clenched, her chest heaving. Luc recoils from her display, stepping back. "I don't want to do it again, okay? I can't. I can't."

The silence fills with the sound of the breath rasping in her throat. Elle shakes her head rapidly and swipes her tears away with her arm.

"What do you mean," Luc says quietly, not approaching her. Something isn't adding up. Elle hadn't broken her own laes. "What do you mean by again?"

Little by little she shrinks in front of him, going cold, the heat from seconds before dying away.

He repeats himself, though the worst-case scenario is already unfolding in his mind. The comfortable dinner in his stomach sours and begins to rise. "Elle, what do you mean by again?"

When she speaks, it's subdued, defeated. "There was a fight. Yiwú was tired of failure. Tired of grieving people he couldn't save that Tony could. But Tony didn't want to go home. So Yiwú took Tony's jade. To control him. I couldn't let that happen. I was . . . desperate. Not thinking. You don't . . ."

She draws a tremulous breath, then lifts her hand and taps her chest repeatedly. "I love my brothers, okay? I always will. They were going to hurt each other. I had to protect them."

"Elle." The back of Luc's throat burns. "What did you do?"

She turns, giving Luc a view of her profile, her head bowed, eyes downcast. Two tears fall, twinkling, to the ground. "I can't help you," she says at last. "Because I was the one who broke Tony's jade all those years ago."

Luc can hardly breathe. Everything he thought he knew about the Jiang case—the foundation on which he'd built his assumptions—has been wrong. He'd thought it was about jealousy, frustration, anything but Elle and her love for her family. "You . . . what?"

"You heard me. I destroyed Tony's jade."

He has the sensation of a freezing wind rushing by, chilling the sweat on his skin, leaving him numb and clammy. He's light-headed.

She glances at him. "You were so upset after the Oldcastle mission. You weren't yourself, didn't want to talk. I thought about this. Didn't want you to know I did the same thing. Didn't want you to think less of me. I almost killed Tony."

"You aren't Oldcastle," Luc says, hoarse.

"No," she says. "But I did something unforgivable, like him. So you get it, yeah? Why I can't do it? When you told me about your laes in your apartment. I was standing right there in front of it. I couldn't move. Panicked. Couldn't think about anything but what Tony went through. Because of me."

She hunches into her coat, a fading ember. "I don't want to do it again."

The world tilts and shifts, disorienting him before it snaps into hard focus. Luc hadn't understood why Elle had gone to such extremes, spending nearly three decades keeping herself small, giving everything to protect her brother. He hadn't understood why her final gambit was to sacrifice her magic and her ancestors and her god, hadn't understood why Tony accepted it so easily. He hadn't understood why she thought she deserved all the things that had happened to her.

Now he does, and it breaks his heart to know how deeply and for how long she's been hurting. Elle has been in atonement for twenty-six years, unable to forgive herself, unable to heal. And he's asking her to revisit her trauma.

"You did what you thought was right." Luc speaks low and soft.

"Yeah," Elle replies, hollow. "Tony thought so too."

The grim calculator in his mind starts working. This new information changes nothing for him. Elle's still a miracle worker, one who singlehandedly dragged her brother back from a sure death. Twice.

"Shouldn't it matter what he thinks? You will never be Oldcastle. He wasn't trying to save anyone. You were. You chose the hardest path and succeeded. Tony lived. That's *your* victory. You made sure of it."

"I can't make sure of it now. I have nothing. I can't."

"You didn't die when you gave your own laes up either."

"I have Tony and Lira to thank for that."

"So it stands to reason," Luc continues, "that if you ask for their help, I have a very good chance of surviving."

Silence. Elle stares at him, aghast. "How can you . . . ?"

He closes his hand so he can't reach out and fold her into his arms. "Because I trust no one else to do this. You are, as it turns out, the world's foremost expert, with a survival rate of a hundred percent. There is no higher confidence."

Elle sobs, crumpling, and Luc sweeps forward to catch her. "What the hell is wrong with you? What the fuck kind of plan was this?" she says between hiccups.

Luc's eyes sting. "A disaster, but the only one I had."

"You really thought . . . you really thought you'd butter me up, speechify, and then ask me to kill you?"

He laughs. It's all he can do. "Merry Christmas?"

"I can't win!" Elle digs her forehead into his chest, shoulders shaking, and wails. "I give up! I thought I was bad, but you can be president of the chapter. You really are the most terrible prospect."

He hugs her until her ribs creak. "It's a position I will assume with the gravest of responsibility."

Eventually Elle lifts her head. "I still don't want to kill you."

"My heart." He releases her, nudging her chin up with a finger. "I have to be honest. I don't see much of a choice. I will die, or spend the rest of my life incredibly miserable, which would be worse. My aunt asked me what made me happy, and it's you. I want you and the future I see each morning I wake up next to you." He wipes away the tear threatening to spill onto her cheek. "I can't tolerate being under Oberon any longer."

"But you can't leave because he'll use the Right."

The certainty of it sits like a stone on his chest. Or perhaps that's his compulsion binding him, forbidding him from discussing what Oberon has done. Luc chooses his words carefully. "Yes. If not for this, then for something else. Because there will be a something else. My only chance at being free lies with you, and I don't know for certain whether it'll work. I'm past caring. Either my life is a living hell because of him, or I die by your hand, next to you. I know which one I'd prefer."

She shoves his shoulder, sniffling. "Is that supposed to be fucking romantic?"

"No." He loves her so much, in a way that's greater than himself. "Realistic. Will you help me?"

"I love you," she whispers. Luc tastes her fierceness when she kisses him. "This is nuts. I'm terrified. No, I don't want to do this, but I can't come up with an alternative. Yes, I'll help you. I know what worked before, and I can get Tony and Lira in on it."

He lets out a shaky breath of relief. "I'm terrified too," he admits. "As long as I'm with you, I can face it."

Elle takes both of his hands in hers and squeezes, determination settling onto her features. "So, about that group chat you hate . . ."

"I'll stay in it. For planning."

"Now I know you're really serious. First you let Tony have your private number, and now you want to stay in a group with him."

"It's temporary. Once this is over, I'm leaving the group and blocking his number."

"Once this is over, you're taking me to Chicago for a pizza crawl."

He laughs despite himself, pulling her into a hug. "Okay."

"Like right away. You wake up and I'll wipe the snot off my face and we'll go to Chicago. Promise?"

"I promise."

Chapter Twenty

*T*he familiar, cozy smell of charcoal and ash hangs in the air of Oberon's smithy, clinging to the wool of Luc's jacket. He hasn't been here in ages. The smithy is personal, the space Oberon retreats to for solitude and reflection, and is off-limits for work meetings. Except this one.

He seats himself on a stool, folding his hands in his lap as he waits. Overhead lights illuminate an anvil and a dormant forge in the center of the room, and a huge table with an attached lamp sits in one corner, positioned to catch the light from the south- and west-facing windows. Shelves holding hundreds of trinkets and inventions line the walls except for the left side, where there's a tool-laden workbench, a belt sander, and a band saw. Oberon used to spend hours designing the next magical wonder for the agency with Luc beside him, a witness to his genius. When Oberon built the port ring prototypes, it was Luc who helped test them. When Oberon invented the remote charm system, it was Luc who first used it in the field. Half the magic that agents take for granted at Roland & Riddle is a product of Oberon's mind.

Luc can no longer take pride in any of his contributions. All he's been to Oberon is a project. On a shelf by the door is a silver puzzle toy made of interlinking loops, enchanted so it will never tarnish. Luc had sat where he is now, his bottom lip tucked under his front teeth, trying to take it apart faster and faster as Oberon watched. Other memories rouse, shaking off the long-settled sediment of time. Here is where Luc studied English, reading weapons treatise after weapons treatise, testing each technique against Oberon in grueling, rigorous training. That, he won't miss. Nostalgia can't paper over the times Luc has been yelled at for being clumsy, or shamed for being slow, or thrown onto the stone floor, bruised and bleeding. Oberon had been a proponent of live steel and full contact sparring as a teaching technique.

"You're here. Good." Oberon emerges from the original port ring prototype at the other end of the room, a raised wooden grate surrounded by faintly glowing orbs. He steps down, his fine surcoat rippling around his soft leather boots, and gestures carelessly. His glamour disappears, revealing what he's actually wearing: plain workman's clothes, a stained leather apron. Durandal flickers in and out of existence at his side. His aura of power pulses through the room.

"Sir." Anger flares at the sight of him. Luc has to stuff it into a box, but it won't fit. It's taken every last drop of his discipline to hold onto his stoicism at work, and only the thought of Elle keeps him reeled in. He has to be able to return to her to carry out their plan.

"You might be wondering why we're conducting this meeting here. This is of the highest sensitivity." Oberon places his hands behind his back. "I won't mince words. A critical mission in Geneva has lost its head of operations. I've recommended you for the position. They'll brief you once you arrive."

Luc is on standby for another mission, there are tasks related to his move that he hasn't finished, and there's a mountain of paperwork that needs his signature. He's also expected at Elle's tomorrow evening. "I'm currently overseeing other affairs, sir."

"Drop all of them. This is more important. An assassin is targeting the heir of a royal elven family. I need someone I can trust in Geneva, and that's you."

Oberon hasn't said it, but he's likely related to that family. His line is ancient, with deep roots. "When do I need to be there?"

"Now."

"How long is this assignment?"

"Thirty days minimum."

There is no way Luc is leaving Elle for a month to guard Oberon's distant cousin. He's already guarded one piece-of-shit distant cousin, and that's enough. "I have tomorrow off, per our agreement."

"That's over." Oberon waves a dismissive hand. "Effective immediately."

Luc stands, disbelief rising out of his chest to grab him by the throat. "We had a deal."

"And I've just ended it. This mission is more important than whatever you do on Fridays."

"Your family is more important than what I do on Fridays?" She may be somewhat recovered, but Elle still has bad days when she needs him. He's fought for his scraps of time, and he won't give them up.

Oberon levels a piercing look at him. "Always. They're waiting for you. Time is of the essence."

"I prefer not to go." The anger escapes again. He slips his hands into his pockets. His switchblade provides solid, visceral comfort.

"Your preference has nothing to do with it. They requested my best and most trusted agent. That's you. Handle it."

If there's one thing Luc has learned from Tony, it's how to be flippant in the face of authority. Luc adopts a little of that attitude and amends his statement. "I misspoke. I'm not going."

Oberon pauses. "What has brought this on?"

Luc exhales, centering himself, finding his balance. Perhaps he should try an appeal first. He owes Oberon an explanation for how he feels at least, as thanks for the centuries together. "I realized I am, and have been, profoundly unhappy here. I don't have much time to myself, I'm overworked, and my colleagues don't treat me as a peer. I have made decisions that I've regretted, and I've questioned my performance in several operations."

Oberon doesn't move a muscle. "This isn't about that harpy again, is it?"

"No. This is about the job overall. I couldn't care less about the work you assign me, or any concern related to the Bureau."

"So you're burning out." Oberon shrugs. "I can assign you to a desk job with regular hours after you've completed this mission. If you do well, a director-level job can be created for you."

Luc bites back his retort. He has to stay rational. Oberon refuses to listen to anyone who is too emotional. "I'm beyond burnt out. I was burnt out years ago and didn't realize it. I'm resigning my position."

"A bit premature, don't you think?" Oberon's face softens, but Luc has seen this play enough times not to be fooled. "Try the desk job. It'll be a decent break. Do this last mission for me, and I'll reward you."

It's getting harder to douse each flash of emotion. "Have you heard anything I've said? I am refusing this assignment. I am refusing the director job and any other job you think will suit me. None of them suit me. I don't want to do this work anymore."

Oberon draws himself up, a dangerous gleam in his piercing blue eyes, which are the same shade as Luc's. Or, rather, Luc's eyes are the same uncommon shade as Oberon's. "Have a care with your tone, Luc. It isn't about what you want."

"No," Luc says, bitter, thinking about Jacqueline and Dominic. "It never has been."

"This is Maryam's doing, isn't it? She's too soft with you."

He almost hisses in reflex. "You leave her out of it."

"What did she convince you of this time?"

"I said leave her out of it." He enunciates the last word sharply. Luc won't hear anything negative about his aunt.

"Well, go on, then. You said it's never about what you want. That isn't true, but I'll entertain it. Let's make it about you this time. What is it that you want? To go play house with your little girlfriend? At least with your boyfriend there weren't any children. I do hope you've been careful."

The anger returns, undeterred, and ignites. Of course Oberon knows about Elle, just as he'd known about Baptiste. "I've told you what I want and you haven't listened. If you want to bring Elle into this? Fine. I love her and want to be with her."

"You love her?" Oberon smiles, thin-lipped and razorlike. "You think you love her because she's been nice to you. It will fade, trust me. You'll see soon enough that she's a diversion."

Luc stands, his hackles rising. "She isn't a diversion."

"On the contrary, she is. There are better matches for you than some human with a fraction of your worth who you'll outlive four times over. I didn't think I needed to counsel you on having human affairs, but since this is your second, here is my advice: do what the rest of us do, and let it be short. Don't stake your future on someone you'll tire of in a year."

He has to take a long breath before responding. Luc hadn't been the one to end his relationship with Baptiste. "You assume I want something temporary."

"If it's settling down you want, there may be a few elves who'll be nice to you."

Luc's anger erupts, then compresses, granting him the curious calm of battle. That's what this is; that's what he excels at. He smiles, the vista of possibilities unfurling before him, scenario after scenario passing through his mind until he knows without a shred of doubt how this fight will end. He will leave. Oberon will use the Right.

The situation isn't optimal, but he and Elle, and by extension Tony and Lira, have been preparing for this. The sphinx has already given him her blessing. Whatever happens, he'll face it without fear. Without regrets.

Oberon turns his back, going to the forge, leaning over to look into the firepot. "It will never work between you two," he says to it. "I've been generous while you've had your fun, but it seems I've been too sentimental with regards to . . ." He looks up, meeting Luc's eyes. "Your wants. I do take them into account." Oberon returns his attention to the firepot, picking out a few clinkers. "That ends now. You are done with her starting this second."

"No."

"No?" Oberon repeats, sounding amused.

"Shall I spell it for you?" This must be why Tony acts the way he does. It's downright gleeful to say no. "I'm done with you. Find someone else to take this mission, then find someone else to take this job."

"You'll throw all of this away?" Oberon spreads his hands wide, gesturing. "All that I've given you? Your education, your training, all the luxuries money can afford? Your position here at this company. You'll throw that all away for a bit of skirt?"

"You can believe that if it makes you feel better. Say whatever you'd like, but this has been a long time coming. If she weren't in my life, we would still be having this argument in a year's time, or ten, or twenty."

"You don't understand." Oberon approaches, shaking his head. "I must admit fault in this area. I haven't made it clear who you are. You are made for greater things. It would be negligence on my part to allow you to waste your talents."

"You've made it perfectly clear who I am and how much I'm worth." He's a foundling, a fatherless half-elf charity case. A lab rat picked up for cheap.

"Then you understand why you cannot leave."

"I understand why I must. I'm taking my talents elsewhere."

Oberon prowls closer step by step, the power in his aura growing solid, battering at Luc. Durandal begins to materialize, called by its master. "After all I've done for you, this is how you'll treat me?"

"Yes," Luc replies. "After how you've treated me."

Oberon reaches him, his face inches away from Luc's. "I have given you the world. I did not have to. I have saved you. I did not have to. I have shaped you, invested in you. All I ask for is a return on that investment. You cannot even do that much for me."

Luc doesn't flinch. "I've kept your secrets and given you two hundred years."

"And now you'll give the rest to a human who has no understanding of you?"

"She knows me better than you." If there's one thing Oberon hates, it's being second best. "She wouldn't betray my trust by—"

He cuts off, mouth forming uselessly around imagined words.

"By invoking the Right?"

Luc can only glare.

"I betrayed nothing. But if that's how you feel, go ahead. Blame me. Walk away. Claim the life you think you want."

Oberon has never looked small to Luc until now. He stares down at his boss, feels nothing but grim satisfaction. "I will."

"Lucien. I will invoke the Right again."

Durandal appears in its entirety, tantalizingly within reach. The idea that comes to him is madness itself. He shouldn't be able to touch Durandal, much less wield it, but Luc doesn't give himself time to second-guess. He removes his hands from his pockets. As quick as a snake striking, he grasps Durandal's hilt, backsteps, and yanks the sword free.

Light bursts behind his eyes, and in his hand Durandal sings in triumph, the leather wrapped around the hilt warming as if alive.

Something in him sings back, and a strange power rushes out, shocking him the way it did when Elle unknotted his energy. This time, however, it isn't painful. It's heady, making him feel like he's flying although his feet are rooted firmly to the ground.

There's a sense of recognition from the sword. Durandal molds to him, sussing out his needs. The heft of the blade changes in his hand, balancing itself perfectly as he levels it at Oberon's neck. The point of it caresses his skin, bringing forth a bead of blood.

To his credit, Oberon doesn't move. All he does is stare at Luc, his blue eyes lit from within, boring into Luc like awls. "You wouldn't dare."

"Try me."

"Lucien Châtenois."

Luc freezes. Despite himself, nausea rises in his throat. Knowing what's coming doesn't stop the chills from crawling up and down his spine, or the instincts screaming at him to run. He wonders if Durandal is sharp enough to slice the spoken word in half. "Do it, and get it over with."

"I will use it as many times as I have to without regret. In future, when you beg me for death and I refuse to let you go, recall the choices you could have made. This is your last chance. Do what I ask, and I will forgive you and forget this ever happened."

"No." Oberon will have to live with knowing how much Luc loathes him.

"Lucien Châtenois, I speak your truename and invoke the Right of Dominion."

Luc closes his eyes as nettles tighten over his skin, an iron band slamming into place around his heart. He flexes every muscle, trying to fight the compulsion which grips his body and holds it so strongly that his breathing stops, but it's no use.

"You will return Durandal to me and never touch it again. You will not quit Roland & Riddle. You will end your relationship with Elle. You will go immediately to Geneva and take the month-long assignment I have just given you, and return to London as soon as it is over. Am I understood?"

Luc gasps as he's released. His arm lowers of its own accord, and he flips his grip on the sword, presenting it pommel-first. "Yes, sir."

Oberon reclaims his sword and dismisses it. His voice returns to its usual tone. "Good. I will inform them that you are on the way."

"I'll need . . ." Time. What Luc needs is time. ". . . an hour to pack my things, pick up a glamour, and arrive at the rendezvous point."

"An hour?" Oberon snorts. When he speaks, he sounds bored. "Lucien Châtenois, I speak your truename and invoke the Right of Dominion. You will arrive in Geneva within forty-five minutes. Got it?"

"Forty-five minutes," Luc manages, closing his eyes to better withstand the pain.

"I will call you soon. If you do not answer, I'll send the Wrecking Crew after you and look the other way if harm is dealt. You're dismissed."

He won't dignify Oberon with a response. Luc turns, stiff, and heads for the door.

"Agent Villois."

He halts mid-stride. "What."

"Let this be a lesson to you."

Chapter Twenty-One

Luc yanks the door open and strides out, checking his watch, then spinning the bezel to set a timer for forty-five minutes. Forty-five minutes until the compulsion is in full effect. Forty-five minutes until the end of his life, or the beginning of it.

There's a plan, which is supposed to be reassuring. He doesn't know whether it can be condensed into the time given him. A real possibility exists that he won't make it. But he can't think about that right now. All Luc can do is go forward minute by minute as best he can.

He runs through his list of destinations, using ten seconds to savor the ability to breathe freely, fixing his itinerary in his mind. From London he needs to go to Paris, then from Paris to the oasis. After the oasis, New York, and then hopefully, under his own power, San Francisco. All in under three-quarters of an hour.

Thinking about his final destination causes a slight hitch in his breathing. Shit. That's a complication for certain, likely caused by Oberon commanding him to go immediately to Geneva and then commanding him to be there in forty-five minutes. He may not even be able to think about it for any length of time, and he has no idea whether he'll be able to control his own actions.

He has to get through as many tasks as possible before it's too late. *Geneva*, he tells himself, speed-walking through the hallways, taking the stairs two by two to avoid the lift. *I'm going to Geneva.*

His heart rate is up when he gets to the port rings located on the other side of the building, on the fifth floor. He flashes his FID at the hobgoblins, skips to the front of the line, battles a reluctant mouth before he can tell the conductor where he's going. In a blink he arrives in Paris and is swinging open the glass door, his phone in hand, dialing Elle, regulating his breathing. He'll need every bit of air soon enough.

Luc checks his watch. Five minutes down.

It takes several rings for her to pick up. It's pre-dawn in San Francisco, and she's mostly asleep when she answers. "Hey. What's up?"

"Elle, listen closely. I don't have a lot of time. I just quit."

"What?!" Now she sounds alert. "What happened?!"

He responds more levelly than he feels. "I have approximately forty minutes to gather my things and go to Geneva. I have no choice. Oberon did what we thought he'd do. Get Tony and Lira. Send them to Manhattan." He has to be careful with his words, but even so, his chest constricts.

If there's difficulty now, there's no way he's going to make it. Damn Oberon for using the Right twice. Luc has to ease the compulsion on himself. "Whatever happens, I love you. Do you remember when I said I wouldn't lie to you except when I had to?" His steps slow as his voice grows pinched.

"Yes." She's hushed, and Luc can tell she's apprehensive.

"We cannot see each other anymore. I'm ending this relationship."

"Wait, what? Are you—"

Luc hangs up and gasps in sweet air, breaking into a loping jog. Seconds later, his phone begins buzzing with messages. He ignores them, shouldering open the door to his apartment, kicking it shut, skidding into his bedroom to lift his mother's rosary off the cross. A thrill shivers through him as he touches it, along with a burst of strength.

He loops it a couple of times around his right wrist, returning to the living room where the full-sized sphinx statue is. There are three things in his apartment that need to be moved, and the return point is one of them. The call rune nestled over his ear is not.

He checks his watch. Thirty-two minutes left and counting.

Luc works the rune off his ear as he scoops the figurine of the sphinx into his hand. For a few seconds he stands frozen at the point of no return, the rune in his left hand still warm from his body, the miniature of the sphinx in his right, cool in the cup of his palm.

Oberon will call soon, and when Luc doesn't answer, he'll have hell to pay in the form of the Wrecking Crew. Likely, they've already been roused and are prepping right this minute. Luc needs to be as far away as possible, has to buy enough of a lead to do what needs to be done. After that, he doesn't know. He's bringing danger with him to Elle, and as skilled as Tony and Lira are, there is no scenario in which the Crew is defeated.

There is still no turning back.

Luc drops the rune on his coffee table, lays his hand on the full-sized statue, and activates the magic that will teleport him to the oasis.

He's in motion the second the soles of his shoes touch down, leaping off the stone and landing with a spray of sand. He weighs the consequences of running, decides he has no choice. Luc sprints toward the compound, pulling power from his laes, the desert air evaporating sweat before it has a chance to bead. The sphinx's mind touches his as he passes the guard tower, and in half a second he's relayed all that has happened.

The compulsion grips him when he enters the main building, making his diaphragm spasm. Breathless, Luc trips, catching himself with his left hand before he crashes to the floor. He staggers to the doorframe and leans on it, grappling with himself as time slips away. *Geneva. I'm going to Geneva. I'm going to Geneva.*

His aunt arrives mid-litany. « *Lucien!* »

She offers her shoulder, and he supports himself against her, letting her guide him to the gazebo. With the telepathic channel open between them, he feels the mix of her emotions as his own. There's fear layered over a long-simmering anger, and beneath it all, love.

He sends all the affection he can through their link. « *J't'aime très fort, Tatie. Mille mercis.* »

Another fit overtakes him. She practically carries him across the stepping-stones, propping him up so he can bid farewell to the children. He stands stoop-shouldered between the beds, the burden of three Rights a crushing weight that tests the strength of his bones. *This isn't the end*, he promises them. *I will be back as soon as I am able.*

The sphinx nudges him. Twenty-five minutes left.

Luc pockets the figurine, touches his forehead to hers, readies himself. There's a tug on his stomach, a sweep of sand-laden wind. He and Maryam appear on the dais in New York City amid the morning rush. Luc looks around, ignoring the shrieks of surprise, not seeing any faces he recognizes. He checks his phone for messages.

They're here. Maryam points Luc in the correct direction. There, lancing through the crowd, are Tony and Lira. Tony is in pajama pants and a T-shirt, feet in slides, hair disheveled, while Lira, as always, is put together in a sleeveless garnet romper.

"Hey, Lukey!" Tony greets him, then stops short.

"Don't call me—" Luc holds on to the sphinx, fighting against the compulsion, his neck tightening with the effort.

"Oh, you're in some serious trouble."

An understatement. They have twenty-three minutes to get to Elle. There's a swell of compulsion at the thought of her, and Luc takes several steps toward the port room before he can stop himself. *Geneva. I'm going to Geneva.*

Lira gets the slight faraway look that means the sphinx is talking to her. "Got it. Can you make it, Luc?"

"Maybe. Don't know. Don't trust me. Don't let me talk."

Maryam hisses suddenly, her head coming up, her fur standing in a ridge all the way down her back. "Go now, all of you!"

Luc's feet hit the marble floor, the impact juddering up his shins. The compulsion eases as the three of them hustle toward the port rings, Luc several steps behind, trying gamely to keep up. Just as they arrive, simultaneous beeps and buzzes fill the air. A good percentage of the fae in the room check their phones.

He can guess what it is. Now that Oberon knows he isn't coming back, he's put out an advisory on Luc. He reaches out for Tony's shoulder, his fingers digging in like claws, his other hand holding up his FID. "Get me through now. Or else I won't be able to port."

"The line—" Tony says.

"Fuck the line!" Lira grabs them both and hauls them toward one of the conductor goblins, shoving her way through the fae in line, phasing through them when they start complaining. "San Francisco!" she yells, just as another goblin looks up from his phone.

"Wait a second," he says, his objection getting lost in the uproar of the room.

With a surprising amount of physical strength, Lira jams Luc into the ring and slams the door shut.

Luc falls out on the other side, hanging onto the latch of the door as it swings open, tumbling over his feet and off the grate, landing in a heap on the floor. He groans, pain spiking throughout his body as it tries to draw breath. There's nothing he can do but lie there as his vision starts blanking out. Unknown seconds tick by.

"Isn't that . . . ?" an unfamiliar voice says.

"Yep, but it ain't your business though."

Someone hoists him to his feet.

"So, Lukey, where are you going? Geneva?" Tony sounds mildly strained but pleasant, like he's having a conversation while moving something heavy.

He sneaks a big breath as the compulsion relaxes for a second and keeps his eyes closed. He has to fool himself for as long as he can, an impossible task. "Geneva."

"Can't believe you broke up with my sister. Now you're running away to Geneva. I oughta kick your ass."

The compulsion relaxes even further at the sound of the conviction in Tony's voice. Elle was right. He's a good liar.

"Tony!" Lira interjects.

"Don't worry about me, I'm helping him. You call Elle."

Luc stumbles at the mention of her name, losing the line of his thoughts. His eyes open reflexively as he falls. Tony grabs him by his suit jacket, the material bunching in his fists. Stitches pop and snap.

"Shit!" Tony then mutters something in Chinese.

Luc is barely able to stand, the walls of his vision narrowing before Tony does something and Luc can breathe again. He and Tony stagger toward the main doors of the San Francisco branch, Lira running ahead.

There isn't enough air for him, but it's important that Luc warns Tony. He takes a breath that sends pain knifing through his chest and stomach. "Should've mentioned. Wrecking Crew coming."

"Oh, great," Tony responds. "Fucking great. You know what? It's fine. We'll deal with that when it happens."

Luc closes his eyes, concentrating on exhaling as much as possible, clearing the carbon dioxide from his system. He hears the slam of To-ny's hand on the handicap button, smells the wetness and heaviness of the San Francisco fog as the doors whir open. Any pretense he has of being in Geneva burns away.

Tony's temporary measure fails as they wait for Lira to perform a miracle and show up with transportation, and a wave of sweaty dizzi-ness brings him heavily to his knees. Luc loses his fight to gain breath.

Tires screech in the distance. He has the faint sensation of being laid down. The world lurches hard.

"Hold on, Luc," Lira says. He can barely hear her. "Almost there."

"To Geneva," Tony pipes up, but it's not working anymore.

"Time?" Lira barks.

Tony lifts Luc's wrist, then swears as Lira barrels around a corner. "Nine minutes."

"Can't—" Luc starts.

Tony puts a finger to Luc's lips, shushing him tenderly. "You focus on breathing so you don't get brain damage. We'll handle the rest."

He can't summon enough energy to be annoyed. There's a lot of swerving and cursing from Lira, which rattles Luc around in the back seat. In his weakened state, he can't fight the compulsion, his willpower draining away. All he needs to do is start the journey to Switzerland and he'll be able to breathe again. The pain will stop. He'll have a month to recoup, and when he's back in London, he'll leave without telling Oberon. Elle can wait a month.

It's logical. Tactical. It makes the most sense.

Lira brakes to a stop. "Fuck! Red light!"

Luc throws himself into motion, twisting up from the seat like a cobra, scrabbling for the lock. He jerks on the handle, punching the door open.

"Hey!" Tony yells, seizing Luc's ankles, wrenching him back inside with a grunt. The door slams. "Fuckin' gun it!"

Geneva. Luc tries for the door again as Lira stomps the gas, tires squealing. Honks fill the air.

"You're insane!" Tony whacks Luc in a few strategic places until Luc goes limp. "Lira, I'm gonna have to carry him."

"Gods save us," Lira responds, braking again, jamming the clutch forward into park. "There's Elle, let's go!"

He's lifted like a child and put over someone's shoulder. The movement jostles his stomach, but he can't breathe anyway. Dizziness claims him first, joined by fiery, shooting pain and the light of a thousand swarming fireflies.

"Elle!" Tony hollers, stomping up the stairs. "Everything ready?"

"Put him here!" At the sound of Elle's voice, the compulsion gives him a vicious squeeze. He's going to suffocate.

"We're out of time!"

No, he is suffocating.

Luc is lowered until he's stopped by cool hardness. All around him, the world spins and heaves, even the floor. He's on the floor of Elle's apartment. People are talking.

"Elle, do it now, he's dying—"

"I know, shut up!"

"We've been tracked. I'll head them off. Lira?"

"No, you stay. Take these. I'll set up a barrier downstairs—"

"They have an enchanter—"

"Tony, I need you now! Luc, I'm here."

It's all he can do to open his eyes a sliver. The blurry figure of Elle leans over him. Fingers scrape at his wrist. Pain needles into him when she touches his laes.

"I love you." She turns away. The beads of his mother's rosary click together. He sees the cross swinging back and forth in time to the frenetic beat of his heart. *Lucien*, he hears his mother whisper. He used to kneel with her in their church, lifting three fingers to touch his forehead, chest, left shoulder, right shoulder, copying her. *Credo in unum Deum, Patrem omnipotentem—*

Elle grips the rosary in her hands and yanks it apart.

Luc's body jerks, going taut as the rosary snaps. Elle's fear whines like a drill in her teeth; there's metal on her tongue. *Breathe*, she prays. To whom, she doesn't know. Anyone who will listen. *Breathe, please breathe.* She drops the laes onto a cutting board she's prepared and grabs the hammer.

She lifts it high and brings it down hard. Wood cracks, the sound splintering through her. Luc convulses, much like Tony did, and for a second Elle can't move, gripped with panic. They've been wrong about his chances. She's killing him. Killed him.

"Yíyǎ!" Tony snaps as he muscles Luc onto his side. "Finish it!"

Elle smashes at the rosary, blinded with tears, then raises her arm and does it again until the beads lie crushed into slivers. She shoves the board away as Luc whistles in one breath, then another.

Tony presses one of Lira's runes to Luc's neck, his eyes closed, his mouth moving. Magic streams in ropes of white light from him, dissipating into Luc's body. There's nothing Elle can do but watch as Lira runs into the room and drops to her knees beside Tony, runes sparking and flashing in the air around her.

Something strikes the door downstairs with so much force that it sends vibrations up through the floor. Elle gets to her feet, slamming her door shut, locking it though it probably won't help. Another strike, and the street-level door gives way. Footsteps tramp up the stairs. She scrambles to the cutting board, snatches up the hammer, cocks her arm back. She's not a fighter, but she'll be damned if she doesn't fight for him.

Her apartment door blows inward, the doorframe breaking as easily as a piece of celery. A huge man, black-haired and pale, barrels through with a roar. Elle whips her arm forward, the muscles of her torso contracting, and throws the hammer at him.

It connects with a thunk and falls to the floor. The man puts a hand to his face, dazed, bright red appearing in two spots on his jaw. She scuttles to the cutting board, bending down to grab it, and puts herself between the man and all the people she cares about.

He takes a step forward, his eyes rolling white and crazed, veins bulging in his neck. He must be a berserker, but she has no space left in her to be afraid. Yelling, Elle swings for his head.

He backhands her like she's nothing. She goes airborne, dropping the board, landing in a heap by the dining table. He lumbers into her apartment as she forces herself upright, ignoring the pain. Three more people, two women and a man, pile in behind him. "Stop!" she screams. "You can't have him!"

"What—" The huge man halts so suddenly he almost falls over.

"—the fuck—" one of the women continues.

"—is going on?" another one of the women finishes. "Tony?"

"Not now," Tony replies curtly, turning Luc onto his back.

Elle grabs the nearest object—one of her folding chairs—and gets ready to brandish it at the nearest person, an Asian man. "Don't touch him," she snarls.

Slowly, he holds up his hands in the universal sign of surrender. "We won't."

"Ken!" The woman who protests is short and brown-skinned, with curious golden eyes.

Elle redirects her ire. "Don't."

Ken shakes his head, casting looks at the other three members of his group. "Stand down, crew."

One of them, a tall Black woman, relaxes her stance.

The big man scowls and points to his face, which is bleeding. "She hit me!"

"We attacked her. Obviously, we don't know what's happening here." The Asian man lowers his hands. "I'm Ken."

"Uh, not to bust up this little party, but I need help." Tony assumes control of the situation, his voice firm with command. He points at the Crew, snapping his fingers. "Gill, pick Luc up and bring him to the bedroom without accidentally crushing him. Fern, Emi, you're on life support duty. Ken, keep my sister away until I say it's okay."

"Tony!" Elle takes a step forward, only to be blocked by Ken. Gill, still bleeding, lifts Luc as if he's a doll and carries him away. Elle watches Tony, Emi, and Fern follow behind, unable to take her eyes off the limpness of Luc's arms and legs, or the lolling of his head.

"He's right." Lira stands, sweat glistening on her temples. "We have your plan. He'll be okay, I promise."

She enters the bedroom and shuts the door with a soft but decisive click. Elle puts down the chair, wanting to run in five different directions at once, agitation flapping wildly in her stomach. She has to do something, anything. She has to be with Luc. She has to help him.

Ken shakes his head. "I knew he wasn't joking. The Crew owes me money."

"What?"

"You must be Stella."

"Elle, now."

"Elle. Tony always spoke highly of you." Ken regards her, his brown eyes thoughtful, the very picture of zen. "He said you were more gifted than you thought. Perhaps more gifted than he."

"That's a lie." Elle folds her hands into fists, but they shake along with the rest of her. The floor shakes too. Maybe it's an earthquake. They're supposed to be common in California. "He'd never admit it."

"Not to you, but he was quite boastful of it to us." Ken puts a hand on her shoulder, directing her toward the couch. She tries to resist, but it's futile. Behind his unassuming appearance is a will stronger than iron. "I must conclude that Villois is in good hands, if you've laid out the directions."

"I broke his laes." The shakes intensify. Tears brim in her eyes. Someone is gasping like they've just run a marathon, and after a second Elle realizes it's her. She's hyperventilating.

Distantly she hears Tony, his voice raised. She tries to stand, but her legs are weaker than matchsticks and won't support her. "I broke it. I have—have to—"

"Tea? I see you have a good clay pot. The old ones are a treasure." Ken goes to her kitchen, checks the water level in her electric kettle, and toggles it on. "I used to have one, but it got dropped in the move. I almost set up an altar to it."

The idea of praying to a picture of a shattered teapot is so logical and ludicrous that she can't help but smile briefly.

"When you're able, you'll have to fill me in on the details. I suspect we'll be here for some time. Maybe not seventy-two hours, but long enough to get the full story."

"He didn't do it," she tries to tell him, but each word is interrupted by an involuntary breath.

"That much is apparent, if you're willing to risk your life to defend him. We'll have some reassessing to do, starting with our contract with our boss." The sound of the water in the kettle rises to muted applause. Unrushed, Ken turns it off and opens a canister, spooning balled-up leaves into her pot. "This calls for calming jasmine tea, don't you think?"

She doesn't want calming jasmine tea. She wants to spill the truth, even if each word she speaks heaves and drops like a boat in a storm.

"You can't take him back to Oberon. He knows Luc's truename and has been using the Right. Luc's been forbidden to talk about it."

Ken exhales noisily, his nostrils flaring. His skin takes on a bluish tinge. "I suspected as much. What else do you know?"

"The kids are alive. Luc never hurt them. Will Oberon come looking?" The effect of her demand is ruined by the trembling of her jaw.

"That will depend on my report to him."

"That's not good enough. Get Oberon off Luc's back."

"You're right." Ken hmms, low and rumbly. "I can delay. For how long, I don't know, but I'll do my best. As for Luc, it seems we owe him an apology."

"Apologize later. Take action now." Elle stands, wobbly but sure, and moves to the dining table. Ken pours her tea. Despite herself she inhales the scent of jasmine, closing her eyes, letting it infuse her. The shakes remain, but they're manageable. She can no longer hear anything from the bedroom, which could be good or bad. Either way, if she tries to barge in, Tony will definitely knock her out. Her job now is to take care of everything outside that room.

"You said your name is Ken?"

"Yes."

"You need to fix my doors. I want my safety deposit when I move out of here."

"They'll be good as new." A carved wooden rune, identical to Luc's, appears in his hand. Ken fits it around his ear, bowing slightly to excuse himself. "I need to make a call. I'll be right outside."

Elle leans over the bed, her folding chair creaking, and kisses Luc's forehead. Beneath his Moroccan blanket, his chest rises and falls, almost imperceptibly. The last day has been a roller coaster, and though she's spent hours dozing next to Luc, keeping him warm with her body, hyperaware of the cadence of his breathing, she hasn't gotten any rest. In the middle of the night his heart had stopped, and it wasn't until Elle had performed an eternity's worth of CPR, bolstered by Lira's many runes and Tony's energy techniques, that it had restarted.

The irony is that CPR had been a mandatory class at Roland &

Riddle, in a small way, it's Oberon who has saved Luc's life. The rest depends on Luc.

"I love you," she whispers. She lays her head lightly on Luc's shoulder, avoiding his bruises. Grant, glued to Luc's side, swivels his ears to listen to her. He's been guarding him ceaselessly, a hunter lying in wait to catch Luc's life the moment it slips away. "Come back to me."

"You should take a break." Tony walks in, looking much more refreshed than how she feels. "You too, Grant."

The big cat doesn't move. Elle shakes her head, her fingers finding Luc's pulse, pressing against his wrist. It's uneven and weak, on the verge of guttering out. But at least there's a pulse. "He's in bad shape."

"You being in bad shape isn't going to help that."

"I know, but . . ."

"But nothing. What's he going to think when he wakes up and sees you all gross and anxious and smelly by him? Ew."

"He's not going to care," Elle replies. "Unlike you."

"Fine, shoot me down." Tony pats the jade pendant on his chest, fingers drawing a thin stream of white mist from it. He takes a seat, dislodging her from her chair by virtue of sitting on her, and directs his magic to Luc's heart, allowing it to sink into his body.

Elle looks at the poster she's tacked on the wall next to the bed. It's a detailed map of Luc's qì that she's drawn herself, with annotations from Tony. During the planning process, the two of them had sat down to collaborate for the first time, sharing many pots of tea between them as they figured out how she'd saved Tony all those years ago. The laes, they've determined, is the key which binds magical energy to the body, and when it's broken, the energy no longer has a locus and escapes. Without constant, careful direction, the loss of energy results in death.

In truth, having Tony as her first patient had been pure luck. Elle's known his energy patterns since she was a child. As for Luc, she's been lucky there too, having performed so many pulse examinations on him. Then there was Paris.

"It runs the opposite direction over there." She points to the meridians going through Luc's chest.

Tony looks at her. She can tell he's trying not to be annoyed. "I know. We've gone over this, and I can see it for myself. Go eat before you faint. I signed on for one patient, not two."

"Half of one. Lira's here too."

"Yeah, her containment runes are helping a lot. You aren't. Shoo."

Elle makes her exit, joining Lira at the dining table, where there's a bowl of food waiting. Lira slides it across the table. "Courtesy of the Crew. They got you covered for at least two weeks. Apparently, Ken has family in the area, and they made recommendations."

"Please tell him I said thanks." The food is tasteless, but she needs fuel.

"Will do, if I can get back into the agency."

Elle pauses, her chopsticks halfway to her mouth. "If?"

"Yeah." Lira sighs. "Looks like my FID is flagged. I'll be facing some serious disciplinary action for helping Luc, even though he's Bureau. We really pissed Oberon off."

"So that means you can't go back."

"Probably not."

Elle's mouth pulls into a frown. "I'm so sorry."

"Don't be!" Lira flicks a dismissive hand. "I already told you I wanted to retire, right? I was already closing out. This is a good way to go. There isn't anything at the agency that I really need. Just a few tools, and even then, I can always craft more. Besides, now that I know Fern, she can help me get the things I need. Overall, I think we came out on top."

Not if Luc dies.

Well, not exactly. If what happened to her after she gave up her laes counts as dying, then Luc has already died once. She won't allow it to happen a second time.

"He isn't dying." Lira's expression firms. "Your care plan is flawless. He's got Tony and me, plus Fern and Emi, who said, and I quote, 'We're sorry for being dicks to him.' With all that help, the miracle will be if he *doesn't* live. But I'm feeling way more confident. Tony too." Lira folds her lips in, lifting both eyebrows. "And most importantly, he has you. You'd probably snatch his soul as it's leaving and stuff it back into his body."

She would. If his spirit tries to sneak out, she'll know. "I'm grateful for their help." And true to Ken's word, Fern had fixed both doors and added reinforcing.

"Same. Now they've got some figuring out to do. It isn't every day you find out your boss is a heinous villain twice over."

Elle makes a confused face. "Aren't *they* heinous villains multiple times over? They're called the Wrecking Crew."

"No, just regular villains." Tony breaks into the conversation and assumes a place like he's always been there. "Heinous villainy is doing things like abusing a truename. Regular villainy is blowing stuff up for the hell of it."

Lira gives up her seat to Tony, who takes it. "How's he doing?"

"Stable. Day one isn't the worst though." Tony's voice softens with sympathy. "We'll need to be on our game tomorrow. If we can get him through day two, the next twenty-four hours start looking up. Elle, you're gonna owe me for my multiple heart attacks."

It's a joke, and she should laugh, but she can't find it in herself to do it. Instead, Elle glances at the remains of Luc's laes, collected in a shallow dish. She hadn't been able to throw it away. It isn't her decision to make.

She puts her bowl down, discomfited. "What needs to be done?"

"Nothing," Tony replies. "Everything is clean, his qì is where it's supposed to be for the moment, and the Crew is running interference on his boss."

"Ex-boss," Lira corrects him. "Emi said she left some unpleasant surprises attuned specifically to Oberon's aura, if he comes calling. She said they should buy you and Luc enough time to get away."

Tony puts his hands on his hips and leans back in his chair until it creaks. "Oberon will do the cost/benefit analysis. That's the kind of person he is. You'll have a bit of time. You're done here anyway, right? Go find a tropical island. It's too expensive to live in this city."

"That's for damn sure." Maybe not for the tech people, but the locals Elle has gotten to know over the past six months all share a common fear of rising rent and predatory real estate conglomerates looking to develop historic land.

"Maybe you should move down south," Lira suggests.

"We've already been there." Tony picks up Elle's abandoned bowl. "Should choose somewhere else."

Lira scoffs. "Raleigh isn't, say, Atlanta. I heard some parts of Tennessee aren't bad either. Lots of ghosts."

Elle leaves Lira and Tony to their discussion and goes back to her vigil.

Day two brings with it the predicted bumps in the road. Before the sun can rise over the horizon, Luc's energy begins dissipating, searching for its focal point. Tony sits with him, lit up like a beacon, glowing pale blue as he uses acupuncture needles to direct qì to the correct paths. He does it all in silence, which is how Elle knows it's more serious than he's letting on.

"It's similar to what happened to you." Tony slumps in the chair by the bed, wiping sweat off his temple. Elle gives him a hand towel and a mug of tea. "But different, because he's half elven, and his qì is looking for places that don't exist anymore. I have to keep tying him back to his own body, and he doesn't like it. If he were a full elf, he'd be dead by now."

Tony heaves a sigh and takes a long pull from the mug. Elle has fortified his tea with as many herbs as she can. She's doing the same for Lira, tailoring each formulation to their needs, which change by the hour. "I thought he was being hyperbolic, but he really wasn't lying when he said only you could help him. You drew a hell of a map."

Elle looks at it, thinking of Luc unbuttoning the cuffs of his shirt, holding out his wrists for his customary exam.

"Goddamn." Tony stands. "Where do you keep your needles? I need more."

"There's a spare set downstairs."

The tips of the acupuncture needles already in Luc's skin start to quiver wildly. Apprehension fractures through her. "Tony?"

"Better run. He's gonna take a dive in three, two, one . . ."

She bolts for the door.

Luc takes several dives as she and Tony perform triage, tackling wave after wave of critical moments. After a while Tony substitutes Lira in, benching Elle, sending her to run errands. Elle suspects it's because Tony doesn't want her to see how hard he's fighting for Luc's life. When she comes back, she's given menial but necessary tasks like sanitizing used needles, changing sheets, and giving Luc a sponge bath.

"You're the one who loves him, so you get to do it. Does Lukey have any nurse fantasies?" Tony jokes tiredly as he and Lira file out of the bedroom, leaving Elle with him.

"If you do," she murmurs once she's done, crawling into bed to be closer to Luc, "you'll have to tell me in Chicago. Because you're going to make it out of this. We're so close."

Luc will live, and they'll do whatever they want in the future with no regrets. She's gone through gauntlet after gauntlet in her life to learn many hard lessons, and she's going to apply her knowledge. She's drunk bitter medicine over and over. She's better, she hopes.

Her mind goes back to Paris and the way Luc had looked at her so tenderly, the city lights casting him in warm gray tones. He'd loved her already. *I'd like to see that,* he'd said. *You without anything holding you back. I think you'd be magnificent.*

He will. Elle's going to be magnificently happy with him. She deserves this. She's worthy.

"Look, I'm getting my phone out." She gropes around under the covers until she finds it. "We can rent a car or something. I'm gonna book a hotel. I don't even know how to do that and I'm still gonna do it."

Someone lets Grant into the room. He jumps onto the bed and makes himself comfortable, tucking himself against Luc's waist, activating his purr. "You're a good boy," she tells him. "See, Luc? Grant's helping. Did you know that cats purr to help each other feel better?"

She reaches out to pet Grant, feeling the three of them pressed together as if they're a pack. Grant purrs louder, and sudden exhaustion washes over her. She changes position to better scroll the search engine results, frowning at the prices. "This one looks cute," she murmurs. "Pineapple-themed. Cool building. Cheapish. Let's take a look."

Day three dawns.

Elle wakes the instant Luc takes a deep breath, like he's surfacing from the ocean. She holds herself still as he takes another and another, stirring beneath the sheets. With trembling fingers, she checks his pulse. It quickens under her touch, each part of his heartbeat growing more and more distinct.

"Luc?" she whispers, tears starting at the leaping joy within her.

His eyes open, clear and blue, focusing on her. Slowly, a smile blooms on his face. "Hi," he mouths.

She can't seem to stop crying. "Hi," she says back to him, dashing tears away left and right. "Hi. Welcome back. I love you."

He clears his throat several times. When he speaks, his voice is raspy with disuse. "Am I dreaming?"

"No. You're really awake, and I'm really crying on you. Grant's here. I love you."

"I love you too. Hello, Grant."

The softness of his expression makes the tears come out faster. "How do you feel?"

He considers. "Like shit."

Elle laughs, then sniffles. He isn't up to standard, that's for sure. Her bedroom smells like a sickroom, with the faint oniony aroma of sweat, and his hair is greasy and sticking out in various directions. "But living shit."

"Yes. Living shit, grateful to be alive, happy to be awake. I've had strange dreams about going to Chicago."

"Did they involve me having to use my phone to book a hotel?"

Alarm shows on his face. "Did you?"

"No, because I couldn't figure out which one was the cheapest. There are all these fees."

Luc starts laughing. "Never change, my heart."

"Okay. Let's get you up so you can—"

"Elle."

"What?"

"Say my truename."

She blinks. "Lucien Châtenois."

He sips in a breath, lets it out just as slow. "Use the Right."

Elle inhales, sharp. "I don't know the words."

There's love in his eyes when he looks at her. "You say, 'I speak your truename, and invoke the Right of Dominion.'" Luc takes her hand, lacing their fingers together, and somehow, strength flows into her.

She lifts his hand to her mouth, kissing each knuckle. "I love you."

"I know."

"Lucien Châtenois." Elle swallows. "I speak your truename, and invoke the Right of Dominion."

His hold on her tightens. "Command me to do something."

"Uh. Um. I command you to get up and dance."

"No." A smile spreads over his lips. "At least, not without you. Say my name again, command me to do something different."

She racks her brain for something ridiculous even as a delirious glee fills her. "Lucien Châtenois, I speak your truename and invoke the Right of Dominion. I command you to tell me Alsatian cuisine is bad."

"Never."

"Did you feel anything?"

"Not a single thing." He grins bright enough to light the room.

They can rejoice for real later. "Okay," Elle says again, flipping the covers back, chasing Grant off. She's gotta help Luc up. He's been in bed too long. "I'm going to get Tony and Lira. You go use the bathroom and take a shower. I'm gonna wipe the snot off my face, just like I predicted, and you're gonna—"

"Elle."

"What now?"

"I need to say something important. I had a dream about this."

She freezes in the middle of climbing off the bed. "Okay, but if you're going to speechify—"

"Marry me."

Elle stares at him open-mouthed. "What?"

"Marry me. Please."

"Don't you have to pee or something?"

"Yes. Elle, will you marry me?"

It's her laughter that brings Tony and Lira charging into the room, where Elle is covering Luc's face with kisses.

"Yes," she says.

Epilogue

"Luc, quit moving."

He scowls at her from his spot on the patio. "I'm cold."

Elle would normally feel sympathy for him, but today she's focused and on task. Luc has survived a Russian winter; he can survive this.

"It's finally sunny. I'm not wasting my chance. Stop making me talk." She squints at him, twisting her piece of charcoal between her fingers, then resumes drawing.

"You couldn't do this inside?"

"No. Not the same." A few more strokes of the charcoal, and Luc's face jumps out at her from the paper. She nods at it, a sense of deep satisfaction starting in her, keeping her warm in the chilly Bay Area spring.

"You look like you're done." Luc starts to get up.

"Sit!" Elle snaps at him, then points. "And fix your face."

"I'm cold. I don't see why I couldn't wear a shirt. People will be arriving soon."

"It's called life drawing. And no one ever shows up on time." Her hand moves swiftly over the paper, giving shape to Luc's neck and shoulders, the trimness of his waist. "Hold still."

"Did it have to be on the patio?"

"Aren't you French?" Elle matches his glare with one of her own. "En plein air ringing any bells for you? The backyard is fenced. I remember you specifically liking it because it'd give you privacy."

"I didn't think you'd use it for nefarious purposes, and you can't abuse the definition of en plein air like that."

She bursts into laughter, setting her charcoal down. "I'm just drawing you!"

"You've drawn me at least a dozen times already."

"Yes, and they've all been okay, but this time I think I got you."

"Let me see."

She doesn't protest when he gets up, moving aside instead so he can view her easel. He spends a good thirty seconds observing it, his gaze traveling from one part of the paper to another.

His voice gentles. "Is this how I look to you?"

"When you think no one's watching, yeah. And when you look at me, sometimes." Elle smiles up at him. He's wearing that same expression now, a hint of a smile curling the corners of his mouth, blue eyes soft with affection, all traces of hardness and stoicism gone.

He leans down to kiss her. Elle closes her eyes, melting at the tenderness of it. She cups his cheek so she can return the kiss.

When he pulls away, he murmurs, "And you needed me shirtless for this because . . . ?"

"Can't I ogle you in the privacy of our own home?" She giggles at the smudge of dark gray across his cheek. "I got some charcoal on you, sorry."

"I'll clean up when I go in. Can you check the tarts while I get dressed?"

"Sure." Elle unclips her paper carefully, weighing it down on the patio table before folding up her easel and stowing her supplies. Soon, Luc will finish building her backyard art shack so she can, in his words, contain her mess there, but for now, she has to march everything to and from the corner in the living room.

She maneuvers the sliding door open, humming with pleasure when the scent of lemons and fresh pastries wafts out, then closes it without dropping anything. The tarts are sitting on cooling racks on the counter beside the range, which is displaying a timer for the baeckeoff in the oven. Elle passes by, wanting to deposit her things first. She walks through the kitchen toward the living room, then pulls up short at the sight of Luc, bristling and still shirtless, facing off against Tony, who looks like the cat who got the cream.

"Hey, sis," Tony greets her, a grin stretching from ear to ear. "You didn't tell me clothes were optional."

"You're early," Luc growls at him. "Come back when it's time."

"Is that any way to talk to the guy who saved your life? Give me a break. I'm tired. I just got here from the desert."

"You teleported."

"Exactly, and you know all about the time weirdness in the oasis." Tony grabs the hem of his T-shirt like he's going to take it off.

"No!" Elle shouts in unison with Luc.

"Rude," Tony says, obviously insulted.

Grant materializes from behind the window blinds and meows.

Tony puts a hand to his chest. "Wow. Dagger to the *heart*, Grant. I thought we were buddies."

"Just give Luc an update, will you?" Elle walks over to her chaos pile and drops her easel on the floor, then unzips a portfolio and slips the portrait in. "A quick one. He wants to get dressed."

"A pity." Tony eyes Luc. "Seems a waste to hide it."

"Tony," Elle says, warning lifting the tone of her voice.

"Okay, okay. Maryam and I had a long talk, and I did diagnostics on both Dominic and Jacqueline." Tony nods at Elle. "You were right about me being the only one who can fix this, but it's going to take some time and planning to do it right. There's a lot of really fiddly energy work. Hope you can wait, Lukey."

"I can. Thank you." Luc exits the living room for the master bedroom.

"That's it, huh?" Tony shakes his head.

Elle gestures for him to follow as she goes back to the kitchen to wash the charcoal off her hands. She talks as she removes the tarts from their pans without cracking the crusts, placing them on cake stands. "He actually said thank you, which is pretty good. I'm just letting you know that I'm going to ask you more questions later." She slaps Tony's hand away from one of the tarts. "Don't you dare."

"I'll keep that in mind. Have I ever mentioned what a good decision you made to hook up with someone who really knows how to cook?" He sighs at the tarts, the sound wistful.

"Speaking of, where's your contribution to this party?" Elle stares at him meaningfully.

"What are you talking about? I'm here, aren't I?"

She rolls her eyes. "It's a potluck, Tony."

He shrugs. "Put me to work, then."

That's new and different. Pleased, Elle gives Tony a smile and a list of chores to do as she puts the finishing touches on arranging the living room for eight. Lira has flown in from New Jersey, where she'd moved in temporarily with her family after being fired, and the Wrecking Crew—though they've transferred to the Pacific division and aren't called the Wrecking Crew anymore—have picked her up and are driving her over.

Elle goes to peek in on Luc when she's done, knocking on the door to announce herself before entering. "You okay?"

It had been quite the effort to convince Luc to agree to a housewarming party, especially with his former colleagues. He's wary of them, understandably, but Elle is sure Ken and Emi won't let Fern or Gillen get out of hand, especially without the ridiculous insurance policy they used to have at the Bureau.

Luc glances at her as he works his fingers through his hair. He's donned a lightweight olive wool sweater, the collar of a patterned shirt peeking out from the neckline, and medium wash jeans. On his wrist is a silver watch with a light brown leather strap. "I fully expect to make a tactical retreat to the kitchen before the night is over."

"That's all right." She gives him a reassuring smile. "I'll come keep you company if that happens. It can get overwhelming, especially with Tony and Lira. You've never seen them let loose, have you?"

Luc shakes his head, checking his reflection as he does so.

"They're the life of the party. Don't worry about them. You just be social tonight, even if it's only for a little bit at a time." Elle wants everyone else to see Luc's real personality, but the years of isolation mean the change won't happen overnight. "Besides, once they eat your food, it's all they'll be able to talk about. I have the best personal chef on the planet."

He snorts, but smiles regardless. "Thank you."

The doorbell rings.

"I'll get it!" Tony hollers from the dining room. A second later, there are squeals of excitement from the front of the house.

"Elle!" Lira yells, her voice muffled by the bedroom door. "Girl, get out here!"

"Just me?" Elle yells back, grinning.

"Bring your fiancé with you!"

A chorus of juvenile *ooooh*s goes up from the Wrecking Crew. She swears she hears Tony as well.

Elle laughs and grabs Luc's hand. "Feeling ready?"

He nods. "With you, my heart, always."

A Note on Language

There are, you may have noticed, three main languages in *Bitter Medicine*: English, Chinese, and French. When I first wrote this book, I had meant it only for myself, and so I let my characters be characters and flow in and out of the languages I was most familiar with. I grew up as Taiwanese diaspora in a multilingual environment where English, Mandarin, and Taiwanese Hokkien were spoken regularly. Add in the Japanese spoken by my grandparents, many years of French study, years of singing in ecclesiastical Latin, decades of Western classical music study (where knowing some Italian, German, French, and English is necessary), and living in environments where African American Vernacular English, Hebrew, Cantonese, Korean, Portuguese, Spanish, and Bulgarian were spoken, and you get a world full of languages. Therefore, to mirror my world, Roland & Riddle had to be an international corporation.

Code-switching is a part of daily life in many countries. I have fond memories of being in Taipei with my family, listening to people flowing seamlessly from Mandarin to Taiwanese Hokkien and back to Mandarin, with the occasional Japanese thrown in. Television programming is also multilingual: Korean dramas, Japanese dramas, and Japanese animation are often left in their original languages, and everything is subtitled in Chinese regardless. The Taipei metro has announcements in English, Chinese, Taiwanese Hokkien, and Hakka. There were many instances where I'd be listening to a conversation or be in a conversation only to have my conversation partner switch languages. Sometimes, they'd switch into a language I didn't speak.

When that happens, it feels like a door shutting.

When that happens, it's okay.

I wanted to bring some of that experience to *Bitter Medicine*, which is why I did not provide translations. There isn't anything in the non-English dialogue that's critical to the overall understanding of the text, but I wanted explicitly for readers to experience the shutting of the door, the dropping of the portcullis. The English-speaking West operates on strict English accessibility (and likewise, Mandarin-speaking China operates on strict Mandarin accessibility). The only acceptable language to speak is English because the dominant culture has an imperialist desire to know everything. If it cannot be known, it must then be conquered and colonized. People of the dominant culture can and do get upset when they suddenly no longer understand what's happening because they've been denied the access they believe is theirs. But that's a discomfort I'm willing to bake into my book.

Specifically, *Bitter Medicine* operates on some rather fine rules when it comes to English and non-English. Native speakers of Chinese will have dialogue in both characters and pinyin. Non-native speakers will speak with pinyin, but without accent marks for tone. When a character speaks in their native tongue, the quotation marks change: guillemets for French; brackets for Chinese. When it comes to Elle and Tony, the modern mainland Chinese media they consume will be in simplified characters, but because they were born before standard simplified Chinese was implemented, their dialogue uses traditional characters.

It's my hope that the language switches help demonstrate the breadth of the Roland & Riddle world. It's also my hope that, for those of us who speak the languages in the book, you get a little happiness when you see your language on the page. Because sometimes, code-switching is not a door shut. It's a door opened and a gift given.

Acknowledgments

Writing a book is a group effort; this book is no different. I could not have done this without the participation of many people. To Tachyon Publications: to J-cubed (Jacob, Jill, Jaymee); to Elizabeth, Rick, Kasey, Su-Yee, and Nino—thank you so much. I landed in exactly the right place with you all. Thank you especially to my editor Jaymee Goh, whose edit letters were a hoot and should be used as sample/ website material.

Thank you to my agent Anne Tibbets, who laughed at all my jokes and whose agenting style is an excellent match for me. Get you an agent as warm, caring, and ambitious as Anne, who sets her eyes on the horizon and then takes off toward it. Thank you to my agency, DMLA. I could not ask for better.

Mille mercis à mon brilliant and invaluable critique partner Casey Berger, who is a polyglot, polymath, author, and a literal physicist, who prodded me through my drafts and whose instincts were always correct. I am eternally grateful for friends and readers like Jen, who is the most tireless cheerleader I know, and Gabriella, whose excitement and enthusiasm kept me afloat. 謝謝 Rebecca, Sheryl, 跟 Yilin. Katje, to-siā for all the naming help.

The writing community has been my rock. I couldn't have gotten this far without the Loon Slack. Special thanks go to Mel for her wisdom, Faye for the French, Val for her encouragement and guidance when I was first dipping my toe into the waters, and Marianne, whose experience, level-headedness, and complete chill were what I needed to reframe my perspective when it came to the highs and lows of publishing. I would not be where I am without you. Thank you to all my beta readers, and thank you so, so much to the authors and editors who have supported me: Gwynne, Janet, Anne, Deborah. Huge thanks go to Alyssa Cole, whose romance class got me to dust off a draft and start rewriting.

And then there are the folks in your life who go through it at the granular level with you. Jannelle, you're a real one. Larissa, Grace, D. Ann, and Soumi, thank you. To my cats, Gremlin and Pooka, thank you for keeping my legs warm and my heart full. I wish you were still here so you could chew on the final product. To my kids, who watched me move furtively and secretively around my work, thank you for putting up with the nonsense. Lastly, and most importantly, thank you to my husband Brian for being my first reader, for supporting me when I flagged, and for taking care of me when I could not take care of myself. I love you.

Mia Tsai is a Taiwanese American author of speculative fiction. She lives in Atlanta with her family, and, when not writing, is a hype woman for her orchids and a devoted cat gopher. Her favorite things include music of all kinds (really, truly) and taking long trips with nothing but the open road and a saucy rhythm section. She has been quoted in *Glamour* once. In her other lives, she is a professional editor, photographer, and musician.

Mia is on Twitter at @itsamia and on Instagram at @mia.tsai.books.